TRIBUNAL

OTHER BOOKS AND AUDIO BOOKS
BY SANDRA GREY:

Traitor

TRIBUNAL

SANDRA GREY

Covenant Communications, Inc.

Cover photography by McKenzie Deakins
For photographer information please visit www.photographybymckenzie.com.

Cover design copyrighted 2009 by Covenant Communications, Inc.

Published by Covenant Communications, Inc.
American Fork, Utah

Printed in Canada
First Printing: January 2009

15 14 13 12 11 10 09   10 9 8 7 6 5 4 3 2 1

ISBN 13: 978-1-59811-671-7
ISBN 10: 1-59811-671-1

This book is dedicated to Nazh-Mama,
and all like her who have lived through the horror of Communist rule
and emerged strengthened by their experiences.

Sandra Grey wishes to extend heartfelt appreciation to . . .

Kat and Eliza, at Covenant Communications—for their patience and meticulous care of this story

* * *

Roy Wilcox—for his assistance with Russian phrases, names, and pronunciation

* * *

Shirley Freeman—for her advice on Russian history, pronunciation, and names

* * *

Nazh-Mama—for sharing her memories of life in Eastern Europe as a young woman under Red Army control

* * *

Samara (name has been changed)—for her courage to flee the Soviet Union's oppression

* * *

Gene Gammon—for his descriptions of conditions in Frankfurt after the war

* * *

Ret. Air Force Major Jerry D. Wilcox—for his insights into military life

* * *

LDS Bishops Mike Simpson, Raymond Webber, Jim Maner, Steve Crosby, and Jerry Wilcox—for their advice in matters of LDS doctrine

* * *

Registered Nurse Laurette Platt—for answering medical questions

* * *

Lieutenant Colonel Whaley, retired army chaplain and head of the Church Military Relations Department in Salt Lake City, UT—for his patient discussion with me in April 2007 of army chaplain services

* * *

David F. Boone, professor of Church history at Brigham Young University, Provo, UT—for his continued friendship and assistance with my Church history questions for both *Traitor* and *Tribunal*

* * *

Robert Hill—who helped me research the atomic bomb

* * *

. . . And my new friend Logan—who lives in California and who suggested several great ideas for this book

PROLOGUE

Over the gate of the Sachsenhausen Death Camp, steel bars are bent to form letters, and the letters are welded into a phrase that reads, ARBEIT MACHT FREI.

Work makes you free.

One of the prisoners spat at the foot-high reminder of the paradox that was Nazi Germany. He clutched his treasures to his chest—a bundle consisting of a blanket and a few possessions: a book, a cup, and a toothbrush. He'd been lucky to steal a coat, and in the early morning darkness he held it tightly around his thin shoulders as he passed through the gate.

Chaos still reigned on the *Appell-Platz* as frustrated SS guards battled to funnel an impossible mass of humanity into orderly groups. The Czechoslovakians had already passed through the gate. Political prisoners and habitual offenders waited farther back in line, followed by the Polish, criminals, Jehovah's Witnesses . . . In the darkness, prisoners fought for blankets, coats, and shoes, tearing them from friends' backs or guarding them with every ounce of energy they still possessed.

In a shirt several sizes too large, a child stood alone in the midst of the confusion, his cheeks stained with filth and his feet bare. Eventually he migrated with others toward a group of Polish prisoners at a gathering point. The boy sat in the dirt and clutched his stomach, staring blankly at the passing feet.

Questions raged throughout the *Appell-Platz* like a whispered storm.

"Where are we going?"

"Someone said we are marching north."

"For what reason?"

"The Russians are coming."

"And the Americans."

"Why don't the guards just leave us and save themselves?"

"I heard they're planning to dispose of the evidence."

A group of German prisoners passed the Polish group on their way to a spot farther back in the line. Criminals, habitual offenders, and deserters blended anonymously—as castoffs from the Fatherland, they migrated together in the confusion.

Rolf Schulmann clutched his coat securely around his neck with one hand and guarded his blanket with the other. His emaciated face turned in the direction of the whimpering child sitting in the dirt, the tiny sticks that used to be the boy's arms wrapped around a stomach bloated with starvation. Rolf inched his way closer, cautiously watching the SS guards nearby. He bent and spoke through cracked lips.

"What's your name?"

The boy stared at him mutely.

"Are you cold?"

The child nodded.

Rolf dropped his blanket in the boy's lap. "Hold onto this with all your might. Don't let anyone take it from you. Understand?"

The boy's dull eyes registering a spark of life at the kindness, he gathered the thin blanket in his arms and held it tightly against his chest.

"Schulmann!" Rolf straightened at the sound of his name and waited silently for his punishment.

"The commandant wishes to see you."

Rolf followed the SS guard toward the brick administration building. He didn't waste energy wondering why Anton Kaindl wanted to see him; he'd learned to accept whatever came and not worry about the future. If this was finally his moment to die, he would die. Nothing he could do would change that.

But his heart told him this was not his moment to die. Why would Heavenly Father save him from a firing squad and protect him through a year of torture in the Punishment Company only to allow him to be executed for befriending a child?

He climbed the steps and followed the guard into the commandant's office. Anton Kaindl stood in the center of the room, gathering papers and stacking them in piles along the edge of his desk. Periodically he chose one, peered at it through his wire-rimmed spectacles, then returned it to its stack. He glanced up as the guard entered with Rolf, and then he returned his concentration to the papers.

Rolf stood at attention and waited for the commandant to speak.

"Rolf Schulmann?" The commandant continued to shuffle papers.

"Yes, sir."

"You used to be a major in the SS, am I right?"

"Yes, sir."

"You were charged with treason."

"Yes."

Kaindl turned to face him, leaning back against his desk. "Why were you spared the firing squad?"

Rolf lifted his chin. "June sixth—last year—the Allies were bombing production centers. The former commandant postponed the execution, anticipating they'd come after our factories."

Kaindl folded his arms and studied Rolf. "Postponed indefinitely, it seems." Then, to no one in particular, "Seems strange to postpone an execution on the slight chance a bomber might pass overhead . . . Didn't you ever wonder why you were spared?"

Rolf's blistered lips twisted. "I kept forgetting to ask."

Kaindl was not amused. He peered at Rolf over his spectacles. "You're a Mormon, aren't you?"

"Yes."

"Your God must think highly of you to save you from the firing squad."

Rolf said nothing.

"I hate Mormons." Kaindl scowled. "I hate Mormons and I hate turncoats. I should've had you executed along with the Russian POWs at Station Z." The commandant shook his head in wonder. "I've missed several opportunities to rid Germany of a traitor. I should be shot myself." He turned back to his papers. "But since you're still here, you'll be put to good use. Do you know where we're going?"

"No, sir."

Kaindl turned again to face him. "To the Baltic Sea. You and the other prisoners will be loaded onto barges and drowned."

"Why?"

Kaindl smiled. "Cheating death has made you bold. I could shoot you for asking."

"What am I supposed to do to help?"

The commandant nodded to the guard, who stepped forward and handed Rolf a rifle. Kaindl spoke. "You are to select several men from among the other German criminals and form a 'camp people's unit.' Your assignment is to assist the SS guards in maintaining order on the march. Since I don't trust a traitor"—Kaindl scowled—"I'll assign an SS guard to each unit. You might have escaped the firing squad, but one false move and your carcass will be picked clean by Red Army buzzards. Understood?"

Rolf fingered the rifle and nodded.

"Get out of here." Kaindl waved his dismissal and turned his attention to his papers. Rolf followed the guard from the building and returned to his group. He felt hundreds of eyes staring at him as he passed his fellow prisoners. He felt awkward and foolish—a skinny shadow of a man holding a useless weapon. He didn't imagine for a moment he'd been allotted any bullets.

* * *

At the end of the first day, when Rolf's assigned group moved toward Neuruppin, Rolf noticed the guard limping slightly, as if the boots he wore chafed and bothered his feet. Rolf's own feet burned from eighteen hours of walking, and he knew many of the prisoners in his care were feeling the same. He glanced at an older man near the back of the group. Johann was beginning to lag behind the others, his thin legs trembling with every step he took, and Rolf knew if the man stumbled the SS guard would shoot him and leave him by the side of the road. Rolf slowed his pace to walk next to the man. "How are you doing, Johann?"

The man's face betrayed his fatigue. "I'll make it. I have to see my grandchildren again."

"Where are they?"

"I don't know. Before the war they lived in Belgium."

"You'll find them. But for now, we need to concentrate on keeping you on your feet. Can you do that?"

"Yes, sir."

"Good for you." Rolf smiled at the man and moved forward. The SS guard stared angrily at him, warning Rolf with a shake of his head.

Three kilometers later Johann fell, curling into a fetal position in the middle of the road. Rolf lifted him onto the SS supply cart, ignoring shouts from the guard. Within seconds the guard confronted Rolf, his face mottled with anger. "You're disobeying my orders, Mormon. Why'd you help that man?"

"Because of your feet, sir."

"My *what?*"

Rolf pointed to the guard's boots. "That limp is getting worse, and this man's a doctor. If he dies you'll have no one to look after your feet."

The guard glanced down at his feet, and then at Johann huddled on the back of the cart. He swore at Rolf and walked away.

* * *

Johann died before they reached Neuruppin. His body was left at the side of the road with others who had also lost the strength to live. Rolf Schulmann concentrated on placing one foot in front of the other. The column of thirty-three thousand prisoners—men, women, and children—moved slowly. Rolf didn't notice much around him. He mostly watched his feet—left foot, right foot, left foot, right foot—so he was aware when the soles of his shoes gave out and his feet began to bleed.

International Red Cross trucks arrived one afternoon and distributed packets of food to the prisoners. Rolf held his portion reverently and fingered a tiny square of chocolate. He placed it in his mouth and relished the sweetness before letting it melt down his throat, and then he watched as his column ate ravenously, tears of gratitude streaming down filthy faces and mixing with the food in their hands.

They traveled steadily northwest, and the guards forced them to move faster, averaging twenty to forty kilometers per day. The pace proved too much for many, and they lagged behind and were shot.

Rolf found a dead prisoner and stripped him of his boots while the guard occupied himself with an escaping prisoner. One night Rolf's group found a barn to shelter them from the cold, and in the morning the farmer's wife distributed bread to the starving men before they continued their march.

Once while passing through a village, a second-story window opened and a potato flew through the air toward the marching prisoners. Panic ensued: prisoners threw themselves bodily at the object until a large pile of struggling, desperate humanity clogged the street. Calmly the guards began shooting, and when Rolf passed the location the potato had disappeared—replaced by three lifeless bodies in the mud.

When Rolf found blood in his stool, he tried to limit his contact with the other prisoners, but the dysentery that attacked him spread throughout the column and weakened the weakest until prisoners were dropping at an alarming rate. Rolf began watching his feet again: left, right, left, right . . .

Near the Belower Woods, Rolf and sixteen thousand prisoners dug holes for themselves and burrowed in for the night. Shaking with fever and cold, Rolf pulled tree roots out of the dirt and chewed them until he could imagine he was no longer hungry.

In the morning the SS guard in charge of the camp people's unit stood over his hole. "German prisoners are being released," he said without preamble.

Rolf decided it must be a trap, meant to catch him trying to escape. He knew the guard would not pass up any opportunity to shoot him.

"As far as I'm concerned, you're a traitor and should have been executed long ago." The guard adjusted his rifle over his shoulder and folded his arms. "But much as I hate you, I admire the way you've kept your column in line. I've shot fewer escapees from your group than from any other, and there's been little insubordination on your part. So I'm going to give you one last command: find your countrymen and give them the order to report to me. You've got fifteen minutes."

Still unbelieving, Rolf stumbled through the woods, conveying the message to all the German prisoners under his care. The prisoners met his announcement with blank stares or disbelief, but eventually a crowd had gathered near the SS guard. Rolf listened while the prisoners were ordered to march to a nearby village for instructions, and then he followed the group through the trees to a cluster of homes where a group of SS officers recorded names and handed out freedom passes.

Rolf held his pass in one trembling hand and stared at it, his mind refusing to register his good fortune. Then abdominal cramps forced him to his knees and he crouched in the dirt while around him prisoners celebrated their freedom.

* * *

Early in the morning the road still teemed with refugees fleeing the advance of the dreaded Red Army, and Rolf waited for a bicycle loaded with suitcases, bags, and a wilted houseplant to pass before he struggled to his feet. He brushed dirt from his clothes and stood weaving, trying to catch his balance. His body was on fire yet his flesh felt clammy. His boots rubbed in all the wrong places, and he felt blood between his toes. Gritting his teeth against the pain, he followed the multitudes of people migrating west.

When the sun hovered directly overhead, he fell by the side of the road to rest. He stayed there longer than he'd planned, and when evening approached he struggled to rise. Two young men with a loaded wheelbarrow stopped to assist him, and when he finally stood on his feet they gave him water and bread. Gratefully, he ate and found the strength to continue his journey.

He continued to walk, certain the next time he fell would be his last. Throughout the night and into the next day he walked steadily forward, following the masses of refugees and thinking about the two most important people in his life: Alma, with his eager, bright-eyed face and deep love for his father, and Marie, the woman Rolf loved with all his heart and would never see again.

He pressed forward, ignoring the excruciating pain in his feet, legs, and abdomen. Several concerned passersby offered him water, but he vomited violently whenever he tried to drink. He fell to his knees and couldn't rise, so for hours he crawled forward on his hands and knees. Razor-sharp gravel sliced through the fabric of his trousers and embedded itself in his flesh, but he didn't register the pain, didn't even notice the red stains he was leaving on the road.

Then, when he was sure he would collapse at the top of the next rise, through the fog of his delirium he thought he recognized the sound of someone calling his name. He continued to crawl forward, his fever-burned mind refusing to accept what he'd heard. Even when strong hands detained him and tried to help him drink, he didn't recognize the voice of his lifelong friend. Hans Brenner picked up Rolf's body and laid him in the back seat of a small car. Rolf huddled there and stared blankly at the man who had helped him. He heard none of what Hans said about the war being over, and his brain didn't register Hans's tears. But when he was pulled from the car and placed on a stretcher in the back of an Allied truck, he heard the words of the medical officer:

"He's too far gone. This one won't make it."

ONE

Hans Brenner had no idea when he walked through the hospital doors that this particular visit would change his life forever.

It seemed new medical staff had arrived from the United States, and there was a curious changing-of-the-guard in process. The bustle and excitement of old and new friends meeting after months of separation, and recently arrived nurses chatting and comparing notes with their established colleagues caused Hans to overlook the middle-aged British woman with the clipboard trying to get his attention. He was surprised by the unexpected pandemonium, intrigued that such a depressing place could be infused with such enthusiastic energy.

She tapped his arm firmly. "You need to sign in, love."

Even though he had been immersed in the strange language for months, it took a moment before Hans understood the woman's thickly accented English. He took the clipboard and a pencil from her and signed quickly.

"Who're you here to see?"

"A patient. Rolf Schulmann."

"Wait here." The woman indicated a waiting area for visitors, and then she shuffled away toward the mass of humanity in the inner recesses of the building.

Hans watched her go. Apparently the hospital had incorporated new procedures for visitors since yesterday, and he shifted impatiently from one foot to the other, irritated at the delay.

There was no need to wait. Hans knew where to go, and so he set out on his own. He made a purposeful beeline through the medical crowd toward the room his friend shared with other comatose patients. He sidestepped an auburn-haired nurse who glanced up at him briefly with pretty blue eyes as he passed, then he walked down a busy corridor and turned right. He opened the door and his heart stopped beating. Rolf's bed was empty.

Suddenly panicked, he turned and began searching the hospital, ignoring the exclamations of staff as he invaded their domains and raided patients' rooms. Finally he stopped a doctor. "Where's Rolf Schulmann?"

The man shook his head, peering at Hans over wire-rimmed spectacles. "I don't know the man. Is he a patient here?"

"He was in that room over there." Hans pointed down the hallway.

The doctor looked where Hans pointed and his face softened. "I under-stand we lost several patients from the ICU last night. I'm sorry."

Hans stepped back, stunned. He took a deep breath. "Where can I find someone who will know for sure?"

The doctor nodded toward the approaching form of the British recep-tionist, and Hans saw that her expression was livid as she zeroed in on him.

"She's your best bet," the doctor said and moved away down the corridor, leaving Hans to his fate.

"I told you to wait," the woman accused, descending on Hans like a thunderstorm.

Hans's worry for Rolf had dulled his combat tactics. All he could think of was Rolf's empty bed. "The doctor said several patients died last night. Was Rolf Schulmann one of them?"

The woman shook her head and seemed to relax somewhat. "Come with me. I'll show you where he is."

"Is he better?" Hans was suddenly hopeful. "Is he awake?"

"All I know is that he's been transferred." She shuffled back down the corridor with Hans in tow, and he felt a relief as profound as when he'd first seen Rolf crawling along the immigrant-choked road just outside Berlin. He didn't know what he would have done with himself if he'd lost the man who had been his closest friend since childhood.

"He's in here." The woman opened a door for him and then walked away.

Hans stood in the doorway and studied the silent room. The smell of sterile alcohol invaded his nostrils, and the white walls smelled of fresh paint. Wooden floors had been polished until they shone in the light from the fluorescent bulb above his head. Six beds filled the small room, with walking space at a premium between each one. Every bed was occupied, and every patient lay silently, in slumber as deep as death. Hans felt a sharp jab of fear at the comparison and swiftly approached the beds.

He found Rolf in the third bed, apparently still in the coma he'd lapsed into just days after Hans had brought him to the hospital more than two months ago. Rolf's tall frame was so thin it barely made a mound under the sheet. His breathing came shallow and irregular, and the curve of his once-strong jaw had a grayish hue. Hans reached and touched his friend's forehead and then quickly withdrew his hand. Rolf's forehead was cold.

Hans turned and sprinted from the room, grabbing the first person unfortunate enough to cross his path. He shook the man sharply. "There's something wrong with my friend. Where's the doctor?"

The man stuttered, surprised by the attack. "I—I don't—"

"Get me a doctor, mister! My friend is dying, and nobody's helping him."

The man glanced at the room Hans indicated. "You need to speak with the nurse in charge of hospice, sir. I'll point her out to you."

"Hospice?" The word was new to Hans.

Hans's prisoner cleared his throat awkwardly. "You'd better speak with Nurse Allred." He pointed through the pandemonium at the young auburn-haired nurse Hans had noticed earlier. "Miss Allred, I believe."

Hans released his captive and made a beeline for the nurse. She was in merry conversation with another nurse and didn't see him approach. He grabbed her arm and swung her around to face him, his worry for Rolf so great he didn't care what she thought of either his intrusion or his thick German accent. "There's something wrong with my friend and I hear you're in charge."

Nurse Allred stared at him, and he noticed the fright in her wide blue eyes at his unexpected attack. "Depends on who your friend is."

"Major Rolf Schulmann."

She carefully pulled her arm free. "Major . . ." she reflected, then her eyes widened in recognition. "Oh, yes. Rolf Schulmann. They said to expect his friend to visit at least once a day to check on him."

Hans scowled. "You're new around here."

"That's right."

"My friend needs help."

The nurse nodded, her expression softening. "I'm sorry, sir. He's dying. There's nothing we can do for him except keep him comforta—"

"What do you mean, 'he's dying'?" Hans's panic intensified. "That's not possible! He was healing, the doctor said yesterday, and—"

Nurse Allred shook her head. "He took a turn for the worse last night." The nurse indicated for him to step aside with her. She glanced over her shoulder at the other nurse and then turned her attention back to him. "Look, sir, I can imagine how much you care for him, and I'm sorry to have to be the one to tell you . . ."

"Tell me what?"

"Your friend is not going to recover. His condition has deteriorated to a point that his internal organs are refusing to function properly—"

"I was told yesterday he still had a chance."

"I understand, but that was *yesterday*. I'm sorry."

"No you're not."

"What?"

"You're not sorry." In his panic Hans lashed out thoughtlessly. "You threw him into a room to die alone and washed your hands of him. He's still breathing, and in my opinion that means there's still a chance!"

"You need to understand—his body is *shutting down*."

"I understand, all right. I understand that you're young, inexperienced, and heartless, and that there's a man dying in that room who might stand a chance if one senseless, stubborn *drache* would quit socializing and do her job."

Her blue eyes flashed, making her seem even more like what Hans had just called her—a dragon. "You have no right. I don't know what you called me, but I'm sure it wasn't civil. I'm only trying to tell you how things are. There's no reason to bite my head off for doing so."

"And I'm only trying to tell you to help my friend or I'll *really* get angry." Hans felt his fear for Rolf's safety constrict his throat, making it difficult to breathe.

"Look, I know you're distraught, but there's no need for rude behavior." She was clearly perturbed at his words. "To be honest, you're frightening me. You need to calm down. Talk to me politely, or I'll have to call security."

"You'll go to the effort of throwing me out—the only friend that man has in this entire shell of a city—but you won't help a dying man live again."

"Sir, I'm sorry, but he would need a miracle."

"One you're obviously incapable of giving, I see." Hans lashed out against the woman in front of him in an unreasonable attempt to stifle his fears. "Why'd you come over here, anyway? So you could watch us Germans die and gloat over your victory?"

She gasped. "Of all the insensitive—"

"You're the one who's insensitive, telling me you're not going to do anything to help my friend!"

She took a defensive step backward. "I know this is hard for you, but I don't have to listen to this."

Hans glared at her. A portion of him felt bad about treating her as he was, and with the threat of forceful eviction looming over his head, he took a deep breath and forced himself to be civil. "Look, Miss Allred, I'm just worried about my friend. He's been through a lot—more than you could ever imagine. And now his son and the girl he was going to marry are praying for his safe return . . ."

His attempt at civility had an immediate effect on the young nurse. She studied him. "What is your name, sir?"

"Hans Brenner."

"I'm sorry, Mr. Brenner. I really am. And I wish I could help your friend. Like I said, it would take a miracle to bring him back, with the way he's shutting down . . ."

Hans mumbled, "And to think he believed in miracles."

She gave him a sympathetic smile. "He must've been a religious man."

He frowned. "Don't speak of him like he's already dead."

"All right." She gently tried again. "He seems like he *is* a religious man."

"He's a Mormon, if that makes him a religious man."

Nurse Allred blinked. "A Mormon?"

"That's right."

The nurse's brows puckered and she seemed deep in thought. "From a medical standpoint, the doctor is convinced he's beyond hope . . ."

"What do you mean, 'from a medical standpoint'?"

She hesitated. "I just arrived, so I don't know much about his medical history, other than what the doctor told me when your friend was delivered to my station."

"What are you trying to say?"

"I have some friends—"

"Yes. And I do too. One of them is lying in this hospital, dying."

"Will you *please* let me finish?"

He repented, folding his arms and waiting silently for her to continue.

"You said he's a Mormon?"

"What's that got to do with anything?"

She touched his arm absently, as if her mind was still far away. He wondered if she would have dared touch him if she had not been preoccupied with her thoughts. "Wait here with the patient."

"Where are you going?"

"To get my friends. I think they can help—at least they can help *you* . . ."

"Help with what?" Even though he was frustrated with her, he didn't want her leaving him alone to care for a dying Rolf. "Why can't you just bring a doctor?"

"To be honest, Mr. Brenner, your friend needs more than a doctor." She smiled sadly. "And if he were awake, he might tell you the same."

"I don't understand . . ."

She moved off down the hall. "Wait here."

Why was everybody telling him to wait? Hans said a few choice words under his breath as he returned to Rolf's room.

Rolf had paled considerably in the few short moments of Hans's absence, and Hans found a chair and pulled it close to the dying man's side. He dropped his head into his hands beside Rolf's still form. The major's once-muscular chest now barely moved, and Hans found himself leaning close to Rolf's face more than once to check for breathing. He rubbed his own throbbing forehead and ignored the angry grumble in his midsection as he mentally tried to compose a letter for Rolf's fiancée: *Dear, darling Marie, I regret to inform you that, after struggling courageously for weeks, your sweetheart finally succumbed to disease and passed away . . .* Hans felt his emotions rising threateningly. *Don't die, Rolf—not after all you've been through . . .*

Rolf was his best friend and the closest he'd ever come to having a brother. Rolf's family had taken Hans in as a lonely orphan boy and raised him as their own son, giving him the same love and the same advantages as any young son of a well-to-do businessman and his wife, and Rolf and Hans had been as close as biological brothers could ever be.

Even during the war they had been close, and when Rolf had decided to protect Marie, the beautiful American operative he had captured in his *département* in France, he had involved Hans in the perilous scheme. Hans and Rolf had worked together to hide her from the Gestapo and help her escape to Switzerland.

And they had both fallen in love with her.

But much as Hans had once adored Marie Jacobson, she was not his and never would be. Her heart belonged to Rolf Schulmann as entirely as if it beat next to his inside his chest, and Hans Brenner had to accept the fact that his own feelings for her had been misplaced. She did love him, she insisted—but like a brother.

Perhaps that was one of the reasons he'd left Switzerland. Some friend, Hans thought ruefully, who would plot to steal away from Rolf the priceless treasure that had become the very reason for Rolf's existence. Thank goodness for Marie's stubborn refusal and for the faith that had shone in her eyes when she told Hans she would hold out for the possibility of an eternity with Rolf Schulmann and his son, Alma.

Hans heard the heavy tread of military boots behind him and turned dejectedly, certain Nurse Allred had been true to her promise to summon the brute squad. Instead, he was met by two young Americans in army uniforms entering the room with smiles on their faces. Their demeanor both cheered him and drove him mad with their seeming thoughtless ignorance of death hovering so close. Behind them Nurse Allred breezed into the room, her eyes betraying her excitement to introduce him to the new arrivals. "My friends, Curly and Gregory—the ones I told you about."

Hans stared at the assembly, unmoving. He struggled to suppress his frustration. "Are they doctors?"

"No, army pilots. But you don't need a doctor—"

"I'm not the one you should be worried about." Hans stood and indicated the motionless form on the bed.

One of the young men eagerly spoke. "We're Mormons, Mr. Brenner—like you."

Hans raised his hands defensively. "*I'm* not a Mormon."

"Your friend, then . . ."

"His name is Rolf Schulmann. And, yes, he is a Mormon, for all the good it's doing him now . . ." Hans trailed off dejectedly.

"We'd like to give him a blessing from God."

"A what?" Hans stared at the two men. "A blessing? Is that supposed to be the 'miracle' this woman has been talking about?"

"Your friend believed in God's miracles, sir."

Hans didn't know how to respond. Mutely, he stepped aside and watched the two young men approach the bed. As they laid their hands on Rolf's head, Hans felt an unexpected peace envelop him, shocking him with its suddenness.

One of the men said gently, "Rolf Schulmann, in the name of Jesus Christ and by the power of the priesthood which we hold, we lay our hands on your head and give you this blessing . . ."

Hans watched, stunned, as a young American stranger told Rolf that his Heavenly Father loved him and was mindful of him, and that it was not yet his time to return home. He said that Rolf's body would again begin to function properly and that it would fight off this ailment that threatened to shorten his mortal existence before his earthly mission was through.

Hans stole a look at Nurse Allred and saw that she was crying, with her arms folded and tears streaming down her cheeks. Awkwardly Hans followed her example and folded his arms, then turned his attention back to the Americans.

". . . Your family and friends love you and will be comforted until you can be with them again . . ."

The man finished his prayer, and both men removed their hands from Rolf's head. In the hallway somebody walked past the room laughing and talking to a friend, and a patient moaned in the distance. But in the hospice room everything was still.

Finally Hans cleared his throat. "Is something supposed to happen?"

One of the Americans laughed. "Only if God wills." He glanced down at Rolf and then back at Hans. "A blessing comes from God, and it is up to God to decide—"

"So we're back where we started," Hans interrupted, rolling his eyes. "Look, I appreciate the gesture, but—"

He stopped. In the bed Rolf had begun to moan softly, his head turning slowly and his eyes moving under closed lids. His hand moved under the sheets, and Nurse Allred started, turned, and bolted for the door, calling for a doctor. The two young men looked at each other, and then quickly moved out of the way as several medical personnel invaded the small hospice ward and descended on a still moaning Rolf Schulmann.

TWO

Lieutenant Viktor Nikolayevich Rostov did not have to be here tonight to watch this man suffer. He was, after all, resident operations officer for the Soviet NKGB in Berlin. He answered only to Colonel Mikhail Sergeyev, who in turn received his orders directly from Commander Korotkov, under commission of Military Governor Zhukov.

Lieutenant Rostov could easily have delegated the dirty work of this humid July evening to his subordinates. But for this last assignment, this last mission before his return to a more serene life in Moscow, Rostov wanted to personally observe the procedure to make sure everything went smoothly and nothing transpired to obstruct his return to his daughter's side.

The Soviet officer waited in the car, watching along with his driver for the German scientist to appear. Rostov's most trusted agent, Petka Vasilev, with his tousled blond hair and watchful, dark blue eyes, leaned one shoulder against an unlit lamppost and smoked a cigarette, the tiny glow visible in short bursts each time he lifted the cigarette to his mouth. He kept his body hunched, an effectively convincing portrayal of an unimpressive street beggar—or a homeless German refugee.

Two other operatives, a man and a woman, relaxed together on a bench across the street. Vasik Zelenko came from Ukraine and was Rostov's most effective muscle, his massive size and build an impressive deterrent to any escape attempted by his victims. Rostov had purchased his unquestioning loyalty and gratitude by providing Vasik's wife and infant son with a comfortable room in a community apartment in Moscow and a few rubles and a loaf of bread each week. Now Vasik waited silently, his expression unfathomable in the darkness, but the tapping of one beefy hand along the back of the bench portrayed irrepressible proof of his anticipation.

The woman lounged calmly next to him, her body close to his but her face turned away as though she were a bored lover. Young and sassy, Angelina Blanc was pretty in a futuristic way, with her unnaturally silver-dyed hair and green eyes. During the war her family had been terrorized by the Nazis in France, and she was a recent recruit from the Communist breeding grounds of the French Alps. But Rostov knew Angelina well enough to guess that her continued postwar devotion to the cause stemmed more from her affection for the handsome Petka than from her hatred of Nazi fascism.

Within the next few minutes the acclaimed German nuclear scientist Klaus Lichtermann would leave his apartment to walk his dog, Komödien. According to Rostov's agents, the man would cross the street at this point, pause at the corner of the unused and partially destroyed clothing shop, and allow Komödien to water the tiny bush that struggled to push its way up through the fractured concrete of the sidewalk. That was when Rostov's men would make their move.

The wind turned brisk, coming from the east with a subtle evening chill. Rostov rolled down the window a fraction of an inch and breathed deeply of the night air. It reminded him of the winds from the Siberian Steppes that invaded his homeland throughout the year.

His driver gave an almost imperceptible grunt, and Rostov brought his thoughts back to the task at hand. As he watched, Klaus Lichtermann appeared across the far end of the street and moved toward where Petka waited. Bent with advancing years and unimpressive with his walking stick and long trench coat, the man was being pulled along by a frisky puppy no bigger than a house cat. Lichtermann scolded the dog in German, and then he stopped and waited patiently while his pet watered the bush.

"*Entschuldigen*—Excuse me, sir. Do you have a light?" Rostov could barely make out the murmured exchange between Petka and the older man in that momentary pause by the bush. The scientist patted his coat pockets, inside and out, and finally produced a small, gold-engraved lighter case, which he flipped open and extended toward Petka. In that moment Vasik attacked from behind, one beefy arm imprisoning the man's neck and the brute force of his other fist connecting with Lichtermann's lower back and toppling him as easily as one might fell a tower of children's building blocks.

With the scientist immobilized, Petka and Angelina moved to restrain his arms in front of him. They tied his wrists with twine, disengaging the dog's leash and allowing the frantically barking puppy to dance free. Petka and the massive Vasik then lifted the uncomplaining captive and carried him toward Rostov's car. Rostov made room in the back seat for the gasping, disoriented German, noting the blank look in the man's eyes as he struggled to breathe around the pain in his lower side. The scientist didn't complain as his handlers tossed him roughly onto the back seat beside Rostov, nor did he respond when Rostov, cool and composed, smilingly offered him a cigarette. Instead, Klaus Lichtermann stared wide-eyed back at the Russian, his eyes glazed with pain and his jaw working as he fought for air.

"I'm delighted to finally meet you, Professor Lichtermann," Viktor said in flawless German, smiling cordially at the stunned man. "I regret that it has to be under such harsh conditions. I do hope you will forgive my agents their enthusiasm."

The man coughed, gasped great lungfuls of air, and struggled to form the words, "What . . . do you want . . . with me?"

Rostov waited politely for the scientist to finish his tortured inquiry, then responded calmly. "I have been asked to extend the Soviet Union's gracious invitation for a *second* time, Professor, seeing that you were unwilling to accept it in the first place." Viktor glanced at his agents and they closed the door and dispersed into the shadows, leaving Rostov to speak in private with the captive. "You were treated fairly, and you were given a generous offer by my government—an offer which, unfortunately, you chose to decline."

The man was slowly regaining the use of his vocal cords, and he wheezed, "I will never . . . help the Soviets."

Rostov's expression turned sorrowful. "And that is why we had to treat you with such energy, Professor Lichtermann. It was for your own safety that we met you here this evening—otherwise the Americans would have kidnapped you as you walked to work in the morning."

The man's face colored, and Rostov noticed the disbelief in his eyes. "That's not true." His voice had almost returned to normal. "They promised me that my family and I would be moved to Great Britain, and then possibly to America."

"And that, I'm afraid to tell you, is a fabrication, spawned by American Intelligence in a misguided attempt to entice you away from the true source of your satisfaction in the Soviet Union. Did they tell you that they do not allow your wife and sons to be with you for *years* after you're recruited? Your precious family is forced to wait in special military barracks for you to complete certain assignments, in dark, dusty Los Alamos, where the sun rarely shines and your beloved wife and sons are not allowed to go."

"No!" The man was in an argumentative mood, Viktor noted, despite the debilitating blow he had sustained to his sensitive interior organs and nervous system. "That is not what they promised me! They will give me a home, a car, money for food, and even money for my sons to go to college."

"Capitalistic propaganda." Rostov shook his head sadly. "And you wouldn't have realized the falsehood until it was too late."

Lichtermann huddled silently against the door, his face distressed and his chest still rising and falling as he breathed deeply, contemplating this new information. He reached with one manacled hand and scratched the side of his head near his receding hairline. He glanced out the window to where his dog waited forlornly in the gutter, sorrowfully watching the car that had swallowed his master and ruined his outing. Then Lichtermann turned to Rostov. "What are you offering me?"

"A comfortable apartment, your family with you at all times—except when you're needed in the laboratory, of course—money for necessities, and the chance for your sons to attend college."

The man shook his head. "The offer is the same, so therefore I must go the way my conscience dictates—I must choose to help the Americans."

Rostov tapped the back of the driver's seat. "I never said you had a choice, Herr Lichtermann. The Americans want you, and we want you, and in this race it is the one who wants you the most who wins the prize."

The man reached desperately for the door handle, and Rostov said calmly, "If you jump, my men have orders to shoot you." He made his voice sound hopeful. "But if you decide to stay in the car, then by this time tomorrow you will be safely in Russia, and before the month is over—if you're responsible, dedicated, and trustworthy—you will be reunited with your family and receive all of the benefits I have described to you for your faithful service."

* * *

Major James Matthews, officer in charge at the Frankfurt branch of the Office of Strategic Services, slammed the phone into its cradle. His heavy eyebrows scowled over normally gentle gray eyes that had finally found a reason to storm. Bushy hair prematurely white capped his head and framed a forehead creased with worry. Normally a pleasant, middle-aged grandfatherly type, Matthews was presently fuming.

He frowned at the telephone on his desk. It was not the fault of his men in Berlin, this disastrous failure to procure the German scientist Lichtermann. Matthews should have known that Rostov would discover his plans and strike before Matthews could contact Lichtermann and finalize the American government's generous offer. After all, the young Soviet lieutenant had recently made a career out of thwarting the OSS, the Americans, the U.S. military, and Major Matthews personally.

Matthews realized he should have placed less trust in the American government's fledgling intelligence capabilities and more trust in the Soviets' abilities to discover OSS secrets. The Soviet NKGB was already light years ahead of the Americans, and Matthews had to admit that the Russian he had been forced to play man-on-man defense against in this nerve-wracking game of intelligence was not a man to take lightly: Lieutenant Viktor Rostov was the epitome of Soviet socialism, communism, control, manipulation . . . duty . . .

Matthews fingered Klaus Lichtermann's file, open on his desk. He remembered the first time he had met Viktor Rostov. They had met at SOE headquarters in Britain, back in the days when the United States had had the misguided assumption that the Soviets were allies and that it didn't matter what was discussed between allies . . .

Matthews had been impressed with the Russian—his fine command of the English and German languages, his intelligence, his willingness to help with the problems the OSS faced of what to do with captured enemy scientists, artists, mathematicians, engineers, and doctors after the war, and how to best divvy up the resources of a floundering superpower. Rostov had made several very viable suggestions for the cooperation of the Americans, the British, and the French with their eastern ally—suggestions that would have rendered obsolete any complaints from Matthews's peers that the USSR was attempting to interfere with America's nuclear program.

But after V-E Day Rostov had betrayed him—abducting several of the scientists Rostov and Matthews had planned to recruit jointly and making them disappear. Rostov's true colors had shown through.

Lieutenant Rostov was a Jekyll and Hyde, Matthews thought grimly, still awestruck that a man so congenial and personable on one hand could turn and kidnap or murder reluctant Germans on the other. For most of Rostov's targets, accepting Matthews's offer of an assignment to work for the Americans became their only chance to survive.

Matthews's secretary knocked on the doorframe. "Sir, Berlin is on the line, wanting to know what you plan to do about . . ." The young woman's face colored slightly. She was embarrassed for him. "About this latest disaster."

He waved her away kindly. "Tell them not to worry about it. Win some, lose some."

The woman left. Despite the temperance of his reply, Major Matthews was far from ready to let this thing go. He reached for the phone.

After a series of complicated diversions and connections, his call was finally patched through to the phone on the desk of Lieutenant Viktor Rostov in the Soviet sector of Berlin. Rostov answered on the third ring.

Matthews clutched the receiver. "They say you're an expert at hunting game in the Urals, Lieutenant." He spoke in English—his adversary spoke it as well as he.

For a moment there was complete silence at the other end of the line and Matthews imagined the triumphant smirk that would play across the face of the tall, handsome Russian when he recognized who had called him this morning.

"Some types of game are more enjoyable to hunt down than others, Major Matthews—especially if more than one hunter has the prey in his sights." The Russian's words remained calm and respectful, and Matthews again marveled at his rival's ability to control and command, even when he was on the line with his enemy.

"What are the chances of a negotiation, Lieutenant?"

"There is no chance, Major. I'm sorry. The rabbit has already been skinned, cleaned, cooked, and eaten."

Matthews shuddered. Did the Russian's cold words mean that the scientist had resisted and had been killed, or was this yet another ploy to keep Matthews in the dark? Rostov would never intentionally admit to having abducted anybody, especially a scientist as destructive in his knowledge of the fledgling nuclear program as Lichtermann.

Major James Matthews would have to accept that German nuclear scientist Klaus Lichtermann was gone. He was either dead or sequestered away somewhere deep in the laboratories of the USSR, his capabilities already at the mercies of his new, compulsory government, and his dreary, dismal future made sure.

Slowly, gently, Matthews hung up the phone.

THREE

As the morning light filtered through the ill-fitted boards of his ramshackle lean-to, Hans rolled onto his side, groaning as his body complained of another night on the hard-packed ground. He brushed aside the tattered coat he used each night as a blanket and drew his knees up under him, his six-foot frame kneeling on the trampled grass out of necessity—even with his shoulders stooped and his head bowed, he had to be careful to keep from bumping the back of his head against the rough planks of the ceiling, with their twisted, rusting nails and occasional termite. For a moment Hans stopped moving and grinned wryly, realizing that to someone watching from the outside he might seem the religious sort, rising from slumber to thank a benevolent Maker for His watchful care throughout the night.

Rolf was that pious sort, Hans knew. And the prayer of those two American pilots two weeks ago had certainly seemed to be the trick that finally drew Rolf out of his coma and saved him from the brink of death. He definitely wasn't out of the woods yet, but at least now the hospital staff acknowledged that there was hope for his recovery. That in itself was a miracle.

And maybe that miracle hadn't been the first one, Hans admitted to himself. Hans had returned to Germany to search for Rolf on the minutest of chances that a bullet had not found his friend's heart before the end of the day the Allies had invaded Normandy and changed the outcome of the war. And Hans had found Rolf, sick with dysentery and beyond emaciated from his internment in the Sachsenhausen Death Camp, crawling along the road in the direction of Berlin with the indelible spirit of a life that without a Supreme Being's care would already have been spent several times over.

On this morning, the thought of Rolf made Hans hesitate on his knees, the absurdity of finding himself in such a posture still playing at the corners of his mouth. Suddenly he had a thought: *Why not say a little prayer for Rolf myself? What could it hurt?* Who else in this cold-hearted, tumultuous shell of a city teeming with refugees from all parts of Germany would think to say a prayer for an SS major struggling to hold on to a thread of life?

Once Hans had told Rolf, "The day I pray is the day I die." Hans had said it in jest, but to be honest, he figured that even if there was a God in heaven looking down on His shattered people and doling out miracles on a whim, there wasn't much reason why He'd listen to Hans Brenner, a former Nazi who had never had much use for religion. Certainly God would know that Hans was the vilest of sinners and had been ever since his college days, when he'd discovered that women found him very attractive. For years Hans had taken advantage of that discovery. With his dark hair kept on the long side and his body well built from working on the farm before the war and then from navigating the mountain slopes as a Gebirgsjäger officer in Hitler's Mountain Elite, he had attracted more than his share of female companionship. And yet Rolf, even though he had never appreciated Hans's pleasurable debauchery, had always insisted that Hans was a good man—one whom God loved and would listen to if Hans ever decided to go against his immoral nature and bow his head in prayer.

Hans swallowed, and with his voice bordering on sarcastic he said out loud, "God, you have every right to strike me down, but you know I'm not praying for myself—I'm praying for my friend Rolf Schulmann. So even if I'm not the best person, please help Rolf to get well . . ."

Suddenly Hans felt a warm breeze envelop him like the most comfortable blanket he had ever used. After nights spent shivering under his useless coat, it was a welcome, if rather unsettling, feeling. He licked his lips and glanced outside his shelter at the surrounding shantytown, his eyes searching to see if any of the other awakening refugees had also felt the warm stir of air. But he saw nothing out of the ordinary. In fact, the cool fog had not yet dissipated, leaving several early risers clutching blankets or thin jackets around themselves as they awaited the full force of the rising sun.

He shook his head, confused. But suddenly he thought of something else he wanted to mention to God, and the words that left his mouth next surprised him. "I think I made a promise to you on the road to Berlin." Hans almost choked on the words, feeling as if half of him was standing to one side, watching in disbelief and derision while the other half knelt in the dirt making a fool of himself. "And I want you to know that I've kept my promise so far . . ."

Hans paused awkwardly. "If you really are there and you really do know about me, then you know how hard it is for me to keep a promise like this. But I'm willing to continue to keep that promise if you're willing to help Rolf."

Suddenly embarrassed, Hans abruptly ended his impromptu prayer and slid out of the shelter. He stood, stretched, and glanced around to see if anyone had noticed. He felt the warmth slip from his shoulders and disperse, replaced instead by his usual layer of cynicism and depression.

Hans walked past his pilfered *Kübelwagen,* useless without petrol. The car had lasted from the moment he'd pushed it out of a ditch near the Belower Woods until the day he'd transported a suffering Rolf Schulmann to the care of an Allied mobile hospital unit near Berlin. Then it had promptly died as he'd pulled to a stop near this overgrown, refugee-choked park. It was out of petrol, and there was no chance of getting any more in the near future—at least, not for a lonely German soldier in conquered Berlin. Not for the dirty, useless tramp he had become.

He walked across the rubble-strewn street, sidestepping a muddy pothole spacious enough to bathe in and trying not to show too much notice of the old woman and young boy sifting hopefully through piles of refuse. He passed them almost every morning as he walked to the hospital to visit Rolf.

In the street, the stench was unbearable. American GIs had conscripted German POWs into street-cleaning service, but still the smell of decaying bodies not yet discovered in the bombed-out piles of rubble that used to be Berlin's Kreuzberg district permeated the stale air and made Hans's stomach churn. It didn't help that he hadn't eaten since the day before yesterday— and then, only half a loaf of stale bread handed to him by a kindly pastor distributing meager rations near the corner of his half-demolished church. "Come in and worship with us," the pastor had said hopefully, and Hans had laughed. He felt bad about his reaction now; the man had just been trying to dispense comfort in the way he knew best. And Hans had to admit that at times he'd considered doing just what the man had suggested.

He waited as a military vehicle crawled by, negotiating the hazardous road. He watched it as it continued past him down the street, past destroyed buildings with half-walls rising hopefully out of mounds of bricks, past German prisoners sorting and salvaging bricks and twisted steel reinforcement, past demolished city parks and filthy alleyways, and past desperate shantytowns constructed of plywood, blankets, rope, and fallen concrete.

Entire families lived under those sheets of plywood or in bombed-out stairwells or dirty alleys. Hans knew he should consider himself lucky to have the shelter he did. The weather was decent, and his living conditions, although not much better than a rat's, at least allowed him a place to close his eyes at night and forget the nightmare that had become his and thousands upon thousands of homeless individuals' waking existence.

His search for a better place to live, however crowded and dilapidated, had so far been fruitless. Those who possessed housing clung to it tenaciously, and those who didn't—like Hans—couldn't hope to afford the high rents exacted by desperate landlords trying to feed their own families.

He saw an informal message scrawled in charcoal across a crumbling wall: HEIL HITLER. What a mockery. Hans shook his head as he negotiated the uneven sidewalk. The Führer had rallied his troops to the last, pulling the youngest of boys and the oldest of men into the battle and admonishing them to give their lives for their country. And, unfortunately, many had. The Hitler Youth and the ancient Volkssturm had fought valiantly at the end, twelve-year-old boys and seventy-year-old men flinging grenades and manning machine guns and anti-aircraft weaponry until the last commander either deserted or took compassion on his loyal troops and told them to go home. *What a waste.*

Finally he reached the corner of the huge theater that had been partially destroyed, hastily repaired, and then transformed into a military hospital. Hans glanced up at the structure and grimaced at the memory it inspired of a long-ago summer, when he and Rolf and several college friends had frequented this very establishment. They had watched all the latest films, letting Hitler's New Order doctrine wash over them and transform them into fighting men and women that the Fatherland would be proud to call its own.

Back then it had been so easy to believe in a society in which a worker had job security and a housewife could be a national hero for bringing children into the world. Hans had to admit that even his subtle introduction to anti-Semitism had not seemed disagreeable—the Jews as an enemy of the Reich—until the deportations of many of his Jewish friends had caused him to wonder if the Jewish Question might not be more of a diabolical Jewish "resolution."

It had been easier to not think about it and to avoid discussing his concerns with any of his military colleagues. It had been easier to just let it flow by him like a river of sewage that would eventually empty itself into the ocean and be forgotten. Hans guessed he had been luckier than Rolf— Hans's job had never required him to take direct action against the Jews. But that didn't change the whisper of guilt that had nagged him ever since Rolf had told him that Hitler's trains didn't necessarily transport their unhappy passengers to work camps.

Hans paused to let a heavy stretcher carried by two American GIs pass. Watching them ascend the steps into the building, he wondered what all the fuss had been about for the past few years. Americans and Brits could not be as bad as Hitler had led his followers to believe. These American boys seemed decent enough fellows, if a bit outspoken and impetuous.

Impetuous and outspoken? A little like he had been, Hans thought with a smile, and he followed the soldiers into the building.

* * *

With the worst of the danger past, Rolf had been moved to a convalescent ward on the other side of the hospital, where he continued to make a slow, torturous recovery. In the two weeks since he'd pulled out of his coma, Hans had often asked him what he remembered about his march from Sachsenhausen, his release, and his walk toward Berlin. At first Rolf recalled nothing except how his feet hurt, but then as the days passed he began to remember details of his experiences, and he shared them with Hans. But Hans noticed that no matter how Rolf's health improved, his memories stopped short of Hans's arrival on the scene.

Today Rolf asked, "Hans, where's Marie?"

Hans folded his arms and leaned back in his chair. His friend's mention of the woman who had once held both of their hearts caught him momentarily off guard. "Switzerland, of course—with your and Hélène's son."

Rolf smiled weakly. "You're a traitor, Hans Brenner. I told you to get her home."

"Did you really think she'd go?"

"I hoped she would."

Hans hesitated, and then he said, "What would you think if I told you I asked her to marry me?"

For several moments Rolf remained silent. Hans could see he was trying to discern whether this was one of Hans's numerous jokes or if the threat were real. Hans felt his betrayal wash over him again at the realization that his words had affected Rolf so deeply.

Finally Rolf whispered, "What did she say?"

"She said no. Then she kicked me out of the house for asking."

Rolf gave a faint smile. "She missed out on a good man."

With Rolf's words Hans realized his friend had forgiven him, and the heavy load he carried on his heart lightened somewhat. He smiled. "That's what *I* told her. But she insisted she was waiting for one even better."

Rolf closed his eyes and said nothing.

"Anyway," Hans continued, "I've been meaning to write to her . . ."

"Don't."

Hans looked at his friend, surprised. "Why not?"

Rolf spoke slowly. "I don't want her to know until—"

"Until what? Until Alma's a grandfather?"

Rolf's laugh dissolved into a fit of coughing.

"I'm not sure I understand, Rolf."

"I don't want her to be hurt."

Hans stared at his friend, bewildered. "Hurt? She's hurting every day, Rolf, not knowing if you've been found or if you're ever coming back to her. And Alma . . ." Hans hesitated.

"What about my son?"

"He's praying that you'll come home. He prays every day that *that* particular day will be the day you'll appear. You don't want to *hurt* them?"

"I don't want to raise their hopes and then end up dying anyway."

"You're not going to die."

"I still could, Hans. The doctor told me there are a lot of problems, complications . . ."

"And you're making things even more complicated by not letting me write to your girlfriend and son." But Hans could see the determination on his friend's tired face, and he shook his head. "I just hope you have a very good reason."

"I do." He turned his eyes away from Hans.

"Tell me why you'd do such a cruel thing to the woman you love."

Rolf shook his head. "It would be more cruel for her to be here with me now, to see what I look like, and to realize I'm not going to make it."

Hans snorted. "That's a terrible excuse, Rolf. I can't accept it as a reason for keeping Marie in the dark any longer."

"Hans . . ." Rolf hesitated, and for just a moment Hans caught the anguish in his friend's voice. "Promise me."

"I don't know if I can keep a promise like that, Rolf."

Rolf turned and gazed at Hans, his eyes pleading. "Someday you will understand what it means to love someone so much that you'd want to do anything for her—including saving her from a sight that might be more than she could take, and from problems that might have no solutions." He glanced down at his body, lying useless under the sheets. "If Marie were to see me like this it would be devastating to her—and to my innocent son." His voice wavered, but he continued. "But that wouldn't be the worst of it, Hans. What if I can't ever marry her because of the part I played in the war? What if the Allies continue to forbid Americans and Germans to marry and, even if I'm never imprisoned for war crimes, we never have a chance to go to the United States and take the step we so desperately want to take? *What if I never have a chance to marry the woman I love for eternity?*"

Hans stared at his friend, stunned. He felt the anguish of Rolf's words and realized the emotions behind them, and he dropped his gaze to his large, dirty hands, clutching them in his lap.

"All right. I'll try to remember not to write to her—at least for a few more days."

Rolf relaxed, although his blue eyes still showed his worry. "I guess that's the best I can hope for from you."

* * *

August 6, 1945

Lieutenant Viktor Nikolayevich Rostov gazed back steadily at the man in front of him. He did not question the colonel's orders, nor did he allow the anxiety he felt to show on his face and betray his concern.

Colonel Sergeyev's soft-spoken Russian had a way of making even the most encouraging words convey threat. "The High Command is aware of your talents, Lieutenant. Stalin is placing his trust entirely in men like you for this assignment." The colonel hesitated. "You understand, of course, that there is no room for failure."

There it was: the lessons of Stalingrad again being taught to the Motherland's unworthy soldiers. There was no surrender. No turning back. No possibility of failure. Rostov felt again the familiar pain at his loss three years before, but he kept his gaze steady. "I understand."

"Sasha would have been proud of you, Lieutenant Rostov."

Sasha had never returned from Stalingrad. And Rostov's wife had died on a lonely city street, riddled with bullets from a passing German plane.

His burdens seemed so heavy—first his son, and then his wife, and now *this*.

At the very moment he entertained the thought, he inwardly scolded himself for its inception. He had lost much, it was true, but he still had his lovely daughter, and his sweet Lucya's existence gave him purpose where otherwise there would be nothing but despair and death. The image of his seventeen-year-old daughter comforted him. If it were not for his beautiful Lucya he would be without a reason to continue this magnificent fight for a new and powerful Russia.

Rostov watched as his commanding officer turned and left the room, and he felt again the gloom that had been his companion ever since the news reached him of the Americans' assault on Japan. If the Japanese didn't state their intent to surrender to the Westerners within the next few hours, he knew Stalin would officially declare war on that country, perhaps prolonging this diabolical conflict indefinitely. It never seemed to matter how many fathers gave their sons to the Motherland—she always demanded more of her people. So they gave their sons, and then they gave their other sons, and then they gave their daughters, and still the bloodshed continued and the enemy did not retreat.

Viktor sank wearily into a chair, resting his head in his hands. Now that his search for Klaus Lichtermann had reached a successful conclusion, he had been looking forward to washing his hands of this war, leaving the maintenance of a shattered enemy nation to his younger, more enthusiastic countrymen, and again taking upon himself the responsibility of enlightening a new generation of students. But now this new assignment had filtered down through the ranks from their glorious leader to him. Alyona would have been proud of him . . .

It didn't take much to summon his wife's image to his mind—her dark hair tinged in the sunlight with the red that flowed through his country and his soul, her full lips, and the stunning eyes that reminded him of the sky above his parents' village in the Ural mountains. Her gaze had always seemed to see through any façade he managed to portray, piercing through any man-made deception to the little boy hiding inside. She had been the light in his dreary wasteland of duty, and over the years of their marriage her love and acceptance of him had carried him out of the gutters of self-doubt to the heights of happiness and self-fulfillment that only a man who had a woman like her for a bride would ever be allowed to experience.

With her image in his mind, he could more easily see the good in all things. He would stop questioning Stalin's purposes and would focus on the light that still filled his life: his daughter—his Lucya—stunningly beautiful like her mother, and a partial balm for the loneliness that clutched at his heart. Lucya would soon marry a young hero of the battle of Stalingrad— the same battle that had taken Viktor's only son, Sasha—and the marriage would help Viktor make sense of two senseless losses and perhaps make his heart begin, finally, to heal.

Today Commander Zhukov, supreme commander of the Soviet Occupied Zone in Germany, had thrust him far away from his anticipated return to his daughter, into a situation that would continue to entail many half truths and veritable falsehoods on his part—and perhaps even murder— in the line of duty and for the benefit of the Motherland. This particular service to the Soviet Union was not of his choosing, but he knew that his background and continued successes for the atomic future of Russia made him perfect for this last assignment. Besides, no one ever refused a commission from Comrade Zhukov.

Viktor knew that his daughter would be well cared for as a result—she would not lack the necessities that many others lacked. At Viktor's small *dacha* outside the city, Lucya had a warm cottage, a generous garden plot, and a place for the one goat. Viktor was confident that she would never go without food or the wherewithal to subsist while she waited for him to return to her. And Lucya and Anton's wedding would take place in the summer of this next year, now that Anton had been released from his wartime duties. Viktor would make sure that this last assignment was complete, and his superiors satisfied, long before the summer of 1946.

Viktor's mother would have said his life was blessed by God. Viktor himself didn't know about blessings from any deity, but he did know that his loyal service to Stalin had given his small family warmth, food, and security while many of his countrymen lacked all three of these things. Right now that was all that mattered.

The German fascists had finally been forced into submission, and even though his military service was not drawing to a close as quickly as he had been led to believe, Viktor knew he had been handed one last opportunity to make his country strong again—to help Russia neutralize the death threat posed by the United States with its sadistic, prideful display of supremacy this morning in Japan. And that opportunity alone made this last, dreadful assignment worthwhile.

FOUR

As the days passed and Rolf struggled to heal, he had a spell of breathing problems and Hans found himself pacing the corridors while the doctors worked over his friend. But after several days of extra attention from the medical staff, Rolf stabilized and Hans was back at his side.

"Did you give her the book?" Rolf's voice was finally starting to sound like his own.

After days surrounded by Allied medical personnel who expected him to communicate in English, Hans was relieved for the opportunity to revert back to his mother tongue. "What book?" he asked.

"My Book of Mormon. You were supposed to give it to Marie."

"She refused to take it. Told me she was leaving the Mormon Church."

"Be serious, Hans."

"Okay, she gave it back to me and told me to read it. Made me promise I would learn more about eternity."

Rolf smiled. "Have you read it?"

"I've been a little busy, Rolf. Looking for a friend. Besides, you know how I am about keeping promises."

"Will you read it to me?" Rolf tried to raise his head, but after several seconds of struggle he abandoned the idea. "I'm still feeling a little tired. My eyes aren't working right."

"They will."

"Do you still have the book?"

"I'll bring it tomorrow, if you want."

"And you'll read it to me?"

Hans sighed dramatically. "If I must."

"It would mean a lot to me."

* * *

Hans read from Rolf's tattered book every afternoon, his deep voice hesitating at each of the unfamiliar words, sounding each one out like a schoolboy until Rolf would come to his rescue and say it for him. Sometimes Rolf didn't come to his aid, and then Hans would lay the book quietly on the edge of the bed and leave his friend to his healing slumber.

Sometimes Hans spent entire days at the joint American and British hospital ward, not because his friend needed him every hour of every day but because he had nowhere else to go. While he visited Rolf at the hospital, there was no way for him to safeguard the shanty that had come to be rightfully his, and it had finally been dismantled by refugees more desperate than he was. His roof planks, complete with rusty nails and termites, became the fuel for some desperate family's cook fire, his coat became someone else's blanket, his spot on the moldy park grass became somebody else's turf, his stolen car was again stolen away, and he now had few earthly encumbrances other than the frayed clothing on his back, a Luger, and Rolf's book, which he now kept on Rolf's bedside table.

When the British receptionist with her clipboard shooed him from the building along with the other visitors the first night he tried to stay, he wandered for hours through the darkened city until he discovered a crowded, filthy basement bomb shelter with room for one more homeless soul. In the morning he realized his new accommodations placed him dangerously close to the Friedrichshain and Treptow districts located in the Russian zone, and he didn't want to spend any more time than necessary in the neighborhood. But that night he returned to the same shelter out of necessity rather than any attachment to the place. He looked into the eyes of his forty-odd disheveled and desperate bedmates and saw the same necessity mirrored in their eyes.

Over the weeks Rolf continued to mend. First his eyesight returned, although he neglected to mention that fact to Hans. Hans realized the change when he noticed Rolf's hooded interest in the goings-on of the hospital ward, but Hans continued to read to him day after day, amused at his deception. It was obvious that Rolf wanted Hans to finish the book for himself.

Hans had to admit he was intrigued by the strange, complicated epic he was reading. He was now in a section entitled, "Mosiah," and as he read, several things became clear to him. Obviously the story of the rebellious Alma in chapter 27 had once had an impact on Rolf—he had told Hans once of his conversion to the Mormon Church, and Hans could see the parallels between Rolf's experience and that of this Alma character in Rolf's book. And after reading several chapters into the section entitled, "Alma," he could see why Rolf and his now-deceased wife, Hélène, had decided to name their son after the man.

Sometimes Hans wished he could experience a conversion like this Alma— or like Rolf had. He had to admit that, for him, it might take a whole heaven full of angels pummeling him to overcome his stubbornness, pride, and bad habits. But what if he ever did decide he wanted to change? What would it take to transform him into a man of conviction like his friend Rolf, who was alive today only because he believed in a God of miracles and in the gift of healing?

Rolf should have been dead. He should have died when he confronted the Gestapo in Izieu. He should have been executed at Sachsenhausen. He should have perished in that tortuous march toward the Baltic Sea. He should have succumbed to his illnesses in this hospital. If Hans had pulled even one of the traitorous shenanigans Rolf pulled during the war—in the name of either religion or love—Hans would already be rotting in the ground with a bullet in the back of his skull.

* * *

Hans Brenner didn't have anything useful to do besides read to Rolf and haunt the corridors of the hospital hoping for a glimpse of the American nurse with the auburn hair and pretty blue eyes. He craved something constructive to fill his hours—not because he wanted to be away from Rolf, but because he felt like he would go mad if he didn't have a purpose.

He sometimes felt like he was rotting anyway. He knew he certainly looked and smelled that way! How long had it been since he'd had a decent bath? Long before picking Rolf's carcass off the road to Berlin, that was for sure. Of course, he'd splashed water on his face a few times since then, but a clean, hot bath was not exactly readily available in filthy basement shelters teaming with rats, lice, and crying babies. Still, Hans rarely felt self-conscious, even though he'd seen a few noses twitch as he passed nurses on his way to read to Rolf. But he realized with chagrin that he was quite conscious of his body odor and lack of personal hygiene in the strangely mesmerizing presence of Nurse Allred.

"How's he doing?" was her usual greeting as she passed Rolf's room, pausing fairylike in the doorway for just a few seconds.

"Fine." It was usually all he could think of to respond in English and all she ever seemed to expect. Then, with a fleeting smile, she would disappear down the hallway to more pressing duties and he would not see her again for several days.

One morning, immediately after this profound exchange with the American nurse, Hans turned to see Rolf's supposedly useless eyes studying him thoughtfully. But Rolf made no comment, and Hans picked up reading where he had left off:

"Alma chapter ten. Now these are the words which Amulek preached unto the people who were in the land of A . . . Am-mo-ni-hah, saying, I am Amulek; I am the son of . . . Gid-do-nah, who was the son of—"

"Hans Brenner, you smell horrible."

Hans stopped reading. He laid down the book. "I beg your pardon?"

Rolf reverted to German and expounded delicately. "You smell foul. Like a decomposing corpse."

"Since when do you care, Rolf Schulmann?"

Rolf shrugged, his lips twisting in amusement.

Hans scowled at his friend, who was grinning at him from the pillow. "Now Rolf, is that any way to thank me for reading to you? I come here day after day, week after week, and all the thanks I get is a 'you stink'?"

"I'm trying to break it to you lightly."

"I can tell. Thanks a lot, Rolf."

"You really should take a bath."

"I hate baths. Every day I turn on the hot water in my porcelain tub, grab a new bar of soap and a soft, clean towel, and decide, 'No, I don't want to take a bath today. I prefer to smell like a rotting corpse.'"

"Well, it's working."

Hans exploded. "How do you expect me to take a bath, Rolf? Have you seen what it's like out there? Where do you think I'm staying?"

"From the looks of you, in a gutter."

"Just about."

Rolf sobered. "And yes, I *can* imagine what it's like out there. Besides, the hospital staff can't stop talking about the bombed city, the Russians, the beggars . . ." Rolf shifted position on the bed, wincing as he stretched a stiff back. "And every night I see them throwing you visitors out, and I wonder where you go until morning."

"A bomb shelter."

"I figured it was something like that."

"I have my own little corner, and no rodent, pest, or human dares invade my privacy."

"I'm glad you're so comfortably housed."

Hans detected the worry in his friend's voice, and he hated it. He detested anyone feeling sorry for him. "Hurry up and get well and I'll make room for you," he said. "I'll throw some mother with her crying baby out."

Rolf's lips twisted again. "You're such a friend, Hans Brenner."

FIVE

On his way to his basement retreat, Hans Brenner was passed by a convoy of trucks leaving the hospital compound. He caught a whiff of rotting food and other refuse, and on a whim he picked up his pace and trotted after the retreating vehicles. His body complained from the unaccustomed exercise and lack of nourishment, leaving him light-headed and breathless, but his stomach convinced him to continue.

He turned the corner in time to see the trucks, now several blocks ahead of him, disappear behind the crumbling façade of a department store. His lungs ached with the physical exertion and dust inhalation, yet he pressed on, willing his burning limbs to move faster as he followed the trail of dust.

The sun was beginning to set as he passed a family squatting around a campfire in the street, preparing their scanty evening meal. The children watched him pass, their eyes wide with interest and their bellies protruding with hunger. He turned where he had seen the trucks disappear and then slowed to a stop and stared down the deserted street. He was too late. No dust hung in the air to indicate the direction the trucks had gone. He leaned against the corner of the department store, dropping his arms to his sides and fighting for breath.

He felt foolish. What had he supposed he would find at the end of the journey? An ever-growing pile of miraculously preserved food, rising like the French Alps in front of his famished eyes? Hans licked his lips and contemplated the idea of food. After his foolish sprint through Berlin, his fantasy also included a tall glass of clear, cool water, heaven-sent to alleviate his ravenous thirst. He slid to a crouch against the wall, his back against the irregular bricks, and then stretched his long legs out across the sidewalk and into the open gutter.

He rested while the street grew ever more silent and the sun faded into the crumbled city's profile, the horizon orange with dust and evening moisture. A scattered whispering of clouds that promised much and delivered nothing stretched like crooked fingers across the sky. He leaned forward with his face in his hands, and as he rested he found himself wondering what the beautiful and mysterious Nurse Allred would be doing that evening.

What a strange thought to have at a time like this! He cursed silently and kicked at a chunk of concrete near his feet. Why would the American nurse invade his consciousness when all he desired at the moment was a bite of bread and a sip of water?

He heard the rumble of returning trucks then, and he leaped to his feet, watching the convoy turn into his street, solving the mystery of where it had disappeared. He began to run, ignoring the stares of the drivers as the empty trucks passed him by and returned in the direction they had come around the corner of the department store. Hans rounded the new corner and found himself finally facing the mountains of army refuse he had imagined.

He let neither the overwhelming stench nor the fact that food was not the most prominent product discourage him. Looking around, he saw a multitude of desperate humanity appearing from all points of the compass, moving in the same direction as he, with empty baskets and wooden boxes and filthy burlap sacks clutched in their hands. The race had begun.

Hans found a withered apple and consumed it in two bites—seeds, stem, and all. Next he snatched a stale crust of bread and stuffed it into his mouth. He was still chewing when he discovered an entire crate of potatoes and peelings, almost completely edible. He didn't hesitate—he snatched up the crate from the refuse pile, turned his back on the melee, and walked away. He'd found his treasure, and he no longer had any desire to wrestle against the determination of the other desperate refugees.

Hans noticed the envious glances of the new arrivals, and he shifted the crate of potatoes in his arms, feeling triumphant. As he turned past the department store, he again saw the family in the street. Again the children's eyes followed his progress, and this time they licked their lips, eyeing the crate he now carried. They didn't say a word, but he couldn't help stealing a glance in the direction of their cook fire as he passed. There was nothing but a thin liquid in their bowls and in the pot still simmering over the fire.

He hesitated, and at that moment he saw a slender figure on the other side of the street—a young woman with a paper in her hands that held her attention as she passed. Even in the fading light he recognized Nurse Allred. The crate in his hands felt heavy as he watched her glance down at her paper and then back up again, as if searching for something as she walked down the street.

He felt a sudden suprising desire to protect this woman, and he made a decision. He bent and deposited his crate with its irreplaceable treasure on the sidewalk in front of a tiny girl. She stared down at it as if he had just laid the treasures of the Orient at her feet. Then she crouched and reached with one grubby hand into the box, and soon she was joined by the remainder of her family.

Hans ignored them and followed the woman into the fading light.

SIX

Nurse Natalie Allred fingered the worn envelope in her hands as she had every day since she had arrived in Germany. She stared again at the address, the writing smudged from age and inattention: Bernaur Strasse 8-145, Berlin.

Natalie had not intended to be out alone this late in the day. But she had never told anyone but Curly her real reason for coming to Berlin, and Curly was on a temporary duty assignment to Nüremberg. If he'd known she was trying to find the address without him, he would have tried to dissuade her, saying it was too dangerous for a woman to be walking alone in Berlin—especially with her walk leading her directly toward the Russian sector. But Natalie couldn't afford to wait any longer.

She tossed her head, letting the cool evening breeze catch her auburn hair and blow it around her face. She could take care of herself. Fifteen years of hard work on a cattle ranch, then nursing school, and finally a career with the U.S. Army Nurse Corps had made her strong and self-sufficient. She could hold her own in this bombed-out shell of a city, and as much as Curly meant to her, she wasn't about to let his hesitant, careful nature interfere with what she had come here to do.

She slipped the letter into her pocket and picked up her pace. Her shift had gone late because of an old Frenchman's death. She'd had to take care of the body, bathing it and labeling it and turning it over to the morgue, then filling out an impossible mountain of associated paperwork before her supervisor would allow her to leave. The delay had cost her precious daylight.

This errand had been relegated to the back burner long enough, and she had vowed not to let another week go by without looking for her aunt. She'd deal with Curly's displeasure later. Right now, she needed to find Bernaur Strasse.

It frustrated her that every street looked the same. No matter where she turned, all she saw were bombed-out buildings, twisted steel, rats, and filth. What street signs remained were often buried in piles of rubble and refuse on the street corners, and she had to stop and dig them out before she could verify that the words did not match those on her envelope.

At times while she walked she imagined she could hear footsteps behind her, and she would turn, concerned at the thought that someone might be following her. But all she ever saw was the inexhaustible supply of dirty refugees going about their dreary existence: families clustering over their evening fires, children playing forlornly in the gutters, and individuals huddling together for warmth under makeshift shelters. Each time she turned to look over her shoulder, her fear was quickly replaced by amusement at her tendency to jump to conclusions, and eventually she convinced herself to stop looking over her shoulder and to simply ignore everything but her errand. So when the drab sunlight gradually faded to darkness and human noises died away, she didn't notice the growing solitude until she rounded a corner and found herself completely alone in an unfamiliar street.

Now she hesitated and glanced around her, trying to ignore the tiny prickles that had returned to pester her. She had no choice, she reasoned with herself. She had to find this address before the army started getting any ideas about relocating her and her unit—and they seemed to do some sort of rotation every month with other bases around Europe. Until today Natalie had not even considered the possibility that she might lose her chance to find her mother's sister. Then this morning her friend Hannah had been transferred to Frankfurt with just a few hours' notice, and Natalie had realized that her stay in Berlin was precarious.

She pulled out the envelope and glanced again at the address and then around her in an attempt to find the name of this street she was on. At that moment she heard the sound of footsteps rounding the corner of a half-demolished structure, and she turned in the direction of the sound, hopeful of some assistance with the address. Three figures materialized across the street, but they headed in the opposite direction from her position. She squinted, trying to make them out in the darkness, and again she berated herself for being out so late.

The three men laughed and talked, and one of them weaved a bit as he walked. They wore uniforms, and two carried rifles loosely in their hands. Natalie could not quite make out what they were saying. She realized that it was not English they spoke but something that sounded disturbingly like Russian.

Natalie's heart immediately started to pound. She could have sworn she was still in American Berlin, in the Neukölln district south of the hospital.

A young commissary officer who made deliveries to the hospital had insisted that the address on her letter was in that area. How could she have crossed over into the dreaded Red Army sector without realizing it?

She stepped backward and, in her haste, promptly tripped over the gutter. Desperately she grabbed for anything to stop her fall, but her hands closed on thin air. Her backside hit a pile of rubble, and she slid down the side into a pitiful heap. Loose bricks tumbled and slid around her, bruising her shoulders and limbs and clattering like little bombs onto the sidewalk and into the gutter.

All three soldiers stopped in their tracks, turned, and looked in her direction, and for one terrifying moment the earth stopped turning as she stared into the faces of the three soldiers. She scrambled to free herself from the rubble.

"Wait, Fräulein—I help!" The words were German, and spoken terribly. Even with her rudimentary knowledge of the language, Natalie could tell that the tall officer was slaughtering the phrase. He approached her, trotting across the street with his companions, their footsteps echoing as their boots struck the uneven street. He tossed the bottle he'd been carrying to his comrades and paused next to her, offering her his hand.

Natalie hesitated, and then carefully took his hand and allowed him to pull her to her feet, his enthusiastic heave bringing her momentarily within inches of his face. She smelled the vodka on his breath before she moved farther away, brushing dust from her clothes and adjusting her skirt. The man and his companions watched her with unveiled interest.

"Danke," she managed, although the German word came out with difficulty. She didn't want them to know she was an American, and she hoped their own dismal German would keep them from realizing that she was a foreigner. She didn't want to speak to them at all—she only wanted to turn and run. But she noticed that two of the men had moved, casually positioning themselves on her left and her right, cutting off her escape route—unless she could sprout wings and fly over the wall at her back.

The man who had assisted her smiled, displaying several mended teeth. His face was crisscrossed with scars, and someone somewhere had broken his nose. He wore his uniform cap at a jaunty angle over hair bordering on the long side of military regulation. The fine wrinkles at the corners of his grey eyes suggested he was in his mid-thirties, but since she had arrived in war-destroyed Europe Natalie had realized that wrinkles did not necessarily indicate age.

She glanced to her left and met the smiling young face of the other officer, blond-haired, blue-eyed, and clearly not even into his twenties. He tipped the bottle of vodka to his mouth, his eyes never leaving her face.

The first officer spoke again. He had not missed her deception. "You—not German." The man's brows puckered, and she caught a curious flicker of humanity in his eyes as he studied her. He was honestly trying to communicate with her, she realized, and suddenly she wondered if she should allow herself to trust him. She knew her safety hung in the balance: if she feigned ignorance or refused to communicate, the men might lose interest in her and leave her alone. Or the opposite might hold true, and they might decide to dispense with all attempts at chivalry and attack her right here, right now—she glanced around at the empty, darkened street—without wasting any more time trying to converse.

Nurses returning from the war had cautioned her before she came to Berlin to steer clear of the Russian soldiers at all costs, and Natalie had accepted their warnings without question. Working at the hospital, those warnings had become etched more deeply into her soul with each sad medical case she had witnessed. But certainly not all Russians would treat a woman with such disrespect. Certainly there would be more than just monsters among these tentative allies of the United States who had suffered so much at the hands of the Axis powers.

"American?"

Natalie realized she might be making a terrible mistake, but she decided to give diplomacy a chance. She nodded.

The officer stepped closer, reverting eagerly to her tongue. He patted his chest proudly. "I study English on the Moscow University."

"I'm a nurse, working for the Americans," she replied. She had heard that Russian men admired intelligent women, and the look in his eyes told her that perhaps her profession elevated her a little above the masses. She hoped that admiration would inspire him and his comrades to treat her like a lady—at least until she could talk her way out of this mess.

He reached out his right hand, and she reluctantly allowed him to take hers in a very American handshake. "I am Oleg," he introduced himself. Then with his free hand he indicated each of his companions. "This Misha," he said, pointing to the other officer, "and this Yarik."

Natalie acknowledged them but did not volunteer her name.

He sensed her reluctance, hesitated, and then dropped her hand, sobering somewhat. "I am happy to meet American woman intelligent enough to be nurse—but I still must ask you what you are doing in Russian zone."

"I'm *not* in the Russian Zone." Out of the corner of her eye Natalie caught Misha glancing at Yarik and she felt her heart skip a beat. She was certain these Russians were outside their area. She had not passed any checkpoints, American or Soviet, and she doubted it was possible to cross over otherwise. Most likely these soldiers had been trying to slip unnoticed back into the Treptow district before they could be discovered. She licked her lips nervously and wondered how to proceed.

"You are young," Oleg said. "How old?"

She hesitated, then added four years to her age. "Twenty-eight."

"Show me papers, please." The officer remained cordial. Reluctantly she reached for her passport and military ID, and he took them, brushing his fingers deliberately against hers as he did so. He looked from her military picture to her face, his eyes hooded. He studied the documents slowly and deliberately, and Natalie's anxiety intensified with each passing moment.

"The papers say you born in 1921." Oleg had caught her lie, and she could see that it amused him. She dug her fingernails into her palms.

"Why you here?" Oleg handed her documents to the younger officer, and Misha took them and studied her picture with interest.

"I was assigned here by the American army . . ." She pretended to misunderstand his question, but Oleg did not let her get away with it.

"You know what I mean, nurse. Why you here, now—alone?"

"I . . ." Natalie swallowed hard. She didn't want to tell the man about her letter, her possible connection to a German, and it took a moment for her to remember her rehearsed excuse for her excursion: she had been sketching scenes of the ruined city, hoping to sell them to an American newspaper that had seen her talent and shown an interest in her work. "I'm an artist—see?" She fumbled in her purse and took out her portfolio, opening it and producing a pencil sketch. It was her latest masterpiece, a drawing of a grandmother sitting in the gutter with a baby in her arms, leaning on a pile of rubble, the woman and the baby bowed against each other in shared slumber.

Oleg took the sketch from Natalie's outstretched hand, his eyes lingering on her face and hair before gazing down at the picture. A moment later he handed it back to her, uninterested. He glanced once at his companions and then back at her. Then he shook his head as if chiding a disobedient child. "You should not be in Russian zone, Nurse Allred."

She felt a retort on her lips but forced herself to answer humbly, "I'll go home now. Thank you for helping me." She turned to the younger officer and held out her hand for her passport and ID. But with a sneer on his lips, he deliberately slipped her documents into his uniform pocket.

Natalie's jaw dropped, and she protested, "Give me my documents!"

Oleg spoke, his voice forced politeness. "You will come with us. We need to ask questions before we give you documents. *Ponimayetye?* Do you understand?"

She understood. She stepped backward, shaking her head. "No. I—I have to get back to the hospital."

He might admire intelligence, but the spark in Oleg's eyes warned her that insubordination drove him mad. "You will come." He stepped toward her and reached for her arm.

She batted his hand away, her adrenaline rising, and suddenly Yarik attacked from behind, twisting her right arm painfully behind her back and attempting to throw an arm across her shoulders. Without thinking she whipped her free left elbow upward and backward into Yarik's nose and mouth. He released her with a vicious string of Russian curses. He staggered backward, disoriented, clutching at his face and tripping over the broken curb in his shock. Then Misha lunged at her with great enthusiasm, grabbing her hair and sidestepping her flailing fists, determined not to allow her the same advantage over him that she had had over his comrade. Animal-like, Natalie turned her head and bit his finger deeply, breaking skin and bringing a dreadful howl from her tormentor. He released her and stumbled backward, crying like a baby. Stunned by what she'd done, Natalie didn't notice Oleg until it was too late. He stepped forward and punched her in the midriff with unbelievable force. She gasped, doubling over and fighting for breath. Her purse fell to the road and her sketches caught the evening breeze and scattered in all directions. Several were mangled under the boots of her attacker as he moved closer.

Yarik came toward her as well, one hand trying unsuccessfully to contain the bleeding from his broken nose and the other producing a small, evil-looking knife. He held it expertly and advanced toward Natalie, murder in his eyes.

Oleg grabbed her hair and hauled her to her feet, and she felt his foul breath on the back of her neck as he hissed, "You make mistake, Nurse, coming here tonight."

"*You're* the ones trespassing!" Natalie gasped the words, hardly able to breathe and still unable to believe she'd gotten herself into this predicament. *Stupid, stupid girl!* she scolded silently.

"Hush, woman." Oleg's sticky hand wrapped across her mouth, and she fought to free herself from his disgusting grip. She reached upward and backward and managed to drive her thumbs into his eyes. He yelled and slapped at her angrily with the hand that had covered her mouth, and she took advantage of the split second of freedom to scream as loudly as she could before his hand came securely down again.

Oleg's breath tickled her ear. "You hurt Yarik, and Misha's finger. Now we hurt you." He grunted at the knife-wielding Yarik, at the same time catching her by the chin and forcing her head backward, exposing her throat to Yarik's advancing, eager blade.

In that split second of stark reality Natalie's world went cold and unbelievably dark, and she had a desperate, fleeting image of her mother in her mind. Her mother needed her. How would her mother ever survive the news of her death?

Her head thundered with the suddenness of it all, and in her shock her mind was slow to register the sounds of a gunshot, the knife hitting the pavement, and Yarik's scream as he fell to the ground, clutching the hand that had held the knife to her throat. Oleg released her and stepped backward, grabbing for his rifle. From his huddle near the bricks, Misha shrieked, high pitched and shrill, before staggering to his feet, leaping over Yarik, and sprinting down the street.

"Don't do it."

The deep voice behind her sounded familiar, and Natalie turned to see Rolf Schulmann's friend standing on the corner of the street less than twenty paces away, grungy, ill-clothed, and scraggly-haired. Natalie's first irrational thought was that the German looked like a beggar—and her second, even more irrational thought, was that she desperately wanted to run weeping into that beggar's arms.

Instead, she stood where she was and squeaked, *"Hans Brenner?"*

He ignored her and glared steadily at the two remaining Russians with his gun leveled at Oleg's head. He spoke deliberately, in the thick English he always used with her. "I said, 'Don't do it,' and I mean it. Drop your weapon and step away."

Oleg hesitated, shifted uncomfortably, and then tossed his rifle into the gutter.

Hans stepped closer, his gun trained on the officer's head. "You sure know how to treat a lady. Now leave." He gestured with the weapon. "Take your cowardly friend and leave."

Without argument, Oleg helped the wounded Yarik to his feet and moved away down the street, glancing behind him as they retreated. Stunned, Natalie stared after her tormentors, and then revulsion made her shudder and she turned aside, dropped to her knees, and retched into the gutter. Only after emptying her stomach was she able to straighten and turn to stare at her rescuer.

Her eyes dropped to the Luger in his hand, and Hans quickly concealed the weapon beneath his tattered shirt.

Trembling, Natalie whispered, "They ruined my sketches." It sounded absurd even to her.

"They were planning to ruin something else, Fräulein."

Suddenly she gasped. "They have my passport and military ID!" She pointed accusingly after the escaping soldiers, realizing as she did so that she sounded like a blubbering child on the playground, complaining to the teacher that a bully had stolen her lunch pail.

"You'll have to get others."

Numbly she rubbed at her throat, her eyes again falling to the knife on the street. Blood from Yarik's wounded hand stained the handle and blade, and Natalie could not help imagining that in another second the blood would have been her own. Her hand clutched nervously at her still-intact throat.

"You saved my life," she moaned, and she hated that she sounded so vulnerable. But the fact was, she could not get her brain to function properly— let alone her voice. She was on the verge of tears, fighting against the urge to howl in frustration.

"What are you doing all alone?" The German was incredulous. "At night? In Berlin? I can't imagine anything so idiotic—"

"Look, Mr. Brenner, it's really none of your—"

"Yes it *is* my business, Nurse Allred. I almost killed three men, and I have a right to know the reason why."

She blinked back hot tears, angry at herself for her lack of control and frustrated that this German was here to see it. "I was sketching Berlin."

"What?"

The tears she had fought to suppress began to fall unchecked. "I'm an artist," she sobbed. "I was sketching Berlin."

He was incredulous. "Are you mad? *Sketching Berlin?* At night? Right next to the Soviet zone?" He stepped closer. "Not enough Berlin in the Allied district, is that it?"

Natalie tried to glare at him through her tears, but instead she wilted, her shoulders slumping and her hands covering her eyes. "Actually, Mr. Brenner, I'm lost."

Hans's voice softened. "You sound lost, Nurse Allred."

She turned her back on him and tried to pull a blood-stained sketch out from under Yarik's knife, but it came apart in her hand. Suddenly the harsh reality of what had just happened—and what *might* have happened— overwhelmed her, and she crouched next to the abandoned knife and bawled.

Behind her, the German gave an exasperated sigh. "This is not the time or the place, Miss Allred. We've got to get away from here before those soldiers return—with reinforcements."

"They almost killed me!" Natalie rolled to her knees and crawled dazedly after a sketch that turned over and over in the breeze. "Oleg stepped on my drawings."

Hans stomped heavily on the paper as it passed, stopping its escape but at the same time grinding it into the dirt with his tattered boot. He ignored Natalie's outraged gasp at his blatant damage to her art. "Get up, Miss Allred. This really isn't the time." He grabbed her arm and hauled her to her feet, handing her the paper. "Your pictures are gone, and we've got to get out of here now or we're dead." He shook her arm. "Do you understand me?"

"I can still save them."

"Listen, woman, half of your pictures are destroyed and the other half are on their way to Denmark."

"They're important to me." She knew she was being irrational, but she still couldn't stop herself.

Hans dropped her arm and sprinted after three papers that had already crossed the street and were making their way up and across piles of twisted rubble on the other side. He swept them up and sprinted back the way he had come and thrust them into her hands. "There. That's all I can find. Now can we go?"

Suddenly she stared up at him as if she had just recalled who he was. "What are you doing here, anyway, Mr. Brenner?"

"Walking," he said. "Thinking." His words were vague, noncommittal.

"Walking? You mean following me, don't you."

His face flushed. "I had a feeling you might need help, Nurse Allred."

She studied him thoughtfully, and then she said, "Natalie."

"What?"

"My name is Natalie." She looked up at him and saw the world begin to tilt sideways behind his head. She reached out to him and felt his arms catch her before she could fall.

"Listen—Natalie—we really don't have time for introductions." He moved her away from the scene of the attack, his arm supporting her. She forced her legs to follow his lead while her stunned brain still tried to evaluate his reason for being there, but she didn't resist as he led her through the darkened streets of bomb-ravaged Berlin, weaving through alleys, around corners, and across a park overgrown with weeds and rubble, with clusters of campfires and refugees huddling against the night's chill. She didn't protest when he led her down a flight of steps, through a heavy door, and into the rank, stale air of a basement shelter.

"Sit here, Natalie." He handed her a dirty blanket. "You need to rest until you're better."

"I'm all right."

"No you're not. You've been babbling."

"Listen—I'm a nurse. And I'm not stupid. I'd know if I was all right."

"I wouldn't say that too loud, Natalie. Any woman who wanders alone at night near the Soviet sector could very easily be mistaken for stupid."

She opened her mouth to retort, but something in his expression made her realize it would be useless.

Brenner persisted. "What were you doing?"

"Where are we? This is disgusting."

"Home."

"Certainly not the home of a human being."

"Of course not. Just me. And forty other gutter rats."

Natalie looked around her. She was sitting on an overturned crate next to a moldy concrete wall, and as her eyes adjusted to the gloom she noticed her curiosity mirrored by at least a dozen pairs of eyes, situated in faces ranging from the very old and infirm to the tiniest of babies. A mother with twins held against her chest stared back at Natalie with desperation so great that it broke her heart. A tiny girl clung to her father and pulled a coat over her small frame in an attempt to stay warm. Babies cried and men and women talked in groups, their voices low. The place reeked with suffering humanity.

"I—I'm sorry, Mr. Brenner. I didn't know . . ."

"We're lucky to be here, Miss Allred."

For several moments she silently studied the room, watching as a woman stirred something in a small iron pot suspended over a miniature flame, a bewhiskered ghost of a man smoked the stub of a cigar, two children fought over a broken toy truck, and a white-haired grandmother read to a young girl in the feeble light of a candle.

"Where do all these people come from?" She said it with a mixture of pity and awe, as if the plight of these homeless souls was tempered by the obvious resilience and determination to survive evident in their simple routines.

"Refugees," Hans murmured. "Most of them came from the east— they were trying to keep ahead of the Soviet army's advance. There are hundreds of thousands of them in the city. They can't find places to live, and they can't go home. Probably most of them had family—or at least distant relatives—here in Berlin before the war. So they came here to find their family members only to discover that their relatives are dead or have disappeared."

Natalie turned her gaze to Hans. She studied him. "Do you have family here, Mr. Brenner?"

"Only a brother."

Natalie looked at him thoughtfully. "Rolf Schulmann."

Hans nodded. "His parents took me in when I was young, and we've been like brothers ever since."

He cleared his throat and suddenly changed the subject, and Natalie realized he was uncomfortable talking about himself. "Tell me what you were doing, Natalie. And don't tell me you were drawing pictures."

She hung her head. "I was looking for someone." She was surprised at herself. The only other person she had ever told this information to was Curly. Why would she confide in this untidy, dark-haired drifter?

"Looks like you succeeded. You found a group of misplaced, excitement-starved Russians."

She shook her head. "I was looking for . . . Oh no . . . *no!*" Suddenly her voice rose to a distressed wail and Natalie flew to her feet, the blanket sliding from her lap. Several refugees turned to stare at her, startled by her outburst.

"What is it?"

"My letter. *My letter!*" She turned and clutched Hans by his shirt front. "We've got to go back!"

"Not for all the gold teeth in Germany—or Poland either, for that matter."

"You don't understand—"

"That's right. I *don't* understand. You're becoming more of a riddle every second."

"My letter . . ." It was a desperate howl, welling up from deep inside Natalie's chest. She dropped once more to the crate and buried her face in her hands. "I need that letter!"

"This one?"

She looked up from her hands and saw him extract a letter from inside his shirt, one corner of the envelope shredded from the heavy tread of a boot.

She reached for it with another cry, this one of pure joy. "You found it!"

He held the envelope at arm's length. "Not until you tell me what this is all about." He waved it in front of her, just out of her reach. "Why did I almost have to kill tonight?"

"You have no right." She lunged for the letter. "Give it to me!"

"Yes, I do," Hans retorted. "I saved your life and I saved your letter, not to mention your precious sketches. So tell me why this envelope is so important."

Natalie hesitated. She studied Hans for a long moment, trying to discern whether he would safeguard her secret. Finally she sighed and relented. "My mother has a younger sister who lives in Berlin." She hesitated. "At least, she used to before the war . . . This is the last letter we received from her."

Hans studied the letter. "This was mailed more than seven *years* ago."

"That's right. We haven't heard from her since then. And because of your war"—Natalie stopped herself, then altered her wording—"*the* war, we haven't been able to contact her." Natalie reached again for her letter, and this time Hans didn't pull it away. "I came to Germany to find my aunt and her family."

"I thought you came to help us bury our dead."

"That's not funny. Don't joke about what I do."

Hans scowled. "The address on that letter is in the middle of the Treptow district—in the Russian sector. You'd never have made it."

"You're wrong, Mr. Brenner." She lifted her chin stubbornly. "I have it on good authority that this address is in south Neukölln, well inside our sector of Berlin."

"No, that's wrong." Hans swiped the letter back from Natalie's grip and pointed to the address. "Bernaur Strasse runs east and west, perpendicular to the American–Soviet division. Besides, this particular address would not even be connected to the Bernaur Strasse several kilometers south of here. Whoever gave you directions probably had you heading south." Hans's lips twitched as he suppressed a smile. "I know Berlin, Miss Natalie. You were headed the wrong way."

Mortified, Natalie glanced down at the letter from her aunt and felt depression settling in the pit of a stomach still aching from Oleg's blow.

Hans's voice softened. "You came all the way across the world only to have your mission of mercy interrupted by a demarcation line and a group of drunken criminals."

Natalie recalled she was speaking to a former German officer and drew herself up. "Don't call them that, Mr. Brenner. I'm sure they're just lonely and frustrated by all this." She wiped at a running nose. "Besides, they've been pummeled and victimized so badly by you Germans, they probably think they deserve a little of their own back."

"Yes, and those deserving victims were going to kill you."

Natalie shuddered and clutched the letter to her chest. She could feel the German's dark eyes studying her, and she tried not to feel uncomfortable. After all, he'd just saved her life. Certainly his actions spoke louder than his appearance—and made more of an impression than his *smell*. "Mr. Brenner . . ."

"Hans."

She turned and managed a half-smile. "I know. Your friend told me."

"You talk with him a lot?" His voice had a sudden, curious edge to it.

"No. Just a word or two when I pass by."

Hans lowered himself to the floor beside Natalie's crate, then glanced up at her. "Look, Natalie, I . . ." He hesitated. "I've wanted to thank you for what you did for Rolf . . ."

She shook her head. "It wasn't me."

"Your friends, then. For giving Rolf a—a blessing."

"It wasn't them, either. God honored their blessing."

She could see that he was confused, so she tried to explain. "Curly and Gregory try to live their lives so that God will honor them for their use of His priesthood power. They are only messengers from God."

"Like missionaries? Rolf said missionaries taught him about God."

"That's right." Natalie nodded. "In many ways, they are like missionaries— they are ordained to hold God's priesthood, and as long as God is happy with the way they are living their lives, God will honor the requests they make in His name."

"I wish I could understand what happened in that room." Hans shook his head, something still baffling him. "I wish that I—" He broke off suddenly and folded his arms across his knees, apparently not planning to finish the thought.

Natalie watched him and felt an inexplicable camaraderie with the man who had just saved her life. "Rolf will make it, I'm sure." Suddenly, impulsively, she touched the rough hand that rested so near her own, and she was surprised when he captured it tightly. And then, as if the touch of their two hands had affected him more deeply than he had expected it to, he abruptly pulled away.

Natalie tried to take her mind off her embarrassment. "Tell me more about your friend Rolf."

Hans shrugged. "He has a young son waiting for him in Switzerland. Rolf's wife died a few years ago, and he has an American girlfriend now— Marie Jacobson—watching out for the boy and praying that Rolf is still alive."

"The war separated them?"

Hans nodded. "Rolf spent the last year of the war as a prisoner at Sachsenhausen concentration camp—now *that* would make an interesting bundle of sketches for your collection—and Marie escaped to Switzerland to find Alma."

"Rolf's son?"

"That's right."

"And what about you, Hans Brenner? What have you been doing for the last year?"

"Looking for Rolf. Running from the Nazis, the Americans, and the Red Army. I'm a deserter, you know."

"Can you tell me about it?"

Hans leaned back against the concrete wall behind him and glanced at Natalie sitting on the crate. For just a moment his eyes met hers, and she tried to ignore the way the connection made her feel. Hans hesitated, and she realized he probably hadn't shared his experiences with anyone before, let alone an American nurse with a knack for getting herself—and him—into deadly situations.

Finally Hans shook his head. "You're the enemy, remember?"

"Thanks a lot."

"No. I mean it. You think the war is over. But look around you." Hans's arm swept the depressing room. "These people have a long way to go before the war ends for them."

"We're here to help, that's all."

"Whose side are you on?"

"What?"

"Whose side are you on, Natalie? You're an American—"

"—with German blood," she interrupted. "My grandfather was born and raised here. My mother and her sister—"

"But *you* are an American. And you're here with the Allies to subdue, reconstruct, and rule what you've destroyed."

Natalie bristled slightly. "Destroyed because of a stubborn madman."

"I'm not going to argue with you. Hitler *was* a madman."

"How long did it take you to figure that out?"

"That's not important."

"It's very important. When did you desert? After you'd killed a few American soldiers? Or as soon as you realized Hitler was terrorizing the Jews?"

"That's none of your business. Besides, what does it matter to you? You're not a Jew."

"Yes I am."

Hans fell silent, and again he studied her, this time with a mixture of admiration and pity. "You're courageous to tell me, Miss Allred. I might be a vile anti-Semitic."

"*Are* you a Jew hater?"

"How much of a Jew are you?"

"What do you mean?"

"What percentage?"

"This is disgusting. I can't believe we're discussing this."

"Half? Quarter? Eighth?"

"What does it matter?"

"You don't look like a Jew. I would never have known."

"Quarter. Do you hate me now?"

"No. Why should I?"

"Nazis hate Jews."

"I don't consider myself a Nazi anymore."

Natalie leaned back. "I'm not a practicing Jew. My mother expected me to follow my father's religion, and he was a Christian."

"Was?"

Natalie nodded. "He died two weeks before I came out here." She shrugged and ignored the familiar emptiness that threatened to bring tears to her eyes.

"Do you miss him?"

She brushed at a lock of hair. "To be honest—no, I don't."

"Why not?"

"He was never a big part of my life." She picked a piece of lint from her skirt. "He was always away herding cattle with the other outfits, and when he was home, he never paid me much attention."

She could feel him studying her. After several moments of silence he said gently, "I said I don't hate you, Natalie. It doesn't matter if you're a Jew or not. And you can practice whatever religion you want." Hans smiled wryly. "Hey, my best friend's a Mormon. How much worse can it get?"

Natalie laughed hesitantly. "So am I."

Hans stared. "I'm confused. You just said you're a Jew."

"I am. Jews can be Mormons."

"So you're a German, but you're an American. And you're a quarter Jew, but you're also a Mormon. You're quite the breed, Miss Allred. Tell me you're anything else and you'd belong in a zoo."

Natalie smothered a giggle and felt a sudden, growing kinship with the man sitting on the floor beside her.

"How'd you become a Mormon?"

"My friends are Mormons—Curly and Gregory."

"After what they did for Rolf, I guess I assumed that."

"They taught me about the Church."

"How did you meet them?"

"The taller one—Gregory Jameson—he's from back home. Curly Miller I met in the army."

"So when did you become a Mormon?"

"Curly baptized me a few months ago—before we left the States."

"Where are you from?"

"South Dakota. Wait a second." Natalie punched his arm. "We were talking about *you,* not me. You were telling me why you deserted."

Natalie felt her companion's mood change, as if he suddenly wished she would change the subject. She obliged by saying quietly, "Are you sure it doesn't bother you?"

Hans smirked. "Your Jewish heritage? Or the fact that you're a Mormon?" He shifted position on the hard concrete. "I have to be honest with you, Miss Allred. I've been indoctrinated pretty thoroughly by the Führer's anti-Jewish propaganda. But, for some reason, I never felt a need to form an opinion of my own one way or another."

"But you helped him implement his policies."

"No. I just shot enemy soldiers who were trying to shoot me."

Natalie shuddered. "How many did you kill?"

"I don't remember. One, at least."

"Only one?"

"I said 'at least.' And I'm sure he deserved it. Why are you asking me such a question?" Hans scowled at her. "How many Germans has your friend Gregory shot? Or Curly?"

"I see what you mean." Natalie's voice softened. "I'm sorry."

"Look, Natalie . . ." Hans took a deep breath before continuing. "There are some things better left alone. Better forgotten. Understand?"

"Maybe. But I've always felt it was better to get things out in the open. Then they're not festering inside and destroying your future happiness."

"I don't have a future."

"A lot of people feel that way right now, Hans Brenner. Don't worry. Someday it'll all work out."

Hans gave her a faint smile and stood. He said nothing for a few moments, and she could hear the muffled sobbing of a baby at the far end of the shelter. She looked up and met his gaze.

Hans spoke softly. "I think it's time to get you home."

"Hans?"

"What?"

Again she reached for his hand, and this time he did not pull away. "Thank you for saving my life."

SEVEN

August 16, 1945

Rolf struggled against the confines of his blankets, tossing his head urgently back and forth. His panicked contortions displaced his coverings, sending them sliding to the floor in a tangled heap. Over and over he moaned, and the sound was more than Hans Brenner could endure.

The doctor had said there was nothing they could do—he surmised that some horrific inner turmoil held Rolf in its subconscious grip. But Hans stubbornly shook Rolf again, urgently this time, and finally Rolf's body relaxed until nothing remained of the episode but a sheen of sweat on his brow. Rolf opened his eyes, and Hans breathed a sigh of relief.

Even though the episode had frightened him, Hans forced himself to be cheerful for Rolf's sake. "How's the eyesight today?" he asked with a grin, falling into a chair next to Rolf's bed and giving an exaggerated stretch.

"Terrible." Rolf's voice was little more than a whisper.

"Really."

"You'll have to read to me again. I'm so sorry." Rolf suppressed a weak smile. "Where were we?"

Hans reached for the Book of Mormon next to Rolf's dinner tray. "Somewhere in 3 Nephi, I think. I'll have to find the marker." He began thumbing through the book, his long fingers leaving smudges on the pages, and Rolf watched him silently. To Hans, Rolf seemed extra tired lately, as if his health were deteriorating. Hans didn't mean to ask, but his eyes betrayed his concern, and Rolf answered his unspoken question.

"I've been having trouble sleeping."

"They can give you something for that."

"I'm sure they can. I just haven't asked."

"Why? You look terrible. How do you expect to leave here if you can't get well?" Hans nodded in the direction of Rolf's food. "You've hardly touched your food. How do you expect to heal if you don't eat?"

"Want it?"

"Of course not. Eat it yourself."

"I'm not interested, Hans."

Hans set the book down, scooted his chair closer to the bed, and reached for a sandwich. Rolf watched him, his eyes wary. "What are you going to do with that?"

"I'm going to shove it down your ungrateful throat, Mormon. I'm going to make you get well whether you like it or not. And then I'm going to write to that woman of yours and tell her to get over here immediately and talk some sense into you."

Rolf scowled weakly. "You promised, Hans."

Hans stretched out his hand. "Eat. That's an order."

"You're so persuasive."

"Eat it, Rolf."

Rolf took the sandwich and stared at it listlessly. Then he set it back on the tray. "I'm really not hungry, Hans."

"I didn't ask if you were."

"I can't eat with you sitting there staring at me."

"Why not?" Hans demanded, his voice rising several decibels.

"Because I can't keep it down, and I know you're starving."

Hans smirked. "That's not true. I had a fine lunch today: Russian caviar from the Black Sea, a fine Bratwurst, and fresh-brewed coffee."

"You're a terrible liar."

Hans stood and walked resolutely toward the door. "I'm going to go get Nurse Natalie to talk some sense into you."

Rolf smiled. "She's a handful, isn't she?"

"I wouldn't know."

"She keeps asking questions about you."

Hans paused. "What questions?"

"Subtle, vague ones—like 'So when is that friend of yours going to take a bath?' and stuff like that."

"Funny, Rolf."

"When you find her, will you do me a favor?"

"Depends on whether that sandwich is still sitting there in three seconds."

Rolf picked up the sandwich and took a small bite. He chewed deliberately, and Hans realized from the look on his friend's face that Rolf had been telling the truth—he was having a hard time eating. Hans felt the familiar worry-knot in the pit of his empty stomach, the same feeling he always had when he allowed himself to wonder if Rolf was going to make it. He forced himself to smile encouragingly. "That's it. Keep going. Now what do you need me to ask the dragon?"

Rolf laughed, a muffled sound around the food in his mouth. He swallowed—with difficulty, Hans noticed—and said, "I need a chaplain."

"Last confessions? You're not dying, Rolf."

"No. Nothing like that. I need a *Mormon* chaplain. I—I need to ask him a question. Do you think you could ask Natalie if her friends . . ."

"Of course." The knot in Hans's stomach worsened.

* * *

Hans found Natalie in the lunchroom with the American pilot she had called Curly. They seemed deep in an emotional conversation, and Hans loathed the thought of approaching the table. But Curly saw him and straightened, waving at him over Natalie's shoulder. She turned and smiled, and he knew he was trapped. He approached the pair.

"Hans Brenner!" Curly rose to his feet and slapped the German's shoulder companionably. "How're you doin' today?"

Hans was not in the mood for boisterous American greetings. "Rolf's not eating," he said without preamble. He glanced at Natalie and saw his concern reflected in her eyes.

She said, "I'll get the doctor for him."

She began to rise, but Curly shook his head. "No, Nattie, stay and finish—you need a break. I'll find him." Curly reached for his visor cap, hesitated, and touched Natalie's shoulder. "Just think about what I said. You're getting too emotionally involved in this thing . . ." He stopped and glanced up at Hans.

"Mr. Brenner knows about my aunt, Curly. He—he found me looking at that letter." She caught Hans's eye, and he realized she had not told her friend the whole story.

Curly studied Hans with new respect. "You agree with me then, don't you? She could be getting herself into trouble."

"Natalie's pretty smart. She can take care of herself."

"There's no doubt she's smart," Curly said. "I just want her to be safe, that's all." He didn't take offense at Hans's contradiction but just smiled at Natalie, and Hans wondered what exactly their relationship entailed.

Natalie returned Curly's smile and Curly bent and kissed her cheek. Hans didn't like the way that made him feel and he looked away, feigning interest in the other tables and their occupants.

Curly slapped Hans again on the shoulder, a friendly gesture that never ceased to irritate Hans about the Americans. "You're a good man, Hans Brenner. You've been a great friend to Schulmann. He owes you one."

One what? Hans ignored Curly's strange reference to debt and turned to Natalie. "Rolf wants you to find him a Mormon chaplain."

Natalie's brow furrowed, but Curly was the one to speak. "What's up, Brenner?"

"I think he's giving up." The thought made Hans sick, but he shrugged, trying to feign indifference.

Curly nodded soberly. "All right. I'll get one. Tell your friend I'll find him a chaplain." Curly glanced one more time at Natalie. "You going to be all right?"

Natalie nodded. "I'll see you after work."

Curly smiled at Hans and then turned and walked away, waving at an acquaintance across the room as he did so.

Hans turned back to Natalie. "He's a nice fellow."

"He's one of my best friends."

"You're going to marry him, aren't you?" He was surprised when the thought made his stomach churn.

Natalie's cheeks blossomed red. "I don't know. He says we should get married . . ."

"Do it. You can marry him for eternity."

"Eternity?"

"In your Mormon temple." Hans slid into the chair Curly had vacated. "Rolf's girl told me all about eternal marriage."

Natalie smiled sadly but didn't respond.

Hans studied her closely. "Did your father ever meet Curly?"

"No. I don't think he would've liked Curly."

"Why?"

"Dad hated Mormons. Had an argument with a Mormon neighbor once over property boundaries. He wouldn't have approved of my joining the Mormon Church, either."

"Why did you let Curly baptize you if you knew your father wouldn't have approved?"

"I *asked* Curly to baptize me, Hans." She was suddenly thoughtful. "I let him baptize me because I knew it was right."

"You didn't get baptized just so you could marry Curly in the temple?"

"Of course not." She shook her head. "What an awful idea, to join the Church just because I aspired to marry someone in the temple. As far as I'm concerned, that's like lying to God."

"How?"

She shifted in her chair and glanced at him uncomfortably. "Because when we're baptized we make promises with Heavenly Father—we promise to keep His commandments even if it's difficult. If I'd decided to join the Church just to fulfill a selfish ambition, it wouldn't have been honest—to me, to my husband, or to God."

"But I thought being a member of the Mormon Church was the only way to marry someone for eternity."

Natalie nodded. "But joining the Church just so you can convince someone to marry you seems a bit manipulative—especially if deep down in your heart you know you're not converting for the right reasons."

"What are the right reasons, Natalie?"

Natalie hesitated, studying him. "Curly says they would be following the Savior's example, repentance, obedience. I think it would also include a desire to change one's heart."

Hans asked, "But in spite of these fine-sounding principles, you believe your father would not have approved—of your baptism or your boyfriend."

Natalie's eyes misted, and Hans knew he'd hit a sore spot. She lifted her chin in the way that made her irresistible. "I never really cared what my father thought, really . . ."

"Really."

Natalie glanced at him sideways. "He wasn't necessarily the best of fathers, and he got angry at my mom a lot."

"Your mom anything like you?"

Natalie slugged his arm in protest, and Hans didn't mind. She sobered. "Anyway, Curly tells me he loves me so much that he's sure we'll get married in the temple someday. We're not engaged, but he feels God has prepared us for each other." Natalie paused. "But he wants the Mormon chaplain to marry us first, so we can be together right now."

Hans's eyes widened. "Can Mormons do that?"

She nodded, but she looked uncomfortable.

"A civil marriage? For eternity?"

Natalie shook her head. "No, just 'til death do us part.'"

"So a temple wedding is more important to you than to Curly." Even though Hans didn't completely understand this whole marriage-for-eternity thing, he felt a twinge of respect for the woman.

She tried to explain. "There are situations where it's impossible to get to the temple, Hans, and it wouldn't be right for a couple to decide not to get married and start a family just because they can't afford the passage to America or they're unable to go because of a war, or they're denied exit visas by their government . . ." She hesitated and looked away. "Curly just says he loves me too much to wait."

Hans's brow puckered. "I don't know much about eternity, but that doesn't sound right. Seems like if he really loved you, and he was able to get to a temple, he'd want to hold out for the highest marriage available. Rolf's girl told me once that *that* would be the best indication of a man's love."

"I think Curly just worries about how long it will be before we'd be near a temple. I don't doubt he loves me."

"You love him, don't you?"

"He's a really good guy." There was a prolonged silence. Natalie studied Hans closely, her blue eyes clear and thoughtful, and Hans found he was uncomfortable under her close scrutiny.

It was Natalie who finally broke the silence. "You've really been a friend to me these past few days, Hans Brenner." She touched his arm lightly, and Hans felt his flesh tingle. "I wish there was some way I could repay you . . ."

"There's no need," Hans mumbled.

Natalie studied him thoughtfully, and he willed himself to meet her gaze. She said, "Hans, I've been trying to decide how to tell you . . . to ask you . . ."

"What?"

"Maybe I should just show you . . . I've got a little time on my hands . . ."

Warily, he asked, "What do you have in mind?"

"Come with me?"

Hans's brow furrowed. From his experience, her request sounded like the hint of an invitation—the type of invitation he thought Mormon girls wouldn't consider giving a man, especially when they were contemplating marriage for eternity. And the color heightening her cheeks just now seemed a dead giveaway—at least it would be if this mess hall were a tavern, and they had just shared a round of drinks, and it was beginning to get late . . .

She led him out of the building, down the steps, and across a large courtyard toward a row of hastily constructed barracks and piles of cleared rubble. An occasional army Jeep passed them en route, and several American soldiers waved at Hans's companion as they passed. He glanced over at her and felt an almost uncontrollable urge to touch her hair.

It all seemed a little strange and sudden, and he was still confused by what it seemed she was suggesting, being that she had just been telling him of promises, and repentance, and changes of heart. Rolf had mentioned once that he believed sexual relationships belonged only in marriage, and Hans was beginning to see the reasoning behind that idea. But a part of him argued that it wasn't like Natalie was *promised* to Curly, and whenever he thought about her it wasn't like he hadn't considered the possibility. Besides, she *did* have the most stunningly blue eyes and the cutest little nose . . . and it had been a long time . . . and perhaps she was trying to thank him for saving her life . . .

"I've been thinking about you lately, Hans Brenner, and . . . well . . ."

Suddenly Hans recalled a chilly night in a secluded, darkened forest, and a cold, filthy hole in the ground. He remembered his anguished petition for assistance and a bargain he made with a Being he didn't know. As he thought back on the memory his steps slowed. "Natalie . . ."

They were close to the barracks now, and Natalie sensed his sudden hesitation and turned to him with a kind smile. "Don't worry, Hans—it's really all right. Besides, you need it dreadfully."

Hans swallowed hard. He shook his head. "No, Natalie."

She looked confused.

"I mean, even though we're away from home, lonely, thrown together like this . . ." He hesitated, perplexed at the surprise that was gradually blossoming into embarrassment in her wide eyes.

He did not want to hurt her feelings, and he tried to explain. "I don't want you thinking I don't *like* you, Natalie, because there's nothing further from the truth. In fact . . ." He finally reached and touched her hair, his fingers lingering in the way he had been anticipating ever since he first met her. "I think you're the most beautiful woman I have ever met, and the thought of holding you in my arms, and, and . . ."

His voice trembled dangerously, and he forced himself to drop his hand. "But I—I don't think it would be fair to Curly . . ." He wet his lips nervously, and the little demon that had been his companion for as long as he could remember screamed at him, stabbed him, and condemned him for his stupidity in turning her away. He took a deep breath. "I'm honored that you thought of me. But the answer is still no."

Natalie was staring at him now, wide-eyed and open-mouthed. Her face had turned several shades of red as he spoke, and now her voice sounded strangely tight. "Hans, you misunderstood me completely."

He stared at her, confused. "What do you mean?"

Suddenly Hans recognized the sound of water running nearby, and he glanced at the wooden structure near where they stood. Steam billowed from the open entrance into the outside air.

"We're at the men's shower room, Mr. Brenner." Embarassed, she took his hand, squeezed it reassuringly, and pointed inside. "You'll find towels in the locker room and fresh clothing in locker 43. I've explained the situation to the captain. Since you're obviously determined to stick around the hospital to see your friend through his ordeal, it's a consensus among the medical staff: we'd like you to consider"—Natalie's face showed the depths of her embarrassment—"taking a shower once in a while."

* * *

Rolf Schulmann shook the outstretched hand of the young American officer standing by his bedside.

The man smiled pleasantly. He removed his visor cap and secured it under his arm, exposing thinning blond hair meticulously combed to cover the beginnings of a bald spot. He had a recently healed shrapnel scar running across the right side of his neck, just above the collar of his uniform jacket. He wiped an arm across his forehead and said, "August in Berlin can get sticky, can't it?" He smiled again and searched for a chair. "Chaplain Morris, at your service, Mr. Schulmann. I understand you wanted to speak with me?"

"Thank you for coming, sir."

"May I sit down?"

Rolf nodded, and the man settled himself into a chair. Suddenly Rolf felt awkward, and he took a deep breath, wondering how to begin. This man had obviously fought against Rolf's countrymen in the war, and Rolf realized he might have strong feelings about Rolf's situation—and, because of Rolf's Nazi affiliation, about Rolf's membership in the Church.

Chaplain Morris spoke pleasantly. "Captain Miller tells me you're LDS."

Rolf nodded. "Schwarzwald region. A branch in Baiersbronn."

"I've been to Baiersbronn—it's beautiful. How long have you been a member?"

Rolf told him briefly of his contact with the missionaries in 1939 and of his baptism in France. He kept it simple and straightforward, leaving out the more dramatic aspects of his conversion story.

Morris listened intently, and as Rolf spoke he could sense that the chaplain was not going to judge him. He was relieved.

The chaplain asked, "You were a prisoner in a concentration camp?"

"Sachsenhausen."

"And before that?"

Rolf's hands clenched beneath his blanket. "A major in the SS."

"I see." Morris sat back thoughtfully.

"I was stationed in southern France." Rolf breathed deeply, trying to maintain his calm. "That's one of the reasons I need to speak with you, Chaplain . . ." He swallowed. "I have been worried about how my membership in the Nazi Party and my participation in the war will affect my ability to receive certain temple blessings . . ."

EIGHT

August 17, 1945

When the military truck shuddered to a halt near the entrance to Hans's basement shelter, he found himself on his feet, poised and ready to do combat, his Luger in his hand, before he was fully awake. He maneuvered his way through the sleeping forms and flattened himself against the wall beside the door.

"What is it?" Someone else had heard the sound, barely audible through the thick, humid walls, and Hans warned the speaker to be quiet.

He had worried this would happen. They were so close to the division between Soviet and American territory that he figured someone would someday report them to the Soviets, and he and every former German soldier in the shelter would be carted away to some labor camp in the east. He wasn't about to let that happen. At least not tonight.

Tentative footsteps sounded outside the door as someone descended the concrete stairs. Whoever approached was trying to keep the noise at a minimum, and Hans tensed to spring on the intruder as he opened the door. He heard the footsteps hesitate, and then the heavy door swung ever so slowly inward on hinges that could have used a good oiling. At the first offending squeak the door paused in its advance, as if the person on the other side were trying to analyze the sound's damage to his surprise approach. After a few moments the door began to move again, slowly and carefully. When a hand curled around the edge of the door, Hans reached out and grabbed the exposed wrist. Quickly he jerked it into the room with its owner attached, then twisted the arm mercilessly until the small figure was forced to its knees, letting out a high-pitched howl that pierced the air.

Startled, Hans quickly let go. *"Natalie?"*

"You broke my arm, you big brute!"

Hans pulled her to her feet. *"Was tun Sie?"* In Hans's bewilderment he had forgotten to speak her language, and he quickly corrected himself. "What do you think you're doing?"

"Earning myself a *dis*honorable discharge from the army, that's what."

Hans realized he was still brandishing the Luger, and he swiftly hid it inside his clothes. A baby began to cry in irritating shrieks. By now most of the residents of the basement had awakened and were watching the spectacle with sleepy interest. "You startled me, Miss Allred."

"What did you just do to me?" She looked about ready to cry, and she rubbed her arm tenderly. "I'm going to have to explain how my arm got broken . . ."

"It's not broken. I didn't twist it that hard."

"What do you know about it? It's my arm."

Hans grabbed her arm and bent it back and forth at the elbow. She stifled another howl and pulled it away. "What are you now, a doctor?"

"No. But in the war I had to take care of my men. I could set a broken arm faster than—"

"I'm not interested, okay?" Natalie scowled up at him, her blue eyes smoldering.

He tried to ignore the daggers her eyes were throwing at him and his own irrational desire to respond by taking her into his arms. He stammered, "Why are you here? It's long after curfew—*and* your bedtime."

"I'm not a child, Mr. Brenner."

"I don't want you to be in any danger . . ."

"Then we'd better hurry." Gesturing for him to follow her, Natalie started back up the stairs.

Once outside the shelter, Hans saw the army truck parked on the street with several GIs unloading boxes into neat piles along the curb. Natalie turned to him and whispered, "Just thought you and your friends could use a few supplies. Food rations, soap, medical supplies—stuff like that."

Hans felt his stomach growling at the thought of food. "Does the commander know you're here? Are you allowed to feed the Germans?" He realized it sounded like he was describing animals in a zoo with a sign posted that read, DON'T FEED THE ANIMALS.

"Like I said, they'll be shooting me at sunrise." She smiled at him for the first time that evening. "Actually, I have my supervisor's go-ahead, but I had to wait until my shift was over. Let's get this unloaded as fast as we can so we can both get some sleep tonight."

Hans sprang forward, followed by several of the bomb shelter's residents whose curiosity had brought them wandering up the stairs after Hans. They hefted the boxes and again descended the stairs, and more residents assisted in opening the containers and distributing the welcome supplies among the different families. Hans watched the joyful pandemonium with a curious feeling in the pit of his empty stomach, and he tried to imagine what the feeling might mean. For several minutes he and the others worked feverishly at their task, and when he passed the last of twenty boxes down the stairs the feeling inside had grown until it seemed to envelop him with a tenderness all its own. He turned to face Natalie.

"You didn't have to do this."

"Yes, I did." She smiled at him. "Last night we had cheesecake with our dinner—*cheesecake!* Can you imagine?—and I thought about you here with all your friends and these children, and I just *had* to do something."

His stomach growled at her mention of food, but he forced himself to ignore his hunger as he made a decision. "Listen, Natalie, I need to ask you about something. Will you let me walk you back to the hospital?"

"You realize we'll be executed on sight, don't you?" Her grin softened the dire warning.

Hans returned her smile. "No one will see us. I'm used to evading the lookout."

Natalie's eyes twinkled. "My life is once again in your hands, Mr. Brenner." She waved a dismissal to her escorts, and they drove away with the truck. Hans and Natalie walked together down the middle of the empty street.

Hans was comfortable with the silent camaraderie they shared, and even though he would have liked to discuss yesterday's embarrassing misunderstanding at the shower room, he didn't want to run the risk of ruining this perfect evening.

"So how did you get permission to come tonight?" he asked.

"I help out when the army makes deliveries on weekends—you know, food, bedding, fuel—to some of the more destitute refugees." She glanced apologetically at Hans. "I don't mean to imply that you can't take care of yourself, but—*you* shouldn't be expected to look out for all those people . . . and . . . all those children and *babies* . . ." Hans hadn't had any idea before tonight that the Americans were even helping the homeless, starving refugees, and he was both surprised and impressed by the thought. He felt the compassion and concern in Natalie's voice as she continued. "I mean, do you have any idea how many undernourished babies we see in the hospital? Sometimes the poor mothers are on the brink of death themselves, and they are still trying to nurse their infants. Just yesterday a baby—a *five-week-old baby*—died in my arms as I tried to get him to swallow a few drops of milk from an eyedropper . . ." She choked on her words and couldn't continue. For several minutes Hans walked silently beside her, studying the slender American woman who seemed to have such courage and such a desire to make a difference. The Americans trying to feed and clothe all the starving Germans was like trying to shear a sheep with a pair of tweezers—it was just not possible—but it impressed him that Germany's conquerors were at least giving the impossible a try.

"Natalie, I have been meaning to ask you . . ." Hans hesitated, suddenly embarrassed about his request, but then he forged ahead. "I need something to do. I need something to work on. I have nothing to fill my days other than visiting Rolf, and with him sleeping so much of the time I find myself going crazy . . ."

She wiped at a stray tear and glanced up at him.

He continued awkwardly. "Is there something—*anything*—that I can do to help you at the hospital?"

"What do you want to help me with?"

He shrugged, feeling foolish. "I don't know . . . Something like what you do with these boxes, maybe?" He gestured back down the street in the general direction of his basement abode. Then he straightened, encouraged by the idea. "I could help the American soldiers deliver these boxes to the poor starving mothers."

Natalie laughed softly, and Hans met her gaze, instantly happy at the thought that there might be something he could do to make his existence worthwhile.

"I'll talk with my supervisor. I'm sure they could use your help, Hans. What a kind thing to offer."

He was relieved, and he impulsively took her hand in his.

She squeezed it, then changed the subject. "Your friend, Rolf—"

"What about him?"

"How did his wife die?"

"Hélène? Childbirth. Rolf has never discussed it with me, but I know he grieved desperately for her."

"Is he still grieving?"

"For Hélène? No."

She hesitated, and Hans didn't like the worry he saw on her face. "His doctor said he's losing his will to live," Natalie began. "It's as if he's lost any hope for the future. He seems listless, his blood pressure is rising, he won't eat enough to keep a rat alive, and he sleeps more than he's awake." She took a deep breath. "And when he's asleep, he struggles like he's having the most dreadful nightmares."

Hans nodded. "I've seen that. He tosses and turns and cries out constantly. Sometimes he doesn't even know I've been there. And one time when he was coherent he asked me why God would want to keep him alive. Imagine that—a Mormon asking *me* what God was thinking!"

Natalie studied Hans thoughtfully. "This morning he called out in his dream, and he said the strangest thing, Hans." She hesitated. "He kept repeating something in German, so I asked a friend what it meant. She said it was something about betraying children. Have you ever heard him say anything like that?"

Hans frowned. "Once he said, 'Don't kill them—they're only children.'" Hans shook his head and felt sick in the pit of his stomach. "There are a lot of things that happened in the war, Natalie—things he had to be involved in that he never told me about. But I know he would never harm children."

"I'm worried about him, Hans."

"So am I," Hans agreed. "And he made me promise not to write to her . . ."

"To who? His sweetheart?"

Hans nodded. "Marie Jacobson." He briefly told Natalie about Rolf's relationship with Marie.

"So why won't he let you write to her?"

"He told me he doesn't want to hurt her."

"*Hurt* her? If it were me, I'd be overjoyed to know that the man I loved was still alive!"

Hans Brenner watched her closely. "He said Allied law might keep them from traveling to America to be married in the Mormon temple—"

"You need to write to her, Hans."

"I know I do. But Rolf's my best friend. I've broken plenty of promises in my lifetime, but never one to him."

"He's not in his right mind—or just incredibly foolish—if he'd make you promise a thing like that."

"He's an intelligent man, Natalie. Extremely so. If you only knew . . ."

"All right, then," Natalie blurted. "Tell me where she is and *I'll* write to her." She picked up her pace, her decision seeming to infuse her limbs with new strength and purpose. "Somebody's got to do something before Rolf decides there's no reason to go on living. And if you're bound to a silly promise made to a man who might not be in his right mind, then it's up to me to make sure Marie Jacobson gets her letter."

Hans opened his mouth to protest and then closed it again, his face thoughtful. He studied Natalie carefully. "If you did write to Marie Jacobson . . ." He tried to sound noncommittal. "What would you say to her?"

NINE

They say a Soviet labor camp is one of the most dismal, terrifying places in the Soviet Union. Lieutenant Viktor Rostov didn't necessarily agree.

He preferred to look at Stalin's forced work camps as places of enlightenment—the perfect location for a man to see the error of his ways and plot a new course toward personal reform and social compliance.

But for this particular German unfortunate, Viktor believed that confinement in the camps should be a last resort, to be offered only when he failed to respond to more conventional methods, such as respectful questioning, polite persuasion, and, finally, physical coercion.

Unfortunately, the middle-aged German scientist seated across from him had not responded to the first two methods, and it seemed very likely that Viktor would soon have to introduce him to the third, unless he soon shared the information Viktor needed . . .

Viktor leaned forward and offered the man water from a pitcher on the table. The man merely stared back at him with a mixture of fear and loathing in his eyes, so Viktor forged right ahead to the matter at hand.

"I have been polite with you, Professor Farber. I have not threatened you with physical harm. And yet you have insisted on repaying my kindness with silence, when you could show your gratitude by answering my questions. Why won't you tell me where your colleague is hiding?"

Otis Farber did not respond, nor did he take his eyes off the Soviet officer sitting in front of him.

Viktor shook his head. "I'm baffled by your lack of cooperation. You, of all people, should understand how strong a bond can exist between professors, and I have told you that long ago Professor Edwin von Hausen was my particular friend. He probably told you of the exceptional work we accomplished together at the university here in Berlin before the war . . ."

Again the German stayed silent, and Viktor had to force himself to remain civil. "Professor, you visited with von Hausen the night before he and his wife disappeared, just after my countrymen invaded Berlin. You carried a letter from von Hausen to the American military. You have been safeguarding his belongings in your apartment, and you have been attempting to speak with the American representatives of the Berlin Operations Branch on von Hausen's behalf." Viktor paused. "I believe you have been trying to negotiate von Hausen's safe passage through Europe, and possibly his future cooperation with the Americans."

Even though his fear was obvious, the man's eyes did not waver, nor did he break his silence.

"If you cooperate, I can promise you your freedom." Viktor frowned. "Just because I'm a representative of the Soviets does not mean you have to fear me, my friend." He forced a congenial smile. "You should not look upon me as your enemy just because you and I have different political feelings and ideas. We're both professors of science." Viktor watched the man closely. "You are interested in discovering new medicines to benefit mankind. I am concerned with protecting mankind's survival—defending the very existence of the humanity you profess to shelter from harm . . . And Herr von Hausen . . ." Here Viktor hesitated for emphasis, analyzing the wavering emotions in Farber's eyes as he did so. "*Professor* von Hausen was my colleague in that undertaking, my comrade."

Farber continued his silence. Finally Viktor sighed, placed his hands palms down on the table, and pushed himself wearily to his feet. He knocked on the door of the small room, and Vasik Zelenko, his Ukrainian bodyguard, slipped inside. Viktor glanced once at the mirror on the opposite wall and then back at Farber, whose expression was now one of primal terror as he contemplated the physical size of the newest threat.

"Do you have anything you wish to tell me, Herr Farber, before I leave you and my friend to get to know each other better?"

Still the German didn't speak, but Viktor imagined he heard the small professor's breath beginning to rattle strangely in his throat.

Viktor shrugged. "Very well." Turning his back on the two men, he walked through the door and closed it gently behind him. He moved into the observation booth and stood silently next to Colonel Sergeyev. Viktor was intimately familiar with Vasik's methods and was not necessarily interested in witnessing them again.

Vasik stepped toward the terrified prisoner, and as he did so, Otis Farber did something neither Vasik Zelenko nor Lieutenant Rostov had been expecting: with a strangled sob, the small professor turned and launched himself with incredible momentum directly into the brick wall. He struck his face against the unyielding surface with a force that knocked awareness from his body. His unconscious form slumped to the concrete floor into a pitiful heap.

Vasik stood in the center of the room and stared at the inert form, his large hands loose at his sides and his expression a mixture of shock and confusion. Then he looked up at the mirror, his sunken eyes wide and apologetic. He moved to the form huddled against the wall, bent down, and straightened it almost gently on the floor, laying the professor's limp arms at his sides and checking for a pulse. He turned and nodded at the mirror.

Viktor cursed softly. "I am sorry, Colonel Sergeyev." He forced a smile. "Perhaps a few weeks in the camps will remind Professor Farber of the wonderful life he had before he defied the Soviet Union." He rapped on the glass, signaling Vasik to step away from the prisoner. "And I will make it clear to him that his freedom will be returned to him the moment he tells us of von Hausen's whereabouts."

"He has proven he has no intention of speaking." Sergeyev's displeasure was evident. "It could take months for his sufferings in a work camp to convince him to change his mind. Why not continue your persuasions here, until his defenses crumble . . ."

"It *could* take months," Viktor acknowledged. He studied the inert form. "As you can see, his mind is strong, but I fear Vasik's type of persuasion might kill him. As you said yourself, von Hausen is integral to the plans of the atomic commission. A few months in the camps may give Farber time to reflect, and time to repent of his stubbornness." Viktor smiled. "Besides, I'm a patient man."

"Korotkov may not be, Professor Rostov." Sergeyev stood. "He has not reached his position by being patient—either with the enemies of the Motherland . . ." The colonel paused to show that he was choosing his words carefully. "Or with those of his subordinates who do not share his same sense of urgency."

The colonel's threat was obvious. Rostov clenched his fists behind his back and gazed steadily back at the other officer, ignoring the dangerous acceleration of his heartbeat. "Farber will tell me where von Hausen is hiding, Colonel Sergeyev. You can be certain that I'll not fail. I always do what I must, for the glory of Stalin."

TEN

Natalie Allred knew of several very pleasant things to do on such a lovely late-summer afternoon. Many of her friends were attending a party hosted by the British and American Army Nurse Corps in a park on the convergence of the Havel and Spree rivers in the British sector. Other nurses had chosen to take the afternoon to sunbathe on the balconies of the hospital, congregated in groups and armed with the latest gossip and plenty of carbonated beverages. Her British roommate, Mabel, had opted for a long afternoon snooze.

Sorting, packing, lifting, and hauling supplies might not top any lists delineating pleasant weekend diversions, but to Natalie Allred there was nothing else she would rather do—especially with Hans Brenner at her side and hordes of grateful refugees surrounding the loaded army truck. The driver opened the tailgate and climbed inside with Hans, and then Hans turned and reached for Natalie, hauling her up effortlessly beside him.

Germany was on the brink of starvation and Eisenhower couldn't feed them all, but Natalie was grateful to be allowed to help where she could. She wondered how long it would be before a child would not be required to go to bed hungry, or a farmer would have the seed and fertilizer he needed to provide for his family. Or a new mother would again have sufficient nutrition to nourish a newborn.

Hans brushed by her with a crate of potatoes. He hopped from the bed of the truck and carried his treasure into the crowd. He returned empty-handed and picked up another crate. He was a hard worker, Natalie observed, and she found herself glancing at him more than once, grateful for his assistance and uncomfortably aware of her growing attraction to him.

Halfway through the distribution, Hans moved to Natalie's side. "There are so many of them."

Natalie's gaze swept the mountain of boxes still to be distributed, and she sighed, "I know, Hans. I'm sorry. I couldn't find enough volunteers. There's a party going on and that was more interesting than distributing food to starving refugees."

"I meant the people." Hans wiped a sleeve across his face. "There are so many people. How are we going to have enough for everyone?"

"That's the most difficult part of this job—when we've finished distributing all the supplies, there will still be people waiting for food. Word spreads, and each week there are more refugees waiting." Natalie's arm spanned the multitude surrounding the truck. "Look at them, Hans—there must be over a thousand people already—and they're still coming. We *never* have enough, and it's distressing to have to drive away and leave so many people with nothing."

"Can't we just bring another truck?"

She shook her head. "There's not enough food in the warehouse. There's not enough food in *Europe* to feed these people!"

Hans studied her soberly. "You really do care."

"What?"

"You really do care about my country." He gave her a faint smile. "I accused you of the opposite once—and I'm sorry."

She returned his smile, and as she made eye contact her heart danced a little jig before returning to its normal rhythm. She looked away quickly and busied herself with a box. "Come on, Hans, let's take care of a few of your countrymen."

The truck was eventually emptied, and Hans hoisted a lonely crate of potatoes into his arms. He glanced at the crowd and then back at her. "This is the last of it, Natalie. Who should I give it to?"

She smiled sorrowfully. "Someone with a lot of children. And I guess that narrows the choice only a little."

Hans nodded and then turned to study the crowd. He climbed down from the truck, and several youngsters tugged at his sleeve and clamored for the potatoes. Others flocked to his side, and soon he was surrounded by children of every age and description.

Natalie watched as Hans faced the children, their eager, pleading faces upturned and their hands stretched imploringly toward the load in his arms. Hans hesitated, looking down at the crate and then back at the hopeful, dirty faces of the children. There must have been at least fifty of them congregating around the German, begging for his crate. The scene tugged at her heartstrings, and Natalie wondered how in the world Hans was going to choose who should get the potatoes.

Hans deposited the crate onto the ground and knelt beside it in the dirt. He began to talk to one of the children in German. "What is your name?"

"Zelda."

Hans ripped open the crate with his large hands, and even though Natalie had been diligently studying German conversation with her roommate, it took all her skill to understand the subsequent dialogue.

Hans asked gently, "How many potatoes can you eat tonight, Zelda?"

The miniature fräulein giggled hopefully and held up two pudgy fingers.

"Two?" Hans gave her two potatoes and turned to the next child. "Who are you?"

"My name is Emile, Herr Soldier."

Hans smiled. "How many potatoes?"

"Two, *bitte.*"

Hans continued until the potatoes had all been distributed, and Natalie forgot all about boxes and distribution, war and refugees and suffering, as she watched Hans interacting with the children.

Hans stood and retrieved the empty crate. He turned and saw the look on Natalie's face.

"They won't have food tomorrow, but at least they won't go to bed hungry tonight." He hopped into the truck and grinned at her. "Now what?"

* * *

Natalie had a difficult time sleeping that night, and she found herself recalling the evening's activities again and again. She couldn't get the image of Hans Brenner out of her mind: Hans crouched at eye level with a group of dirty street children, handing out potatoes two by two into eager waiting hands, satisfying hunger for only a few hours but offering kindness that the children would remember forever.

If Curly had been in town, she would have gone with him to the party. Instead, she had spent one of the most fulfilling, peaceful, and satisfying afternoons she could remember in the company of a man whom she barely knew but who had unexpectedly become one of her favorite people in Berlin.

The thought that she was developing feelings for Hans Brenner worried her—not just because the army discouraged such relationships with Germans but because she understood that his morals were probably at odds with the teachings of the gospel. Deep down she knew he shouldn't be more than a friend to her, and even though she accepted that realization as prudent, deep in the recesses of her heart she fought stubbornly, desperately against it.

She couldn't stop thinking about him. He had saved her life, and she was still not sure if she liked being indebted to him for that. At one time he had been a Nazi like his friend Rolf, and that meant trouble in the near future if what she had heard in the officers' mess was in any way to be taken seriously. She wondered if she should warn Hans. Rolf was not hearing much of anything these days, and so she doubted it would make any difference to him. But Hans should probably be notified, although, to be honest, she didn't want him to leave . . .

She threw the covers aside and sat up. Across the room Mabel snorted and mumbled something unintelligible before rolling to her side. Natalie tiptoed across the cold floor and searched her desk for a piece of paper, a clipboard, and a pen, and then she tiptoed out of the bedroom, through the parlor, and out onto the porch.

There was only a fingernail of moon visible, but in the still air of the midnight sky a vast array of brilliant stars danced. The medical compound was dark except for a faint glow in the window of the nurses' station and the single bulb flickering over the guarded entrance to the courtyard a hundred yards from where she stood.

She felt the crisp night air tickle her toes and creep under the hem of her nightgown, and she smelled an unexpected scent of flowers. She hugged her arms close about her body. Apart from a lonely shadow pacing forlornly back and forth at the guard shack, she seemed to be the only human being not asleep in bed.

Natalie sat on the edge of the porch and began to write. *"To Miss Marie Jacobson,"* she began, *"You don't know me, but I wanted to write and tell you about a mutual friend of ours who is a patient in the military hospital where I work . . .*

ELEVEN

Marie Jacobson knelt by the edge of the bed, her head resting against the headboard and her eyes half closed as she contemplated the little boy sleeping next to her on the pillow.

Today was September seventh—Alma's sixth birthday. She'd made a cake for him out of her meager rations and placed six candles on top, and when she'd asked him to make a wish as he blew out the candles, he'd wished for his father to return home.

Now Marie caressed his soft forehead, pushing the brown locks away from a face that reminded her more and more of the boy's father.

It had been almost two years since Alma had last seen his father. His birthday wish had intensified her worry that Rolf might be dead, and she remembered the pang in her chest when Alma had suggested they pray for Rolf's return.

"Does Heavenly Father listen to my birthday wishes?"

"Yes, Alma, He does."

"If I kneel down and pray—like you taught me—do you think He will bring Papa home?"

She hadn't known how to answer him. She hadn't wanted to crush the budding faith growing in that tiny little body.

"Heavenly Father, this is Alma. Today is my birthday and I'm six years old. I love my mami very much, but I wish Papa would come home and be with us too. Mami says you answer our prayers—and even our birthday wishes!—like the one I made today that Papa will come home. Please let him come home soon."

She ached for the sweet, innocent little boy. His determination and faith humbled her. But the thought that tiny Alma might be all she would ever have of her beloved Rolf Schulmann made her ache inside, and she realized it would be some time before she could come to terms with the pain.

Hans had eventually stopped writing, or his letters had stopped finding their way to her doorstep, and she could only imagine that meant nothing good. Certainly Hans would have written if he had found Rolf . . .

Alma stirred in his sleep, whimpering. His tiny hands clutched the wooden tank his father had carved for him the last Christmas they had been together, and now as he slept Alma held it close to his chest with both hands. He never played make-believe with it anymore, Marie reflected, although he would sit for long periods of time with it in his hands, pressed to his chest, a faraway expression in his eyes. The boy missed his father with a pain at least as acute as Marie's, and the realization tore her up inside.

How she longed for a healing ointment for wounds that refused to heal! She realized that her prayers for Rolf's safe return just might not be what the Lord intended for her and for Alma. Now, with her beloved charge sleeping peacefully, Marie decided it was time to stop waiting for news in Switzerland. It was time to move on.

After the war ended Marie's father had moved back to Paris with the new president of the provisional French government, General Charles de Gaulle. Professor Jacobson was there now, waiting for Marie and Alma to join him, and now Marie was finally ready to do just that.

She had spoken with her father several times since her move to Switzerland, and each time she became even more anxious to see him, to explain to him in person all that Rolf Schulmann had done for her. Somehow her words over the phone never seemed to convince her father of the Nazi major's goodness, and she was heartbroken at his insistence that she forget about Rolf. No matter how she expressed all these feelings in letters and in phone conversations, Professor Jacobson had never been willing to see past the unpleasant fact that Rolf Schulmann was a Nazi.

Marie knew her father was happy she was alive. He was proud of her for caring for the small boy in her charge, and he was grateful to Major Schulmann for having had the decency to spare her life. He realized Rolf was a member of the Church, and he had even conceded that Rolf probably had much good in him. But he drew the line when this Nazi dared to suppose that he could marry Marie.

Now Marie whispered her own prayer, leaning her head against the wall without disturbing the sleeping Alma. "Dear Father in Heaven," she whispered. "Please help us to be strong, to accept Thy will. And please bless little Alma, and me . . ." Suddenly she sighed deeply, her breath wavering as her emotions broke near the surface. "And please, Father, if there is any possible way that Rolf could still be alive and Alma's prayer could be answered with a miracle . . ."

She kissed Alma's forehead and felt the warmth of his breath on her cheek. Then she stood and left the room, leaving Alma to his slumber. She would finish this last load of ironing tonight and then tomorrow return it to its owner and collect payment. Then she would pay the remaining rent and close up the house and take Alma with her to liberated Paris.

She had no fear now of the situation in France. Her father had said that postwar France was always in some crisis or another: the devaluating franc, the political spats between de Gaulle's government and the French Communists, the continued witch hunts for Nazis and the French traitors who had collaborated with them, the trials, and the constant hunger and fuel shortages. But Marie didn't fear France or anything France could throw at her now that the war was over. She only feared her father's inability to accept her love for a German officer.

When a knock came later that evening, Marie had been on her way through the cottage toward the front room, and so she answered quickly. Her prompt response startled the woman on the front porch.

"Oh, Marie, I'm so glad to see you!" the tiny nun exclaimed. Her round cheery face shone red with the exertion of her walk up the hill from the orphanage, and her kind eyes crinkled as she gave Marie a happy smile.

"Sister Bernadette!" Marie's eyes widened at the sight of her friend standing in the doorway in a wool wrap bundled over her blue habit. Elated at the unexpected visit, she ushered the woman into the small cottage and pulled the door shut behind her before hurrying to the kitchen for cups and the hot chocolate left over from dinner.

When she returned, the two women chatted in the parlor, exchanging news and pleasantries. They had become fast friends while Sister Bernadette cared for Alma in the orphanage until Marie had been granted custody. Marie had helped several times a week with dinner at the orphanage—at first as a condition of Alma's nighttime release to her care, and then as a favor to an overworked friend.

When their conversation slowed, Sister Bernadette set down her cup and said, "I cannot stay. Dinner is over, but I left the kitchen a disaster, and my new helper doesn't take such pride in cleanliness as you. I must go home and have her scour the pots again if necessary."

"I wish I could've helped you more these past months, Sister Bernadette."

"No, no. You helped me for longer than any other volunteer, and I understand that it's in the evenings that you must work to keep food on the table for you and Alma." She paused, then reached inside her voluminous wraps to extract a small envelope. "I didn't come all this way to complain, Marie. I have a letter for you." She held out the envelope. "I have no idea if it is important, but it is so difficult for mail to arrive in a timely manner these days, and I thought it might be of some comfort for you to have a letter. Besides"—her eyes turned sorrowful—"I know you're considering leaving Switzerland—and I didn't want you to miss this letter, in case it might bring news . . ."

Marie took the letter with a grateful smile and turned it over in her hands to read the return address.

"Natalie Allred . . ." The name was not familiar. She began to tear open the flap, and Sister Bernadette rose to her feet and moved toward the door.

Marie also stood. "Don't go, Sister Bernadette. I'm sure this envelope contains nothing I need to keep secret. I haven't a clue who this Natalie Allred is, and I'm sure she wouldn't mind if you heard—"

"Nonsense." Sister Bernadette opened the door. "It is your letter and I'll not intrude."

"Sister Bernadette." Marie touched the woman's sleeve. "I have decided to leave this week."

The sister turned again to face Marie, and even though her lips smiled, her eyes were sorrowful. "You will be sorely missed, Fräulein Jacobson, and I wish you the best in your new adventures in Paris. I'll miss you, dear friend. I will pray for you, Marie, and for Alma." Sister Bernadette touched Marie's shoulder and smiled kindly, and Marie could see the understanding in her eyes. This woman must know what it was like to lose a loved one, and to wonder if you'd ever recover from the emptiness the loss caused.

"Your prayers will be much appreciated, Sister Bernadette. And I'll miss you, too."

The sun had finally set, distorting the surrounding homes and scenery in misty gray. The nun's figure faded into the descending darkness as Marie watched, her feelings of gratitude for Sister Bernadette keeping her on the porch as the woman disappeared from sight.

Then she turned toward the light and opened the envelope that was still in her hand. She extracted the letter and began to read.

"To Miss Marie Jacobson, You don't know me, but I wanted to write and tell you about a mutual friend of ours who is a patient in the military hospital where I work . . ."

Marie's heartbeat accelerated until it beat against her ribs hard and fast. That opening line from a complete stranger in Berlin made her hands holding the letter tremble, and the very next sentence changed her life forever:

". . . Your fiancé, Rolf Schulmann, has been convalescing in our facility for a number of months, but he has refused to allow his friend to contact you, purportedly to keep you from worrying about his failing health. You must know that Hans Brenner believes that your presence here might improve not only Mr. Schulmann's spirits, but also his chances of recovery.

Rolf Schulmann is a good man, and I believe it is because of his faith in God that he is alive today. In my opinion, it would be a pity for that to change because he is languishing for his loved ones. Do come if you can.

Sincerely,
Natalie Allred, U.S. Army Nurse Corps

* * *

Rolf Schulmann sat up in his hospital bed and listened carefully. He was sure he had heard someone calling his name. It had been a little girl with a voice as sweet and musical as the summer stream that ran through the woods near his farm in the Schwarzwald. He pulled back the blanket and stepped to the floor, ignoring the cold hardness on his feet as he walked in the direction of the sound. Outside his room his footsteps echoed eerily in the empty corridor, and he squinted to see through the darkness.

Turning a corner, he saw an open door with light pouring from inside the room, cutting a path across the corridor and up the opposite wall. He walked toward the light, aware that he felt happy inside, and strong. His legs no longer ached, and the bottoms of his feet no longer burned where the soles had been worn away, exposing the raw flesh to each horrific, painful step. He reached the lighted doorway and looked inside.

He was looking into a schoolroom, with row after row of benches and tables. Contented children sat with their backs to him, swinging their legs as they busily and quietly worked at their lessons. One girl stood and walked toward him, her clear eyes smiling at him with startling intensity. She held out her hand, offering him a paper. He took it and read,

God? How good You are, how kind, and if one had to count the number of goodnesses and kindnesses You have done, one would never finish . . .

Rolf stepped back in horror, looking up from the letter at the little girl. She smiled at him again, turned, and was gone.

Rolf jerked his eyes open and stared at the ceiling of his darkened hospital room, and he felt the cold sweat on his pillow. How many times had this dream haunted him, with the young girl Liliane, who was the author of an innocent letter to God pleading in behalf of her parents and all the other children at *La Maison d'Izieu . . .* ?

He remembered the children's home situated in the mountains above the tiny Rhône-Alpes community of Izieu. But more, he remembered the horror he had felt when he'd realized that every child had been removed from the home and deported to concentration camps by Captain Bernard Dresdner and the Gestapo, under the direction of Klaus Barbie in Lyon.

Now, terrified that the dream might repeat itself, he lay with his eyes open the rest of the night, pouring out his heart to his Father in Heaven and begging Him to forgive him and to care for his sweetheart, Marie, and for Hélène's little son, Alma.

* * *

When Lieutenant Viktor Rostov accepted the document brought by his aide, he gave it only a cursory glance before setting it to one side. Not that he dismissed its significance—just that he could see from the date that it was an older report, which meant that he had time to finish reading a cheerful letter from his daughter, brought with the mail that came whenever there was space in the military supply convoy from Moscow.

Lucya wrote that she filled her days with work on their dacha and her evenings with preparations for her wedding. Anton and his parents had invited her to come with them on a trip to Samara, where she hoped to be able to find material for her veil in one of the higher class department store districts. She told her father that she missed him, and that she hoped he would be able to complete his assignments soon and return to Moscow and be reinstated at the university in time for the wedding next year.

She told her father that she was proud of him for his service to the Motherland.

Viktor read the letter one more time, folded it carefully, and slipped it into the breast pocket of his tunic.

He stood and reached for the new document and skimmed it impatiently, his mind already skipping ahead to more pressing matters. He wondered why his superiors had sent him a copy of a routine border incident report. The idiotic rampages of Russian soldiers didn't necessarily constitute danger to his government, nor did a bullet in a hand or a severely bitten finger represent a threat to Soviet national security.

He was about to throw the document away and assume it had been routed to his desk by mistake when his mind registered the name of one of the perpetrators of the crime. Suddenly his hand froze with the paper halfway to the wastebasket. He brought it again to his desk, his heart beginning to race. He looked again at the wounded officer's statement: *The American nurse turned at the sound of the shot, and I thought I heard her say, 'Hans Brenner!'* . . .

Viktor felt his heartbeat begin to accelerate dangerously, and he slowly lowered himself back into his chair. Perhaps fate had finally intervened in his behalf, he mused, as he read the entire report again, carefully, thoroughly, from beginning to end.

TWELVE

September 10, 1945

Natalie settled behind her desk in her office and reached for a pen, and as she began to update her log for the day she heard her supervisor's voice in the doorway of the nurses' station. "Nurse Allred, this gentleman needs to speak with you, if you have a moment."

Natalie looked up from her paperwork and studied the man standing next to Dr. Hayes. He must have been in his late thirties or early forties, clean-shaven, brown-eyed, with dark hair trimmed short. He was tall—close to Hans Brenner's height—and his face displayed the strong, pronounced features of Slavic heritage. He wore a businessman's suit and silk tie, accentuating his broad shoulders and trim waistline, and he carried a new hat and a light raincoat under one arm. The pin situated in the center of his left lapel sported the sickle and hammer of the Soviet Republic, and she noticed the incongruity of combat boots protruding from under his slacks.

Why would a representative of Soviet Berlin want to speak with her? She asked, "Is something wrong?"

The man stepped forward, and for a split second she saw his dark eyes waver, as if something about her surprised him. For a furtive moment he seemed to study her face, as if he had suddenly realized she was familiar to him. It startled her, and she mentally shrank from his advance.

He must have read her unspoken fear, because the warm expression in his eyes disappeared behind a cool mask of politeness. He smiled and thrust his hand toward her in a very American gesture he accomplished with very Soviet rigidity. She accepted it, wincing as his strong fingers crushed her slender ones before he released her.

"Miss Allred, my name is Lieutenant Viktor Nikolayevich Rostov, and I'm here to apologize to you in behalf of my government." His voice was pleasant, and his English near perfect. If he had not displayed his nationality so prominently on his lapel she might have mistaken him for an American.

"Apologize to me?" she asked. "Whatever for, Lieutenant?"

The man shook his head sadly. "It seems we have a long way to go in our labors to befriend our neighbors in this country. We're constantly improving our efforts, and constantly making errors . . ."

"Excuse me, sir, but I don't see what this has to do with me." Natalie felt uncomfortable under this man's intense scrutiny and wanted to condense the conversation as much as possible. Curly was coming to get her after her shift for a night on the town, and she still had to change her clothes, curl her hair, and repair her makeup.

"May I sit down, Miss Allred?"

Reluctantly she offered the visitor a seat and sat down again behind her desk, facing the Russian and Dr. Hayes.

Lieutenant Rostov smiled at her, his expression courteous. He cleared his throat and proceeded to explain the reason for his visit. "Not long ago two of our officers and a comrade had a little too much to drink and became lost from their outfit. They wandered a good distance from their district and found themselves a few kilometers from this hospital—still in the Soviet zone, of course . . ." The lieutenant glanced sideways at Natalie's boss before continuing. "It seems they encountered a woman—a young American woman, with very pretty auburn hair—who was also wandering lost in the vicinity." He looked at Natalie and smiled affably.

Natalie felt her heartbeat accelerate, and she swallowed uncomfortably. But she met the Soviet officer's gaze and said nothing.

"My officers remembered their manners and asked for the woman's documents so that they could be of assistance in helping her return to her home before nightfall. It was dangerous for a woman as pretty as this American to be out alone after dark . . ."

Natalie nodded. "Of course." The room was slowly beginning to spin.

"Unfortunately, an accident occurred . . ."

"An accident?" Had the visitor heard the catch in her throat?

"An unfortunate, unimaginable accident." The lieutenant's handsome face clouded. "One of the men was shot, and another was badly wounded."

"*Shot?*" Dr. Hayes bolted upright in his chair, his eyes wide. "Were the men all right?"

"Luckily, they survived. But it was a tragic, *tragic* accident. They escaped as fast as they could—I'm sure they imagined they might be killed. I don't blame them." Here the lieutenant paused, glancing sideways at Natalie. "One of the men's fingers had been bitten almost completely through!"

Natalie felt her stomach heave at the memory. She felt dizzy and clung tightly to the edge of her chair.

"Shocking!" Dr. Hayes exclaimed, looking like he would turn green.

Rostov agreed. "And apparently the poor man was quite frightened by the whole incident. He waited so long to request medical attention that a good portion of his hand was lost. And, unfortunately, he ran away from his attacker with this young, pretty American's documents in his pocket. I have not yet seen them, but the officer mentioned Miss Allred's name . . ."

Natalie sat silently, her heart exploding in her chest and the room spinning ever faster around her. She had to work hard to focus, and she found herself trying to convince her terrified brain that it was not she to whom the Russian officer referred.

Lieutenant Rostov's voice penetrated her consciousness. "What a tragic, terrible accident. We can't imagine this woman was the person who attacked the three men. It would be inconceivable that she would do such a thing. So we have to assume it was the tall, dirty beggar who joined her soon after the men stopped to help her."

"Natalie?" Dr. Hayes stared at her, incredulous. "Is it *you* he's talking about?"

Natalie opened her mouth to protest, but nothing came out but a strangled squeak.

"Were you walking in the Russian zone, Natalie?"

"Of course not!" she managed.

Her superior was satisfied. He addressed the Soviet officer. "Perhaps you should speak with personnel over at headquarters. Give them the documents, and they will assist you in locating the woman. I can't imagine she would be one of ours. You must have been mistaken when you assumed she was a medical officer . . ."

"For the moment," the Russian lieutenant interrupted, "we have to retain the documents the wounded officer gave us. We're not finished with our investigations, and it seems that the man who joined the beautiful American woman is important to the investigation. So, until we have received positive identification of the man and have detained him, we cannot return the documents." He looked intently at Natalie, his meaning significant only to her.

The Soviets knew it was her. They knew, and they would punish her. But first they wanted her to tell them that it was Hans who had pulled the trigger. They would not care that he had done it in order to save her honor and her life. They would only care that a Nazi had been involved and therefore should be turned over to the Russians to be tried and executed. Or maybe they would dispense with the trial and Hans would just be executed. She felt icy fingers of fear creeping up her spine.

With superhuman effort she stood and faced the sitting lieutenant. "You have your work cut out for you, it seems, Lieutenant Rostov. My condolences on the suffering of your soldiers."

He seemed unwilling to leave. "Do you understand, Nurse Allred, that if the man is not found, we will have to assume that the soldiers were too drunk to tell their story straight and there really was no other person involved other than the woman? Do you understand how unpleasant that could be for that woman?" The lieutenant finally stood, towering over her and locking his eyes with hers. "Or if this man were to be warned of our interest, and foolishly helped to escape, the Soviet government might decide *both* are guilty . . ."

Natalie felt her throat go dry. "I understand. Best of luck to you in your investigation."

"No luck will be needed. I imagine soon I will have all the answers I seek." For an uncomfortable moment he studied her, and she saw a return of the strange emotion in his eyes that had unnerved her in the first few moments of his visit. He turned to go but hesitated at the door. "Perhaps, Miss Allred, you would join me sometime for dinner?"

Past the terror that was beginning to strangle her, she forced herself to ignore her revulsion and answer the Russian politely. "Thank you, Lieutenant, but I don't believe that will ever be an option."

"Maybe, when you have had enough time to reconsider the offer?" The man smiled at her, nodded a farewell to Dr. Hayes, and left the room.

* * *

Natalie walked past the door to Rolf Schulmann's room and willed herself not to even look inside. She could hear Hans reading the Book of Mormon to Rolf in his low, comfortable accent, and even through the effects of her recent encounter with the Soviet lieutenant it warmed her spirit. She remembered again the children, and the potatoes, and Hans Brenner kneeling in the dirt, and it was all she could do to keep her feet walking down the hall and not turn in at the door.

She was afraid—both for herself and for Hans. Luckily Dr. Hayes had seemed oblivious to the Soviet officer's threats. But Natalie realized that Lieutenant Rostov's interest in her experience with Hans on a darkened Berlin street had suddenly transformed an uncomfortable memory into an ongoing nightmare, and under no circumstances was she going to catch

Hans's eye and get him following her out the door with some excuse or another that they spend time together. She suspected she was being watched, and she did not want Lieutenant Rostov to find out about Hans.

She walked toward the front exit and absently waved to her British roommate at the reception desk. She would not have paid any attention to the man sitting in the waiting area had it not been for the fact that this was the third time she had seen him sitting there, his blond hair tousled, a magazine unattended on his lap and his dark blue eyes brazenly watching her as she passed.

Shaken, she pushed open the exit and left the hospital, turning into the residential section of the medical compound. She walked rapidly across the courtyard to the women's quarters, trying to shake off the fear that still clung to her insides.

She should not have been wandering through Berlin on her own, and she should never have kept the incident a secret. The fact was, she'd been humiliated, and she'd been nervous about what Curly would think of her, worried about what her superiors would say, and, most importantly, fearful that she would be transferred without another chance to find her relatives. Except for her nighttime trip to Hans's shelter with supplies, ever since that night she had remained close to the medical compound, avoiding situations in which she might be called upon to produce her missing documents. So there was no record of her having lost them or requesting to have them replaced.

She desperately wanted to talk to somebody about her predicament, but for some strange reason she could think of no one she could trust more than Hans.

* * *

Lieutenant Viktor Rostov ordered his driver to turn into a deserted, garbage-strewn alley and stop the car. Face flushed and sweat building under the frayed collar of his shirt, he leaned his head against the back of the seat and tried to calm his breathing, feeling the pulse in his chest and neck pounding against his skin as if his heart would leap from his body. He pulled open his own door and exited the Renault, then bent over with his hands on his knees and gulped deep lungfuls of stale Berlin air. He finally straightened and paced slowly up and down the street, his shoes noiseless on the wet cobblestones and the idling of the Renault's engine behind him the only sound in the empty alley to rival the frantic beating of his heart.

He tried to think through this latest shock that threatened his health. He had been favored throughout his life—with loving parents, a good education, great responsibility given to him for the security and well-being of his country, remarkable children, and, most dear to his heart, his memories of a beloved, beautiful wife who had adored him and who had been torn from his side in the midst of this terrible conflict.

He could not think of his Alyona without feeling again the mixture of triumph and agony that accompanied her memory. She had loved *him!* Above all others and in spite of the reluctance of her parents—why should they be overjoyed at their beloved daughter's choice to marry the lowly son of a poor mountain farmer? And then, after years of married bliss, how was it possible that she should be so brutally taken from him, the only woman he had ever loved and who had ever loved him?

And what cruel fate had brought the memory of her back to him, today, in the form of this young American woman who looked so much like his Alyona, and who must, out of necessity, act as a pawn in this vicious nuclear struggle between himself and the dangerous American, Major Matthews?

Viktor retrieved Natalie Allred's military ID from the pocket of his suit coat and leaned against the nearest wall, studying her picture carefully. The black-and-white snapshot could not do her justice: the dark eyes in the photograph did not capture the deep expressiveness of the living woman's sky-blue gaze, and her hair in the picture seemed pitch black, whereas in reality it undulated with the same auburn highlights as his Alyona's. As he held the picture, his heart beat through his chest with a fury that would certainly put him back into the hospital if he didn't find a way to deal calmly with this new shock.

Sergeyev would understand, once Viktor reminded him of Zhukov's promise and of the doctor's warnings of Viktor's weak heart. The doctor's orders stated that Viktor was not to allow himself to become emotionally distraught. Even though he was young and strong in most things physical, Viktor's lot in life was not only a weak heart, prone to episodes related to intense stress and physical exertion, but also a deep emotional attachment to the young wife who had left him alone and had, with her death, taken away the remaining strength of his heart.

He would explain to Colonel Sergeyev that his heart could not survive another Alyona.

THIRTEEN

September 17, 1945

Natalie awoke in the middle of the night to the sound of persistent knocking on the door to her barracks apartment. She sat up, disoriented, and fumbled for her slippers. She could hear Mabel shuffling across the front room floor, cursing in her heavy British accent as she struggled with the latch. Then Natalie heard the front door open.

"You?" Mabel's voice rose with annoyance. "What do *you* want?"

The thick, comfortable accent of the answering voice rumbled in Natalie's ears and initiated the strange, fluttering sensation in the pit of her stomach that she had begun to experience every time she was near Hans Brenner. "I know it's the middle of the night . . ." He was anxious, Natalie perceived, and it made his efforts to speak English excruciating. ". . . and I really don't want to bother her . . ."

"Then don't." Mabel was welcoming Natalie's visitor with her usual charm, and Natalie abandoned the futile search for her slippers and grabbed her bathrobe.

"I don't think this can wait until morning, Fräulein, and I do not mean to be rude . . ." She could hear the controlled tension in Hans's voice, and she knew Mabel would hold out 'til the death, so she hurried for the door.

"Not at this hour of the night."

"It's important."

"It can wait until morning."

"Let her decide that."

"This is the women's facility, and you're trespassing. Leave now or I'll holler for security."

Hans glanced past the irate Brit and locked eyes with Natalie, and Natalie saw the appeal in his gaze. Natalie patted the older woman on the arm. "It's okay, Mabel. He's harmless."

Mabel mumbled something about Germans being a far cry from harmless and shuffled back to bed. Natalie leaned into the screen door and met Hans's steady gaze. He was different tonight, she mused, as his dark eyes met hers with a seriousness that aged him. She felt a sudden, strong urge to touch that face, so scruffy and battle-worn yet becoming so inexplicably dear to her. She knew he was also drawn to her, and the way he acted toward her sometimes made her wonder if he felt a need to protect her.

"Hello." She knew it sounded foolish. She *felt* foolish, standing here in the middle of the night in her bathrobe and bare feet, meeting Hans at her front door as if he were here to pick her up for a night at the opera or a stroll under the stars.

"Harmless?" Hans scowled at her. "I'm a seasoned military officer, Natalie. I fought for the Fatherland for the entire war, and more than a handful of the enemy cowered at my feet in terror. And you think I'm *harmless*?"

"Will you come in?" she asked sweetly, pushing open the screen door.

"Not with that dangerous battle-ax defending your honor."

"I thought you were a seasoned military officer, Hans Brenner." She couldn't suppress a smile. "Maybe she'll do you the honor of cowering at your feet in terror."

Hans glowered at her.

She sobered, realizing that he was not in the mood for trivial banter. "What is it, Hans?" Self-consciously she retrieved a hairband from her pocket and pulled her rumpled hair back into a ponytail. She knew it made her look like a teenager, but she didn't care. "You know, people will talk if we keep slipping off together after dark."

Hans couldn't suppress a slight grin, but he erased it quickly. "What I need to tell you is not funny, Miss Natalie."

"I'm working in a few hours. Can't it wait?"

"It's about your relatives."

Natalie froze, her hands still pulling the band around her hair. "Aunt Clara . . ."

"You need to hear this."

"All right." Natalie stepped onto the porch and let the screen door swing shut behind her. She moved to the edge of the porch and sat down on the uneven, rough-hewn planks. She burrowed her bare toes into the dirt, wrapping her arms around her knees. Hans sat down beside her, and she tried not to think of the way his proximity made her feel.

Hans looked down at his large hands, and Natalie could see that they were worn and calloused. She knew from experience that they were the hands of a hard worker.

"I found your aunt's address . . . or, I should say, what's left of it."

"Hans Brenner." Natalie stared at him, her eyes wide. "You didn't go into the Soviet—"

"I just got back."

"But Hans, you know they'd kill you if they found you. After that night—"

"I can stay invisible if I want to."

"That's quite a talent. I'm just so glad you're safe." The light in his eyes said he was pleased by her words. "How did you find the place?"

"I lived in Berlin in the years before the war. I went to school here . . . at the *Universität zu Berlin* . . ."

"You're full of surprises." She was impressed. She hadn't known he had attended college. He had an excellent command of the English language, although his thick accent would have given away his German heritage to anyone, and she had heard him speaking French with Rolf. But she hadn't realized that his background might include a university degree.

"I remembered the address from your envelope," he continued, "and I found the location where the address should have been."

"What do you mean '*should* have been'?"

"There's not much left, Natalie."

Natalie's face fell. "I guess I was hoping that they would still be there—that they had survived . . ." She trailed off.

Hans turned and faced her, his eyes sober. "Your aunt and uncle owned a leather goods store, and they lived in an apartment above it."

"And it was bombed?"

Hans nodded. "The whole street was deserted—every building practically leveled to the ground. But according to a neighbor I found camped out nearby, they moved away before that."

He leaned forward. "In November of '38, almost seven years ago—and three months after your aunt sent that letter to your mother—Nazi storm troopers raided your aunt and uncle's apartment in the middle of the night." Hans continued gently, watching her closely the whole time. "The attackers smashed the windows, broke furniture and threw much of it out onto the street below, and beat your uncle to within inches of his life. Then they went down to the leather goods store, looted the merchandise, stole the unopened safe, and set fire to what was left."

Sickened, Natalie said nothing. She just clenched her hands in her lap and silently watched Hans.

"This woman said she used to know your aunt. But she spoke about the incident as if it were no concern. She—she said some thoughtless, unkind things about the Jews . . ."

Natalie heard the anger that had crept into Hans's voice, and she broke in, her own voice a frightened whisper. "What happened to my aunt? Where did they go?"

Hans shrugged, his expression apologetic. "The woman didn't know. She said the whole family disappeared a few days later. I asked her if there was anyone else who might help me know where they went, and she said the other neighbors were all gone."

He hesitated, then pressed forward with what Natalie realized must be the most difficult part of his narrative. "I *knew* of the events of that night, Natalie." He took a deep breath, letting it out slowly as he tried to formulate his explanation. "I was a Nazi back then, and I didn't think what happened to the thousands of Jews that night—*Kristallnacht*—was any big deal." He stopped suddenly, and she could see the remorse in his eyes. "Everywhere they were burning, beating, looting, killing . . . and I was a Nazi just like them."

Natalie sat silently, her hands clasped tightly as she stared out into the cold darkness. She suddenly felt small and scared, as if Hans's revelations had sapped her of her normal vivacity and purpose. She took a deep breath and faced him squarely. "Did you help?"

Soberly Hans shook his head. "I didn't get involved."

"Why not? What made you any different from the other monsters that night?"

He looked at her then, anguish in his eyes. "I don't resent your description of my countrymen, Natalie." He shook his head. "I've seen too much to think anything else about many of them. And while I'd liked to tell you I am different, my reason for not getting involved was not virtuous. On that particular occasion, a Jew had murdered a German embassy representative in Paris, and news of the murder had reached SS Command shortly after. The order for the Nazis to retaliate against all Jews came from Reinhard Heydrich, chief of Reich security, in the middle of the night, and I—didn't hear the order until late the next morning."

"Why not? Where were you?"

He shrugged, and his cheeks flushed slightly at some embarrassing memory. He looked down at his hands. "I was drunk . . ."

For a long time Natalie said nothing. She watched Hans's head droop and his eyes close, and her heart went out to him as it had never warmed to anyone before. Silently she slipped her hand around his upper arm, and without a word he reached up and covered her fingers with his own. The welcome contact warmed right through her hand, and she leaned close to him, resting her head on his broad shoulder and lacing her slender fingers through his large, rough ones.

"I'm so sorry, Hans."

He didn't look at her. "I cannot imagine why." He sighed. "My membership in the Nazi Party is part of the reason for your suffering."

"And part of the reason for *yours,* Hans Brenner." She squeezed his hand gently. "You've had to deal with the consequences of your actions for the whole war—even though I believe some of the things you did were required by your government."

"You don't need to feel sorry for me." He sounded subdued.

"I'm not feeling sorry for you, Hans. I'm grateful for all you've done for me, and I'm indebted to you for not only your kindness, but also for your timely protection in a moment of my recklessness."

He said nothing, and after a moment she continued softly. "You saved me from a group of drunken soldiers, and you put your own life in danger to bring me news of my relatives. I can see that you're suffering, Hans, but instead of letting all your adversity get you down, you've continued to be there for your friend Rolf, watching over him and praying for him—don't look so surprised, Hans Brenner. I know you pray for him, even if you don't ever ask God for anything for yourself." Suddenly, impulsively, Natalie reached up and touched the face that was so close to hers. "I can see in your eyes that reading Rolf's book has been good for you. If only *you* could see the good it has done, the way it shines through your spirit."

"Natalie . . ." His voice sounded anguished, and she felt his hand trembling against hers. "I don't know what to think of God, or prayers, or scriptures that teach of eternity . . ." He shuddered. "Do you realize what you're doing to me right now?" With his free hand he touched her cheek then followed the line of her jaw and the slender curve of her neck, and then he slid his hand behind her head, gently pulling her face toward his own. And in that instant Natalie thought about the embarrassing misunderstanding at the showers, and the fact that Hans was not a member of the Church, and she saw the sweet face of Curly Miller in her mind. She pulled away and stood abruptly. Hans rose to his feet also, and they faced each other warily.

"I was *thanking* you, Hans—nothing more." She felt her heart beating traitorously against her ribs. "Please don't think I would give myself to you so easily."

"I don't think anything like that, Natalie." His voice had a strange edge to it, and Natalie tried without success to read the emotions in his eyes. He continued softly. "I know you're confused—you care for Curly, but at the same time you know that you and I are drawn to each other, and because of your religion you think there's nothing you can do about those feelings."

She turned halfway away from him, suddenly wishing he would leave. "I can't ever fall in love with you, Hans. I—I wish you'd stay away from me." She swallowed, remembering that her fear that she would develop feelings for him wasn't the only reason he should stay away. Lieutenant Rostov was searching for Hans and was quite possibly having her followed in order to discover him. And she'd been instructed not to warn Hans about the situation—she was in an impossible position. "You need to stay far away from me, Hans—for your sake as well as for my own."

Even though the look in his eyes betrayed his frustration at her words, Hans's voice remained level. "That's not possible, Natalie Allred. If you honestly want nothing to do with me, then you're going to have to stay away from *me*." And he turned and walked away, leaving Natalie standing alone on the porch.

FOURTEEN

September 20, 1945

Hans had just arrived at the hospital when they came to arrest Rolf.

It was a formality, because Rolf could not be moved and he obviously posed no immediate threat to the new German government or anyone else. He rested quietly, his eyes half closed, as the American sergeant read the arrest warrant and Hans stood helplessly to one side, guarded by a military policeman who watched his every move.

"Major Rolf Schulmann, under orders of the Joint Chiefs of Staff of the Allied Control Council, you are under arrest for suspicion of Nazi Party membership and multiple war offenses against the safety and security of the German nation. You will be incarcerated until you're ready to face trial. You will be granted the right to hire an attorney or accept a court-appointed advocate to speak in your defense. Is that understood?"

Rolf nodded weakly, and the sergeant folded his warrant and turned to face a glowering Hans Brenner.

"You his friend?"

"Of course. And I'm a Nazi too."

"Hans Brenner?"

"You men have done your research."

"The hospital superintendent told us about you. However, your name doesn't appear on the official list."

"What's that supposed to mean?"

"With the help of Nazi records, we've compiled a list of criminals who may need to stand trial for war crimes. You're not accused of being a 'major offender' or 'offender'—like your friend here. Therefore you're a 'lesser offender, follower, or exonerated person.'"

"That's a relief." Hans couldn't help the sarcasm.

"However, I must ask you not to leave the city."

"All right."

"You're not to be employed as anything other than a common laborer. You've been stripped of your military rank, and you're not allowed to retain any personal property until your name has been cleared of any and all criminal charges."

"I wouldn't mind a job as a common laborer right now."

The officer ignored his comment. "As long as Major Schulmann is in military custody, you're not allowed to visit him, and you will clear all messages, written or otherwise, with the MP."

"Now wait a minute. That's not right." Hans's voice rose threateningly. "He's not doing too well right now. He shouldn't be left alone."

"Orders, Mr. Brenner. You will have to leave."

Hans looked past the officer to his friend and met Rolf's eyes. Rolf smiled faintly at him as if to say, *it's all right*. But Hans felt an unreasonable panic at the thought the he might not see his friend and brother again—at least not alive. He clenched his fists angrily. "You're going to make Germany whole again," he said bitterly. "You're going to eliminate the vile offenders that have corrupted the German nation. I wonder, in fifty years, what people will think of *your* methods."

"Leave, Mr. Brenner."

"Won't they just say you were another Third Reich?"

"Now that was uncalled for. You have no idea the extent of the damage done by you Nazis."

"I've heard about Hiroshima." Hans resisted the hand on his arm. "Don't tell me about 'major offenders.' You used a defenseless people to prove your superior might—just like Hitler."

The MP brought the butt of his rifle up sharply under Hans's ribcage and Hans doubled over, gasping for air.

"You've made your point, Brenner." The officer spoke firmly. "Now leave, or I'll arrest you and send you where you'll never see your friend again. Do you understand me?"

Hans nodded, unable to speak. Slowly he straightened, looked one more time into his friend's eyes, turned, and left the room.

* * *

Later that evening Lieutenant Hans Brenner noticed the two figures following him as he stopped to allow a truck loaded with German prisoners of war and American guards to pass before he crossed the street. He looked back and saw the man and woman pause to study a group of children playing in the rubble, the youngsters laughing as they tossed and dodged a half-inflated leather ball.

Hans continued down the street, wondering what to do. He realized he was in trouble. He had no papers and no possibility of getting any from the Americans because of his Nazi affiliation. He had two bullets left in the Luger he'd carted since '44 and no chance of another round in the near future. He was not his old physically fit, self-confident self and doubted he could subdue the powerfully built gorilla of a man following him this cold evening, even if the gorilla's attractive silver-blond female companion would not pose a threat.

Finally he sprinted, eating up the sidewalk as if his life depended on it, which it may very well have, except that his two shadows did not try to follow.

FIFTEEN

When she finally reached Paris, Marie Jacobson did not discuss with her father her joy that Rolf Schulmann was alive. Miss Allred's correspondence had rekindled the spark of hope that, even in the long absence of news from Hans, had always burned ever so subtly deep inside a heart that was trying to mend. It had confirmed her most sincere, innermost hope that Rolf would still be found alive.

But now that she knew Rolf was alive, still her father refused to discuss it with her. He did not, however, impede her efforts when she petitioned him for his help to work through the military red tape to receive permission from the American authorities to travel into military-controlled Berlin. He even seemed incensed when permission was finally denied after two weeks of torturous waiting. When Marie received unexpected assistance in the form of an official letter of introduction from de Gaulle's interim government, signed by President de Gaulle himself and handed to her by her father, she felt a glimmer of hope that the professor might be experiencing a change of heart.

But when Professor Jacobson told Marie what de Gaulle expected her to do while in Berlin, she felt her hopes fade. Her father gave her a government car, knowing that it would be impossible for her to make the trip into war-ravaged Berlin without it, and he insisted on a driver who would also act as a bodyguard and a separate *gendarme* escort to the American sector of Berlin.

Marie wondered if he secretly hoped that this would be a journey to see Alma's father one last time—and that Major Rolf Schulmann might indeed die. Perhaps, because of that horrible thought, he didn't feel a need to discuss the situation further with his headstrong daughter.

Her driver glanced into the rearview mirror. "We're almost to the hospital, Miss Marie."

Alma's body tensed, energy tightening his muscles and catapulting him from Marie's arms. "I'm going to see my papa!" he yelled.

"A few more minutes, sweetheart." Marie searched in her bag and produced a comb. "Let's get you cleaned up a bit, Alma, so your papa will recognize you."

"He's going to be happy to see me."

His joy filled her heart. "Yes, darling, he is."

"Will he be surprised at how big I am?"

Marie nodded. "And he will say, 'Whatever happened to my little Alma?'"

Alma giggled. "I'm going to show him the tank, Mami. The one he gave me."

"What a good idea." Marie pulled it from her purse and handed it to him, and when he immediately began playing with it in his lap, the sight gave her a surge of hope that there was finally going to be healing.

* * *

Hans looked up from the outdated copy of *Time* that filled his days in the waiting room of the hospital—the closest he was allowed to come to Rolf—and saw her standing there. He stood abruptly, spilling the magazine onto the floor and earning the disapproving glare of Mabel at the reception desk and the attention of the silent Russian occupying a seat against the far wall.

But neither the receptionist nor the Russian could affect him; Hans had eyes only for Marie.

She didn't see him at first, intent as she apparently was on searching for someone official who might help her navigate the hospital to Rolf's bedside. Her brown hair had been cut short, curling and waving about her head and throat. She wore a hat and mesh accent, set stylishly at an angle and drawing attention to her wide brown eyes and red lips. Her red suit was tailored perfectly to her slender curves, and her hand held that of Rolf Schulmann's son.

Alma turned and saw Hans first, and the little boy stared, one hand clutching Marie's and the other a toy Panzer tank. Hans smiled when it became apparent that Alma was having a difficult time remembering where he had seen him before.

Marie handed a document to Mabel, the receptionist, who read it, glanced up at Marie, and nodded. "Wait here, love." She left to announce Marie's arrival to Rolf's guards, but not without sending a "stay where you are, you rat" glare in Hans's direction. Marie noticed the look and turned, curious to see its recipient.

Her eyes went wide and she breathed Hans's name. Then she flew across the room, and Hans found his arms naturally pulling her close in a long embrace. For many moments she said nothing, her arms crushing his neck, and then Hans felt her body convulse and he knew she was crying.

It made him feel uncomfortable. He was not used to drawing out such emotions in anyone, and he wished she would stop. But he didn't want to have her move away and never come back. So he said nothing and let her cry.

Finally she whispered, "How can I ever repay you?"

That was a trick question. Last time she'd asked him that question he had offered what he'd thought was a suitable answer—that she marry him. But she had flatly refused. Hans didn't want to make another mistake like that one, so he kept quiet.

"God bless you," Marie sobbed, "for giving me back my Rolf. And for bringing Alma's father back from the dead."

A smile played at the corners of Hans's mouth. "I guess Natalie wrote to you."

Marie nodded against his neck. "And she told me he's in a bad way."

"He's not well, Marie."

Suddenly she pulled away, brushing at her tears. "I have to go to him. I have to see him and be with him. He needs to see his son." She looked up at Hans imploringly. "Will you come with me?"

Hans shook his head.

"Why not?"

"I'm not allowed to get close to him, Marie."

"Why on earth not?"

Hans shrugged. "Rolf's and my Nazi crimes are catching up to us. I'm a 'lesser offender, follower, or exonerated person' and Rolf is a major war criminal."

Marie stared at him, confused. "What do you mean?"

Hans explained briefly about Rolf's arrest and the restrictions surrounding Hans's own activities. "Maybe they're afraid we're going to conspire to overthrow the new German Republic if they allow us to be in the same room together."

"That's preposterous, Hans. That can't be right."

"Right or wrong, that's the way it is."

Hans saw rising panic in her eyes. "Hans, I need you there. I need you with me when I see him! I—I can't handle it alone."

"He's been through a lot," Hans agreed. "You won't even recognize him."

Mabel returned with a smile for Marie and Alma followed by a grimace for Hans. "You're permitted to see the prisoner, Miss Jacobson."

Hans scowled at the woman. "I thought he was a patient."

Mabel opened her mouth to retort, but Marie laid a soothing hand on Hans's arm. "It's all right, Hans." She stepped toward the receptionist. "I'll be taking Mr. Brenner with me."

"He's not allowed."

"Yes, he is." Marie straightened. "You obviously didn't read my letter. If you will notice, it says I'm supposed to keep a bodyguard with me at all times."

"And my orders say I'm to keep him out."

Marie smiled sweetly at her. "Please tell the commanding officer of this hospital that a representative from General de Gaulle's government is here from Paris to see one of his patients, and that I'll take Mr. Brenner with me." She pointed to the letter on the woman's desk. "And make sure you take that with you."

Mabel stared at Marie, open-mouthed. Then with one final icy glare in Hans's direction she snatched up Marie's letter and returned to the inner recesses of the hospital.

Marie turned her attention back to Hans. "You've been through a lot, Hans."

"Nothing compared to him."

"Where are you staying?"

"An apartment not far from here," he lied.

"Are you getting along?"

"Don't I always?"

Marie studied him thoughtfully, her eyes gentle. "I meant it, Hans, when I said you'll be my friend for eternity."

"I really don't want to talk about that right now."

She touched his arm softly. "Are you really all right?"

"I'm fine." He said it a little too quickly, though, and he could see that it worried her.

"Are you fine—about us . . . ?" She trailed off.

He frowned. "I've gotten used to it. I've had plenty of time to work at getting used to it, Marie."

"I didn't ever mean for you to feel—"

He interrupted, feeling reluctant to allow her to see any more of his feelings than she already had. "Look, Marie . . . Don't worry about me. I was wrong to ask you to marry me—I see that now. You're a great girl, but not for me. Understand?"

She looked into his eyes and nodded soberly. "I understand. Thank you, Hans."

The embarrassing awkwardness of his ill-received offer of marriage was finally out in the open, and now that he had seen her again and had talked to her, he realized he could be free of the nagging worry that she would harbor ill will toward him for ever thinking that they could be together. He realized his old romantic feelings had changed to sisterly affection for her, mixed with a profound relief that she was finally here to take Rolf's mind off his troubles. Perhaps, with Marie here, Rolf would find new reason to live.

"You're rather brash, woman, saying you're a representative of de Gaulle."

Marie laughed. "But I am." She told him about her father's work as a consultant to the provisional French government, and of her use of a government vehicle. "I think he was worried about me and wanted to make sure I didn't have any problem getting safely home. He sent me as a representative of de Gaulle's military tribunal."

"Military tribunal?"

Marie nodded soberly. "Rolf was an SS major in southern France. President de Gaulle sent me to ask if Rolf would be willing to come to Paris and provide him with a list of Frenchmen who collaborated with the Nazis in Belley."

Hans stared, incredulous. "You're not serious. You realize it's just a ploy to capture Rolf, don't you?"

She nodded soberly. "I would never recommend he do it."

"And how do you explain the boy? Or your feelings for Rolf?"

Marie smiled lovingly down at Alma. "He is Rolf Schulmann's son. I would not tamper with that fact for all the riches in the world. And I'm in love with Rolf. The commander can accept it or not. It doesn't matter."

Hans crouched in front of Alma. "Do you remember me?"

Alma nodded soberly. "You helped us get away from the bad man. The one that hurt Mami and made us swim in the freezing water."

"That's right." Hans knew the boy was remembering a cold night in the Schwarzwald, when Alma and Marie fell into an icy river in their desperate escape from the pursuing Gestapo. Hans had found them later, hidden in a farmer's barn, soaked through and nearly frozen. Hans glanced up at Marie and met her solemn gaze. None of them would ever forget that night.

"And now you're going to see your papa. Right?"

Alma brightened. "Heavenly Father answered my prayers!"

Hans grinned. "I guess so. Make sure you keep praying for your papa."

"So he can get well."

"Yes. So he can get well. Good for you." Hans hugged Alma and stood to face Marie. "I read Rolf's book, like I promised I would."

She smiled. "I never doubted you'd keep your word, Hans."

"It gave me a lot to think about."

"Have you had a chance to talk with Rolf about it?"

Hans shrugged. "Not really. Just a little, while I was reading it to him."

Hans waited under Mabel's disapproving glare while Marie talked with the hospital commander. When Marie reappeared she told Hans that the commander had made a series of phone calls, culminating in a discussion with personnel in Frankfurt. Hans was allowed to accompany Marie to Rolf's bedside.

As they approached Rolf's room Hans tried to prepare her for what she would see. "He's lost a lot of weight, Marie. He's wasting away."

"I understand."

"He might not even recognize you."

Marie glanced at Hans in alarm, and then down at Alma. But after a few seconds she swallowed and lifted her chin. "I'm ready."

She hesitated in the corridor outside Rolf's door. She looked past the military policeman into the darkened room, saw the still form on the bed, and began to cry. But she squared her shoulders, took a deep breath, wiped at her tears, and smiled down at Alma. "Let's go see your father. Shall we?" And Marie took Alma's hand and with the little boy stepped bravely into the room.

Hans watched as Marie reached for Rolf's limp hand, her tears falling as she drew it close and kissed it. Hans hung his head, staring at the floor and scuffing the tile with his boot as he tried not to let the touching scene affect him. It had been a long, horrifically excruciating road for all three of them—all four of them, actually, Hans corrected himself, glancing at the little boy on the edge of Rolf's bed, his hands on his father's chest and his eyes imploring him to wake up and notice him there.

Finally Rolf's eyes opened and he stared at the ceiling, disoriented for a few moments. He blinked a few times, then finally looked down, his senses probably registering the caress on his hand and the tiny weight resting on his chest.

"Papa!" Alma threw himself across his father, his little arms grasping the man's neck as he kissed his cheeks. "Papa! It's me—Alma!"

Rolf stared back at the boy, and Hans noticed the tiny flicker in Rolf's dark blue eyes as he registered his son's voice. Rolf reached his free hand up and across Alma's prostrate form, pressing him closer against him. "My dear, sweet Alma . . ." His voice was weak, but it had a joy in it that thrilled Hans.

Then Rolf turned to Marie. His eyes searched hers for a long moment and then he whispered, "Marie . . . My darling Marie . . ."

"I've missed you, Rolf Schulmann."

Rolf gave a shuddering sigh, as if the weight of the whole world had just been lifted from his shoulders. His eyes moistened and he whispered her name again, this time with wonder. She leaned close and kissed him, and the emotion that swelled between them was more than Hans could take, and he had to leave the room.

He aimlessly roamed the halls of the hospital, stopping briefly to stare at a duty roster tacked to a bulletin board on the wall without really seeing it. He exited the building and walked across the courtyard, and he didn't even notice that the evening cold penetrated his thin clothes and made the hair on his wrists stand on end. He did notice Natalie approaching from the opposite end of the courtyard, from the direction of the barracks, and he paused, his heart leaping into his throat and his mouth suddenly dry. He didn't know what he would say. It had been over a week since she'd talked to him.

"Hello, Mr. Brenner." She nodded at him briefly and continued past him on her trajectory toward the hospital.

He turned to follow her, feeling a surge of frustration at her seeming indifference. "Look, Natalie—you've been avoiding me . . ." She didn't stop, so he grabbed her arm and halted her determined march. She glanced quickly to the left and then to the right as if she were afraid, and Hans's brows knit at her strange reaction. He moved closer to her, concerned. "Are you all right?"

"I really need to go." She hazarded a worried glance in his direction. "I have to get to work."

"Stop acting this way, Natalie." She was literally jumping out of her skin, and her eyes canvassed the courtyard, anxious, haunted. "What's wrong? You haven't talked to me in days. You'd think we didn't even know each other."

"I'm sorry, Hans. It's just that . . ." She trailed off.

"What, Natalie?" Hans leaned close and touched her cheek, and he felt her trembling. "You're frightened. Who are you afraid of?" Suddenly an awful thought occurred to Hans. "Are you . . . afraid of *me?*"

Natalie bit her lip. She shook her head and tried to smile, but the attempt failed miserably. Instead, her eyes swam and she whispered, "I'm not afraid of you, Hans . . . It's just . . . I can't—" She broke off as two men in business suits passed their location. Hans noticed the cautious glance she sent their way, followed by another fearful sweep of the courtyard.

Curious, Hans also looked around the courtyard. "Is someone bothering you?" He felt a surge of anger at the thought.

"No," she answered a little too quickly. "Of course not." She backed away and forced a polite smile.

"What *is* it, Natalie?"

Natalie sighed. "Hans, I should have told you before . . ."

"Told me what?"

She met his gaze, and Hans could read the turmoil in her beautiful eyes. "I don't think it's safe for us to see each other again . . ."

"Safe?" He stared at her. "Safe for you or for me?"

"Hans." Her eyes swam with unshed tears. "This is important, for both of us."

"You're not telling me something." He felt a strange knot forming in the pit of his stomach as she continued to watch him steadily. Something was dreadfully wrong. His voice sounded far away as he whispered, "It's Curly, isn't it."

She gallantly fought her tears, but her gaze wavered. She took a deep breath. "Yes. It's Curly." She straightened, lifted her chin, and faced him. "I've decided to marry him."

Hans was stunned. "You don't even *love* him, Natalie!"

"Yes I do! Whatever gave you that idea?" She tried to look incensed through her tears.

"He has you all molded into something you aren't. He has your future together all planned out . . ."

"Maybe that's not as bad as I originally thought."

"And what about marriage for eternity?"

Natalie cringed. "I think he's coming around. He understands how important it is to me . . ."

Hans realized he was angry—at her, at Curly, and most of all at himself. He should have listened to his feelings and not left her alone for so long. He stooped and picked up a loose brick, lofting it angrily against a wall so that it disintegrated into powder and debris. "I can't accept that you love him enough to—"

"What, Hans?" Natalie's voice rose defensively. "Love him enough to what? Marry him? He's a good man, Mr. Brenner. Better than—" She stopped short, mortified.

But Hans understood. "Better than me."

Natalie dropped her gaze. "I'm sorry. I didn't mean for it to come out that way . . ."

"Yes, you did." Hans felt defeated. "You've been feeling that way for some time, haven't you."

She looked up at him, her eyes pleading for him to understand. "It's not as if we've had a relationship or anything . . ."

"What would you call it?" Hans knew his voice sounded cold.

She shrugged. "A good friendship, maybe?"

"You mean 'a project,' don't you?"

"Stop it, Hans."

"You've been cleaning me up and feeding me and trying to make me into your little laboratory experiment—so that your guilt about what you Americans have done to my country could be appeased."

"That's not true. You know that's not true. I *like* you."

"How much?"

"What do you mean, 'how much'?"

"Enough to marry me?" His bold words surprised both of them.

"Hans!" She finally lost her battle with her tears and started to cry softly.

He wished he could join her in a good cry. "Do you have *any* feelings for me?"

"Of course I do, Hans—but I'm engaged to Curly now, and—"

Impulsively Hans reached and gripped her shoulders, and his words sounded harsh, even to himself. "How can you become engaged to Curly Miller when you have feelings for someone else? How is that going to be fair to any of us?" Anguished, he asked, "Who do you like better, Curly or me?"

"Don't make me answer that, Hans Brenner. That's not a fair question."

"What about honesty, Natalie? You told me that it's important for two people to be honest with each other." Hans could hardly think past the fear of losing her that now engulfed him. "Are you being honest with me? Or Curly? Are you being honest with yourself? Or *God?*"

She lifted her chin and met his gaze unwaveringly. Then she took a deep breath and turned her head away.

He felt a curious emptiness eating away at his chest. He had lost her. The realization ripped him apart inside, and he dropped his hands to his sides and turned to go.

"Wait. Hans . . ." Suddenly it was Natalie grabbing at his arm. "Don't leave like this. Let me explain what I meant."

"You've said enough." Didn't she realize how dangerous it was for her to touch him like that? He was frustrated, disappointed, and crushed beyond words, and that, in conjunction with her proximity and her touch, made for a hazardous combination. He continued to walk away, but he couldn't help taking one parting shot. "You and Curly deserve each other."

"Hans, please . . ."

Hans felt as if a door was slamming shut. He didn't want it to, but he didn't know how to stop it. He desperately wanted to talk to Natalie, to tell her some of the things he felt for her, and to explain how her engagement to the amiable Curly Miller confused and humiliated him. How he wished Natalie wouldn't marry the young, fresh-faced Mormon who had helped prolong Rolf's life . . .

But he knew the time for talking had passed. His usefulness here was pretty much at an end, and it was time for him to leave. Without a second look at the military hospital or at Natalie, Hans walked away. It was Marie's turn to care for Rolf—and Hans had to admit she would probably have much more success at it than he'd had.

For several hours Hans wandered aimlessly around the city, his head lowered and his hands shoved deep into his pockets in an attempt to quell the shivering of his body. He resembled a million other hopeless souls trapped in divided Berlin without hope, purpose, or a future. He watched dispassionately as trucks passed loaded with supplies or weaponry, and he didn't care that the evening cold intensified as the sun set behind the ruins. He walked steadily away from hospital, his mind registering nothing of the destruction and misery around him as it focused inward on his own confusion, defeat, and despair.

What had Rolf said once? That loving a person meant more than nights in each others' arms and bearing children. It meant fidelity, respect, trust, and promises made in a special place. Hans wanted to believe that such a place existed—that such a marriage existed! Marie had promised that if Hans read the Book of Mormon he would learn more about eternity. Hans thought about the book lying on the table next to Rolf's bed. He decided it *had* taught him more about what the Mormons believed about families. He understood his friend's strange religion a whole lot more now than he had when Rolf used to share his feelings with Hans during the war. He understood Marie's and Rolf's determination that nothing less than an eternal marriage would do for them.

And he understood why Natalie would want to marry a man who felt the same.

Several hours after dark, Hans pulled himself out of his melancholy long enough to alter his course. He didn't know how he would make it out of the city without the proper travel permits, but he would worry about that later. He felt an urgency that, as he walked, emerged from the barrenness in his soul to control his motor functions, and his stride lengthened and quickened until by the time he reached his shelter he was certain of where he needed to go and what he needed to do.

SIXTEEN

Rolf gradually recovered. Over the weeks he healed to the point that he could stand on scarred feet with Marie holding him on one side and Natalie supporting him on the other. Alma bounced up and down, screeching with delight and dashing to and fro, grabbing first at his father's shirt and then at Marie's dress, as if he could find no other outlet for the joy that erupted at the sight of his beloved father on his feet. He lost no time asking Rolf to take him fishing, and Rolf, Marie, and Natalie had a good laugh at the impulsive excitement in the little boy's request.

Natalie took pleasure in the transformation and found herself visiting Rolf's room often during her breaks, enjoying the company of both Marie and Rolf. Her anguish for Hans's whereabouts and well-being was somewhat placated by the peace she felt whenever she was with them. And seeing the love and respect they had for each other, combined with the solid determination they shared to be married in the temple, filled her soul and made her determined to develop the same relationship with Curly. She could see that Marie was gloriously happy, and that her happiness had worked wonders in Rolf's recovery. Rolf was also content—but to Natalie there seemed to be an underlying melancholy to his joy, and Natalie could only assume that even though Rolf was grateful to have Marie and Alma here with him, he shared Natalie's concern for Hans's welfare.

Hans did not come back. Natalie found herself thinking about him constantly, berating herself for the words she had said at their last meeting. She also mulled over the night he had rescued her, his confession that he cared for her, so embarrassingly expressed on the way to the men's showers, his kindness when he had risked his freedom to illegally enter the Soviet sector and gather news of her aunt . . . and the almost-kiss in the middle of the night that had catapulted her emotions into a dangerous, irreversible tailspin.

One morning Natalie paused next to Rolf's door and peered inside, past the military policemen who guarded his door. She saw Marie sitting close to

Rolf on the bed, her head leaning against his chest while she read to him from his book. His large hand was entangled in her hair, moving ever so softly against the side of her head while he listened, while at the same time he was contentedly watching his son, who was playing on the floor with the wooden tank. For some reason the peaceful scene overwhelmed Natalie, and she turned and left, striding down the corridor as she fought against her tears.

Soon she heard footsteps hurrying after her. "What's wrong, Natalie?"

Natalie turned toward Marie. "It's Hans." She gave a dismissive wave with her hand. "I haven't seen him for a while, that's all."

Marie's face mirrored Natalie's concern. "Hans hasn't been to see Rolf since I arrived. I saw him for just a few minutes and then he disappeared. It's not like Hans to up and abandon his friend like this."

Natalie's voice wavered. "He talked to me in the courtyard—just before I met you. He—he was upset."

"About what?"

Natalie shrugged, avoiding Marie's gaze. "I'm not sure. We talked about Curly and me, and for some reason it made him angry . . ."

Marie studied her face, and Natalie wondered how much of her turmoil would be evident there. Marie spoke softly. "Hans is a good man, Natalie. A little rough around the edges, maybe, but a good man."

"I know," Natalie whispered. Finally she met Marie's gaze. "To be honest, I'm more than a little worried about him. He was so constant in his attentions to Rolf, and now he just disappears . . ." She couldn't continue.

She didn't mention to Marie the thought that screamed through her head—that somehow the Soviet officer who had visited her and threatened her was responsible for Hans's disappearance. The horrifying thought that her solitary excursion into dangerous territory could be the reason for that disappearance was almost more than Natalie could bear.

* * *

By the middle of October, Rolf could negotiate the vast expanse of the hospital with one hand on a cane and the other on Marie's shoulder. During one of these walks, Alma tore off down the corridor to terrorize the nursing staff while Rolf and Marie followed at a more deliberate pace. Marie remained painfully conscious of Rolf's guards trailing behind.

Rolf spoke to her in a soft voice as he concentrated on his steps. "Have you spoken to your father lately?"

Marie nodded, but she didn't elaborate.

"You don't want to tell me."

Marie knew Rolf understood how Professor Jacobson felt about his only daughter's choice of future spouse. She also knew Rolf didn't blame her father for his concern: Rolf had been part of an organization despicable to the renowned professor and hated by the government Marie's father advised. President Charles de Gaulle would not forgive Rolf easily for his part in France's suffering. Rolf's gentle voice interrupted her thoughts. "President de Gaulle is going ahead with his plans, then?" he asked.

Surprised at his uncanny perception, Marie nodded.

"Tell me about de Gaulle, Marie."

"I'm not sure I understand him."

"What do you mean?"

Marie tried to explain. "When de Gaulle entered Paris last year, he originally acknowledged that the Free French support was necessary to the Allied victory. But now it seems as though he has turned his back on them. They feel he doesn't share their vision of a more equal society, and they feel he is ignoring the good they did for his country during the war. They want more of a say in government—and they feel he is excluding them because they are Communists."

Rolf nodded. "During the war the Free French were his soldiers for liberation. And now that the war's over his fighters are hoping he will recognize them for their efforts and listen to *their* ideas for a better France."

"That's right," Marie affirmed. "But de Gaulle now refuses to acknowledge as heroes some of the greatest Résistance figures of the war. And at the same time he has been pardoning Vichy civil servants and industrialists by the dozens. So the Communists are understandably confused about this new president's loyalties."

"I assume President de Gaulle is still arresting Nazis involved with the occupation. Tell me of his plans for them."

Marie couldn't look at him. "He's organized a military tribunal to try as many Nazis as he can capture." She said the words with difficulty. "And my father supports him in it."

"Your father is a good man."

"Yes. But highly unreasonable at times." Marie's voice was bitter. "I've told him some of what you've done for me—at least what I *know*, since you keep refusing to tell me anything else."

"It wouldn't help matters, Marie."

She turned to him. "There are whole segments of our relationship that I don't know about, Rolf. Almost two years ago you hid me with your sister-in-law while you returned to fight the war in France—I know nothing of what you did during that time—and then when I was captured and you surrendered to rescue me from Ravensbrück . . . After that, it was as if you dropped off the face of the planet until I finally learned that you were here in Berlin. I want to know what you went through—what you suffered . . ."

"I'm not sure I want to talk about it, at least not yet." He squeezed her shoulder affectionately. "I'd so much prefer to talk about you—and Alma."

As if on cue, Alma came charging around the corner with his arms spread wide like airplane wings, his high-pitched voice whining shrilly through the corridor. "Look, Papa, I'm an American bomber." He dipped his right arm and swerved around his father and Marie. "I'm going to bomb the city!" He began making the appropriate sound effects of bombs striking their targets. Each explosion made the little human airplane convulse violently before it righted itself and continued on to its next target.

"Alma. No." The controlled sharpness in Rolf's voice startled Marie, and Alma stopped in midflight, a released bomb disappearing unexploded into thin air. "Don't play that way. Understand?" The distress in Rolf's voice unnerved Marie, and she saw Alma's lower lip begin to quiver.

She took a deep breath and approached the deflated pilot. Kneeling, she touched his shoulders gently. "It's just that bombing makes people hurt, *liebling*—and Papa doesn't want you to play at hurting anyone. All right?"

Alma nodded, and Marie hugged him close. "How about you pretend you're dropping candy for the children in the city. Can you do that?"

Alma contemplated that idea, and after a moment he brightened. "I'll drop candy bombs. And then when they explode candy flies everywhere and all the children in the city can have some. Is that all right?"

"Wonderful."

Alma looked past her at his father. "That kind of bomb won't hurt people, will it?" His voice was hopeful.

Rolf's eyes misted unexpectedly. "No, son, that will make them feel better."

Obviously relieved to have his beloved father's approval, Alma sprang into action and soon disappeared back around the corner.

Marie looked up into Rolf's eyes and saw the fatigue displayed in their depths. "Let's go back to your room, Rolf." She squeezed his arm gently. "You've walked enough for today."

He didn't argue. Marie took his hand and walked with him back in the direction they had come.

"Hans has been gone for a long time," she said after a few minutes. "I've asked around, and I've gone with Natalie to where she said he lived. He's nowhere to be found. No one I've talked to has any idea where he is."

"Hans can take care of himself." But Marie could see the worry in Rolf's eyes as he said the words.

She helped Rolf settle himself in bed. He stretched his legs out and pulled the blanket up to his waist, and Marie again shivered at the physical evidences of Rolf's suffering. She realized that it might take months before he was as he was before Sachsenhausen—and he might never be the same again, but always carry some physical reminder of the war's toll on his system. And she knew he was embarrassed that she had to see him this way. He wanted her to be able to have him whole again, as strong and handsome as he had been before.

It would take plenty of persuasion on her part to convince him of how she really felt—that he was as handsome to her now as he had been when she first knew him, and that he was as powerful to her now in his physically weakened state as he had been when he'd held her in his arms that Christmas in Schönenberg. She knew she would have to remind him often—until his body recuperated to the point that he could believe it himself—but she was willing to do that. She was willing to do whatever it took to be happily married to Rolf for time and all eternity. Whatever it took.

He lay back and she gently touched his forehead. "You're doing well," she said. "The doctor feels you will continue to recover. Soon you'll be walking on your own again. Then you can take your son fishing."

Rolf pulled her close. "I look forward to that." His voice sounded tired, and Marie noticed something else—a shadow of something unresolved lurking behind his words. It wasn't the first time she had noticed it.

"What is it, Rolf?" she whispered near his face. "You're worried about something—something you're keeping hidden inside."

"You've got quite a talent at discernment, Marie Jacobson."

"Is it Hans? My father? Your health? Me?"

"Maybe all of the above."

She persisted. "You're worrying me, Rolf. Please talk to me."

Rolf glanced uncomfortably at the guards, ever vigilant by the door. Marie straightened and looked at the two MPs.

Rolf pulled her face close to his own and lowered his voice. "Marie, I . . ." Something dreadful was forcing his emotions close to the surface.

"What, Rolf?" Marie felt a dread that started as a cold hand at the base of her throat as she waited for Rolf to continue.

"I want to marry you."

Marie relaxed. "I know." She smiled. "The feeling's mutual, believe me."

"And I want to do it right."

"Of course. We'll be married in the temple as soon as—"

"Marie," Rolf interrupted, his voice tired and sad. "You don't think they'll let me go to the United States now, do you?"

Marie sat back, stunned. She hadn't considered the idea. Ever since she and Rolf had been reunited there had been no doubt in her mind that as soon as he healed they would travel together to the U.S. to be married in the temple as they had planned. She glanced again at the guards at Rolf's door. "Surely in your trial they'll find out you're not the hardened criminal they think you are and you'll be released . . ."

Rolf shook his head. "I'm not so sure, Marie. More likely I have years of prison ahead of me—if they don't execute me for crimes against humanity."

"Don't say that!" Marie's words came out more sharply than she had intended, and the guards at the door glanced in her direction. She batted at sudden tears. "You're a good man, Rolf Schulmann! I'm sure they will see that. Crimes against humanity? Impossible!"

"In France, things happened . . ." Rolf shuddered. "I was responsible for things that happened. And I need to accept that responsibility and accept the consequences for my actions—or *in*actions, as the case may be. Marie, even if I could go with you to Utah, I don't feel worthy to take you to the temple at this time, because of my part in the war . . ."

"Stop it, Rolf! Don't talk this way!" Marie could hardly see him through her tears. "You need to stop thinking you're responsible for all the evil your country inflicted on France, or the Jews, or—"

"Marie." Rolf's voice soothed her, even if his words did not. "You're precious to me—you and Alma." He sighed. "And I mean to do everything in my power to clear my name, both with the Allied victors and with God. I may have to stand trial more than once. And I may have to pay dearly for the part I played in this war. But I want to do what is right and I want to feel worthy to enter the temple. And more than anything in the world I want to marry *you* there, Marie Jacobson." He touched the side of her face, his voice soft. "But I don't think it's right that you should feel bound to a man who may never be able to take you to the temple. You deserve—"

"Rolf"—Marie leaned into his hand—"don't turn me away. Don't abandon me. I've already lived without you long enough. I cannot bear to do it again."

"You may not have a choice."

Marie felt her panic rising. "Just tell me you love me," she said. "Tell me you want to marry me."

"I love you. As much as I ever have. And I want to marry you. I cannot imagine a life without you."

Marie touched his hand. "Then I'll be here for you until it's all resolved. As long as I know you love me and want me, I will be here by your side."

"Marie . . ."

"No, Rolf, don't argue with me." Marie shook her head against his hand. "You saved my life—you sacrificed yourself for me at Ravensbrück— and I'm going to be with you for the rest of my days, if you'll have me. It doesn't matter what you have to go through." She shuddered involuntarily. "If they send you to jail, I'll live on the next street and wait for you. Alma will see his father every single day if they will let him."

Rolf kissed her tenderly. "If you only knew how much I want to leave the hospital behind and *really* hold you in my arms."

She smiled and kissed him back fiercely. "Then get well!" Her fingers entwined with his. "And don't you ever try to run me off again!"

SEVENTEEN

October 23, 1945

To an astute observer the voice on the other end of the line might have betrayed its owner's minimal education and a life spent struggling to survive among the less privileged classes of British society. But the man's thick accent and regional dialect revealed more to Viktor than would have been apparent to anyone else eavesdropping on their conversation.

"Connelly and Associates fine menswear and shoes . . ." the voice drawled. "How may we help you?"

"I need a new suit," Viktor informed the man in his perfect English.

The man on the Brighton end gave a martyr's sigh. "I'm a fortnight out at least, gov'nuh." Every word was deliberate. "Y'can't call me at the last bloomin' minute and expect me to up and drop every other job in order to accommodate you."

In Berlin, Lieutenant Rostov tapped his desk with one hand. "You're the best there is. I'm ready to make it worth your while."

"Will you be coming in?"

"Not this time." Viktor tapped his long fingers against the edge of his desk and glanced at Natalie Allred's documents spread neatly across its surface. "I will send you the measurements—the same as before. Hopefully it won't take too long." He hesitated. "I need the details worked out as soon as possible."

"They always want it yesterday," the voice complained to no one in particular. "And they never want to pay me what it's worth."

"This one's worth a lot to me—and I will make it worth your while. Pay special attention to the origin and quality of the fabric." Lieutenant Rostov hung up the phone, slipped Natalie's documents into a large envelope, and addressed it to Connelly and Associates in Brighton.

* * *

Natalie closed the door to the nurses' station and almost collided with the one person she never wanted to see again. Broad shouldered, clean shaven, dark hair neatly trimmed, with the hammer-and-sickle pin on his tailored lapel—she found herself facing the steady, intelligent gaze of Lieutenant Viktor Nikolayevich Rostov. Fear washed over her, and the hand still connected with the door handle went numb. She backed into the doorframe, and her eyes darted to the left and right, as if someone might be available to assist her at 3:00 on a Saturday morning.

"I'm not going to hurt you, Miss Allred." The statement, so polite and steady, only served to heighten her fear. Rostov had not moved. "You and I need to talk."

"We have nothing to talk about." She had to force the words out of her mouth. "Leave me alone."

Lieutenant Rostov shifted slightly as if to step forward, and Natalie tensed. He noticed her reaction and froze, a brief smile playing at the corners of his mouth. He knew what his presence was doing to her. "You need not be afraid of me, nurse."

"You're not supposed to be here." Natalie wet her lips. "How in the world did you get in?"

Rostov shrugged. "Perhaps you'd prefer to know *why* I'm here. How I got here is insignificant. It is easily done."

Natalie finally dropped her hand from the doorknob and forced herself to breathe normally. "My fiancé is going to be here any minute. He's an American officer, and he will report you to—"

"Charles Miller is TDY in Nüremberg. He has an important assignment related to the war crimes trials, and he is not expected back until Thursday. You're a terrible liar."

Natalie's gaze wavered. "I'll call security, Mr. Rostov."

His smile broadened. "You'll have to go through me first. Don't you think it would be a bit more pleasant if you'd just stop panicking and try to relax? I'm really not here to hurt you."

She surrendered, dropping her eyes. "You have no right to keep my identification papers. I've done nothing wrong."

"Maybe not. We shall see."

She raised her head. "Why are you here, Lieutenant Rostov?"

"We need to discuss a few things." Rostov hesitated, his eyes searching the corridor. "But this isn't the place." He turned back to Natalie. "I know of a small establishment near here that will be open for breakfast in a few hours: *Die Biergarten*. I'll meet you there at six." And then Lieutenant Viktor Rostov turned on his heel and strode away down the hall. He turned the corner without a backward glance, and Natalie's legs buckled and she slid down the doorframe until she reached the floor, her knees pulled up to her chin.

* * *

When Natalie arrived at the restaurant, Rostov was waiting for her. He smiled, bowed slightly, and offered to help her off with her coat. She entered the almost deserted dining area and sat with him at a small table draped with white linen and adorned with a single white rose and dual candlesticks. The waiter lit the candles and brought tea for Rostov and hot chocolate for her. She sipped from her mug and tried to calm the butterflies in her stomach.

It was almost as though the lieutenant were trying to alter her opinion of him, she thought—trying to make her forget the fear she had felt since the first moment he had spoken to her in her office. And now that they were sitting here together, at the meal he'd threatened her with in their first encounter, he seemed content to study her silently, his gaze pensive and that strange emotion in his eyes he had tried to mask on their first visit.

She couldn't stand it any longer. "What is this all about, Lieutenant Rostov?" She knew her voice trembled slightly, but she couldn't seem to stop it. "Why are you following me? Why do you keep watching me?"

His eyes widened. "I do no such thing." He sounded indignant.

"Your men, then. Your cronies. It's as if I'm a suspected criminal or a security threat to your country."

"You're no menace to my country, Natalie Allred."

"Then why are you having me followed?"

Rostov leaned back in his chair and considered her carefully before speaking. "You're not a threat to me, Natalie. Maybe it's time you stopped worrying so much."

He hadn't answered her question, so she persisted, determined to find out the truth. "Are you having me followed?"

"No. Why should I?"

"The first time we met you threatened me—remember?"

"Ah, yes." Rostov smiled. "And you hid the truth from me. About your actions that night—and about your companion."

"That man wasn't my companion. I had no idea he was there until he fired that shot."

"So you admit it was he who wounded my men."

"He was defending me, that's all." Natalie shuddered at the memory of that night—Misha's foul breath, Oleg's strength, and Yarik's knife . . .

"Tell me his name."

She felt her face flush hot, and she bit her lip, terrified. "So all of this is about the man who helped me escape from your drunken, depraved, disgusting—"

"There's no need to speak of my country's soldiers in such a derogatory manner, Natalie." Lieutenant Rostov studied her carefully for several moments. He said calmly, "Perhaps my men were not where they were supposed to be that night."

"And they were drunk." Natalie insisted. "Your soldiers have been known to lose control when they are drunk—"

"And when there is a beautiful woman within their grasp." It was said with admiration, even pity, and Natalie sensed that perhaps Rostov might not approve of his soldiers' rampages—or at least he wanted her to believe he disapproved.

She studied him guardedly. "Where are my documents, Lieutenant Rostov?"

He ignored the question. "My men said you showed them sketches you had made—of the situation in Berlin and the suffering of the Germans. I appreciate artistic talent—even if some of my men do not." Rostov smiled cordially. "I would like to see those drawings myself sometime."

Natalie watched him warily. "I want my documents back."

"I'll return them to you as soon as I'm through with them," Rostov said.

"What do you need them for?"

Rostov stirred his tea. "When I look at your identification papers I ask myself, 'What makes a young, pretty American woman travel halfway around the world to a place as dangerous as military-controlled Berlin?' Of course, I understand that your government decides where you will be stationed, but surely you must have some say in that decision. Am I right?"

"I was allowed to express my preferences, yes."

"Each person has a reason why they are here in Berlin: a loved one, curiosity, a desire to help the struggling victims of a madman . . ." Rostov watched her carefully. "And the pull of an individual to return to one's roots can be a mighty force, Nurse Allred. Do you have family ties to Germany?"

"How about duty?" Natalie blurted. "Duty to one's country."

"Of course. Duty to country. Is that why *you* are here, Natalie?"

"I take my duty as a nurse seriously. Why are you asking me this?"

"Does it bother you?"

"Well, yes. It seems you're prying into my personal affairs, and I resent that."

Rostov smiled, amused. "Why not just let us talk to each other and enjoy each other's company. Why can't we be two civilized people sitting down to a civilized meal and a civilized conversation? Why do you distrust me so?"

"Why do you try to frighten me?"

Rostov's smile deepened. "We're getting nowhere if we keep throwing questions at each other like daggers, Natalie Allred. How about a deal: you will ask me all the questions you can think of, and I will answer truthfully every one of your questions. And then after you can think of no more questions to ask me, I'll ask *you* questions and you will answer me in a civilized, levelheaded, honest manner. What do you think?"

Natalie nodded, her eyes flashing as she accepted his challenge.

"Begin please, Miss Allred." Rostov folded his arms and watched her intently, awaiting her first query.

"Where did you learn to speak English?"

"I lived in Washington under a false identity for six years."

"Are you a spy?"

Rostov laughed. "You certainly know how to get right to the point. In a way, I am."

"Why am I so important to you? Why are your men following me? And don't lie to me this time, Lieutenant. I've seen them."

"Two answers, Miss Natalie: I want to get to know you better, and the description my men gave of your companion that night reminds me of a student—a friend—I once had at the University of Berlin. I'm trying to discover if he is the same man."

"You were at the University of Berlin?" Natalie was dubious.

"After I returned from Washington, I was a professor of science at Moscow University. Before the war I was invited by the University in Berlin to teach and do research. For one summer I had the privilege of teaching a guest-lecture series here, along with various other . . . projects. Assuming my conclusions about your companion are correct, I met him that summer. He was one of my students—and he worked as a lab assistant for one of my colleagues. He was a superb, brilliant pupil, I might add."

Natalie realized that if Rostov was telling the truth, he would surely remember Hans Brenner's name. Obviously there was something else Rostov wanted from her besides confirmation that his past pupil was here in Berlin and was Natalie's friend.

"Why didn't you just tell me you were friends with that man?" She refused to use Hans's name, even though she suspected Rostov already knew it.

"Would you have believed me any more than you do now, Natalie?"

She rolled her eyes. "You're the one making this complicated, Lieutenant Rostov. How do you know I don't believe you?"

"If you did, wouldn't you have told me your companion's name by now?"

"Not if I thought you meant to harm him."

"See! You don't believe me. Otherwise why would you imagine I would hurt a friend?"

Natalie said nothing. She was frustrated at this man's banter and incredibly tired. Also, she was afraid that if she submitted to this inquisition much longer she might accidentally give away something important, although with Hans disappeared off the face of the planet she didn't see that anything she said made any difference to his health and happiness.

She rose to her feet, and Lieutenant Rostov immediately followed suit. "Don't run off, Natalie Allred. The day is just beginning, and you can't be out of questions already."

"Lieutenant Rostov, I'm tired. I've been up all night, and I have a shift starting in three hours. I'm going home to bed." Natalie turned and walked away.

Rostov called after her, "Did Hans Brenner find your aunt?"

Natalie froze. Her brain argued with her ears, telling them they had not just heard what they thought they'd heard. She turned and approached the Russian. He was smiling affably at her.

"So you really are a spy."

"I have no reason to lie to you. But I think calling me a spy would be a bit of an exaggeration."

"Either you're a spy or you're not."

"That's not entirely accurate either."

She wanted to throw a chair at him. "All right, then, what part do I play in this exaggerated, slightly inaccurate game?"

"Sit down, Natalie," he said, and his voice was suddenly deadly serious. "Let's discuss this problem like two civilized human beings."

She obeyed him, her heart pounding and her face warm.

"First, you need to understand that if my superiors knew you had called me a spy they would think it a joke worthy of relaying all the way up to Comrade Stalin. I believe the correct term would be 'emissary.'" Again he smiled.

Either this Russian thought everything Natalie said was amusing or he was one of the most charming adversaries Natalie had ever encountered. She clutched her hands in her lap and persisted. "Why are you trying to find Hans Brenner?"

"Perhaps it would be less unpleasant for you, an American who, I'm sure, loves your country as much as I love mine, to accept my previous answer as truth." He spoke to her now with deference, confirming with his words that he would not always be able to answer Natalie's questions truthfully, but that for her own safety she should accept the answers he offered. "Your friend would prefer it that way, if he knew of your involvement."

Her heart pounded, and suddenly she felt Hans's loss so deeply that it was almost impossible to keep her emotions hidden from this man. "My 'friend,' as you describe him, is nowhere to be found. I'm assuming, accepting your previous answer as fact, that you still want to reminisce with a former pupil." How had she ever gotten herself tangled up in this? She said, "I'm sorry, Mr. Rostov, but I don't know where he is."

"And I'll accept *your* answer as truth, Natalie Allred." He took a drink from his cup, his eyes on her face. "But please understand that I would like to talk to him as soon as he reappears."

She remembered the way Hans had touched her cheek and the anguish in his eyes when she'd told him about Curly. "He probably won't come to see me, Lieutenant, so you might as well call off your watchdogs."

"Why won't he come to see you?"

She hesitated. She didn't want to share her personal life with this man, but she did feel a need to say something that would dissuade him from his maddening surveillance. "He and I had an argument the last time we saw each other, and he left rather frustrated."

"He loves you."

"No he doesn't." Natalie wanted to strike out at this man for his interference and arrogant assumptions. "He just thinks he does. I'm engaged to another man."

"Your statement is not logical, Miss Allred. Just because you're engaged to Curly Miller does not mean Hans Brenner does not love you."

He exasperated her. "All right. *I* don't love *him*. I'm engaged to Curly—"

"That's a little more believable, which is what you intend it to be, I'm sure."

"You don't believe me."

Rostov tapped the tablecloth. "I'm accustomed to not believing people— and especially not you." It was said almost with admiration, and he leaned forward, his expression suddenly pleasant. "I have a daughter who will be your age in a few years. She is like you in many ways, Natalie: she has a temper and flashing blue eyes; she is engaged to a good man; and she is a reliable, hard worker. She is beautiful in every way—inside and out—and she is my greatest treasure in this life."

Rostov paused, and then he reached and fingered the single white rose resting in a tiny crystal vase in the center of the table. "You remind me of her, Natalie Allred—and also of someone else dear to my heart."

His eyes again betrayed a curious emotion that unnerved her—the same emotion she had noticed the moment they met.

"Who?"

"Someone who loved white roses." His long finger touched the tip of a petal, bending it ever so slightly. "In a way, you're like this rose, Natalie: beautiful, soft, and a draw for the eyes." He caressed the flower, his hand gentle on its velvet surface, his movements not harming a single petal.

His voice was tender, almost mesmerizing. "I can also be soft, Natalie, and reasonable. I can be a friend to you, and help you when you're in need." His gaze was steady on her face, and his dark eyes carried an intensity in their depths that shocked her. Suddenly, without taking his eyes from hers, Rostov's strong hand enveloped and crushed the bloom in a vicious death grip. When he opened his hand the rose released every one of its petals onto the white tablecloth, and Rostov's hand carried pinpricks of blood from the thorny stem. "But if I'm threatened, or my authority undermined, I can also be dangerous—perhaps even deadly."

Natalie felt a shudder go up her spine, leaving her cold. He was maddeningly unpredictable with her, moving from threats to compliments and from falsehoods to truth, and she couldn't keep track of which was which. He was obviously in the process of blackmailing her this fine morning, but in spite of that unpleasant truth she couldn't make up her mind whether he was a friend or foe.

"If I don't help you find this man, what will you do to me?"

"Oh, you will help me find him, whether you're aware of your assistance or not." Rostov smiled at her.

"And if I find a way to stop you?"

He looked amused.

"And if I report you to the Allies?" She tried to stay as calm as Rostov seemed, but she knew she was failing miserably when she reached for her mug and could not pick it up without her hand trembling.

Rostov picked up his cup again, deliberately taking his time. He sipped his tea, dabbed at his lips with his linen napkin, set the cup down on its saucer in front of him, and replaced his napkin on the edge of the table. "My dear Natalie, I admire your courage." He leaned back in his chair, folding his arms across his chest. "But that courageous act would also be foolhardy." His gaze was a curious mixture of sorrow and triumph. "If you were to mention me to anyone—including your intended, Captain Charles Miller—you would be signing both yours and Hans Brenner's death sentences."

EIGHTEEN

Early November 1945

Lieutenant Hans Brenner stood near a corner of the hospital and watched the courtyard, his tall form hidden in shadows as he patiently endured the cold November drizzle. This morning he had slipped past the border guard and back into the American zone, his military training coming in handy as he eluded capture in the same manner as the day he'd walked away from Natalie, Rolf, and Marie. He felt renewed, invigorated, as if he had just come off a long, much deserved vacation and was ready to take on the world.

By now, Rolf Schulmann would probably be up and about, his body and soul healed by the presence of his fiancée and son. Hans realized his time away had helped him form a new attitude about his life—a positive outlook where he had been so pessimistic before. He had left Berlin desperately wondering if he would ever see Rolf again, and after several weeks with Rolf's friend Horst Wagner in Baiersbronn, he returned now with the absolute certainty that Rolf would be all right. He had left Berlin with a broken heart, one half of that organ sorrowing for Rolf and the other for the auburn-haired nurse who had unknowingly inched her way under his skin until he could not extract her. She had hurt him, he knew, by choosing the American instead of him, but he realized now that his love for her had been one-sided—that his affection for the blue-eyed dragon had surprised and worried her, perhaps even driven her into a hasty agreement with Curly just so that Hans would keep his distance.

He knew he didn't have a chance to win Natalie's heart, but he couldn't shake the desire to watch over her that had finally drawn him back from his self-imposed exile. His draw to her was so intense that he couldn't imagine at least making sure she was safe. Even though he couldn't think of any reason for her not to be, he remembered the fear in her eyes and her furtive glances around the courtyard during their last meeting, and a strange warning had been pestering his heart for the past few days. He couldn't go back to his basement shelter tonight without at least a visual confirmation that Natalie Allred was safe.

She appeared five minutes later, moving swiftly across the courtyard with an umbrella over her head. She clutched her coat tightly about her shoulders and didn't look in Hans's direction.

From the darkness Hans watched her, and he felt the familiar stirrings at her beauty. He fought an almost uncontrollable urge to run into the courtyard and confront her. He imagined the astonishment on her face at first seeing him, but he couldn't decide what her next emotion would be, once she had regained her composure. Pleasure? Joy?

Hans laughed at himself. More likely irritation. *What are you doing here, Hans Brenner? Can't you see I'm busy?*

He swiped at the water that continued to trickle from his hair into his eyes. Perhaps she wouldn't even recognize him, Hans realized. With his hair cut shorter, trimmed fingernails, decent clothes, mended boots, and his stubble shaved mostly away, he was a new man. The transformation made him feel clean, and he realized that he liked the feeling. Perhaps, he reasoned desperately, Natalie would also.

Silently he watched as Natalie completed her passage and entered her barracks apartment, and then he pushed away from the wall and turned to go, a part of him still wishing he could talk to her but his practical side winning out. Natalie Allred was relegated to a chapter in his past, and he was not yet sure that chapter should be reopened. Besides, with the feelings he had for her there was no way they could ever have a normal, platonic friendship—and even if she could return his love, he refused to hurt the good man who had won her affections. Natalie belonged to Captain Curly Miller, and Curly Miller had intervened to help Rolf Schulmann live. Hans would never interfere. He pushed Natalie Allred to the back of his mind.

Hans enjoyed feeling like a new man. His physical absence from all that troubled him had been therapeutic in so many ways, and now, as he moved quickly through the streets toward his old bomb shelter abode, he felt ready to take on the world—or at least take a part of it for himself.

He would go back to the university. He would find his old professor and continue with the education that had ended on such a military note so many years before, and he would try to find a way to survive in a world entirely foreign to the one he had always known. He would make new friends, and after a while he would feel strong enough to renew past acquaintances, but there was no hurry for that. Someday he might even feel strong enough to face Natalie Allred—or Natalie Miller, as she soon would be—and he would be happy for her.

He reached the bomb shelter and descended, sidestepping a pile of refuse someone had pitched down the steps, and he reached for the door handle. He hesitated as he did so, his senses warning him that all was not right. Something had changed since that morning. Why were there no babies crying? It must be about dinner time, and several babies always needed their mothers about now. His hand hesitated on the knob as he contemplated the strange sensation prickling at the back of his neck. He tried to recall when he had felt such a feeling before, but he could not.

He pushed at the door. In spite of his new outlook on life with his visit to the shelter, there came a renewal of his irresponsible feelings for Natalie, and suddenly he felt a deep emptiness at the pit of his soul. He shook his head. Obviously he was tired and confused. He would think about it again in the morning. He opened the door and stepped inside.

In the split second it takes for one foot to move in front of the other, many things can happen. In Hans's case his mind registered the vast empty expanse of the basement's interior, and he felt a bit surprised that it was so big. Then he realized it felt big because it was empty of its usual inhabitants. The old men with their stories and their rheumatism, who always inhabited the corner to his left and played cards with a dog-eared deck every night, had disappeared. The children, with their gaunt faces and eyes bright from hunger and the day's exercises among Berlin's play-yards of rubble, were nowhere to be seen. The women with their skeletal faces and worried eyes, holding ever-hungry and soiled babies in their arms, were not present.

But Hans was not completely alone in the room. And the man with the bowler hat, steady gaze, and hammer-and-sickle pin on his lapel, who stood in the center of the empty room, seemed vaguely familiar.

And then Hans's mind could register no more, because the other man familiar to him—the Goliath with the muscles and the gorilla face who had once accompanied the silver-haired woman in an attempt to shadow Hans—did something in Hans's peripheral vision that did not register in that all-encompassing split second of movement, and Hans felt first the excruciating pain of the man's tremendous fist embedding itself into his kidneys and then into his skull, and finally the dull thud of his own head hitting the unrelenting concrete of the shelter's floor.

* * *

Nurse Natalie Allred finished her shift and dragged herself across the rain-soaked courtyard back to her room, her feet torturing her and her head pounding like bombs exploding across Berlin. She shed her umbrella and her raincoat and then crawled immediately into bed and pulled the covers up to her chin and closed her eyes.

The knock on the door an hour later did little to settle her nerves, and in her sleep-deprived state she tried to ignore the sound. She heard Mabel rousing from slumber, mumbling angrily about night visitors and how if they were going to continue to interrupt her sleep then at least once in a while the visitors should be for her.

Soon the British woman returned carrying a single white rose, which she handed to Natalie with a *harrumph* that could have been heard all the way over in Frankfurt. "You're the female equivalent of the sailor with a sweetheart in every port, Natalie. Let's see, an American pilot, a filthy German, and now, a *Russian?*"

NINETEEN

It bothered Lieutenant Viktor Rostov that he could become so agitated over such a little thing as a bill from his tailor. His hands shook so badly that he almost stabbed himself in the thumb with the letter opener, and he dropped two pages of the invoice before he finally regained control of his emotions.

He carefully studied the lines of figures and sums, and then he moved on to the last page, where he read the following notes from his British contact:

> As instructed, suit fabric will be woven of the finest gabardine wool blend, processed with wool from the finest pastures of South Dakota. Any questions related to the manufacture of said garment to be directed to Mrs. John Allred of Rapid City. It is recommended that client preview manufacture personally to determine if quality is as represented by supplier.

Rostov sent a telegram to Brighton—*Price satisfactory. Recommendation accepted.*

* * *

Rolf finally healed sufficiently to be moved out of the convalescent ward and into a POW camp west of Berlin. With her father's financial assistance, Marie rented a humble one-room apartment a mere kilometer from the camp and, true to her word, brought Alma to visit his father every day.

On the first day, she was informed by the brusque army private guarding the gate that visitors were not allowed into the camp. But each day she came with Alma and waited near the entrance, even though they never caught a glimpse of the man who meant so much to both of them.

At the beginning of the second week the young guard approached Marie and Alma, his face contrite. "Command says to let you in on Sundays." He removed his cap and scratched his head. "I don't understand why, and the commander's been fighting the order—but the word comes from over his head—Commander said someone at headquarters in Frankfurt has taken an interest in Major Schulmann's situation."

The camp was populated with both male and female German prisoners—men and women who had fought for Nazi Germany and had either surrendered or been captured at the end of the war. The prison conditions were not overly harsh, so Marie was shocked by the physical conditions of many of the camp's residents, especially the *Volkssturm,* or senior soldiers, that Hitler had conscripted into his army in a crazy last-ditch effort to hold Berlin. Many of these soldiers looked to be well into their seventies, although Marie was familiar with how war could age a man. The vacant eyes that stared back at her and Alma every Sunday as the two made their way to Rolf's compound tugged at her heartstrings. How many of them would have been safely at home with wives and grandchildren if it hadn't been for Hitler's madness?

Rolf steadily healed. The Americans fed him adequately, and he put on weight and his shoulders and chest broadened. He joined the work crews sorting and transporting rubble in the ruined city, and each week Marie gloried in the returning strength of Rolf's arms as he held her close to him.

And she continuously petitioned both the military powers and a Higher Power for his release.

TWENTY

When Natalie walked Mabel home from the hospital after their shift, Lieutenant Viktor Rostov was waiting for her, bundled against the cold November chill, at the door to her barracks apartment. Mabel said a few choice words as she entered the apartment and slammed the door, leaving Natalie to face the Russian alone.

He had brought her a wrapped gift, which he held out to her with gloved hands. She took it, holding it awkwardly as they faced each other on the porch.

"Open it, Natalie. It reminds me of you."

She made no movement to comply. "You shouldn't have." She meant it.

Rostov retrieved it and removed the newspaper wrapping for her. "I commissioned it especially for you—traded food for it from a starving artist." He held up a painting in a rough-cut wooden frame. Natalie took it and silently stared at the subtle grays, greens, lavenders, and pinks used by the steady hand of a poverty-stricken artist to create an intricate bouquet of white roses. "And besides, I'm a Russian—and Russians like to give gifts."

She ran her finger along the stem of a rose, pausing on the tip of a thorn. "It's lovely . . ." she said, and even though Rostov's persistence in reminding her of her predicament unnerved her, she meant the compliment.

"I came to tell you about my daughter."

"You already have, Lieutenant."

"I have not told you this. I need to tell someone, and I know you will listen."

She was so tired, and because of what this man was doing to her she knew tonight would be another horrible, sleepless night. She studied the lieutenant closely, trying to understand why he would come to her.

"I wish you and I could spend more time together, without you worrying so much."

"I'm always worried that if I go somewhere with you I'll never return," she blurted.

Rostov frowned. "You're wise to worry. But I would never treat you like those hooligans you encountered—"

"How can I be so sure?" She licked her lips. "I can't ever trust what you say."

"Natalie, if you only knew what you mean to me, you would change your opinion of me."

"I know what I mean to you, Lieutenant Rostov." She frowned. "You remind me every time we meet that I'm a puppet in a macabre puppet show—or a trap set for a friend, and there is nothing I can do to warn him."

"This is as difficult for me as it is for you, Natalie Allred."

"But your life is not in danger every time I get close to you."

His eyes locked with hers. "That is what you think."

What a strange thing to say, Natalie thought, and she could not find the meaning to the riddle in his eyes, still intense with the strange light that he never tried to hide from her anymore. "But you've made it all too clear that my existence is precarious." She indicated the painting in her hands. "You remind me constantly that you're not to be trusted, Lieutenant."

"Please stop calling me that. The war is over and I am *Viktor Nikolayevich.* I want you to see me as another human being—just like you."

She recognized in his request a subtle attempt to break down the barrier between them. "You're using me to get at Hans Brenner—*Viktor Nikolayevich.*" She tried to steady her breathing. "Either you're waiting for him to reappear so you can whisk him away to some cold, frozen wasteland in the east, or you have already done so, and the only reason you keep pestering me is so that he will fear for my safety and do whatever it is that you want him to do."

"Russia is not a cold, frozen wasteland—at least not all of it." Rostov's reply answered nothing, and his words were a rebuke. He stepped toward her and tried to take her hand in his, but she pulled away from him and turned to the door. "Please, don't touch me. I can't stand the thought of you touching me."

"I cannot promise I'll never touch you, Natalie."

She reached past him for the doorknob, and after a long hesitation he moved out of the way. Natalie held out the painting to him. "It is beautiful, Lieutenant Rostov—Viktor—but I cannot accept it."

He didn't take it, but stood still, his eyes sorrowful as he looked down at her.

Natalie continued. "You're a danger to me and to Hans, and I cannot allow you to get close to me. Besides, you're an expert at blackmail and I don't appreciate your skills being used on me." She turned the doorknob.

Rostov stepped closer once again, and suddenly Natalie recognized the pain in his eyes. He exclaimed, "My daughter's fiancé—Anton—he was killed in an accident this morning on his way to the factory."

Natalie hesitated, and then she stepped away from the door. She met his gaze and against her will felt a portion of his suffering. She spoke softly. "Your daughter must be heartbroken. I'm so sorry for her loss."

Rostov leaned against the doorframe. "They were to be married soon— how could he be taken from us? How could my Lucya be required to suffer so deeply?"

Natalie didn't know what to say. She knew that his anguish was real—it was the anguish any father would feel if he were required to stand by and watch his child suffer—and yet his actions over the past few weeks made it difficult for her to feel sympathy. With anyone else—a coworker, a friend, even a person she had just met on the street—she might reach and touch his arm, trying to comfort him as a nurse—or a friend—might. And even though as a caregiver her nature directed her to do likewise with this man, a part of her shrank from the thought of knowingly initiating contact. Perhaps if he didn't frighten her so . . .

"My Lucya is heartbroken," Rostov lamented. "She cannot imagine a life without Anton by her side, and her will to live is waning. First her brother, and then her mother"—his voice caught—"and now Lucya's intended has also been taken from her!"

"You came all the way here to tell me this?" Natalie was confused. "Is there no one else you can go to—to receive comfort?"

"No one." He smiled sadly. "I told you that the war has ended, but it really has not. My Lucya's Anton was not supposed to be at work this morning—but he was contacted and ordered to go at the last minute."

Natalie stared at Rostov, her eyes wide. "Are you telling me . . . that you think his death was . . . not an accident?"

Rostov raised is hands in frustration. "I do not know what I'm telling you—I only know that my superiors have recently expressed dissatisfaction with how my work is progressing . . ."

Natalie sobered and bent to lean the painting against the wall beside the door. "Your *work*?" She straightened and frowned at Rostov. "Is your work to spy, to threaten, and to bully an American citizen?"

"Yes, Natalie. If that is what it takes to discover the truth for my government."

She faced him squarely. "Again you're manipulating me, Viktor. You're telling me that my refusal to cooperate has led to the death of your daughter's fiancé." She pointed toward the courtyard. "I was beginning to feel sorry for you and your daughter. How dare you bring me into all this? Please go now."

Rostov's eyes grew wide. "I'm not accusing you of anything, Natalie! I would never imagine you to be the cause of Lucya's suffering." He ignored her invitation to depart. "If you understood my government you would never think such a thing." His eyes pleaded with her. "You're not to blame—it is entirely *my* fault, and the realization makes me ache inside."

He sighed. "Up until now I have not been as responsible as I should have been—perhaps because the things I do are repulsive to me. I cause suffering to the people I care about, I hesitate when I should move forward courageously, and I do not listen to my instincts when they tell me to proceed. And if, as you have deduced, this death is truly no accident, then it is because my superiors are trying to send me a message that I'll never forget—one that will inspire me to move forward without hesitation until my task is complete."

Natalie felt her sympathy disintegrate. Even in his grief he was capable of menace. Rostov was telling her that he was beyond games, beyond any previous attempts at chivalrous coercion. She felt the intended danger in his words.

* * *

November 20, 1945

She didn't hear Curly Miller say her name. Her mind, far away, was occupied with thoughts of her aunt's family, and *Kristallnacht.* The idea that a government would condone what the Nazis did to their own citizens was nauseating.

Natalie Allred still had a hard time believing the reports about the death camps, the bodies, the suffering . . . In fact, the possibility that her aunt and uncle and cousins had died in those camps made her physically ill.

She was standing on a balcony of the hospital, leaning against the railing with her hands clenched inside her sleeves to ward off the bitter evening chill as she watched, unseeing, the street below. She had been in Berlin now for several months and still had no more information about her aunt's family than the news about *Kristallnacht,* given to her by . . . by . . .

She hated even thinking about Hans Brenner. He was like a disease, she convinced herself—a deadly, incurable disease. The emotions she had allowed herself to develop for the German would bother her for the rest of her life, and she worried that there was nothing she could do about it. She had never imagined it was possible to feel a connection to someone she could not even consider spending the rest of her life with, and the unbelievably kind, incredibly handsome, rough-edged German who constantly invaded her thoughts was the last person on earth to whom she wanted to have a connection.

Keep convincing yourself, Natalie.

Why was she thinking about him? She was worried about his whereabouts—that had to be the reason. She forced herself to believe that her feelings for him didn't go beyond that. If Lieutenant Rostov could have read her thoughts, he would have been amused at the turmoil he saw there, she thought wryly.

From behind her she felt a warm breath on her ear and she jumped in alarm, her adrenaline level shooting through the roof. She twisted around, eyes wide and heart pounding, only to find Curly's smiling face close to her own. Her reaction to his presence surprised him, and he straightened, somewhat taken aback. "I'm sorry if I startled you, Nattie. Really, I am. I said your name at least three times."

"You frightened me, Curly. I—I thought you were somebody else . . ."

"Who?" Curly's brow knitted. "Are you expecting somebody else?" He glanced around and then back at her. "This was our night out, wasn't it?" he asked, concerned.

She nodded, her heart still pounding in her throat. How could she tell Curly that she'd been certain for just a moment that the Russian lieutenant had returned to torment her?

Curly slipped an arm protectively around her. "You're a nervous wreck, Natalie Allred. In fact, ever since you said you'd marry me you've seemed unhappy." He hesitated. "You're not sorry, are you?"

"No! Of course not!" She forced a smile. "How could you think such a thing?"

"'Cause it'd just kill me if you backed out now . . ."

She grabbed his shirt front. "Listen, Curly, I'm not going to—" She hesitated as the fact that she had actually questioned her engagement several times flashed through her mind. She rephrased her words carefully. "You're a wonderful man. I'm honored to be your future wife, and I would never want to cause you pain." She realized that she had not addressed his fear that she was getting cold feet, and she watched him, nervous that he would ask her for more.

But Curly seemed satisfied with her words, and he gave her a joyful squeeze before releasing her and taking her hand in his. "Good." He smiled and jokingly assumed a thick Texas accent. "'Cuz I sure am keen on you, Miss Natalie, and I'm glad you feel the same way. Y'know, for the past few weeks I coulda sworn you wuz gettin' a bit antsy."

She smiled at him. "Not at all. I love you as much today as I ever have." And as she said it, she knew that it was true.

But she still could not rid her mind of Hans Brenner, his gun raised, saving her life on that terrible night so many ages ago . . .

TWENTY-ONE

December 14, 1945

Curly surprised Natalie that weekend with Christmas concert tickets. The Berlin Philharmonic was celebrating the return of its concertmaster, Hammond Lieberman, who had been absent from Germany throughout the war because of his precariously Semitic lineage. Rumor held that he had escaped to Holland only to discover that he was in as much danger there as in Berlin, and because he was lucky enough to have a cousin in New York, he slipped across the ocean to become a guest performer with the New York Philharmonic.

Natalie went to the concert with Curly, painfully aware that she had been neglecting him for the past few weeks. She had managed to fill her days so completely as to practically exclude her fiancé from her life. And the whole jumbled mess of her emotions made her moody, irritable, and downright depressed. Through it all Curly maintained his even temperament, showing a patient acceptance and forgiveness that shamed her and made her even more miserable. The fact was, she was spending much more energy on trying to find her relatives and worrying about Hans's whereabouts than she was on cultivating her relationship with her fiancé.

At the concert she finally shared with him some of her worries while they waited for the performance to begin. "It's like I'm being consumed by it all, Curly—as if my search for my family has taken over every aspect of my life." For some reason she left Hans Brenner out of her explanation—perhaps it was the fear that Curly might think her concern for the German more than it really was. And of course Lieutenant Rostov could not possibly be mentioned . . .

Curly rested his arm around her shoulders, his face showing his concern. "Y'know, the army has people who can help you with all this . . ."

"Curly!" She stared at him, aghast. "The last thing I need right now is a shrink telling me I've lost my marbles. I'm not crazy—just preoccupied. Worried."

Curly grinned. "I meant they have people who can help you find your relatives, Natalie."

She returned his smile, feeling sheepish.

Curly continued. "Like I've told you before, the army's got mountains of Nazi documents, and manpower assigned to make sense of it all. Whatever else the Nazis' shortcomings, keeping meticulous records was never one of them. Just give the army the name, the address from your letter, the info Brenner gave you about *Kristallnacht,* and they'll take care of the rest."

Curly's casual mention of Hans made her heart skip a beat, but she leaned over and kissed him. "You always make it sound so easy."

"It's really not that hard. There's bound to be contact info for your aunt and uncle with a bank, a landlord, a neighbor, a prefect, a Nazi relocation list . . ."

"I'm sure you're right."

"I mean, weren't the Jews required to register with the government? And they would've had to get permission to run a business, wouldn't they? What about tax records?"

The musicians began to file onto the stage, moving to their seats and tuning their instruments, the sound at first tentative—a B-flat from a flute, an A from a violin, a low C from the cello section . . . They arranged sheet music on their stands and began practicing, and the sound soon crescendoed, each individual instrument becoming part of a swelling cacophony of sound that rose and ebbed, swirled and eddied, with trills and multi-octave scales, rehearsed allegros and adagios, as they warmed their fingers and their instruments in anticipation of the arrival of the concertmaster.

Curly was not much for concerts—Natalie knew he had done this for her—and he began to fidget a bit after the second movement of the *Stravinsky Symphony in C.* About an hour into the concert Hammond Lieberman played a difficult concerto written by Tchaikovsky, a tribute to Lieberman's mentor and perhaps in deference to the conquerors, and Curly's head drooped. Natalie let him sleep—he'd had a long day, and his duty assignment to Nüremberg must have been exhausting. His head nodded several times, and she finally rested it gently against her shoulder.

During the *Canzonetta* she found her gaze wandering from the stage, over the heads of the audience, across the graceful aesthetics of the concert hall, and up into the boxes above, and she saw *him* sitting there, watching her. It was a bit disconcerting, she thought, to have Lieutenant Viktor Rostov observing her from above and Curly's regular breathing against her neck. Rostov nodded at her, winked, and gave her an amused smile. She turned away quickly, her cheeks flushed.

Curly snored softly while she listened to the remainder of the violin solo, and when the audience erupted into enthusiastic applause at the end, Curly lifted his head, stared dazedly around for a moment, and then joined the applause. He turned and smiled at Natalie.

"Beautiful, wasn't it?" he said.

"Brilliant."

"I'm glad we came."

She returned his smile.

* * *

After the concert, Curly took her for a late dinner, and she asked him about his trip. He told her about the beginning Nüremberg trials and how Justice Jackson and the coalition had managed to get their hands on film footage of the concentration camps. He shook his head, sorrowful. "You and I have no idea what it means to be persecuted, Nattie. The Jews here in Europe have been beaten, demeaned, belittled, dehumanized, criminalized, and butchered. There is no excuse for what the Nazis have done. None at all."

Natalie said solemnly, "I sometimes wonder what I would do if I ever found myself face-to-face with the Nazis who beat my uncle and destroyed his shop."

"That would be devastating," Curly agreed.

"And what if I find out that my relatives didn't survive the war? They might not have, y'know."

"Most Jews didn't." Curly nodded, sympathetic.

Natalie clutched her hands together under the tablecloth. "If it turns out they died in the camps, I almost feel like it would be my responsibility to find the ones who sent them there and bring them to justice. I cannot imagine letting them roam free when my aunt and cousins are dead and buried in a mass grave."

Curly nodded. "Y'know, that's happening quite a bit more nowadays, with relatives of the victims testifying against the perpetrators. Happening all over Europe, and will just happen more if they convict and execute the Nazi leaders they're trying now in Nüremberg."

The waiter arrived with their order, but Natalie had no appetite for the meal placed in front of her. She stared listlessly at the table and mourned, "Curly, I've been searching for them for months, and I've found nothing. *Nothing.* Not since . . . not since . . ." She swallowed hard, and a tear coursed down her cheek.

Curly set down his fork and looked at her gravely. "I'd like to believe your sadness is because of your aunt and uncle."

She stared at him. "Of course it is."

"You miss him, don't you." It came out as a statement rather than a question.

Natalie hesitated.

"Come on, Nattie. I've seen the way you react when I mention Brenner. You try to change the subject, or you get all uptight at me for bringing him into the conversation. You've been thinking about him, haven't you?"

She dropped her eyes.

Curly watched her soberly. "Were you in love with him?"

Natalie shook her head quickly. A little too quickly. "Of course not! It's just that he disappeared so suddenly—"

"When you told him about us," Curly finished for her.

Natalie could not respond. Curly was such a good person. She didn't want to hurt him. Indeed, she saw no reason to hurt him. Curly was the one who could eventually take her to the temple. Curly was the one who could place his hands on a man's head and command him in the name of Jesus to be healed. Curly was the one she should be spending her time thinking about, not the German who had thrown her life and her emotions into a dizzying emotional whirlwind and then disappeared from Berlin and from her life, probably forever.

She felt an unreasonable surge of desperation at the thought of never seeing Hans again, but she smiled and reached for Curly's hand. "Listen, Curly, you're wrong." She took a deep breath. "There's nothing between me and Hans. It's *you* I want to marry. I want a temple marriage, and I want an eternal family."

Curly refused to let it alone. "But if Brenner were a member of the Church . . ."

"Stop it!" She spoke a bit more sharply than she had intended and took a deep breath to steady herself. "He's not, all right?"

"He might join the Church just to please you."

His words twisted her insides into painful knots. "If he did, I would always wonder if he really shared my feelings about the gospel and . . ." she trailed off.

Curly leaned back in his chair and looked at her for a long time. She couldn't meet his gaze. "Natalie . . ." His voice was sober. "I think you're worrying about him more than you will let on. And somehow you've got yourself convinced that you don't have feelings for him." He took a deep breath. "You shouldn't lie to yourself, Nattie—or to me."

"Stop it, Curly."

"No, Natalie, you shouldn't be trying to deceive yourself this way." Curly's voice wavered, and he whispered, "I love you, Nattie—and because I love you I want you to be happy. I want *us* to be happy, and we can't ever be completely happy with this man's shadow constantly between us."

Natalie wiped her eyes and peered at Curly. Carefully, she asked, "Curly . . . what is it you're trying to tell me?"

"I'm saying that it's time you find out what you really feel for Brenner. It's time you decide if it's something that's going to mess us up. And if it is, I'll get out of the way." Curly touched her cheek affectionately. "And if you decide that Brenner is not going to haunt you for the rest of your life, then I think I can live with waiting to marry you until next summer, when we can travel to Utah and do it right."

Natalie looked into his eyes and saw the boyish hope in their depths, and his compromise almost made her feel better.

Curly continued. "But if we're going to stay engaged, Nattie, you need to promise me you'll stop thinking about Hans Brenner."

Natalie opened her mouth to comment but could think of nothing to say. Curly patted her arm and continued. "I believe you were meant for me, Nattie. We were made for each other. But I can't make this marriage work on my own. I need you to return the same feelings, without any misgivings or any backward glances. I don't think I could stand it if"—Curly's voice caught, and he swallowed before continuing—"if Brenner kept filling your thoughts even after we were married."

TWENTY-TWO

December 18, 1945

Viktor Rostov was not accustomed to receiving Christmas presents—Christmas was a Christian holiday, and he really had no interest in participating in such events. But ever since his years in the United States, Christmas had always intrigued him, with its unabashed spending spree that seemed to hold all Americans in its mesmerizing grasp. Westerners chopped down evergreens and decorated them with flammable objects and strings of precious food items such as nuts and candies, sweet breads, oranges, and popcorn strings—and here in Germany the wealthy families even attached burning candles to the delicate tips of branches. Viktor always wondered at the mental health of the person who would light not one, but multitudes of dangerous candles in close contact with such a highly combustible object.

In Russia he and his daughter often prepared New Year's gifts for each other, placing them under a decorated fir tree and reading folktales about *Snegurochka*—Little Snow Person—one of Russia's favorite holiday figures. But Christmas was not a holiday he usually celebrated.

Consequently he was surprised when a package arrived for him the week before Christmas, routed with Allied mail through Frankfurt on a routine courier flight.

The unpretentious object was wrapped in ordinary brown paper and rough twine, but as he began to remove the wrapping he was surprised to catch a glimpse of brightly colored paper hidden beneath.

He opened both the outer paper and the inner Christmas wrapping and fingered the twelve-centimeter-square swatch of fabric inside. His thumb smoothed the navy blue material as he found and read the accompanying note:

It seems gabardine wool might not be sufficiently durable for your needs. It is recommended that threads of Russian cotton be interwoven with the American wool to give it more beauty, texture, and durability. Please see enclosed sample. We really should meet soon to discuss this latest recommendation.

Viktor continued to run the fabric between his fingers as he contemplated this unexpected, startling, and wondrous new development, and suddenly he began feeling strangely, inexplicably generous. As he mulled over the idea of giving one specific holiday gift of his own, he decided that maybe—just maybe—the tradition of Christmas, with its gifts, goodies, and incendiaries, might not be such a bad idea after all.

* * *

December 25, 1945

Marie and Alma received permission to spend the entirety of Christmas afternoon with Rolf in the POW camp. Rolf gave Alma a gift: a stick of gum he had traded from the American guards. Alma stuck it in his mouth, delighted at the fruity burst of flavor that flooded his mouth as he chewed. His delight turned to wonder as the gum didn't deteriorate as did regular edibles but remained chewable and sweet for some time. Marie laughed at the look on his face as he worked his jaws back and forth, up and down, and even removed the wad from his mouth once and studied it, curious why it didn't seem to be disintegrating. Then he popped it back into his mouth and kept it there for the remainder of the visit, sometimes imitating the exaggerated chaw of the friendly guards.

Rolf borrowed a baseball bat, well-worn leather glove, and ball from one of the guards, and he spent a significant amount of time teaching Alma how to play the American game of baseball. Marie watched from a row of rough-hewn wooden bleachers, her arms folded and her mittened hands tucked under her arms against the chill. Snow had fallen early in the morning, followed by clear skies and an almost Indian summer warmth that, as the snow melted and the ground warmed, seemed to have brought out the competitive spirit in the energetic young guards and their prisoners. During the previous summer they had organized two baseball teams in the camp— an American team and a German POW team—and when Rolf arrived he was invited by the POWs to lend them a hand.

Suddenly there was an enthusiastic shout from the army barracks to their left, and over the loudspeaker Marie heard, *"Oh yes, oh yes, oh yes! On your feet, Yanks, and let's teach those Krauts a lesson they'll never forget!"*

Startled, she turned to look at Rolf. He was kneeling next to Alma, showing him the proper way to hold a baseball bat, and he met her expression with a smile.

"Baseball game," Rolf said, his grin widening. "Seems they've forgotten already how we trounced them last time." He stood and patted Alma on the back. "Want to watch your daddy play baseball?"

Marie mused, "Seems a derogatory name for a baseball team."

Rolf shrugged. "Who won the war, Marie?"

Two teams lined up for the opening toss. Marie watched as a guard flipped a coin into the air with his thumbnail, and when it fell to the ground a representative of each team bent to discover the results. The American representative straightened and hollered, "Take to the field, Krauts!" and the American team tossed the Germans their gloves. Alma trembled with anticipation next to Marie, and each time the ball connected with the bat he jumped up and down and hollered around his gum wad along with the crowd of soldiers and prisoners surrounding the field.

Eventually the Americans took the field and Rolf's turn came to bat. He walked to the plate swinging his bat and stretching his arms, and he winked over his shoulder at Marie on the makeshift bleachers. His wink prompted a frenzied moment of catcalls, low whistles, and good-natured comments in her general direction, and Marie laughed. Rolf stepped up to the plate and positioned his feet, and when the pitcher released the ball, he swung, the muscles in his arms rippling as he solidly connected, and the dull crack bounced and reverberated off the low-lying structures around the field. The ball took to the clear blue sky, slicing ten feet over the pitcher's head and continuing to climb. Alma watched in awe as the ball his father had slaughtered climbed out of the field and across the camp fence, much to the frenzied enthusiasm of the Germans and the howling consternation of the Americans.

"Confound it, Schulmann! That was my best ball!"

Alma leaped off the bench and ran to his father, yelling hysterically and punching the air with his fists. Rolf grabbed his son's hand and trotted around the bases with him in tow, and Alma waved at the enthusiastic crowd as if he had been the one to swing the bat.

When Rolf crossed home plate he kept right on going, trotting with Alma's hand still held in his, straight to Marie. He pulled her off the bench, wrapped her in his arms, and pulled her close until her feet left the ground. And then he kissed her, right there in front of the cheering crowd.

* * *

Natalie Allred did not get a kiss on Christmas Day. Curly was off again to Nüremberg, and she found herself pulling a double shift at the hospital. Besides, even if Curly had been here, they were in the middle of a cooling off period that she realized was entirely her fault. Curly had spelled it out for her that evening after the concert, and his candor had made her realize that she really *was* a hopeless basket case, mourning over a man she would never be willing to marry even if he hadn't gone missing three months before. And her thoughts about that man were going to cost her a chance to marry Curly if she didn't find a way to stifle them permanently.

She dragged her aching body across the porch toward her door, trying to ignore the painting from Rostov that still leaned threateningly against the wall, the intricate roses reminding her every time she came home of Rostov's control over her. She had not touched it since the night he gave it to her. She went into her room and fell across the bed, but immediately she felt something hard digging into her ribs. Startled, she jumped away and saw a small package lying on her quilt, still bouncing along with the bed springs. She took it in her hands and studied it, wondering if Curly had somehow found a way to send her a Christmas present. But he had already given her one before he left for Nüremberg, and he hadn't mentioned any gift when he'd called this afternoon—in fact, he had apologized that he "couldn't do something more."

There was no note, no card. The twine came off in her hands and she removed the dull brown paper, her curiosity completely overshadowing her fatigue. Inside the wrapping she found a square lacquer box, brightly decorated and surprisingly similar to one she had once found in a package under her mother's bed. She had been curious about the small box, and her mother had told her that it was a gift from a long-ago Russian friend. She had then proceeded to explain the beautiful ornamentation to her inquisitive daughter.

Just like her mother's treasure, this box was also painted with a *Troika*— a Russian sled pulled by three prancing horses—with a heavily bundled, rosy-cheeked and romantic couple riding along inside.

Around the edges of the box's lid ran a border of intricately painted white roses.

With the subtle message of the white roses still distressing her, Natalie opened the box and looked inside, and instantly she forgot white roses, menacing thorns, her own tired body, and her predicament with Curly.

There was only one item in the box, and she almost couldn't see it for the tears that now clouded her vision. With trembling fingers she reached inside and extracted a photograph, and she held it to her chest and cried. Her desperate tears fell across her flushed cheeks and down her chin and neck, some of them falling on the crisply starched whiteness of her nurse's uniform and others falling on the photograph of a man standing against a neutral grey background with his head slightly inclined and his cheeks pallid. He was looking solemnly at the camera, but to Natalie Allred it seemed as if Hans's dark eyes focused past the photographer, through time, space, and dimension, and into her very soul.

TWENTY-THREE

December 27, 1945

Lieutenant Viktor Rostov flew to London as a guest of Britain's Royal Air Force to inspect conditions at an English-run German POW camp near Brighton. He spent an uncommonly clear winter day touring the facilities at camp number 114 and had a pleasant afternoon tea with the camp commander. He thanked the commander for both the tour and the tea and emphasized the Soviet government's desire to pattern Russian labor facilities after those of their British allies.

In the evening Viktor traveled alone to a nondescript shop in old Brighton to preview fabric for a new business suit. When he boarded the RAF Halifax for his return journey to Berlin a few hours later, he carried with him not only several swatches of an exquisite gabardine wool-cotton blend, but also the documents of the American nurse Natalie Allred and a shocking revelation that both troubled and thrilled him—and that guaranteed Natalie's compliance for as long as Viktor Rostov required it, and perhaps for the remainder of her life.

* * *

December 28, 1945

On any other day a brisk ride through the streets of Berlin on Mabel's grudgingly loaned bicycle would have been an exhilarating escape from the drudgery of the hospital. But not today.

Natalie clenched her jaw against the cold wind that burned her throat and whistled down the collar of her coat. She felt again her anguish as she'd held Hans's picture in her hands on Christmas Day, and she fought against anger directed at Lieutenant Viktor Rostov, who she knew was the catalyst for this morning's dangerous journey.

When she reached the Friedrichshain checkpoint, Natalie dismounted, keeping a death grip on the cold handlebars. She made a beeline for the young Russian sentries standing around the barrel of burning wood on the edge of the street. They stared at her, surprise and curiosity evident on their ruddy faces as they watched her approach. One of the boys leaned toward his comrades and made a comment, and their chuckles escaped in short, cloudy bursts into the bitter air.

Natalie didn't waste precious time on preamble. "Lieutenant Viktor Rostov—please." She prayed they would understand.

"Rostov?" One of the men grinned at her and shook his head. "Rostov—*nyet*." He pointed to himself and grinned.

She clenched the handlebars and yelled at them, "English!" and felt again the horrible fear that had enveloped her that awful night long ago.

She looked past the jeering soldiers and saw another man approaching from the guard shack. He was perhaps no older than Natalie herself, and was dressed impeccably in the uniform of a ranking officer. He was obviously intrigued by her determined presence, and as he advanced he raked her from head to toe with his clear blue eyes, smiling along with his comrades.

"English?" he asked, still smirking, and waved the other soldiers to one side.

"Yes, please."

"I am command. I speak the English."

Her fingers relaxed their death grip on the bicycle, and she repeated her request to speak to Lieutenant Rostov.

"Who are you?"

"Miss Natalie Allred. I have something important to say to him."

Her mention of Rostov's name produced a wicked grin, and now he took a step backward and nodded. "Wait here." He winked at her, glanced at the other soldiers, then turned and trotted toward the guard shack. One of the soldiers gestured for Natalie's bicycle, and even though the offer might have been chivalrous, she shook her head and tightened her grip on the handlebars.

The young officer soon returned, his amusement replaced with a curious mixture of respect and anxiety. "The lieutenant said to wait here—he come immediately. Please"—he gestured with one hand—"you will wait inside? Out of cold?"

"I prefer to wait right here."

The young man's face paled. "No—please come inside . . . out of snow. If you not come inside, the lieutenant think . . ." The officer wet his lips and tried again. "If you not wait inside Lieutenant Rostov think we rude and he will punish." He hesitated. "He said you are important person. He says you are—*gerainya* . . ." The young man struggled with the translation, and Natalie could see that it was important to him. He wet his lips again. "Hero."

Natalie saw the soldiers' expressions change, and she heard the rapid-fire exchange between her previous tormentors and the young officer. Now they looked at her with unmistakable respect, mingled with curiosity that probably mirrored her own. Suddenly they seemed uncomfortable, several of them turning away from her and focusing their attention on the fire, as though all of a sudden remembering that there was an immediate need to warm their hands and stamp their feet.

A hero. Rostov had informed the young officer that she was a heroic person, and from the looks on the soldiers' faces that seemed to mean she was worthy of the utmost respect. Natalie was intrigued. Why would the lieutenant tell this man that?

Natalie relented to the young officer's insistence and followed him to the guard shack.

"Let me put bicycle in the shed." The officer reached for her bicycle. "You can get when you leave."

Natalie pulled it away from his outstretched hand. "It isn't mine. I don't want it to get . . . lost." Natalie was aware of the Red Army's propensity to permanently borrow any items that appealed to them. She could see one of the sentries with at least four looted German watches lining the exposed flesh of his wrist as he stretched toward the fire to warm his hands. Mabel had been irritated enough at her request to borrow the bicycle in the first place. What would happen if it were stolen while in her possession? Natalie shuddered at the thought.

The young man understood the unspoken implication, and he looked genuinely dismayed. "Do not worry—I give you promise that no one will take."

Again she hesitated, but finally she allowed the officer to take the bike from her hands. He guided it to a small shed, and then for her benefit he made an impressive show of removing a key ring from his pocket, selecting a key, opening the padlock on the door, maneuvering her bicycle inside, and then relocking the padlock and returning his key ring to his pocket.

He smiled at Natalie. "There. Safe." He looked satisfied with himself as he gallantly led the way to the guard shack.

He offered her a chair. He offered her tea. He offered her his uniform coat to wrap around her shoulders, and he offered her a bowl of some nondescript sustenance that looked like a mixture of tapioca and black beans, a mixture so curious that she dared not ask what it was. She refused it all and stood resolutely by the window, watching impatiently through the frosted glass for Lieutenant Rostov to appear.

A hero. Gerainya. What a strange title to give her, unless . . .

She swallowed hard. Rostov knew of her predicament, here alone at the guard shack on a cold winter morning, with his soldiers milling around her, cold and bored . . .

Rostov had warned them that she was a hero—to *protect* her. She had heard that the Soviets admired heroes. She remembered how the young officer's gaze had changed from amusement to the utmost deference when he'd returned with the news that Lieutenant Rostov expected them to treat her like a hero.

She shook off the unexpected warmth of the idea and focused instead on her reason for being here. She stood with her hand on her throat, as if she could calm with a touch the pounding of her pulse against her palm. She felt intense anger at the man who insisted on haunting her existence, but at the same time she realized that Rostov hadn't had to do what he'd done—he could have allowed his soldiers to treat her as the three soldiers had treated her the last time she dared to be alone outside the hospital compound. He could have continued to let her worry about Hans's whereabouts and never divulged to her that Hans was with him—and that Hans was alive.

She forced herself to focus on her anger.

When Rostov's Renault finally pulled to a stop next to the guard shack, Natalie ignored the sudden jab of fear that his presence always seemed to produce and was out the door, through a filthy snow bank, and across the open space separating her from the car before Rostov's driver had an opportunity to shut off the motor. The young officer followed her nervously.

Rostov opened the door and rose to his feet, curiosity evident in his dark eyes. "Miss Allred, what a pleasant—"

"You unimaginable monster," she said by way of greeting.

Rostov's lips twisted, amused. "Forgive me, Miss Allred. I'm not familiar with an American woman's taste in Christmas gifts—I have only been exposed to western ideas for a few years, and I apologize that my humble offering was not to your liking."

"You have Hans Brenner locked away in some Soviet dungeon, and I demand that you tell me where he is and why you abducted him." She could feel her body trembling with the emotion that flooded her system, and she hated that her fear for Hans was so obvious to this man. She hugged her arms to her chest, trying to quell their trembling. "You're a despicable, unbelievable—"

"My dear Natalya, you're freezing." Rostov stepped close and placed a concerned arm around her shoulders. He frowned at the young man hovering nervously nearby. "Didn't my soldiers offer you shelter from the cold?"

Mildly surprised at Rostov's alteration of her name, Natalie glanced from him to the officer from the guard shack and saw that the young man's face had turned several shades of gray. She said, "They were more than hospitable."

"I'm relieved to hear it." Rostov signaled for the soldier to leave, and the young officer flashed a look of gratitude in Natalie's direction before scurrying for the safety of the guard shack.

"Where is Hans? Where are you holding him?"

Rostov studied her carefully. "How interested are you?"

She frowned up at him. "What do you mean?"

"Would you get into my car and drive with me, to allow me the opportunity to talk to you privately about the matter?"

Her eyes widened. "I wouldn't dream of getting into that car with you, Lieutenant Rostov."

Natalie was surprised by the sudden splash of color across Rostov's cheeks. He frowned. "I'm not the monster you're imagining me, Nurse. I only meant that we need to discuss this in a place far removed from the curiosity of my soldiers. Please do not think I would force you to compromise your integrity in exchange for news of your beloved."

"What else can I think, from a man who resorts to abduction and blackmail?"

"Good point." Rostov dropped his arm from her shoulders. "You're an intelligent woman to steer clear of me." He sighed dramatically. "For the sake of your honor I'll be forced to evict all my soldiers from the guard shack so that we can discuss this important subject where there will be a dozen pairs of eyes watching us at all times from outside the windows. I promise, with the insatiable curiosity of my soldiers, you will be perfectly safe." He offered her his arm, and reluctantly she took it and allowed him to escort her to the building.

"Have you been offered something to drink?"

"Yes."

Rostov closed the door behind him, sat, and stretched out his legs, the trousers of his uniform shifting upward to reveal expertly knitted, heavy, dark woolen socks peeking above the rim of his combat boots.

Rostov noticed her interest in the socks. "My daughter made them for me."

"She is talented." Natalie meant the compliment.

"She mends my shirts and sends me these socks, made during the winter months when there is not much else to be done because of the cold."

She was struck by the self-effacing picture Viktor was unknowingly painting for her of an unassuming man and his beautiful daughter sitting near a warm fireplace and quietly enjoying each other's company, the girl knitting and the father perhaps reading a worn copy of a book.

Suddenly she felt uncomfortable listening to such personal revelations. Curious, that a pair of homemade socks would illicit such feelings. But when she looked at them she could see the love of a daughter for her father interwoven with the rough wool strands, and it made her wonder if Lucya even realized what her father did for a living. Maybe she knew, Natalie thought, and she loved him anyway. The idea humbled her.

"You're trying to change the subject, Lieutenant." She glared at him. "You have Hans Brenner hidden away from me, and I want to know the reason why."

"You really should sit down, Miss Allred. Continue pacing and gesticulating like that and my soldiers watching from outside will think you're thrashing me."

"You keep changing the subject."

"You keep forgetting that my name is *Viktor.*"

Natalie felt her panic rising. "Please answer my question immediately."

Rostov folded his arms and studied her closely. "I did not hear a question."

Natalie threw up her arms, exasperated. "You *know* what I'm asking, Lieutenant Rostov."

"And now you're beginning to shout at me."

Suddenly, impulsively, Natalie fell to her knees in front of the Soviet officer and pleaded with him. "Viktor, you have no idea what he means to me." Her voice wavered. "Please, sir . . ."

She saw a curious transformation in the Russian's features, as if her sudden act of humility had shaken him, and his gaze locked with hers. For several moments he said nothing, only watched her with that extraordinary emotion in his eyes that she had noticed on his first unannounced and unwelcome visit to the hospital. Then he leaned toward her, his gaze steady and his countenance softening. He spoke quietly, his voice strangely intimate. "I know how it feels to be in love, Natalya—and I know how it feels to be desperate for the well-being of one I love." He touched her hair thoughtfully. "Is that the way you feel about Herr Brenner?"

She nodded, not trusting her voice, and she tried to fight back her tears.

Rostov's fingers lingered against the side of her head. "I cannot promise to return him to you soon, Natalya. First he needs to do something for me."

"Hans Brenner is a good man, Viktor," Natalie implored. "Please don't make him into a murderer, like—" She stopped abruptly, and Rostov's hand stilled on her hair.

He leaned back in his chair. He continued to study her, and when he spoke his voice had a dangerous edge to it. "He will do what I want him to do. And do you know why?"

"What does he have to do?"

"You're brave, Nurse Allred, to ask me."

She lifted her chin and lashed back at him. "And you're a fool, Lieutenant Rostov, to think I'm not going to report you to the Allied Council."

Slowly he smiled, and the menace in his smile chilled her. "Hans Brenner will do everything I ask, Nurse, because of the love he has for you." Again he leaned close to her. "And you, my beautiful nurse, will not go to the Allied Council because of your love for *him*."

"What do you mean?" She could not breathe past the fear that clutched at her chest.

Again his hand brushed her hair. "You will continue as you always do. You will work at the hospital and go to concerts with Captain Charles Miller. You will interact with your friends and write to your mother in South Dakota. Yes, dear Natalya, I know about your mother, Anna— perhaps even more than *you* do—and I know how much she needs you to stay alive." He captured her hand and held her cold fingers close to his mouth, his eyes still locked with hers. "You will think about the way she loves you, and you will think about your love for Hans Brenner, and you will continue, every day and every night, as if nothing has happened." He kissed her hand softly. "And you will think about *me* and realize that it is because I care deeply for you that I do not gather you up right now, carry you out of this building and to my car, and take you away to where you will never see your mother, your friends, or your German vagabond, Hans Brenner, ever again."

TWENTY-FOUR

February 11, 1946

In the beginning he did not remember very much of his confinement—it was just a clouded series of terrifying events and meaningless directives. And now this new ordeal was sapping him of every shred of hope until he was nothing more than a German POW—not unlike the hundreds of nameless forms around him that also lifted and carried, lifted and carried, lifted and carried . . .

Hans Brenner's hand closed around the steel rod and he hefted it, and for a split second he found himself contemplating the possibilities. He glanced at the nearest guard. The small Russian had paused his watchful meanderings, his back to Hans as he focused his attention on another POW down the line.

The guard's attention was elsewhere. This was the moment. Hans lifted the rod.

By now Hans had become familiar with his captors' particular methods of retribution, and when the rifle connected with the back of his neck he didn't even resist the blackness that overwhelmed him. That was the positive thing about losing consciousness—it erased the remainder of the beating from his memory. Only when he awoke would he have to deal with the pain. But for now, at least, he could rest . . .

* * *

Rolf looked up, surprised to hear his name called. He walked forward and accepted the letter from the guard's outstretched hand and moved away so that other prisoners could also receive their mail.

He rarely got mail. The people he cared about most were here with him in Berlin, and he was privileged to see Marie and Alma every Sunday, thanks to visiting hours inexplicably provided them by the Americans. And other than his sister-in-law in Schönenberg, he knew of few other people who would know where he was, or who would take the time to send him a letter.

This particular correspondence had been carried with the U.S. mail bundled into military trucks along with supplies for the prisoners at Rolf's camp. Consequently there were no postal markings on the envelope to indicate its origin.

Rolf pulled several sheets of paper from the envelope and read the signature first. The letter was from Horst Wagner, his branch president in southern Germany. During the war Horst had protected Marie and Alma from the Gestapo, hiding them in his home in spite of the incredible danger to his family. Rolf moved away from the throngs of prisoners and found a relatively quiet location to sit and read.

January 29, 1946,

My dear Rolf, I hope this letter finds you well.

I have received correspondence from Church authorities in Utah requesting that I or a representative of our branch be prepared to meet with a visiting General Authority, Elder Ezra T. Benson, who is scheduled to visit the Frankfurt region on or around the 17th of March of this year. They are requesting that I report on the spiritual and temporal situation of the Saints under my care. Even though my deepest wish is that I could be healthy enough to complete it myself, I am physically incapable of fulfilling this obligation and blessing given to us by our leaders.

My other counselor, Herr Metzger, has not yet returned or contacted me since he was called into action during the last months of the war, which means you are the only member of the branch presidency who can accept this assignment. I know you are a prisoner of our conquerors, but the Spirit whispers that you are the one to complete this task. I ask that you make it a matter of sincere prayer, asking our Father in Heaven to help you find a way to fulfill this assignment.

Enclosed you will find the letter sent to me by the First Presidency, along with my report of the welfare of our members in the Baiersbronn region. I have always had great faith in your ability to accomplish whatever is necessary, even if obstacles to fulfillment seem insurmountable.

I understand from correspondence received at Christmastime from your intended, Marie Jacobson, that your health has improved to the point that you are feeling more positive about your situation. I am pleased that your difficulties are not wearing you down, but that you are rallying your spirits and planning for a wonderful future with a family reunited.

Please accept my deepest regrets for your sufferings and the pain you have undergone at the hands of our own countrymen. May we all learn forgiveness toward those who have transgressed against us, so that we may be worthy of our God's holy forgiveness for our own sins.

I leave this assignment entirely in your hands and will keep you in my prayers, that you might be able to find a way to fulfill this responsibility. As I cannot be certain you will receive this letter in time, or that you will be able to send me a timely response, I will trust in the Lord that His servants' wishes in this regard will be realized.

May the Lord bless you and keep you and your family and sweetheart protected and well.

Sincerely,
Your brother in the gospel,
Horst Wagner

* * *

Hans's tortured body never allowed him as much rest as he needed, and waking up was always excruciating. He fought against his return to consciousness as long as he could, but the bright light focused directly into his eyes pulled him up and up until it forced the blessed darkness to subside and he found himself in a hospital bed surrounded by pretty young nurses. In the fuzziness of his awakening all three of them reminded him of Natalie Allred. Three very fuzzy Natalie Allreds. He tried to sit up.

He groaned as pain shot through his side, his neck, his arms, and his right hip. It was much worse than last time, and definitely worse than the time they captured him as he entered his bomb shelter home in Berlin. He tried to raise his arm to feel the back of his neck, but one of the fuzzy nurses restrained him, berating him in Russian and forcing him to lie still.

The way his head pounded made resting against the pillow worse than resting on a bed of rivets. It didn't help when one of the nurses pummeled the pillow back into shape for him and indicated he was to relax. Sleep, she said in Russian. Sleep. And she smiled at him.

TWENTY-FIVE

March 10, 1946

It took a moment for Viktor to recognize the voice at the other end of the phone line, and even though the camp commandant had tried to prepare him for the shock before putting the prisoner on the line, it still upset him to hear death in a living man's voice. It was amazing what seven months in a labor camp could do to a man; Otis Farber spoke with the voice box of a man who had either smoked more than his fare share of cigarettes or had contracted an acute case of pneumonia through prolonged exposure to less-than-ideal living conditions.

Viktor spoke carefully. "Professor, is there any way you could pinpoint his location a bit more precisely? That covers such a vast geographic region . . ." Now he stood, pulling the telephone receiver up with him, and faced the window behind his desk, but the distress in the German scientist's voice blinded him to the controlled activity of POWs dismantling the factory below.

He listened carefully to the feeble voice on the other end, and even though the geographic region the voice described was vast, suddenly, over-whelmingly, Viktor Rostov felt triumphant. "Professor Farber . . ." He spoke soothingly into the phone, forcing himself to control the tremor in his voice. "You have been more than helpful. And if von Hausen is where you say, then you're not in any danger."

He listened to his prisoner's humble thanks, and then the comman-dant's voice replaced Farber's on the line. "What do you want me to do with him, Lieutenant?"

Viktor replied simply, "Let him go."

The commandant hesitated. "Excuse me, sir—did you mean—"

"I said let him go," Rostov snapped. "He told me where to find my scientist, and I promised him I would release him."

* * *

On the tenth of March, Marie and Alma took advantage of a beautifully warm Sunday and dressed in their best: Alma in green *lederhosen* and crisp-starched white shirt and suspenders, hat, and shined shoes, and Marie in her red suit, hose, and makeup.

Tomorrow was Rolf's birthday, and, with Marie's help and every bit of sugar they could beg with their ration cards, Alma had baked a cake for his father.

Alma insisted on carrying the cake himself all the way through the prison camp gate, past row after row of prisoners' barracks, up a short flight of steps, and into Rolf's building.

But Rolf was not there.

Marie steered Alma back out the door, down the stairs, and past buildings until she reached the camp administration building. She approached the secretary, asked to speak with the officer in charge, and was eventually escorted into the office of Lieutenant Tom Henrie.

He stood behind his desk, searching through a stack of papers on top of a metal filing cabinet, the remaining stub of a cigarette drooping precariously from one corner of his mouth. The blond mustache clinging to his upper lip, and the high cheekbones, thick eyebrows, and thatch of sandy-colored hair gave him a youthful, almost naïve appearance, while his long, lanky body and dexterous fingers reminded Marie of a basketball player from the university back home. He glanced up and saw her, and in one deft movement he swept the cigarette from his mouth and tossed it in the general direction of an ashtray on the desk. He faced her politely.

"Lieutenant Henrie? I'm looking for information on the whereabouts of one of the prisoners in your camp—Rolf Schulmann." Marie glanced down at Alma and then back up at the young lieutenant. "His belongings have been moved and his roommates say he was relocated by military personnel last week."

"Are you his wife?"

She gave him a faint smile. "No. But this is his son, Alma Schulmann."

Lieutenant Henrie gave Alma a kind smile. "You lookin' for your father, Alma?"

Alma nodded enthusiastically. "I made a birthday cake for my papa. Tomorrow is his birthday."

"His birthday, hmm?" The lieutenant crouched in front of the small boy and examined the birthday cake in Alma's hands. "Looks delicious, kid. Wish this were *my* birthday cake."

Alma's eyes opened wide as he stared back at the American. "Is tomorrow your birthday too?"

The man smiled. "No. But last week I had a birthday—and nobody gave me a cake as nice as this one."

Alma said, "It has candles so Papa can make a birthday wish."

"That's great, kid." Henrie stood and returned his attention to Marie. "If you'll wait a minute I can check the prisoner files. Several orders came through here regarding POW transfers. I'll check it out for you."

He returned to his filing cabinet. "You said 'Schulmann,' right?"

"Yes, sir. Rolf Schulmann."

He searched, peered at a name, and then pulled out a folder and slammed the drawer shut with his knee. He brought the file to his desk and leaned his lanky frame over it. "Seems he was transferred to a different location, ma'am."

"Do you mean a different location within the camp?"

"Unfortunately, no."

Marie looked down at Alma and saw his face, sweet and innocent, looking hopefully up at her. She returned her attention to the officer. "Lieutenant, would you be kind enough to tell me where Mr. Schulmann has been taken?"

Henrie studied the document. "It doesn't say." He peered at the paper. "Only says he was transferred to a 'classified location.'"

For several moments Marie stared at the lieutenant. She swallowed against the apprehension rising in her throat, feeling the beginnings of the same anxiety she'd felt when Rolf mentioned in the hospital that he might not be allowed to go free. She whispered, "Do you mean to tell me he is not allowed to see his son?"

"That's correct, ma'am. This says he will be tried for crimes against humanity." He replaced the document and closed the file.

"Do you have any idea what that man has gone through?" Marie was incredulous. "He was a prisoner of the Nazis, Lieutenant. Obviously he did something to incur their disfavor." She pleaded with the man behind the desk. "How does that make him an enemy to the Allies? How does that make him a war criminal?"

"I'm not his judge, ma'am." The man looked suddenly tired. "I wish I could help you more."

Marie forced herself to remain calm in spite of the frantic beating of her heart. "You could tell me where he is so his son can give him his birthday cake."

The man wavered, looking from the boy up to Marie and then down to Alma again, but he shook his head. "I'm really sorry, ma'am. I wish I could tell you. Like I said, the orders don't tell me where he was transferred."

Again he opened the file on his desk and extracted the top document. He looked it over quickly, then held it out toward Marie. "It doesn't say 'top secret,' so it must be all right for you to see." He waited while Marie studied the paper.

It was an order for Rolf's extraction and preparation for trial, and it was signed by a Major James Matthews of the United States Army. There was no indication of where Rolf had been taken—only that the transfer had been authorized by Matthews. Marie handed the paper back to Henrie.

"Thank you, Lieutenant."

He nodded and replaced the paper in the file, then returned the file to the cabinet. "I'm sorry I couldn't be of any more assistance, ma'am. Best to ya." He smiled again at Alma. "Sure do wish I could tell you where your daddy is, son. He sure would like that birthday cake." He moved behind his desk again.

With her hand on Alma's shoulder, Marie steered the boy from the room.

Alma walked obediently from the building, the cake still clutched carefully in his hands and sorrow clouding his features. "Are we going to go to Papa now? Do I get to give him his birthday cake?"

Marie crouched next to the small boy. "Alma—" She sighed. "Your father has been taken to a different camp, and we have to find out where he is."

"Will we find him today?"

Marie shrugged. "I don't think so."

Alma's face fell. "What about his birthday cake?"

Marie put her arms around him gently. "We'll make him another one as soon as we find him, okay?" She kissed his cheek.

"Tomorrow?"

"Alma, I think it might take a while longer. We have to—"

"But it won't be his birthday. He won't get to have a cake on his birthday, Mami." Tears welled in his blue eyes, but he resisted them valiantly. "He will think we forgot about his birthday!"

Marie struggled to find the right words. "Alma, your papa knows we love him, and if he has to have his birthday cake later it won't be a problem. He will be thinking about how much he loves us, and that wonderful thought will be his birthday present."

Alma met her gaze, and Marie felt the familiar sensation of looking into the penetrating blue eyes of his father. Alma said, "What are we going to do with this cake?"

"That's entirely up to you, sweetheart." Marie stood.

Alma studied the dessert in his hands and then glanced at the doors to the administration building. He hesitated, obviously deep in thought, and then he looked up at Marie. "I want to give the cake to the man in that building."

Marie smiled. "The one who had a birthday last week?"

Alma nodded, his enthusiasm escaping past the remnants of his tears. "I want him to know someone loves him, too—just like my candy bombs make the children feel better."

"All right then, munchkin." Marie steered her small charge back up the steps. "Your father will be proud of you for your kindness."

Happier now, Alma negotiated the steps and stepped through the door Marie held open for him. He approached the desk. "I have a birthday cake for the lieutenant."

The receptionist paused his typing and stared at Alma and Marie. "Lieutenant Henrie?"

Marie nodded. "That's right. Will you get him, please?"

The man stood and left the room, returning with the young lieutenant. Henrie seemed a bit perturbed to be bothered by them again, but Alma sprang forward and thrust the cake at his torso. "I want you to have this, Lieutenant! My father can't eat it, and he always says we need to be kind and share, and you didn't get to have a birthday cake from your family on your birthday, and . . ." Alma broke off, breathless, and the man stared at him, obviously taken aback by the unexpected assault. Then suddenly his expression softened and he bent in front of Alma.

"You want to give me your father's birthday cake?"

Alma nodded, his eyes flashing happiness. "And you can blow the candles out and make a wish! And it will come true like mine did that we would find Papa after the bad men took him away during the war."

Lieutenant Henrie's eyes misted and he reached for the cake, his large, rough hands briefly touching the small smooth ones of the German boy as the dessert exchanged hands. "Thank you," he said simply, and Alma beamed.

The lieutenant straightened, the cake small in his hands, and turned to Marie. "Listen, ma'am, I—"

Marie could tell he was embarrassed. "Don't worry about it, sir. He wanted to give it to you."

He cleared his throat. "Actually, I was meaning to talk to you about the boy's father . . ."

"My papa is going to marry Mami!" Alma piped helpfully.

Lieutenant Henrie hesitated. "You're engaged to him?"

"That's right."

He studied her. "You're American?"

Marie lifted her chin, and Alma piped, "She's going to marry my papa in the temple!"

The man blinked. "You're a *Jewish* American? Marrying a Nazi officer . . ." He trailed off, obviously taken aback by the thought.

"I believe most Jews would marry in a synagogue," Marie corrected. "And we're both Christians—more specifically, Mormons. Listen, we've taken enough of your time. We will go." She took Alma's hand and started for the door.

"Wait."

She paused, her hand still firmly holding Alma's.

"Where are you headed?"

Marie looked down at Alma. "I'm planning to take him to his aunt's house in the Schwarzwald for safekeeping. Then I will find his father."

"The Schwarzwald's quite a dangerous journey through Soviet-controlled territory . . ." He glanced at her awkwardly. "We've had several personnel disappear over the past few months and we've never recovered them."

"I'll manage."

"No, miss. I don't think you fathom how dangerous it is for *you*—being an American *and* a woman . . ." Lieutenant Henrie looked embarrassed. "I'll give you a military escort for a few days—an army vehicle and a couple of GIs to discourage any hooliganism until you have the kid safely with his aunt. Then they'll escort you back here." He smiled encouragingly at Marie. "I'm not supposed to interfere, but give me a week or two, and I think I might be able to pull a few strings with the council and find a way for you to communicate with Major Matthews—and maybe even discover where Alma's father was taken."

TWENTY-SIX

March 11, 1946

The mindless drudgery of forced labor might have affected Hans physically, but his mental faculties remained ever intact. His sharp mind kept vigil while his exhausted muscles performed their mandatory duties, and he kept a lookout for any chance to escape.

He could not get his mind off Natalie Allred. Her blue eyes flashed in his mind as vividly as if she were standing next to him now, alternating between teasing him mercilessly and encouraging him if he stumbled, reminding him that he could very easily be shot like the poor soul across the courtyard who had failed to maintain his place in line. *Thank you, Natalie, for helping me to keep my place in line.*

Meal time—at least for the Russian guards. They hollered at the German prisoners and jabbed at them with their rifles until all the prisoners were huddled together in the middle of the courtyard. Hans crouched with his comrades and watched as the guards leaned their weapons against a brick wall and fed themselves from the pot of thick stew, the smell of beef broth wafting cruelly through the group of starving German prisoners, tickling their noses and invading their senses in a torture more diabolical than anything the infamous Gestapo could have accomplished with their straps and metal bars. Hans's fingers curled, and he imagined strangling someone for a bowl of it.

He forced his gaze away from the food and glanced up at the factory's administration offices. He often saw the man standing there, watching the prisoners work from the balcony above them. Now the man stood with his hands behind his back, and his face from this distance remained unrecognizable.

But there was something familiar about him. Even though the brutal attack in his basement shelter, the war, and all its confusion and experiences stood between Hans and the memory, he just had to accept that somehow, before the war, he might have known this man. He fought to recall more, but from such a distance it was impossible to peer into that face and remember. And as the days wore on and the man continued to visit the balcony and watch the prisoners while they worked, he had the unnerving sensation that remembering was going to be very important.

Hans's attention returned to the young Russian guards and their meal. They would not offer it to the Germans even though Hans knew there was more than enough in that pot to at least cover the bottom of each prisoner's bowl and comfort each prisoner's midsection. But the Russians wouldn't feed their German charges until the railroad car stood completely filled with the confiscated parts of a conquered nation's munitions factory.

Even before Hans had thought his actions through, he stood, wavering a bit as hunger-induced light-headedness washed over him, and then he steadied his stance and straightened to his full height. At first the guards didn't notice him. They were preoccupied with pilfered German beer and their view of a young German washerwoman at work, her sleeves rolled above her elbows and her dress filthy from the dirty suds and wet garments that were her purpose in life. She ignored the occasional yells and the laughter, bending to her washboard and scrubbing with all the strength of her wiry frame. And as the guards shared their rough humor at her expense, Hans Brenner inched closer.

They didn't notice him until he had selected a rifle. And when he raised it they stared at him as if he might have lost his mind. It was impossible that a prisoner would have managed to get so close to them and still be alive. They moved for their guns, and Hans trained the rifle on the officer on the balcony. "He will die first," he said in Russian, and it didn't matter that his accent was atrocious—the guards believed him, and they froze.

Hans took a deep breath to steady his breathing. He studied each of the men in turn, keeping the barrel of his rifle trained on the man above them as he did so. He knew his life was as good as over, and suddenly he didn't care.

"*Pisha,*" he said, using another of the few Russian words he knew. With his chin, he pointed first at the kettle of stew and then back at the German prisoners behind him. "*Die-tye . . . pisha.*" He knew he was saying "Give them food" wrong. He added an entreaty: "*Pazhalsta.*"

One of the guards shook his head, but before he could explain his refusal Hans cocked the rifle and took careful aim at the officer standing on the balcony. Several guards raised their hands in panicked surrender, frantically spouting Russian as they tried to reason with him. Hans knew the man on the balcony would have already signaled his guards to train their firearms on the disorderly prisoner in the courtyard below, and he knew he had very little time. "My comrades." He repeated it carefully, firmly. "They are hungry. Feed them. Please."

As if on cue, every guard turned to look at the officer standing silently above them. Hans saw him give a slight nod, and then the guards immediately began to fill bowls with the stew. Hans kept a vigilant eye on both the man standing still as a statue on the balcony above and on the guards as they carried the bowls as fast as they could across the courtyard to the prisoners. With howls of gratitude the prisoners attacked the food, consuming it with a passion inspired by the knowledge that this meal might be their last. And Hans locked eyes with the man on the balcony and suddenly remembered who he was.

"Lieutenant Hans Brenner," the man called down to him in perfect German, his voice conversational. "Lower your weapon. Come up here and visit."

"If I lower this rifle one centimeter, I'm a dead man. You know that."

The man smiled at Hans's words and shook his head. "Unfortunately, you're a dead man if you don't." He straightened his tunic and stepped casually back from the rail, seemingly unconcerned that Hans was still pointing a rifle directly at him. He continued. "If you shoot me, you will in turn be shot. If you do not shoot me, you will be shot—unless, of course, you agree to have a chat with me." The officer gestured pleasantly. "Leave your weapon. Let your friends eat and rest, and come up here."

Hans lowered his weapon and handed it to the closest guard, who immediately whirled it around and trained it on the center of Hans's forehead. Hans ignored him and turned back to the man on the balcony. "I'm coming up. Don't let them shoot me."

The memories came flooding back now of that year at the *Universität zu Berlin.* Hans had been a first-year student then and a new member of the Nazi Party, on fire with the teachings of the Führer. He hadn't paid much attention to his classes, except the amount necessary in order to appease his teachers and advance through the courses. He vaguely recalled the course taught that summer by a young professor visiting from Moscow—an idealistic Socialist with a zeal for his subject and a desire that Germany and Moscow overcome their differences and work together.

The young professor stood in front of him now, at the top of the stairs, and Hans could see how the war had aged him. A Fräulein might still think him handsome, he mused, but would probably be at a loss to guess his real age. The man carried the worries of the world in the lines about his eyes and forehead, and his dark hair displayed hints of salt-and-pepper gray. As Hans approached, the professor gestured for his guards to step back, and they retreated to the other end of the balcony, their hands resting on the guns at their belts. Hans watched the officer steadily.

"Hans Brenner, we meet again." The officer extended a hand in greeting.

Hans took it. "Professor Rostov—Moscow University."

Rostov smiled. "I knew you would remember. Come with me to my office."

Hans followed the professor across the balcony and up another flight of stairs, ignoring the guards following behind. Rostov opened a door and indicated for Hans to precede him into a small, sparsely furnished room with a large window overlooking the factory floor. Hans could see several lines of prisoners passing assorted gadgets hand to hand out the door and through the courtyard to the waiting train cars.

He turned away from the window and faced the Russian officer. "You've been demoted, it seems, Professor."

Rostov laughed a hearty, pleasant laugh that made Hans distrust him even more. How could a man laugh with such enjoyment at a time like this?

"You're probably right, Lieutenant. And yet, I don't seem to mind." Rostov loosened the top button of his uniform jacket and gestured for Hans to sit next to the desk. He lowered himself into a chair across from Hans and leaned back, crossing one leg across his knee, then called for an aide. "Tea for my guest, Petka—and something to eat. Quick, before he keels over from hunger." The professor laughed again and slapped his knee.

But his laughter subsided as quickly as it had begun. "That was a brave thing you did down there, my friend," he said. "Brave, but foolish."

"Hunger will drive a man to do foolish things, sir."

"You remember me, then—from the university here in Berlin."

"Yes, sir. But it took a while."

Rostov nodded. "I can imagine a lot has happened to you since we last met."

Hans didn't respond. Rostov folded his arms and returned Hans's steady gaze. "You Germans disappointed me—you know that, don't you?"

"I can imagine."

"Hitler and Stalin could have made something magnificent of Eastern Europe. It could have been a superpower with the capability of great things. Instead, Hitler went back on his promise to the Soviets."

Hans continued silent. He was not overly interested in his former professor's interpretation of the politics of the war, nor was he interested in chatting with him about their university years. He didn't recall their association as being of any lasting significance, and he couldn't begin to imagine what the man might want of him at this time, unless it was a chance to reminisce with a former student—before he shot the former student.

"You remember, of course, what we worked on that summer."

"Of course I do—although why you think it important right now I cannot imagine."

"And how do you feel about it, Lieutenant? Could Russia—and Germany, for that matter—have the same success as the Americans?"

"I wouldn't have any idea."

"You were more interested than you allow yourself to remember, Hans Brenner. You seemed to have a few good ideas yourself. If I'm not mistaken I seem to recall that you spent several years with Professor von Hausen on the project, and by your graduation you had helped him perfect the process."

"A requirement for the Führer, nothing more. My heart was not really in it."

"And what is your line of work now, Mr. Brenner?"

Hans scowled. "I dismantle munitions factories for shipment to Moscow."

"And before that?" Rostov asked, unruffled by Hans's sarcasm.

Hans shrugged. "I fought the Allies."

"You were a Gebirgsjäger—an Alpine fighter and a tracker for the Führer. You were an uncommonly good one, I understand. Halfway through the war you received the Iron Cross for bravery, and then you spent a significant amount of time assigned to France and the Rhône-Alpes."

Hans shifted his gaze to the food placed on the desk in front of him by Rostov's aide, followed by a steaming cup of light brown liquid. He changed the subject. "Have any water? Tea doesn't do much for me when I've been working all day."

Rostov indicated for the aide to bring water, but Hans didn't wait for it to arrive. He picked up the bowl of stew and drank hungrily, ignoring the spoon and pausing only when necessary to chew, savoring the rich broth and thick chunks of potato and beef. Next he grabbed the black bread and ripped it in half, then downed each half as if the world depended upon its immediate consumption. And when the aide handed him a cup of water, he drank it in deep, desperate gulps, trickles of water escaping from both sides of his mouth and staining his dusty neck and shirt.

Rostov watched him with amused curiosity until he had downed the last chunk of beef, the last crumb of bread, and the last drop of water. Then the Russian spoke. "I need your help, Lieutenant Brenner. I have a special assignment for you to perform for me."

Hans grimaced at the officer. "Isn't lugging steel bars and buckets of rivets across a courtyard so you can reassemble our factories in Russia enough help?"

"Not quite." Rostov smiled. "Do you honestly think we would keep a man with your background—your special skills—alive, unless we had some greater use for you than carting anvils?"

"I haven't given much thought to it." Hans grunted. His midsection was beginning hurt. He had consumed the rich food so rapidly that his stomach, so used to being empty, was beginning to tie itself into painful knots. "In fact, I haven't been doing much for a long time besides getting beat up, recuperating, dismantling assembly lines, and getting beat up again." He grimaced. "That seems to be my lot in life."

"You have to agree it's infinitely better than an execution."

"I'm starting to wonder, Professor." Hans stretched his legs under the desk. "You say I have a higher purpose, and yet you starve me, torture me, leave me to rot for months . . . How many months has it been since you greeted me so courteously at my residence in Berlin?" Hans's voice bordered on sarcastic. "For some reason I cannot seem to keep track of time . . ."

"Almost four months. And the rough treatment was necessary to teach you compliance."

Four months. Hans was shocked, and with the shock came a desperate concern for the well-being of the people who mattered most to him. Rolf would have recuperated by now, under the loving care of his fiancée. And if, by a stroke of good fortune or through one of the miracles God seemed to have in rich supply for Rolf, they had been able to straighten out the difficulties they faced with the Allied victors, then perhaps they were already married and starting a new life together with little Alma.

And what about Natalie? Hans realized that a good portion of his stomach's rebellion was caused by more than hastily consumed food; he was desperately anxious for the well-being of the young American nurse who had become so dear to him, whose memory had sustained him through the ignominy of his captivity and the agony of his existence away from her. He wondered if she had carried though with her threat to marry the American pilot. He wondered if she had been transferred back to the Unites States, or perhaps to a different location in Europe. He wondered if he would ever know what had happened to her after that last night before he was captured, when he had seen her crossing the hospital courtyard in the rain. How he wished now that he had ignored his conscience and left his hiding place, taken her into his arms, and showed her how much he loved her and had missed her . . . *Four months!*

Rostov interrupted his thoughts. "How much do you remember of that project you worked on with von Hausen?"

"Enough." With a wave of his hand, Hans rejected the cigarette that Rostov was offering.

"Tell me what you remember, Lieutenant."

Hans shrugged. "Von Hausen attempted to find a more effective way to purify uranium-235—a vital element in the development of the atomic bomb."

"And you were an integral part of that attempt." Rostov smiled at him. "Your government was right to assign you to be the professor's assistant. He told me that summer that he admired your intelligence and had high hopes for your future."

"Must have been a disappointment for him when I was pulled from the project." Hans was still reeling from the shock of time's passage and could not help the sarcasm. "Seems the Führer had more need for Alpine troops than A-bombs."

"It was a mistake to reassign you, Brenner." Rostov remained unruffled. "Just think: if you'd been allowed to continue, you might have been intimately involved with von Hausen's work throughout the entire war. You and he could have been a deadly, effective team. Perhaps if you had been allowed to continue with the project, there would never have been a Hiroshima. Or a Nagasaki."

"Or perhaps there would not be a Europe."

Rostov smiled sadly. "That is true. There is always the possibility that Hitler would have utilized your research and the war would have ended very, very differently." He folded his arms. "I notice you have managed to hide your intelligence and your background rather effectively, Lieutenant. Who would ever guess from looking at this rough-cut, long-haired, ragged German sitting across from me that he has the makings of a great nuclear scientist?"

"Your establishment has not exactly required a high dress standard." Hans folded his arms and contemplated the Russian. "I'm not interested—in whatever you're offering."

"You misunderstand me, Mr. Brenner. I'm not offering you anything, nor am I suggesting that you continue what you started with von Hausen. I was merely offering a compliment as to your incredible background and what *might* have been."

"Then what is it exactly that you want?"

"You have other skills, Lieutenant." Rostov leaned forward as he spoke. "I mentioned your meritorious service to the German army, and I meant for that to be more than just a compliment. As a matter of fact, those are the skills I have need of at the moment. You are, of course, familiar with the Rhône-Alpes region in France?"

"Whatever could you want in France?"

Rostov shifted in his seat and glanced over at the aide, who backed obediently from the room, closing the door. Then Rostov continued. "Professor von Hausen." He watched Hans closely. "It seems the old professor has found a listening ear in the Americans, and we're concerned they might begin to realize his usefulness and spirit him away like many other Germans they decide are useful."

"I see." Hans realized he had become entangled in a nasty spat between allies, prompted by rising postwar tensions and the United States' audacity in developing and utilizing a working nuclear weapon before Stalin could even perfect the process.

Rostov continued. "Since Hiroshima, Stalin has intensified his efforts to acquire all the commodities Germany has available."

"And by 'commodities' you mean people."

"I mean people, products, raw materials, factories—whatever we can lay our hands on that might allow us to"—Rostov watched Hans carefully—"build one of our own. The Soviet Union is counting on von Hausen's help to simplify the complicated process of uranium-235 production. And if he can produce the same results the two of you produced before the war, than maybe we can eliminate the normal difficulties associated with the accidental production of useless isotopes that are so close in composition to 235. If we can purify 235 without producing so many worthless byproducts, our nuclear program will surge ahead of the Americans and the Soviet Union will be the undisputed leader in this deadly race."

Hans shook his head, disgusted. "You think that if you can get your hands on von Hausen before the Americans, you might be able to produce results similar to those we produced at the university."

Rostov nodded. "Von Hausen's method is the key to faster production, and because you have worked closely with him, and *understand* him, we have decided that you're the one to bring him in."

Hans felt sick. "Why me? And what does this have to do with my war assignments or my knowledge of the Rhône-Alpes?"

Rostov stood and glanced out the factory window. "Back in '37 von Hausen and I struck up a tentative friendship—a truce, you might call it—between a socialist and a fascist teetering between loyalties. It was von Hausen who was influential in getting me to the University of Berlin before the war. I talked to him then about helping us."

Hans was incredulous. "Even before the war he agreed to work with the Russians?"

Rostov shook his head. "Not quite. Von Hausen never betrayed Hitler, although we argued the point on numerous occasions. In fact, Hitler gave him quite a bit of responsibility for German production of 235 in anticipation of Germany's creation of a bomb. Von Hausen was a loyal Nazi throughout the war—and still is, I suppose."

"So what is your arrangement with him now?"

"We have no arrangement," Rostov admitted. "I've had no contact with von Hausen since that summer."

"You must have found some way to convince him to—"

"No." Rostov shook his head. "But during the war we monitored his career as closely as possible—and for some time my superiors have been convinced that he is imperative to our nuclear project."

"If von Hausen is so essential, why have you waited so long for me to recruit him? Four months you've had me here. *Four months.* You plan for me to help you convince an important scientist to join the Soviets, and yet you have not acted." Hans smirked. "A stellar example of Communist efficiency."

Rostov's eyes narrowed. "And we would keep you four more, if we had not recently discovered his hiding place. According to a reliable source, when the Americans and British began their ridiculous roundup of useful Nazis, von Hausen found a way across the border into France. But as fortune would have it, we have discovered that he is now living somewhere in the Rhône-Alpes region."

"Really." Hans's lips twisted wryly. "You're going to kidnap him." He leaned back and stared at the Russian. "You're going to slip past the Americans into France, infiltrate the Rhône-Alpes, grab von Hausen, and spirit him through Switzerland into the heart of Soviet-controlled Berlin, at which point he will be flown to Russia and never seen again."

Rostov smiled grimly. "We would suggest a route through Italy might be less suicidal, but yes, basically that's the plan—what do the Americans say?—'in a nutshell,' except for two minor things."

"What things?"

Rostov sat down in a chair facing Hans. "First, our intelligence tells us he is somewhere near the Swiss border, but other than that . . ." He cleared his throat. "We don't know exactly where he is hiding."

Hans gave a derisive laugh. "The Rhône-Alpes is an easy place to lose a man, Professor. It is very large."

"I suspected as much." Rostov was unfazed. "And second, it won't be me doing the 'grabbing.'"

Hans stared at Rostov, and then he stood and paced the room. "You told me my job would be to *convince* him. You never mentioned that *I* would be the one doing the kidnapping."

Rostov watched Hans pace. "You have the skills, the knowledge of the area, the background necessary for von Hausen to trust you . . ." He stood again and joined Hans at the window. "He talked often of you, Hans Brenner. He said what a good scientist you'd make. And most importantly, he trusts you. All you have to do is find him and convince him, and then bring him safely to—"

"No."

Rostov's lips twitched. "You shouldn't turn down my offer until you've heard the benefits of accepting."

"I said no."

"You're perfect for the job, Brenner. You speak French. You're a talented officer and a skilled outdoorsman. You have intimate knowledge of the Rhône-Alpes region, and you know how to find someone who does not wish to be found. And most importantly, you understand von Hausen, and he knows you and has a high regard for you."

"You said he has been talking to the Americans."

Rostov nodded. "According to my source, that is correct. That is a minor complication that hopefully will not make things too difficult."

"So basically, you want me to abduct him before he has a chance to be abducted by the Americans?" Hans shook his head incredulously. "I would not want to be von Hausen right now."

"The Americans probably don't consider it abduction. I believe the word they use is 'recruiting.'" Rostov kept track on his fingers. "They will offer him a modest home in America, a car, a salary, passage to America for him and his wife . . . maybe even a new identity."

"And what will the Soviet Union offer him?"

"More than the Americans, of course." Rostov smiled. "The Americans will only offer him material wealth. But in Russia, he will work for the glory of the Soviet Union and it will make him a national hero."

"And if he refuses to come?"

Rostov shrugged. "We cannot run the risk that the Americans might convince him to join the United States."

It was said simply. But Hans felt a chill run up his spine. "You'll kill him."

"Again, no. I won't kill him. *You* will, if he refuses to come with you."

Hans shook his head, still reeling from Rostov's plan and the part Rostov expected him to play in it. He spoke carefully. "You've told me the reasons why I would be perfect for the job, and, to be honest, you're right. I could easily find von Hausen, fight off the Americans, and spirit your scientist out of France and into the east. But you've forgotten a very important fact."

"What important fact have I overlooked, Mr. Brenner?"

"I have no desire to help the Russians." Hans folded his arms stubbornly. "To be honest, I cannot think of one thing that you could offer me that would convince me to change my mind."

Rostov walked back to his desk, and his hand fingered the edge of it absently. "That is unfortunate, Mr. Brenner, because I can think of two very compelling reasons for you to accept this assignment."

"I'm not interested, Rostov."

"One reason would be your life . . ."

Hans smiled. "Now what makes you think dangling my existence in front of my face would persuade me to lift a finger for your country?" He turned away from the Russian officer and watched the factory floor below. "The war's over, Rostov, and I'm not in the mood to kidnap a scientist for either the Soviets or the Americans."

". . . and the other reason has very pretty, dark hair and blue eyes like a dragon."

Hans's smile faded, and he felt his chest constrict. The room lurched sideways and he had to steady himself against the window glass. He couldn't look at Rostov because he felt certain the man was watching him for his reaction.

"I thought you might be interested in hearing about your friend—the young American nurse."

"She's not my friend," Hans growled.

"Natalya misses you. She misses you a lot," Rostov said from behind him. "And she's special to you, or you wouldn't have defended her honor and saved her life."

Hans's heart skipped a beat, and he hesitated, then turned to look at Rostov. "Her name is *Natalie*."

"There's no need to try to hide it," Rostov said pleasantly. "She is beautiful. And she *is* a dragon. Like you referred to her that first time you met."

"How would you know about that?"

"She told me. She told me many things about you, Mr. Brenner."

Hans gripped the back of a chair with one hand, and Rostov continued. "She told me about that night, and the soldiers—"

"You're bluffing. She would never confide in you."

"Ah, but there you're wrong, comrade. She *has* confided in me—and she will continue to do so for as long as I wish her to." He smiled and folded his arms.

Hans felt the color drain from his face. He tried to hide his shock, but the Russian was watching him closely. "Did she tell you how ridiculous she thinks I am?" Hans mumbled.

"Not at all." Rostov approached him. "She wept when she told me how she cares for you and misses you."

"She knows I'm alive?" He knew his voice revealed a little too much emotion, and he clenched his teeth and went silent.

"As of Christmas Day, yes, she knows you're alive." Rostov continued, a smile playing at the corners of his mouth. "She is extraordinary, Herr Brenner—soft and sweet, beautiful and pure, like a white rose."

"A white rose?" Hans's face darkened.

"She reminds me of my wife. Alyona loved white roses . . ."

"For your sake, Rostov, I hope you have not touched her."

Rostov's smile disappeared. "I'm not a beast, Hans Brenner. I have never touched her in that way."

"You're a cold-blooded, dangerous man."

"Ah, but I know how to respect a woman. It is only because I *must,* that I threaten her now."

"What have you done to her?"

Rostov said, "What I do to her depends on you."

Hans thought about the blue pools of Natalie's eyes as she looked up at him, her cute, upturned nose, and the way her hair shone in the sunlight. He thought of the night she had been threatened by three drunken men and the way her eyes expressed her gratitude for his intervention.

He thought past the sorrow of her promise to Curly to how much he loved her and ached for her and had wanted to protect her, and suddenly he snapped.

His fist caught Rostov in the stomach, folding him neatly in two, and while Rostov clutched at his stomach and gasped for air, Hans buried his elbow between the older man's shoulder blades with all the force of his fear for a young American nurse. He paid no attention to the approach of Rostov's bodyguards from outside the door but summoned every ounce of strength he could muster and focused it on the punishment of the cause of his fear. And by the time the guards pulled him off of the lieu-tenant and brutally handcuffed him, Rostov cowered in front of him, curled in a fetal position on the floor.

The Russian's voice was little more than a gasp. "There are things about Nurse Allred that you don't know, Hans Brenner—things that give me the legal right to take her back with me to Moscow." He wheezed, the sound awful as he pulled in air. "But I'm a reasonable man, and I understand how deeply you must love her. So I'll give you one chance to save her: bring von Hausen safely back to Berlin, and Natalya will be yours." He struggled to rise. "But if you fail in your assignment . . ." He gasped for more air. "Natalya will go to Russia in von Hausen's place. And I can promise you, my young comrade, that with what I have discovered about Natalya's back-ground, von Hausen's existence in Russia will be far more pleasant and enduring than hers."

"What do you know about her background? Why do you keep calling her Natalya? Where is she?"

Rostov managed to get his feet under him and he stood, wobbling slightly and still hunched over. "Here, safe in Berlin, working at the American hospital. What kind of monster do you think I am?" He faced Hans, his eyes somber. "She is a beautiful woman, and I see no reason to harm her. Besides, I have great confidence in your ability to accomplish this important task, and Natalya will be perfectly safe until you return."

"Professor"—Hans breathed heavily—"what is it about her background that endangers her life?"

Rostov regained his composure and stood erect. "That information will not become a factor unless you fail—and I believe you love her too much to fail." He smiled at Hans. "And when you have supplied Mother Russia with the man who can help us overcome the threat of the Americans and their atom bomb, I give you my promise that you will be set free, that your sweetheart will not be harmed, and that I will never approach either you or Natalya again."

Hans took a deep breath. "How can I believe you, Rostov? What guarantee do I have that you will keep your promise when the time comes?"

"I may be a ruthless man, Hans Brenner, and I may have many faults. But breaking a promise is not one of those faults." Rostov stood eye to eye with the German and his gaze didn't waver. "When I give my word, it is my word of honor."

TWENTY-SEVEN

March 12, 1946

A landscape like this can cleanse and rejuvenate the soul, Marie mused as she stepped from the army vehicle and followed an exuberant Alma toward the two-story farmhouse. *Especially when the vista has magnificent memories attached.*

She shielded her eyes from the sun in order to study the snow-blanketed apple orchard, the garden and fields, the guest cottage, the outbuildings, and Walter Sandler's workshop.

Beside her, Alma quivered excitedly. "Where is he?"

"Who, Alma?"

"My dog." Alma looked about ready to explode with anticipation. "I went away a long time ago. Do you think Bandit will remember me?"

Again Marie scanned the grounds, and as she helped her young charge search for Bandit she was suddenly overcome with her memories of the months she had spent here more than two years before.

She had never felt as comfortable anywhere else. Maybe it had to do with the way Rolf had carried his son on his shoulders that Christmas Eve morning—Alma waving at her exuberantly from his precarious perch and almost tumbling backward into the Christmas tree Rolf was dragging in from the forest. Maybe it was because Rolf had stood in this very spot and held her in his arms, telling her he loved her and wanted to marry her. Maybe it was because the memories from this place were all about *him,* and Alma, and the incredible sacrifice Rolf had made to protect her.

She tried not to worry. She would find Rolf, and the Americans would realize the honorable man he was and release him.

"Bandit! Bandit!"

Marie stood and watched as Alma catapulted away from her side and across the snow, his legs churning until he collided with his enthusiastic, furry friend.

Bandit lost no time giving Alma a wet welcome, his whole body wagging with the delight of seeing his young master again. Alma brought the sheepdog back with him to the porch, and Bandit approached Marie, his tail waving furiously and his tongue hanging out. He remembered her.

The front door opened and Walter Sandler stood in the doorway. His weather-beaten face betrayed his surprise. "Marie?"

"Herr Sandler, it is so good to see you again," she said in German. "I'm sorry to drop in so unexpectedly . . ." She mounted the steps and he pulled her into a bear hug.

Marie saw Berta approaching from the kitchen. Dear, sweet Berta, Rolf's sister-in-law from his marriage to Hélène, and Marie's friend. She was just as beautiful as Marie had remembered, with her blond hair neatly styled and her face serene.

Berta gave a strangled gasp and her eyes grew wide. "Marie!" She threw out her arms, and suddenly the chasm of time and war that had divided the two women completely disappeared. Marie felt like she was home.

She told the older woman about Rolf's disappearance. Berta glanced at the American soldiers standing by the vehicle and asked uncomfortably, "Are you leaving right away?"

"I must find him, Berta." Marie touched the woman's cheek affectionately. "He will be all right, I think. I cannot imagine that God would have protected him through impossible circumstances just to abandon him now that the war has finally ended."

"I believe you're right, Marie Jacobson." Berta smiled. "You're bringing us the boy, then?"

"I need you to care for him." Marie looked affectionately at Alma, who was running and tumbling with Bandit near the steps. "Berta, I don't know how long I'll be."

"Never mind that. We will be happy to have him with us for as long as you need. He is dear to our hearts and will be a joy to have around."

Marie turned and called for Alma, and he bounded up the steps to her side. She then bent down and rested her hands gently on his shoulders. "I need to go find your papa, Alma, and help him. I need you to stay here with Aunt Berta. She loves you very much, and she has been lonely here without you. Will you help her be happy?"

Alma glanced at Berta and Walter and then back at Marie. He was no longer the little boy she had known but possessed a soberness and maturity that amazed her. He nodded solemnly. "You will find Papa and help him come home."

"That's what I'm going to try to do, sweetheart."

Alma studied her carefully. "Will you be gone a long time?" He was accepting the separation without question, and Marie ached, wondering what he was bottling up inside. He had endured more than any child should have to endure, and yet, he had been miraculously protected from much of what the war had inflicted upon other children. He was a survivor—physically and emotionally. And Marie prayed that soon this nightmare would end for all of them and their lives could finally be permanently joined, never to be separated again.

And so she nodded. "I think so, Alma. I don't want to, but I might take a long time." She took a deep breath. "Aunt Berta and Uncle Walter are going to have a lot of work to do here on the farm, and I know you will be a good help to them."

"Promise me you'll find Papa and bring him back."

"I'll find him. I promise."

He wasn't going to let her forget the rest of his demand. "And you will bring him back here."

"Yes," she said carefully, "as soon as he is able to come back, we will return together."

"Will you write to me, Mami?"

His acceptance made her want to cry. But she forced a smile instead. "Of course, munchkin, every week. But remember, letters take a long time, so if you haven't heard from me in a while, please don't worry. I am thinking about you every day, and the letters will come."

She pulled him close, drawing him into her arms in a long embrace. Berta stood with Walter and watched Alma and Marie's farewell, and Marie smiled at them over Alma's tiny shoulder.

She mouthed her gratitude: *"Danke."*

TWENTY-EIGHT

March 15, 1946

Rolf Schulmann waited patiently while the American soldier removed his handcuffs, and then Major James Matthews joined him as he silently faced the row of military officers standing stiffly behind a white-draped table. Rolf had met the major previously, when Matthews arrived unexpectedly to collect Rolf from the POW camp the day before Rolf's birthday. Matthews was pleasant, comfortably soft around the middle, and always cordial with Rolf. At the same time, he had the aura of authority around him and impressed Rolf with his straightforward temperament and operational efficiency.

Matthews greeted him with a cordial handshake. "Herr Schulmann, let me introduce you to the members of the judicial panel who will be discussing your case." He indicated a middle-aged man wearing the insignia of a general, his head balding underneath his visor cap and a patch of color high on one cheekbone. Matthews said, "This is General James Grayson, who will preside at this hearing."

Major Matthews continued the introductions. "This is Sergeant Edward Finley, adjutant to General Grayson and officer in charge of denazification procedures at Rhein-Main." Rolf decided Finley would have had to become a sergeant through rapid wartime promotions common in the heat of battle; Sergeant Finley was a man much younger than Rolf with the air of someone who took his position and rank very seriously. Rolf nodded deferentially in his direction.

"We also have an interpreter here—but it seems you're as comfortable speaking our language as you are your own." Matthews smiled. "It will make this hearing infinitely less difficult for all of us."

Matthews introduced him to the four remaining panel members present, and then General Grayson called for order.

Grayson spoke. "Major Rolf Schulmann, I will reemphasize what Major Matthews has already told you: this is not a trial. It is a *hearing* only, with the purpose of deciding whether or not you're considered a threat to the United States, and whether your Nazi membership and wartime activities warrant a military tribunal. Today we will be hearing only the case against you. If necessary, at a future date you will be granted the opportunity to defend yourself.

"As prosecutor for the United States Government and as judiciary representative of the U.S. High Commissioner in Germany, John J. McCloy, my peers and I must consider the following war crimes in your case: conspiracy to further the agenda of Adolph Hitler, membership and active interest in the Nazi Party's leadership, crimes against humanity committed during the years in occupied France, defying the U.S.-recognized authority of the Vichy government by crossing the Demarcation Line and oppressing the citizens of Vichy France . . ."

Rolf stood resolutely, his gaze steady and solemn, and as he listened to the charges against him the only thing he could think was, *I will never see my son again; I'll never see Marie again . . .*

"In your case, Mr. Schulmann, we see that there are major factors that will affect the outcome of any trial to which you're subjected; mainly, whether there were extenuating circumstances surrounding your participation in the war, the eventual charges of treason against you by the German military, your religious background and values . . ."

Rolf said nothing. After years of unimaginable disappointment and danger, he would not allow himself the luxury of feeling a spark of hope.

"Mr. Schulmann, you were assigned to Vichy France after your government illegally crossed the Demarcation Line into southern France. Do you recall who it was who assigned you to the Rhône-Alpes region of Belley?"

"Yes, sir."

"Will you state the name of your commanding officer for your peers?"

"Yes, sir. It was Major-General Walther Schellenberg."

"Mr. Schulmann, for your information, Walther Schellenberg has been in our custody here in Frankfurt since last year, and we have been asking him questions about, among other things, your responsibilities as an officer for the Reich." General Grayson paused. "We have invited him to join us here today—to testify concerning these charges and your service during the war."

Surprised, Rolf turned and watched as the back door to the courtroom opened and Schellenberg entered and walked forward to face him. He was of average height, with broad shoulders, prominent cheekbones, and piercing blue eyes. His face was pockmarked with ancient blemish scars, and his mouth remained set in an uncompromising line. He returned Rolf's gaze coolly, levelly, the emotion in his eyes unreadable.

It was an uncomfortable moment and an awkward reunion. Rolf remembered his commanding officer's last words, spoken under the brilliant, blinding floodlights of the Ravensbrück concentration camp: *Major Rolf Schulmann, you are hereby arrested and charged with treason against the Third Reich. By order of the Führer . . . you are to be transported to Sachsenhausen, where you will immediately be executed.*

With a grimace Major Schellenberg extended his hand, and Rolf hesitated before taking it. Schellenberg smiled tightly and spoke softly in German. "I'm pleased to see you, Major Schulmann."

"Are you?"

"I was happy to hear you survived."

"I'm sure you were, considering you ordered my execution."

Schellenberg didn't flinch. "I'm glad to see my order was not carried out."

Rolf said nothing, but he frowned down at the man in front of him.

General Grayson intervened. "Mr. Schellenberg, as in all of our previous discussions, Second Lieutenant Smith will interpret for you." Grayson beckoned to a young man standing near the door who hastened to Schellenberg's side.

"Mr. Schellenberg, please describe your relationship with Rolf Schulmann." Smith translated.

Schellenberg replied, "I was Herr Schulmann's commanding officer. It was under my orders that he was transferred to Belley Headquarters in southern France." Smith hastened to interpret for the panel.

"In what capacity, sir?"

"Intelligence. Human affairs. His duties included interrogation, espionage, and interception of Allied agents."

"What else?"

"He was instrumental in the capture and interrogation of enemy resistance personnel."

"I see."

"He was accused by the Gestapo of conspiracy, and he eventually turned himself in." Schellenberg turned to look at Rolf as he continued. "And, yes, I did order his execution." He turned back to Grayson. "As his commanding officer I was not permitted to show favoritism, although Major Schulmann was always a man I trusted." Again he glanced at Rolf. "Schulmann, it seems, leads a blessed life."

"Tell me about his intelligence activities, Mr. Schellenberg."

"In '39 he was assigned to a position as an interrogator in Hamburg. He captured and interrogated several foreign agents who had infiltrated the Fatherland near the beginning of the war, and then in '42 he was transferred at my recommendation to southern France when the Vichy government had outlived its usefulness. He worked to undermine the Maquis movement in the Rhône-Alpes region."

"Why was he accused of treason?"

"He had a moment of weakness, sir. He allowed himself to fall in love with an Allied agent, a woman whom he captured, interrogated, and turned over to the Gestapo, and then, apparently having a change of heart, he sent a team of trusted subordinates dressed as French Résistance to save her. She disappeared for several months and reappeared later with the major's family in Schönenberg. It seems this woman had an impact on the majority of his activities during the first half of '44, although I have reason to believe he was already a traitor to the Fatherland before they met."

"What makes you say that?"

"His convictions, sir, made it so that his activities were never in complete compliance with the Führer's wishes."

"What do you mean?"

"He's a Mormon. He converted sometime in '39, and after that he refused to do certain things."

"A Mormon." Matthews didn't flinch. "I see."

There was an uncomfortable silence in the room for several moments. Rolf looked from one face to another and was intrigued by the mixture of emotions he saw there: Walther Schellenberg stood impassively, his face somewhat cold and distant. General Grayson continued to study Rolf with his face serious, a flicker of dislike in his eyes. Sergeant Finley leaned forward, his fingers laced together on his knee and his studious gaze open and curious, and Major Matthews sat back in his chair, his eyes steady on Rolf with a curious esteem written in their depths.

Matthews asked Schellenberg, "So you believe his religion influenced his service to Hitler?"

"Absolutely."

"He refused to do certain things because of his religious beliefs?"

"Forgive me, Major—I used the wrong term. Not 'refused,'" Schellenberg clarified. "If he had downright refused he would have been arrested a long time before. He would accept the assignments, but then he became adept at circumventing his orders.

Sergeant Finley studied Schulmann soberly before addressing Schellenberg. "If you were still his commanding officer, would you feel you could trust him?"

"I wouldn't trust him with any national secrets."

Major Matthews asked, "Would you consider him a threat to the national security of the United States of America? Would you consider him an enemy to the Americans?"

Schellenberg looked at Rolf, his face a mixture of distaste and reluctant respect. "I would consider him more a threat to the *enemies* of the United States. Except for one thing." He turned back to the panel of American officers. "Keep in mind that if you ask him to do anything that goes against his religion, he will not do it. And that might end up being the greatest threat of all."

TWENTY-NINE

March 16, 1946

Rolf stood resolutely in front of Sergeant Edward Finley, his hands calmly linked behind his back and his eyes steady on the smaller officer's exasperated face.

"To be honest, Mr. Schulmann, you're not in a bargaining position. The fact of the matter is that you're a prisoner of the United States Army. It's as simple as that."

"I want you to reconsider my request."

"The panel has not yet decided your future, and until everything is decided, you're obviously not to be allowed the same privileges as a free man." Finley moved dismissively away from Rolf. "If they decide you're not a war criminal, you'll have your freedom soon enough—and then you can do what you please with your time. What is there to reconsider?"

"I only want to borrow an army vehicle for a few hours tomorrow."

"Whatever for? A scenic Sunday drive?"

"I want to go to church."

Finley stared at him, his jaw slack.

"A representative from The Church of Jesus Christ of Latter-day Saints from Utah is visiting Frankfurt this weekend—and I would like to be there. I want to hear what he has to say—and visit with him. I expect you'll send along a military companion or two. That's not a problem. But I need to be there."

"Now, wait a minute, Schulmann. No way am I going to give you an opportunity to escape."

"I understand," Rolf countered. "Talk to the chaplain and have him send over two LDS servicemen to accompany me. They can report to you when we get back."

Finley continued to stare at him. "This is highly irregular," he said with a frown. "I'll have to run it by Major Matthews."

Rolf deliberately treated the sergeant's words as consent. "Thank you, sir."

* * *

Lieutenant Rostov drove with Hans and Petka to the train station. He left his driver at the car and walked with the two men onto the platform, where he handed Hans a Russian Nagant revolver wrapped discreetly in a newspaper. "I'll send a recovery team for von Hausen as soon as you have located the man." He smiled cordially and shook the German's hand—more for the benefit of the surrounding passengers than for the sake of congeniality. "I don't have to tell you how beneficial it will be to Miss Allred if you do not turn that weapon on your comrades, Mr. Brenner."

Hans glowered at him. "What if I turn it on you?"

Rostov smiled tightly. "No matter how long it takes to find the professor, remember my promise—in regards to your beautiful American nurse."

Hans's eyes smoldered, and he turned and walked after Petka toward the waiting train. Suddenly he paused, turned, and again faced Rostov. "You're a mystery, Professor. I can't quite make out why you're doing this."

"Because it is my responsibility—and my privilege." The words were clipped, dismissive.

"For some reason you're acting outside your comfort zone," Hans persisted. "Even though you threaten with great finesse and skill, it is not who you are. You know how to use blackmail to your advantage and how to bend an individual to your will. You know how to inspire your victims to see things your way, whether they want to or not. But that is not who you are."

"That is what I have been commissioned to be." Hans could hear the tightness creeping into the Russian's voice. "I do not pretend to be better than I am."

Hans's voice remained steady as he met the Russian's gaze. "And yet, I know evil men. I understand how they behave and how they think. And you do not have to be one of them." Hans took a deep breath. "I can understand loyalty to one's government—even an unjust government. But what I do not understand, Rostov, is *why*, with all your intelligence and honor, you would, through your loyalty to this government, aspire to be an evil man."

THIRTY

Rolf watched through the window as the Citroën drove past the *Alte Oper*—or at least what *used* to be the old opera house, which had been built in 1880 by a well-known German architect. Rolf could see where Allied bombs had completely gutted the massive structure, leveling not only a building but also a city's pride.

Frankfurt had virtually ceased to exist. Like Berlin it had attracted a large percentage of the Allies' attention, and the resulting devastation was unlike anything Rolf had ever imagined. Every bridge had been destroyed. Everything that could possibly burn had burned, and above the carnage Rolf saw the old cathedral spire, still standing, watching piously over a city of ghosts.

Rain fell heavily, obstructing his view of the LDS mission home, where he and other district representatives would meet with Elder Benson. He left the car, shielding his face with his hand as he approached the home, and he was surprised to see that the building was functionally intact. As he walked with his escorts up the stone steps he saw a large bombshell buried deeply in the ground in the courtyard. The impact of the bomb had cracked walls and windows on the home, but the bomb had not exploded.

As Rolf entered the mission home with his military escorts, he felt a peaceful feeling envelop him, warming him through his sodden jacket and shirt. He had felt the same feeling when he'd met with those two young men who had taught him the gospel before the war, and he had felt it in Marie's presence. How he wished Marie could be here with him today!

He found a seat in the back of the room and waited with several other men for his opportunity to speak with the Apostle. As Rolf listened to Elder Benson speak, he felt his heart fill with gratitude to his Father in Heaven for making Elder Benson's presence here possible—and for granting Rolf a chance to visit with him. When his turn came to meet with the Apostle, Rolf was filled with a love so profound for the man that at first he could hardly speak.

Elder Benson extended his hand and Rolf took it, amazed at the man's firm handshake. Rolf had met great military leaders—men who had immense power and authority in their respective positions—but never before had he felt the magnitude of power that emanated from this man standing before him. He felt humble in Elder Benson's presence and, at the same time, elated to be in the same room with him.

"Brother Schulmann, I'm happy to meet you. You represent a region farther south?"

"Yes, sir." Rolf swallowed. "I have been asked by our branch president, President Wagner of the Baiersbronn Branch, to report on the affairs of the Saints in that area."

Elder Benson smiled. "Chicago."

Rolf hesitated, surprised. "I beg your pardon?"

"Your accent. You lived in Chicago, didn't you?"

"That's right." Rolf returned the Apostle's smile.

"How many years?" Elder Benson had kind eyes.

"I lived there with my mother and father for three years, moved back to Germany for a while, and then returned to Chicago to attend the university before the war."

"I see." Elder Benson's smile deepened. "You're as much an American as a German."

"My heart is divided, it's true."

Elder Benson took his seat and motioned for Rolf to do the same. Rolf's guards shifted uncomfortably, unsure whether they should stay in the room or wait outside the door. Rolf turned to them. "Stay and listen. I would like you to report everything you hear to Major Matthews and Sergeant Finley."

"You still have a few troubles, it seems." Elder Benson's face remained kind.

"I was an SS officer, sir, and I've been charged with multiple war crimes."

"Will it go to trial?"

"Most likely," Rolf said. "But I'm ready to do whatever it takes to pay for my part in the war."

"Good for you, Brother Schulmann." Elder Benson leaned back in his chair and switched gears. "Tell me about the Saints in Baiersbronn."

"My report comes secondhand, Elder Benson, since I haven't been free to return home. But President Wagner sent me the information he wanted me to pass on to you. He wanted me to express to you his deepest regrets that because of health issues he wasn't able to make the trip himself."

"In that case I hope he will soon recover." The words were said with genuine sympathy.

Rolf proceeded to relate the information from Horst Wagner's letter. "In our branch, to date, seventy-three priesthood holders are listed as missing, prisoners of war, or deceased. Sixty-five percent of those remaining are older citizens who were called up by the German high command in the last months of the war and returned home either sick or wounded. Twenty percent of our members are under the age of eighteen. Eighty-five percent of households are without any priesthood holder age twelve or older. The sisters are rallying to accumulate and provide at least the basic necessities to families with young children, older widows, and those older brethren who are incapacitated. There are more Aaronic priesthood holders than Melchizedek, and most priesthood holders are under constant threat of arrest for the part they played in the war.

"We have many farms in our region, and the members are trying to make sure the crops will be evenly distributed. This past winter was difficult, but for the most part the members of the branch have been very generous with what little they have. No one in the branch has died of hunger."

Elder Benson's eyes misted. "You have no idea how happy that makes me feel, Brother Schulmann. When you have seen what I have seen—Saints so desperate for food that they fight for spoiled scraps in the military land-fills, children with stomachs bloated from starvation, mothers unable to give their babies the nourishment they need to survive—then you understand why the news that the Saints are surviving in Baiersbronn can affect me so deeply. Thank you, Brother Schulmann, for that wonderful news."

Elder Benson sobered. "However, I would hazard a guess that there are necessities that are not readily available. Am I right?"

Rolf nodded.

"What would you say are the biggest needs right now?"

Rolf hesitated. "Clothing. Warm bedding and medical supplies."

"Fine. And what about fuel? Coal?"

"In a pinch they can burn wood, and so far they've got an adequate supply of that." Rolf continued. "Each Relief Society sister who is able cuts enough for her own family and for one more household in the branch, and so far there have been no families without wood for their needs. In this last winter I assume it was the same."

"Wonderful. Do you have anything else to add?"

"No, sir."

"I will pass along your recommendations." Elder Benson leaned forward. "And now, Brother Schulmann, let's talk about you. Do you have a family?"

"Yes, sir. My wife died before the war, but I have a six-year-old son from that marriage, a sister-in-law and her husband, and . . . my fiancée." Rolf knew the man in front of him would not miss hearing the slight hesitation in his voice.

Elder Benson watched him closely, his eyes kind. "Tell me about your fiancée, Brother Schulmann."

Rolf told him briefly about how he'd met Marie, about Félix's death and how he had struggled with the decision of what to do with a captured Allied agent. He told how Marie had cared for Alma in Switzerland until after the war, and about their reunion in Berlin.

Elder Benson's eyes never left him while he spoke, and after he finished, the General Authority said, "Reading between the lines, I would say that you and Marie Jacobson have had more than your share of hardships over the past years."

His comment, spoken so kindly, touched Rolf's heart, and he swallowed hard against the emotions threatening to rise to the surface.

Elder Benson continued softly. "You probably wonder if you will ever get a chance to marry her, settle down, and raise a family."

"Yes, sir."

"Have you ever read the Doctrine and Covenants, Brother Schulmann?"

"No, sir. The missionaries who taught me mentioned something about it once, but I've never had the opportunity to read it."

Elder Benson reached for a book on the table next to him and began to flip through the pages. "The Doctrine and Covenants recounts the history of the Saints during the last century and is a record of the revelations given to the Prophet Joseph Smith. It also tells us a great deal about that prophet, Brother Schulmann—not just his revelations, but accounts of his family, his dealings with the Saints, his emotions, and his trials."

Elder Benson rested the open book on one knee and glanced at Rolf. "Several times he was imprisoned, Brother Schulmann, just like you. And even though the reasons for his imprisonment may differ from yours, you and he have probably shared several of the same feelings of frustration, grief, and maybe even anger at your predicament."

Rolf knew he was going to lose the battle with his emotions if Elder Benson continued to talk like this.

"At one time the Prophet Joseph was being held in Liberty Jail in Missouri and the experience had been so vicious, so demeaning, and so demoralizing that he cried out in anguish, 'O God, where art thou? . . . How long shall thy hand be stayed, and thine eye . . . behold . . . the wrongs of thy people . . . and thine ear be penetrated with their cries? Yea, O Lord, how long shall they suffer these wrongs and unlawful oppressions?'"

Rolf lowered his head, overcome with feeling—both anguish for what he had suffered and guilt for the suffering he had been responsible for causing. Elder Benson continued. "Brother Joseph was a *prophet*, Brother Schulmann! And he, too, had to face pain, and suffering, and disappointment . . . and an earthly tribunal."

"I don't know your situation. I don't know what you did during the war, nor do I make any judgments as to your guilt or innocence. I only say this, Rolf Schulmann: that your Heavenly Father knows you, and He loves you. And you can be assured that no matter what is decided in your earthly trial, it is your *heavenly* tribunal's verdict that matters most. I can tell that the gospel of Jesus Christ is important in your life, Brother Schulmann, and because of that I believe you will be protected. I believe angels will guard you, comfort you, and help you through all of this.

"You will be in my prayers, Brother Schulmann, that everything will go as it should in your trial." Elder Benson paused. "And I feel impressed to tell you that if you're acquitted by an earthly tribunal and are set free, you may hold your head high, go to your Church authority, and be interviewed for and receive a temple recommend. And then you may take that beautiful daughter of God to the temple and be sealed to her for eternity, confident that you are worthy and clean in your Heavenly Father's sight."

Rolf began to sob quietly. Elder Benson leaned forward and said, "Your heart is correct, Brother Schulmann. It will probably never be easy for you and your family, *but I believe you will be all right.*"

THIRTY-ONE

Late March, early April, 1946

Thanks to a tip from a Communist newspaper in Lyon, Hans discovered that a small community of German refugees had settled in the Rhône-Alpes region north of Lyon in '45. Ever since then the settlement had been attracting new residents on a regular basis. It was a small matter to infiltrate the camp and begin preparing for an indefinite stay along with everybody else.

Even though Petka spoke passable German, the Russian kept silent throughout most of their stay, and Hans couldn't decide whether his silence stemmed from fear that his true nationality would be discovered or impatient frustration that Hans wasn't finding the missing scientist in a timelier manner.

Out of necessity Hans joined in the revelry each evening while Petka took his bottle of whatever alcoholic beverage was available and skulked off to bed. Even though he didn't show it to Petka or to the Germans in the group, Hans envied Petka's early retirement each night. He wished he could slip away too and be free of the demons that beguiled him mercilessly, enticing him with memories of the night-long frolics of days gone by.

But somehow Hans kept the promise he'd made so many ages ago on that dismal night on a dreary road north of Berlin—a promise to a God he hadn't yet known. He did not once touch the rivers of alcohol that flowed, nor did he seek out the female companionship that seemed to be in endless supply. Instead, he focused his thoughts solidly on the American nurse who had captured his heart, and in his mind he promised Natalie that, no matter what she thought of him, he would never betray her.

Hans finally received fitting recompense for his suffering. He met a young, intoxicated ex-Gestapo officer who had deserted in the first few months of '45 and escaped to the Rhône-Alpes, who mentioned over a pint of beer provided by Hans that he had been a student of von Hausen's the year Hans left the university. According to the man, von Hausen had mentioned to his class his affinity for the Rhône-Alpes and especially the incredible slopes of the Mont Blanc Massif, where he and his wife had once vacationed, and he had told them of his sorrow that the war would separate him from that location for such an indefinite period of time.

Hans and Petka broke camp the next morning.

* * *

She was detained at the front gate and required to send a message to the young lieutenant. And as he had every day since his promised two weeks had passed, Lieutenant Henrie's response was the same: *To Miss Marie Jacobson: with my apologies, I'm still waiting.*

So it was with a heavy heart that she watched March slip away and April arrive, with its melting snow and blooming lavender, sweet spring breezes and heavenly-scented lilacs.

Near the inside of the front gate the prisoners had planted a small garden with forget-me-nots. Marie studied the delicate blooms and struggled to control her emotions. And she hoped that God would hear her prayer and allow her to find Rolf soon.

* * *

April 15, 1946

Near the base of Mont Blanc and nurtured by the Arve River and the melting of the various smaller glaciers of the Massif, a small communal village hovers in the shadows of the massive Le Brevent and Mont Blanc. Chamonix-Mont-Blanc reigns to the northeast and stately Lyon basks to the southwest, and in its private mountain meadow, the small village of Charé receives only a trickle of the tourism that invades the larger communities of the Rhône-Alpes. Only the most intrepid mountain climbers and campers in the summer and the most foolhardy skiers in the winter frequent its one café and two hotels, and even then, the lure of the larger communities soon drives any tourists onward to bigger and better things.

On the evening of April fifteenth, in the solitary café in Charé, Hans Brenner watched the spectacle he had created with a mixture of envy and disgust. His mouth was dry and he felt an almost uncontrollable urge to grab a mug and join in the revelry he was financing. But he clutched his glass of water and tried to focus on his disgust: a drunken Frenchman was not a pretty sight—especially when his drinking transcended all human capacity and there was still another mug of beer in his possession. Hans had to admit, though, that the inebriated Frenchman's singing was not that bad. He sang jazz and American boogie-woogie with a finesse that would have placed him on the best stages of Paris—had it not been for his unimpressive drunken swagger and the drool escaping the corners of his mouth. Besides, when he sang, Hans had to dodge the spittle that flew and the beer that slopped, and he realized that the man had long ago lost all sense of propriety and reason.

Well, hopefully not *all* reason. Hans still needed this fine entertainer to tell him where the German scientist who had moved into the neighborhood less than a year ago was hiding.

Hans slapped a few more francs on the counter and slid them toward the bartender. The bartender eyed him suspiciously; Hans figured the man was probably a product of the Maquis movement and recognized an interrogation when he saw one. Besides, Hans suspected that the sharp-eyed veteran had discovered his true nationality more than an hour ago, and now he wondered if the man had any inclination to earn himself a substantial award for capturing a Nazi.

But so far the bartender kept his thoughts to himself and his focus on his customers, and now at Hans's insistence he served another mug of beer to the Frenchman.

André never even paused for breath. He had a goodly portion of the new mug's contents consumed before he finished the verse he was singing, and then he stepped away from his stool to add a little dance step to his routine.

Hans brought him firmly back to the bar. "Where did you say your friend is staying, Monsieur André?"

André stared at him as though it was the first time he'd been asked the question instead of the fifth. He took another swallow of beer, and Hans wondered where he managed to store it all.

Hans persisted. "Can you give me directions to his hut?"

Now André spoke, his words slurred and colloquial, and Hans had to muster all of his marginal knowledge of the French language in order to understand him. "You don't look like a Frenchman . . ."

"Neither do you."

André guffawed. "You're not a Frenchman," he persisted.

Hans sighed patiently. "That's right—I'm not. I already told you. I'm here from Switzerland on holiday, and Professor von Hausen is a friend I knew before the war. I'm supposed to meet him."

André emptied his mug and Hans dug into his pocket. "Tell me how to get to the professor's hut, and I'll bring my old scientist friend a draft or two. He must be lonely up there, all by himself . . ."

"Naw." The man was slurring dramatically now. "He's got his nephew to run errands for him. Says he's waiting for the Americans . . ."

Hans felt his heart leap in his chest. He glanced once across the café patrons at Petka, who was nursing a drink and an attitude near the far wall, and then said, "I'm with the Americans."

The Frenchman eyed him suspiciously. "Thought you just said you was from Switzerland."

"I am." Hans thought quickly. "The Americans have me working on a project there—for the restructuring effort, of course."

"Of course."

The man started singing again, and Hans glanced at the bartender. The bartender shook his head and walked away, leaving the room without a backward glance. Hans punched the drunken Frenchman's arm. "Listen. I have to leave now, but I thought you might like one more drink—just for the sake of our friendship."

The man brightened.

"But I won't give it to you until you tell me where—"

"Up the path behind the old church—y'know, the one with the stained-glass window. Survived the war intact, y'know."

"What did? The stained-glass window or the church?" Hans couldn't suppress a grin, although he worried what the bartender might be planning in the other room.

"The whole church, for the love of—" André swayed and managed to catch himself against the counter.

"Good to hear it." Hans tossed a handful of francs in the Frenchman's direction. "You said there's someone staying up there with him?"

André nodded and collected the money. "Strapping lad of twenty or so. They say he's a whiz with a rifle . . ."

Hans stood and reached for his cap.

"He'll shoot you clean through the heart if you try to approach the house."

Hans turned and walked away.

THIRTY-TWO

April 16, 1946

Petka whined until Hans afforded him a few hours' rest under a bridge, and then early in the morning Hans dragged Petka with him to scout out the mountainside behind the fortunate church. He found the rugged trail, gouged by the tires of some motorized conveyance, and he and a reluctant Petka began to climb. Petka's stamina gave out partway into the arduous climb, and Hans discarded him by the side of the trail. "Stay here and wait for me, Petka—I know this is difficult for you."

Petka sank wearily by the side of the trail and leaned into his knees, breathing heavily.

Hans turned to go. "I should be back in a few hours—hopefully with the scientist. If you're still alive, I'll see you then."

"Still alive?" Petka growled.

Hans nodded, his expression apologetic. "It's my fault. I should have told you sooner about the brown bears . . ." He continued up the trail.

Petka caught up to him a few minutes later. "What are we planning to do if von Hausen refuses to come?" he panted.

"We'll give him a day or two to change his mind."

Petka swore. "You mean a day or two for the Americans to get him."

Hans glanced sideways at the struggling Russian. "I don't see that as an option, Petka. Do you?"

Petka fell silent and spent the remainder of their climb focusing any energy on placing one foot in front of the other.

Hans was finally back in his element. After the dirt and grime of a conquered city and the squalor of a Soviet labor camp, Hans finally felt clean and whole again. He loved the outdoors and felt at home and in control there. And as he and Petka ascended through dense trees and underbrush, across beautiful meadows blanketed with lavender and lilies, and past outcroppings of granite and waterfalls formed from glacial runoff, Hans felt rejuvenated. He pressed forward, his wide shoulders bearing the weight of both his and Petka's backpacks and his strong legs remembering their years of training. His only regret was that the person who was the motivation for his presence here was still trapped in Rostov's clutches. Hans's actions over the next few hours could very well determine whether the beautiful blue-eyed American nurse would live or die.

He paused, set down the backpacks, and drank from his canteen. Petka glanced furtively back down the trail. "Why not keep going? There's no reason to stop on my account."

"I want to stop."

Petka stood nervously in the center of the trail and stared pleadingly at Hans. "Let's keep going, Hans . . ."

"Why?" Hans gestured with his canteen. "Von Hausen's hut is right up there." Hans pointed through the trees and across a clearing toward a small stone-and-plaster hut with an old-fashioned thatch. Smoke rose from a central chimney, and there was a motorbike leaning against the south side of the structure. Hans grimaced. He hadn't imagined it would be a simple task for a middle-aged professor to make that climb very often, but a motorbike, on the trail Hans and Petka had just climbed, would have to be almost impossible.

The cottage was tucked into the side of a gigantic granite cliff, with the cliff apparently serving as the back wall. Leading up to the front door lay a long series of stone steps rising from the clearing. And paralleling them was a rutted and muddy track obviously utilized by the motorcycle.

Petka headed for the clearing, but Hans hauled him unceremoniously back. "You ready to get shot, Petka?"

"I don't see any movement—maybe they don't know we're here."

"They know we're here." Hans recalled the distrust on the bartender's face. "They're waiting for one of us to be stupid enough to become the main attraction at a turkey shoot. You stay here, Petka, and draw their attention away from me."

"I don't want to get shot," Petka whined.

Hans ignored him and reached for his backpack, but Petka grabbed his sleeve. "Where are you going?"

Hans scowled. "To negotiate with our scientist. Isn't that why I was asked to come along?"

"What about the bears?"

"Bears? Here?" Hans shook his head as if chastising an errant child. "Wherever did you get that notion? Bears in the Alps are rare. Now, if we were high up in the Pyrenees . . ."

Petka spouted Russian, likely describing in fuming detail what he thought of Hans's earlier deception, but Hans merely shouldered his backpack and headed back down the trail. Petka hissed after him, "Don't you dare leave without me."

"Of course not." Hans didn't even hesitate. "I'm going to find a way around. You make sure you keep their attention right here, Petka—I don't want to get shot either."

* * *

Major Matthews called Rolf into his office that morning.

"Marie Jacobson has been looking for you. For weeks she's been pestering the army to disclose your location. That's quite a determined lady you have there, Mr. Schulmann."

Rolf could not help the smile that played at the corners of his mouth. "You have no idea, sir." He felt warmth envelop him at Matthews's mention of Marie.

"Unfortunately, we cannot let her know where you are, at least for the time being." Matthews seemed genuinely apologetic. "We have something we need to discuss before she can be returned to you. But I want you to send her a telegram and let her know you're all right."

Rolf felt his spirits soar. "With pleasure, sir."

"The less you say, the sooner we can get the two of you back together. Understand?"

"I understand. Thank you, sir."

Matthews leaned forward, his fingers laced together on the desk. "Now, are you familiar with the Office of Strategic Services—the OSS?"

Rolf nodded. "Of course. My assignment in France was to oppose that organization in any way I could."

"And you were good at your job." Matthews smiled wryly. "Thank goodness you didn't have more success."

Again Rolf stayed silent, and Matthews continued. "As I'm sure you know, during the war the U.S. analytic, clandestine, and counter-intelligence functions were organized and administered under the OSS. In fact, you were known to the organization and watched closely because of your operations in southern France."

"I'm not surprised," Rolf said, his voice only hinting at the irony he felt.

"President Truman disbanded the OSS when Germany surrendered. He was of the opinion that intelligence gathering was no longer necessary.

Friends don't read each other's mail, right? Then in January of this year President Truman changed his mind. He responded to a need for the development of a peacetime spy organization to protect our interests in the United States and . . . abroad."

"You mean in Europe. Germany, France, and places farther east—like Russia."

"Exactly," Matthews replied with a nod. "During the war the OSS proved mildly effective in its operations against the Axis powers, perhaps undermining the Nazi war machine just enough so that the Allies could establish an effective foothold in Europe. But we've always had our problems with the other Allied powers. Churchill, for example, had his own organization—the SOE, which I believe your fiancée was involved with, and which at times didn't cooperate with our organization. And de Gaulle had his relatively successful Free French organization, although for the life of me I cannot understand how an organization as divided as the Résistance ever survived, let alone organized into one relatively effective fighting force. We only supported de Gaulle after a time, you understand, because he was so adamantly opposed to Pétain's government in southern France . . ."

Matthews reached for his coffee cup and sipped from it, then set it back on his desk and continued. "But recently our greatest anxieties have been focused on the east, on the Communist entities we once considered friends."

Rolf understood perfectly. "I don't blame Russia; they've probably suffered more than anybody in this war. If I were a Russian I might want to exact my revenge not only on the conquered, but on anyone who might seem unsympathetic to my sufferings."

"It's not that we're insensitive, Mr. Schulmann." Matthews leaned back in his chair. "We understand that their losses have been staggering. It's just that the Communist ideal they're trying to shove down the throats of conquered Europe and the entire Western hemisphere rubs Americans the wrong way. With the close of this war the triumph of superior might is no longer enough for the Soviets. They have their own denazification methods—not just for Nazi Germany, but for the world. And the government of the United States sees both their methods and their ambitions as a colossal threat."

Matthews tapped the edge of the table with his index finger, as if trying to emphasize his next point so that Rolf could not possibly misunderstand. "Our continued presence in Berlin chafes at the Soviets—makes them irritable, unpredictable. They're mad at Truman, de Gaulle, the queen, Italy, Japan, and anyone else who opposes socialism's ideals. And they're determined not to let us beat them to the prize."

"I assume you're not talking just about Germany's factories. Or its resources."

"Intellectual resources!" Matthews thumped the table for emphasis. "Doctors, lawyers, teachers, artists—scientists! Anybody they believe can further their purposes and confirm to the world the superior might of the Soviet Union. And we're caught in the race of the century, Mr. Schulmann, a race so deadly that we cannot afford to lose to the Communists!"

Major Matthews paused, breathing heavily, as if the magnitude of the problem facing his country sapped him of his strength. Rolf didn't need to ask for clarification. He knew Matthews was alluding to the development of the A-bomb and the U.S.'s desire to keep away from the Soviets any German scientists and technology related to Hitler's attempts to perfect a bomb of his own. And he had the whisper of an idea of what he was going to be asked to do.

"Ever heard the cliché 'out of the frying pan into the fire'?" Matthews queried. "It seems that after a cautious cooperation with the Communists throughout the war, we've gotten ourselves into a heated exchange with our once-friends, and the U.S. government is convinced the heat is only going to get worse. And that, my friend, is where we need you."

Rolf kept his gaze steady on Matthews. "I don't have any knowledge of Adolph Hitler's plans for a bomb. Nor do I personally know the names of any scientists. And if I did have any scientist friends, what would you expect me to do about it?"

Matthews laughed. "We are not asking you to rat on your colleagues, Mr. Schulmann. In fact, our intelligence sources are rather talented in that area." He stood and looked Rolf in the eye. "We need you to help us extract a scientist friend of ours who has gotten himself entangled in a very large net. He has been hiding in a small community in the Rhône-Alpes in France, and now he can't get out."

Rolf stared at Matthews, incredulous. "Whatever would inspire him to try to hide in such a dangerous place?" He shook his head. "He couldn't have picked a more Communist-infested spot on the entire European continent. He might just as well try to hide in Moscow. The Rhône-Alpes is a hornet's nest of French Communist Party activity and has been since the middle of the war—or earlier. Are you thinking he might be trying to hide from the Americans? Are you planning to extract him against his will?"

Matthews shrugged his shoulders. "That's what we can't figure out. He's contacted us, expressed his desire to accept our offer—and yet, he goes to hide in the worst place on earth."

"Where is he hiding?"

"Near Chamonix—on the border with Italy and Switzerland."

Rolf shifted his feet. "Are you certain he's not trying to disappear for good? Because Chamonix is a popular place for people who want to cross over into Switzerland. There's a train station there, and a foot path through the Alps, and several routes a desperate man who might be intent on escape could take . . ."

"Yes, I know. Last we communicated with him we instructed him to stay where he was while we arranged his removal to England. But then he cut off all negotiations and we've been unable to determine why." Matthews paced behind his desk, delineating possible breakdowns on his plump fingers. "Perhaps his contact was captured—or killed. Perhaps von Hausen— that's our scientist—has been having second thoughts. Or maybe his wife, who is awaiting him in another location, is sick and he doesn't want to exacerbate her illness with a move. But as of this moment von Hausen is still in France, and up until this morning we were confident that the Soviets had not yet discovered his whereabouts."

Rolf was interested. "What happened this morning?"

"We received a call from one of our men who's been watching over von Hausen—he said a man was asking questions about von Hausen in the café—and claiming to be working for the Americans." Matthews poked absently at a pencil on his desk. "We know all American agents assigned to the von Hausen project, Mr. Schulmann, and this man was not one of them. We can only conclude that Lieutenant Viktor Rostov, of the Soviet NKGB, has finally found von Hausen."

Major Matthews moved around his desk and faced the German major. "We need you to fly to France immediately, Major Schulmann, travel to Chamonix, and make contact with von Hausen tomorrow. We need you to convince him to accompany you back here to Frankfurt and from here to England." Matthews hesitated. "Even if von Hausen doesn't want to work for the United States, his life is in danger if he decides to stay in Chamonix and wait for Viktor Rostov."

"Why me, Major Matthews?" Rolf was curious. "It seems to me that an assignment like this could be handled by any of your intelligence agents with minimal knowledge of the area, a team, and a supply of weapons."

"Perhaps." Matthews hesitated again, and he glanced down at his hands thoughtfully before returning his gaze to Rolf. "But I prefer *you* to do the job for one reason, and if you'll bear with me and hear me out, I'll try to explain it so you'll understand. Please, Mr. Schulmann, take a seat and hear what I have to say."

Matthews settled himself into his chair and Rolf found one of his own.

Matthews began his explanation. "Back in '43 I received a call from my daughter at college, and she told me she had met and fallen in love with a nice young man. Naturally, I was happy for her, but I wanted to know what kind of man was capturing my daughter's heart. So the missus and I invited him to our home for Christmas, and he drove down with my daughter.

"He was a fine young man—tall, handsome, athletic, and very intelligent. He was majoring in engineering at a religious institution in the west and had met my daughter when his basketball team played a tournament at my daughter's school in California."

Rolf listened attentively as the major continued. "They hit it off right away. Love at first sight, y'know. And when we met him we were impressed by him immediately."

At this point, Major Matthews could not remain seated. He rose to his feet and paced. "Of course, I come from the old school of thought—that a father has a right to interrogate his daughter's intended, raking him over the coals and forcing him—on pain of death, of course—to confess all his sins." Matthews smiled at the memory. "The boy stood up well to my abuse and promised me that he would love my daughter not just all his life, but hopefully forever."

Rolf listened closely, intrigued by that last word.

"I asked him what he meant, and he proceeded to tell me about what you Mormons believe—about life after death, and eternal families, and all that. His beliefs surprised me, but I was not against my daughter marrying a Mormon if that was what she really wanted. So I gave my consent to their marriage.

"On Christmas Eve we shared war experiences—my daughter's fiancé had suffered a shoulder injury during the last weeks of his enlistment, and instead of carting him back to the front after he healed, the army just discharged him and let him go home. I asked him to tell us a little about his church, and he told us of his experiences as a Mormon missionary in Germany before the war."

Rolf nodded. "There were quite a few of your country's young men here before the war, but they were all sent home by their mission president."

"That's what he told us." The major stopped pacing and turned to face Rolf. "And then he told us about an encounter he had with a German officer as he was trying to leave the country in '39."

Rolf felt his palms begin to sweat and he could think of nothing to say.

Matthews continued. "He was arrested and taken to be interrogated by a young Nazi officer in Hamburg. He told me that after a rough few days this officer had a change of heart and ended up saving his life. The officer drove him all the way to Denmark and released him, and the missionary knew that this German was risking his own life to help him escape."

Rolf said nothing, his emotions building near the surface.

Major Matthews sank back into his chair, his face suddenly flushed with emotion. He studied Rolf carefully and then leaned close, his voice solemn. "My son-in-law trusted you with his life, Major Schulmann, and because your courage and conviction have saved the life of the man who has made my daughter so happy, I want to offer *you* a chance to be free."

THIRTY-THREE

April 16, 1946

Edwin von Hausen could think of at least a dozen different situations that he would rather be in on this beautiful April morning besides staring through the sights of an ancient Maquis-lauded Stenmark while crouched uncomfortably on the floor below the window. The idea that the man acting so strangely on the low side of the clearing might be trying to divert his attention away from an approaching enemy made the hands that steadied his machine gun require steadying themselves.

"Check the bedroom window, Uncle Edwin," Luther whispered urgently. He moved his head a fraction of an inch from the sights of his rifle to glance at his uncle.

Von Hausen slung his weapon across his shoulder and crawled awkwardly toward the bedroom. "Maybe it's not a diversion," he grunted. "Maybe there's only one, and he's trying to tell us something."

"He's trying to tell us something, all right," Luther growled, keeping his gun steady between the window frame and the curtain. "He's got a companion out there somewhere, and he's trying to keep us intent on his idiotic disturbance while his companion attacks from the side."

"How do you know there's another?"

"Alfred from the café sent a messenger late last night, remember?"

Von Hausen reached the bedroom window. He slid the weapon from his back and took careful aim at the patch of scenery he could see without displacing the curtain, and as he did so he realized he was tired of this dreadful game of cat-and-mouse and was ready for the long, terrifying ordeal to be over. Otis Farber had risked his life to warn von Hausen to leave Germany, and for eight months now von Hausen had heard nothing from his friend.

At least Helga was safe in Spain. Von Hausen fingered the Stenmark and contemplated his options. He could either accept the Americans' offer, or he could hide out here indefinitely and pray that the Soviets wouldn't find him.

If he moved to Argentina he could finally be at peace. But it would be a fragile peace, he realized. Every time he rounded a corner he would wonder what awaited him on the other side. If he refused to work for either the Americans or the Russians he would have to concede the possibility that there might be far-reaching consequences. Either one of those feuding superpowers could decide that he was too dangerous to let live, and an innocent request for directions on a street corner could lead to a bag over his head or a knife between his ribs.

Von Hausen shuddered at the thought and concentrated his attention on the job at hand. Whoever prowled nearby did not mean to let him escape to Argentina.

But what if it was the Americans? The thought made him waver. If he decided to work for anyone it would be for the Americans. He had no love for Communism and no desire to assist blood-thirsty Stalin. He squinted through the opening in the curtains. Because of the sheer mountain cliff at their backs, it would be impossible for anyone to approach without either Luther or himself catching a glimpse of them. Whoever tried to approach would have to know how to fly . . .

The scrape of a kitchen chair brought him up sharply, and he stared through the open doorway at Luther, still crouched near the front window. Luther's face had gone deathly white.

Suddenly, from the recesses of the kitchen came a loud, jovial voice, muffled around a mouthful of food. "Have any jam to go with this bread? On your feet, men! Would you ignore a guest?"

Professor von Hausen and his nephew stood and walked as if in a trance toward the voice, weapons held ready in their hands. Von Hausen entered the kitchen first and stared at the tall man sitting casually at the kitchen table. The trespasser wore the *Bergmütze* of the German Mountain Elite, its soft flaps folded up away from his ears and worn at a rakish angle over tousled black hair. The man's dark eyes glinted mischief as he downed the last of a loaf of bread, his strong jaw chewing with the energy of someone who understood the meaning of starvation. Luther collided with the slack-jawed von Hausen, who stood frozen in the doorframe.

"It's been a long time, eh, Professor?"

Professor von Hausen swallowed, blinked, and stared dazedly at Hans, trying to make sense of the fact that a former pupil had suddenly material-ized in his kitchen. "Hans Brenner?" He took a tentative step into the room.

His gun went slack in his hands and he glanced at his nephew. "Luther, this is a student of mine—Hans Brenner . . ." He frowned. "But now I think you're *Lieutenant* Hans Brenner?"

"I was at one time, Professor." Hans smiled. "Although I believe the conquerors might dispute that point."

"What are you doing here in my kitchen?" Von Hausen couldn't get his mind to stop reeling, and it didn't help that this man was grinning back at him with such maddening confidence. "How did you get in here . . . ?" His eyes swept the room.

"Back door." Hans jabbed a thumb toward the ceiling, and von Hausen and Luther both looked up and saw the attic access panel slightly askew above their heads. "You might want to check your roof for leaks before the next rainstorm, Professor." Hans grinned from ear to ear and speared a sausage from a plate. "If you could only see your face, my dear Professor!" He took an enormous bite and chewed around his explanation. "My associate kept you entertained while I dropped in for a visit from the cliff behind. Got any water? I'm about as dry as I can be without shriveling up and blowing away, and I could sure use a big drink . . ."

Von Hausen moved toward the washbasin and reached for a pitcher. He poured a glass and placed it on the table near Hans, and then he slid numbly into a chair across from him. "I never thought you'd become entangled in this mess, Hans. Tell me who you represent. Are you here for the Americans or the Soviets?"

"If I told you the Americans would you believe me?"

"Should I believe you?"

Hans grimaced. "I wish you would, although I'm not surprised that you have your doubts."

"What did the Soviets do to you, Hans Brenner, to make you agree to work for them?"

Hans's emptied his glass. "They threatened to harm a friend if I don't convince you to come with me."

"I see." Professor von Hausen studied Hans soberly. "The Soviets are meticulous in their blackmail—and effective, if they can convince a man of your integrity." He smiled sadly at his student, and suddenly his eyes were focused far away, into the past. "We were quite a team, you and I." He absently touched the edge of the table. "Together we could have changed the outcome of this war—"

"Professor," Hans Brenner interrupted, "would you ever consider changing the outcome of the Soviet nuclear program? Would you consider moving with your wife to Russia?"

Von Hausen contemplated Hans's words for several moments, and then he shook his head. "The idea is . . . extremely discomforting, my friend."

Hans fingered his glass. "And are you considering an offer from the Americans?"

Von Hausen stood and paced, his eyes first on his nephew and then on Hans. Finally he answered. "The Americans have offered, yes."

"Would you consider the Soviets as an alternative to working for the Americans?"

Again von Hausen shook his head. "I would have to give the idea some thought."

"It would be advantageous to you to accept."

Von Hausen stopped pacing and frowned at Hans. "What are you implying?"

"Only that the Soviets will be annoyed if you refuse . . ."

Von Hausen understood. "They will try to kill me."

Hans didn't answer, and he averted his eyes to glance out the small window above the washbasin. "I would only suggest that working for the Soviets might be the only healthy option, Professor." He stood abruptly, towering over von Hausen, and studied him carefully. "I need an answer soon—and I don't want to have to come up here and risk getting shot at the back door for my efforts." He glanced once at the attic access and then back down at von Hausen at the table. "I expect you to meet me at the café *La Rochette* in Chamonix by noon tomorrow—and I expect to receive your answer then."

He strode to the kitchen door and faced off Luther until the younger man moved out of the way. He moved through the living room, and von Hausen followed him, wringing his hands. "I hate that this whole business has come between me and a cherished pupil." He sighed. "But that is what war will do to acquaintances, isn't it?"

"Sometimes difficult decisions must be made in spite of past acquaintances, before tragedy makes those decisions for us." Hans's smile was a thing of the past. "Don't you agree?"

Von Hausen nodded sorrowfully, and Hans left, closing the door behind him.

* * *

Hans walked down the steps and across the meadow, holding his back straight as he tried to ignore the fear that before he reached Petka a bullet would be lodged between his shoulder blades. His palms were still sweaty and his legs shook both from the physical exertion that had tormented his once-fit form and from the residual fear of his encounter. He tried to discourage Petka's curiosity with a scowl, but Petka was too inquisitive to notice.

"What happened, Brenner? What did he say?"

"He said he would think about it."

"Think about it?" Petka was incredulous. "You gave him time to *think* about it?"

"Why not?" Hans shrugged. "Von Hausen will perform more satisfactorily for Rostov if he's happy, and I saw no reason to toss him over my shoulder and cart him down this mountainside like a sack of onions." He picked up Petka's rucksack. "Tomorrow in Chamonix your curiosity will be satisfied."

THIRTY-FOUR

When the phone rang, Natalie started, jarred from her reverie by the sound. She swiped the receiver from its hook before her brain could caution her, and then she held it in her hand and stared at it fearfully for several seconds.

She put the receiver to her ear. "Nurse Allred's station . . ." she said weakly.

"Nattie?"

She relaxed when she heard Curly's voice on the other end of the line. "Yes, Curly, it's me."

The connection was bad and he sounded far away and muffled. "For a minute I thought no one was going to answer," he said. "Are you all right?"

"I'm fine." Natalie felt her heart rate beginning to normalize. "It's nice to hear your voice. How are things in Nüremberg?"

"Great."

There was a slight pause, and Natalie wondered if Curly had sensed her previous fear and was confused by it. She asked, "Why are you calling?"

"April sixteenth, Nattie." He cleared his throat. "I called to wish you a happy birthday. I'm really sorry I wasn't able to be there for you today—sometimes things get pretty hectic, y'know. I'm at the mercy of the top brass . . ."

"Don't worry about it."

"I really miss you. I wish I could come this weekend. I'm looking forward to next weekend though. We're going to find that family of yours, right?"

Her conscience nagged her, insisting she tell Curly what she had been meaning to for so long—that after all his kindness, after all of his declarations of lasting love, try as she might she couldn't change the way she felt about Hans Brenner.

Hans was alive—and confirmation of his continued existence was more than enough to send Natalie's thoughts into an emotional turmoil, and that, coupled with Lieutenant Rostov's control, kept her stress level soaring dangerously free of healthy parameters.

"Doing anything special tonight?"

Natalie smiled faintly. "I think Doctor Hayes and his wife are planning something covert."

"Wish I could be there with you."

"Me too, Curly."

There was an awkward pause, and then Curly said, "Well, just thought I'd call and see how you were doing . . ."

"Curly—" Her voice came out a little more frantically than she had meant it to, and she hastily explained, "I need to—tell you something important."

Now Curly's long hesitation worried her. When he finally spoke his voice had an apprehensive edge to it. "Do you want to talk about it now? The rest of the guys are off watching the movie in the mess hall. I could pull up a chair and . . ."

She ached inside. Curly was such a good man and didn't deserve to be treated this way. She squeezed her eyes shut against the hot tears forcing their way toward the surface and clutched her hand into a fist. The phone cord was tangled around her fingers, cutting off the circulation. She took a deep breath. "No, Curly. I—I can't talk about it over the phone." She forced a bright smile into her voice. "But when you come next week I plan to dedicate my entire weekend to you and my missing Aunt Clara. We'll talk then. Agreed?"

Curly told her he loved her and hung up, and Natalie untangled her white-ridged fingers from the phone cord. She watched as blood slowly flowed back into each one, changing the color until all that remained were parallel red lines that looked like the bars of a cage. She shuddered and leaned her head into her hands.

The telephone rang again, and she straightened. She picked up the receiver and heard a female voice she didn't recognize.

"Natalie?" the voice asked in a thickly accented attempt at English.

"Yes?"

"Doctor Hayes said there is a car waiting. Come as quickly as you can."

"Who is this?"

The phone clicked and went silent. Natalie stood and stretched. She wasn't in the mood for a party, but she was grateful for the gesture. Her friends would be there—and Dr. Hayes's wife, who was like a mother to lonely young nurses. More than once Mrs. Hayes had offered Natalie or a fellow nurse a shoulder to cry on. The long hours, foreign surroundings, and devastations of war easily took their toll on soldiers and medical personnel alike.

Natalie retrieved her sweater and headed for the door.

She descended the steps and walked toward the idling Renault. The thickset driver opened her door for her, and she slipped onto the back seat, her mind on Curly's phone call. The car rocked as the driver settled his mass into the front seat. He turned the wheel and pulled away from the curb.

She ached for Curly. She had tried to forget about Hans Brenner, but her determination had dissolved instantly when she'd held that picture in her hand on Christmas Day. She wondered how she was going to tell Curly without breaking his heart. He was one of the best men she knew, and his goodness made her failure doubly deceitful and tragic.

The driver was exceptionally quiet as he drove, and the silence made her nervous. "Do you know the way to Dr. Hayes's residence?" she asked.

The driver nodded mutely.

She leaned her head against the back of the seat and tried to relax. Five minutes and they would be there. Five minutes was all she really needed to catch a few winks . . .

Natalie opened her eyes. The car was motionless and the driver had opened her door. "Are we there?" She squinted into the darkness and saw a familiar figure standing near a once-majestic fountain, its potential reduced by the war to a mere trickle of water only identifiable at this distance through its sound.

"Natalya, please come join me."

She bolted upright, all sleep gone from her brain. Warily she moved toward him, her legs suddenly rubbery.

Viktor Rostov held out his hand, urging her closer. "I apologize that I must detour you from your celebration. But Doctor Hayes might not allow me to attend, and I would dearly like to be included."

"Where am I?"

"In the Soviet Friedrichshain district—don't look so dismayed, Nurse Natalya. You knew someday I'd bring you here."

"Lieutenant Rostov, you're scaring me."

"Please—*Viktor*. I insist." His hand captured her elbow. "Please, Natalya, take a seat." He indicated the low stone wall that surrounded the fountain. "I admit I have never been the best at giving gifts to a woman. I can never seem to get the gift right. But I'm determined to try one last time."

"Viktor," Natalie said weakly, "please don't give me any more gifts."

"I have it right here." He indicated his pocket. "But first, I want to tell you a birthday story—Russians love stories, and I'm going to assume that you do also. Will you sit?"

She twisted her elbow from his hand. "I don't plan to stay."

"You will stay until I permit you to leave." To Rostov there was no question of her compliance. "But I think you will want to hear this story. I will tell you a Russian fairytale. I know all American children love fairytales . . ."

"I'm not a child, Viktor."

"Of course you're not. But you still love fairytales—and since today happens to be your birthday, I have created this fairytale just for you. So, how do they begin? 'Once upon a time?'" He smiled. "Once upon a time there lived a beautiful young maiden named . . ." Viktor paused, scratching his chin. "Perhaps we could give the maiden a name easy to remember—like the name of your mother, Anya."

"Anna. My mother's name is Anna."

"Ah, but to emphasize that this is a *Russian* fairytale—and because your mother would be called 'Anya' in Russian—we will use *Anya*." Viktor continued. "Anya was born in Russia, but she moved to Germany with her parents when she was very young. She was raised as a German citizen, and although her family never returned to Russia, she yearned to someday return to her country of birth.

"She fell in love with a young and handsome Soviet naval officer named Ivan Stepanovich Karagodin, who was the son of the war hero Stepan Karagodin. Anya and Ivan married, left Anya's parents and little sister, and moved to Petrograd, near his naval base on the island of Kronstadt—"

"Viktor, I really don't see the point—"

"But you will, dear Natalya, if you will let me continue." Rostov smiled at her, but for some reason the emotion did not touch his eyes. "In 1921, the Bolsheviks were in control of Russia after two bloody years of civil war. They tried to fairly represent the working class, but after years of civil unrest the working class began to demonstrate against the government in the vicinity of Petrograd. To quell the uprisings, Comrade Lenin placed the entire city under martial law. Kronstadt lies to the west of Petrograd, and Ivan Stepanovich and his comrades of the naval base staged a massive revolt against the Bolsheviks. But the government sent an army to crush the uprising.

"Many sailors died." Rostov's voice was sorrowful. "The sailors had massive stockpiles of artillery and guns on the island, and if only they had waited until the ice melted they might have been successful in fighting off the army's advance. But, as often happens when decisions are made in the heat of the moment instead of after careful planning and preparation, the Bolsheviks eventually succeeded in crossing the ice and crushing the rebellion. The armies of Lenin suffered thousands of casualties, and they exacted their revenge on the sailors. Over five thousand insurgents either died in the fighting or were executed.

"Anya was not allowed to know what was happening with her husband. All she knew was that neither her husband nor the husbands of her friends came home. She had seen the government's army leave the city and march toward the seaport. She had heard the guns and smelled the sickening smoke.

She had seen the casualties brought back to the hospitals loaded on carts, and she had smelled the stench of death. She and her friends had watched and waited, and finally, she had seen the Bolshevik army return victorious.

"She was heavy with child, but she joined the throngs of women who swarmed the prison hoping to hear news of their loved ones. For a long time she heard nothing.

"Finally she and thousands of other desperate family members were informed that the majority of the revolutionaries had been executed. The authorities promised an official list of casualties in the near future. Anya felt Ivan's baby move inside her, and she cried for the dashing young man who had stolen her heart, and who might never hold his child in his arms."

Rostov slowly circled Natalie as he spoke, his eyes studying her like a cat analyzing its prey. "Anya waited. Along with the other women she waited. She heard a hopeful rumor that some of the sailors had survived and had been imprisoned in the bitterly cold, marshy, and far away White Sea island labor camps at Solovki, and for weeks Anya survived on the hope that she was one of the lucky ones who waited. She imagined that because she carried Ivan's baby, Ivan's survival would be a priority with God.

"One month after the rebellion at Kronstadt she gave birth to a little girl, and she gathered the infant into her arms, returned to the prison, and continued to wait. For eight more months she waited. Along with hundreds of women who believed their suffering was important to God, she arrived at the prison each morning to await the official list, and she returned home to her bed each evening, ready to do the same the following day.

"And then one morning when the baby was eight months old, the government finally produced a list of insurgents imprisoned at Solovki. Anya and all of the waiting relatives understood what it would mean if the names of their loved ones were not on that list.

"She anxiously pressed forward, shielding her infant from the crushing, anxious throngs, and searched frantically for the name of her beloved."

At this point in his story, Rostov stopped pacing, and Natalie could feel him close behind her. She didn't move. She felt cold fear creeping up her spine between her shoulder blades. This narrative was more than a fairytale to the Russian lieutenant, she realized, and even though the storyline might be foreign to her, the way Viktor told it made it hauntingly intimate.

"Ivan Stepanovich Karagodin was not on the list." Rostov's voice near her ear held sorrow. "Anya took her baby and walked away. She gathered her things and she did the impossible—she escaped from military-controlled Petrograd. I do not know how she accomplished this without getting caught, and she and her baby executed . . .

"For months she traveled by cart, by train, and by foot, until she had left her husband's country far behind. She returned to her mother and her father and her younger sister in Germany, and there in Berlin . . ." Rostov hesitated, and when he continued, his voice was soft. ". . . She married an American tourist, twenty years her senior, who promised to look after her and her little girl. She said good-bye to her father, her mother, and her sister Clara, and she and her baby Natalya moved with John Allred to America."

Natalie whirled on him then, her eyes blazing at the injustice of his malicious tale, and he smiled sadly at her fury. "It is a heartrending account, I admit," he said. "But truth is not always the fairytale we dream it will be."

"How *dare* you, Viktor." She was trembling. "I will not allow you to paint such a falsehood about me or my mother." She faced him. "I'm the daughter of John and Anna Allred, and I'm an American citizen."

He answered evenly, his face solemn. "Your name is Natalya Ivanovna Karagodina, and your biological father was named Ivan Stepanovich Karagodin. Your mother has been hiding the truth from you—hiding *you* in an attempt to protect you from the consequences of having a traitor for a father." Viktor stepped toward her. "She knew that if your real heritage ever became known, the far-reaching arms of the Kremlin could someday beckon you home—whether you willed it or not.

"And now, for your birthday present, Natalya." Rostov reached inside his uniform jacket and produced an envelope. He handed it to her. "I have held on to your documents long enough. It is time for you to have them back."

She broke the seal and pulled several papers from the envelope, and then she stood silently, staring at the identification papers in her hands. It had been months since her documents had been stolen and Hans Brenner had saved her life. Months since that harsh experience that altered her future forever. Months since Viktor Rostov had abducted Hans and turned Natalie into a puppet on a string. Rostov had promised to return her papers when he was finished with them—and in a way, he had kept his promise. The photograph was the same—she had been so excited to begin her career as an Army nurse, a backwoods American girl ready to travel to strange and enchanting lands, and in the process solve the mystery of a family disappearance. Her anticipation and excitement shone in her dark eyes in the black-and-white photo—but this was not the military ID she remembered.

Horrified, she held it away from her body as if it were a venomous snake. "What did you do to my documents, Viktor Rostov?" Her voice rose, fear and indignation making temperance impossible. "What makes you think you have the right to mutilate United States Army property?"

"It is not destroyed, Natalya—only corrected. If you will notice, it now properly lists your place of birth as 'Petrograd, USSR.'"

"No!" She panicked. "You're fabricating this story to manipulate me. How could you know so much about me or my parents?"

Rostov replied calmly. "You named your first puppy *Crawdad*—because once he terrorized a crawdad until it attached itself to his nose."

Natalie stared at him, speechless.

Rostov continued. "You hate broccoli and love Brussels sprouts. You've been an avid artist since you were three years old. You play piano with the skill of Rubinstein and the melancholy of Rachmaninoff. You helped your father break a rogue stallion one summer, and you traveled with your mother to see the world's fair in Chicago when you were twelve years old—I believe you were there on opening day, May 27. Your first boyfriend was named Joseph, and—"

"*Stop,* Viktor, please stop." She swallowed with difficulty. "How can you know those things about me?"

Viktor shrugged. "All it takes is an order to an associate in Sioux Falls, requesting that he make a friendly visit to your lonely mother. Of course Anya Karagodina Allred would brag of her only daughter to a potential neighbor who has considered purchasing the abandoned farmhouse down the street and who wants to become acquainted with his new neighbors. I'm sure you can see how it works."

Natalie gripped the documents in front of her with both hands. "Why are you doing this to me? What more do you want from me?"

Rostov removed his visor cap and scratched his head. "I admit I don't know yet, Natalya. Soviet law says I must immediately repatriate you—but my heart tells me to give Lieutenant Brenner a chance to prove himself first." He indicated the papers in her hands. "These papers correctly declare you to be a Soviet citizen, subject to all immigration and repatriation laws decided upon by the world powers at last year's conference at Yalta. And that means I have an obligation to keep you here with me in the Soviet sector."

"Viktor, no . . ." Distressed, she tried unsuccessfully to give him back the documents. "I'm an American. Ask my commanding officers . . ."

"It makes no difference. You were born in Russia and are first and foremost a Soviet citizen. Your Russian birth automatically places the Soviet Union in control of your future."

"Please, Viktor, please take me back to the hospital."

He said nothing for several moments, and Natalie felt what she thought a captured soldier must experience as he waited to find out if he would live or die. She felt rooted to one spot, standing here in a nightmare as she pleaded with the author of her fate.

"I'll take you back, Natalya Ivanovna—but only because Hans continues to have success on his mission." Rostov did not smile. "And as soon as you open your mouth—to Captain Miller or the American military or anyone else—I will demand that you be released immediately to Soviet authorities as the American government has agreed."

Viktor gently touched her hair, tilting his head to one side as he contemplated her. "Perhaps Lieutenant Brenner loves you enough to fulfill his obligation to me—and if that is the case, your continued silence now means I'll be free to return you to him." He twisted a strand of her hair around one long finger. "But be advised, my beautiful Natalya—if he does not do all I require, then I will immediately come for you. And if you ever return to the Russian zone, you will never again leave my custody."

* * *

The silent driver delivered Natalie to the steps of Dr. Hayes's residence. Natalie stood on the steps and stared numbly after the retreating vehicle. Her hands felt clammy and wet, as if she had just cleaned a fish. She thought about Rostov's story, and the giant claw around her lungs began again to tighten.

It couldn't be true.

Natalya Ivanovna Karagodina. Her mother was Anya Karagodina, and her father was . . . was . . . a *Russian?*

She soundlessly mouthed the name Lieutenant Rostov had given her newly discovered Russian father: *Ivan Stepanovich Karagodin. Russian naval officer and . . . traitor.*

Sounds of laughter and Perry Como albums drifted in waves through an open window and into the peaceful night air, and Natalie sank to the steps and buried her face in her arms.

Mrs. Hayes found her there and called for her husband.

"What is it, Natalie? Are you ill?"

Natalie tried to wave her off. "I'm all right. I just want to go home . . ." In reality she felt like vomiting all over Mrs. Hayes's polished patent-leather shoes.

"But you just arrived, Natalie! Why were you late? Can I get you anything to drink?" Mrs. Hayes hovered solicitously, but Natalie shook her head.

"Oh, what a tragedy!" Mrs. Hayes lamented. "Missing your own birthday party!"

"I'm sure it's wonderful. Thank you, Mrs. Hayes, for your kindness." She struggled to rise. "I wish there was some way I could stay and enjoy it."

"Never you mind, dear." Mrs. Hayes helped her husband pull Natalie to her feet. "You just get yourself feeling better and I'll have Ronald bring you a nice big slice of your birthday cake in the morning."

The thought of her birth and its newfound implications made bile rise dangerously to the surface, and Natalie had to lean over Mrs. Hayes's rose-bushes.

"Oh, my goodness." Mrs. Hayes was mildly taken aback. "My dear, is there any chance you might be pregnant?"

"Gertrude!" Dr. Hayes reprimanded his wife.

Natalie denied the suggestion vehemently.

Mrs. Hayes patted Natalie's back reassuringly. "Don't worry, my dear. If you *are,* and you need someone in whom to confide, you just let me know." She gave Natalie a conspiratorial smile.

Dr. Hayes distracted his wife. "Gertrude, go get Sergeant Patrick and tell him to bring my car and drive Natalie back to the hospital."

Mrs. Hayes left, and Natalie clutched at her supervisor's arm. "Dr. Hayes, is there any chance I could be transferred?"

"Transferred?" He was surprised. "Where?"

She swallowed hard. "I don't care—just somewhere away from here—away from Berlin. Soon, if possible . . ."

Dr. Hayes brows knit. "How soon?"

"Tomorrow?" She winced. She knew it sounded silly.

Hayes stared at her. "Natalie, what's wrong?"

"I don't know." She clung to his arm for support. "I just think it would be best . . ."

He tried to steady her with his hands on her shoulders. "My dear Natalie, there's nothing to worry about. Every nurse feels inadequate once in a while, or lonely, or depressed—it's normal. You'll feel better after a long rest and a day off."

She desperately wanted to tell him about Lieutenant Rostov's threats, and of this new horror that she might actually be subject to a fatal agreement penned by her own government, placing her at the mercy of a man who held her life precariously in his hands. But she thought about Hans Brenner's predicament and kept silent.

She saw the reflection of headlights off neighboring buildings, and Dr. Hayes's car rounded the corner of his home. Hayes gave her a comforting smile. "Go home, Nurse Natalie, and rest." He steered her toward the idling vehicle. "We *need* you here in Berlin. You're an excellent nurse, and we cannot do without you. Take tomorrow off and then we'll talk about all those hours of leave you've been accumulating. I think it's about time you use them."

She mumbled, "Thank you, Dr. Hayes," and slipped into the back seat.

Dr. Hayes bent to look in at her. "Oh, and I guess this is not the best time to say it, but 'happy birthday' all the same."

Sergeant Patrick dropped her off at the hospital, and she made a beeline for the phone in the nurses' station. She called the officers' barracks in Nüremberg and pleaded with the staff duty officer to let her speak with Curly.

"It's the middle of the night," he complained.

"I promise it's important or I wouldn't be calling. I really need to speak with Captain Miller."

"You'd better be his sweetheart or he's gonna have me court-martialed."

Five minutes later Curly's sleepy voice was on the line. "Natalie? Is that you?"

"Curly, I need you to come get me." She swallowed. "Dr. Hayes said I could have some time off, and I need you to fly to Berlin and take me back with you to Nüremberg—"

"Wait a sec, Nattie, slow down." Curly was beginning to wake up. "What's this all about?"

"Come and get me, please, Curly." Natalie could feel the cold fear of her predicament pounding at the base of her throat. She tried to swallow around a lump that was threatening to suffocate her. "I'm in trouble, and I need you to help me."

"Before next weekend?"

"Tomorrow. Please, Curly, I—I can't explain right now, but if you don't come . . ." She let out a sob. Rostov's warnings echoed in her mind, and somewhere Hans was working to keep her safe from harm. She knew she had to find the courage to do the same for him.

"What's wrong, Natalie? Did something happen at the party?"

"No." Natalie hugged the phone receiver to her ear, hunching over it and trying to stop her tears. Her whole body trembled and she could hardly speak. Finally she whispered, "I think my life is in danger."

"What's that, Nattie? I can't hear you very well—this is such a bad connection."

She cleared her throat and reconsidered her response. Raising her voice she said, "I need your help, Curly. Please come and get me."

"All right." There was a pause, and Natalie could imagine the metal gears turning as Curly rethought his flight schedule. "Gregory's got a four-thirty going into Berlin on Friday afternoon—I could hitch a ride and the two of us could be at the hospital that night. I think that's the soonest I could come—"

"That's perfect, Curly." She was relieved. Even though she dreaded passing another three days in constant terror of Rostov's reappearance, the fact that Curly was coming to get her soothed the edges of her fright and made another seventy-two hours of jeopardy seem almost bearable.

THIRTY-FIVE

April 17, 1946

From Auvergne in the west to the borders of Switzerland and Italy, the Rhône-Alpes region of France boasts some of the finest scenery and most rugged mountain ranges in Western Europe. On the northern part of the region, Mont Blanc carries the distinction of being the highest mountain peak in the Alps, an honor the French reluctantly share with Italy and Switzerland, as the nationality of Mont Blanc's summit continues to be a matter of debate. "*La Dame Blanche,*" as she is lovingly nicknamed on the French side, and "*Monte Bianco*" on the Italian, the mountain divides the Aosta Valley in Italy from the Haute-Savoie in France.

But at the northwest base of the wintry Mont Blanc—and unquestionably in France—lies the small town of Chamonix-Mont-Blanc. The Chamonix valley attracts the curious attention of international tourists visiting the region for the Rhône-Alpes' marvelous winter sports. But Hans Brenner was not here for the attractions. In fact, he could think of a hundred places he would rather be at the moment besides sitting in the café *La Rochette* on a too-tiny chair next to a Paris-style table, dressed in a heavy wool coat and ski cap, ski boots, and thick wool slacks. His skis leaned against the table beside him, and he held between his hands a steaming mug. At least in this guise he didn't have to worry about attracting attention. The day was clear and crisp and the powder new, packing just enough to make the slopes interesting, and so like flies to marmalade the sports enthusiasts were coming, flocking to Chamonix's several slopes with their skis, their children, their girlfriends, and their money. The franc had devalued yet again, but this particular economic backlash of the war hadn't slowed the tourists, and Hans felt secure. He could sit here all day, watching the undulating throngs, and no one would think him anything but a tourist.

Hans sipped his drink and watched the woman with silver-blond hair walk by with several other women. The lively group paused near the café, the outdoor tables filled to overflowing with vacationers enjoying a traditional French continental breakfast before heading to the slopes. These women were also decked out for a day in the snow, with their skis over their shoulders and their faux fur hats off so that their stylish curls bounced and shone in the sun. One woman turned and caught Hans's eye, and she smiled coyly. Hans looked away, uninterested.

He briefly made eye contact with his Russian comrade on the other side of the street, his back against a wall and a newspaper in his hands. Petka Vasilev continued reading his paper, and Hans moved his attention again to the milling throng on the street.

As the minutes passed, Hans thought about what he would like to do to Lieutenant Rostov for placing him in this situation. He realized he was not a prisoner. He could stand up right now, set his cup down on the table, and deliberately walk away. And with his background it would require very little effort to lose the silver-haired woman and the other Russian operatives Rostov had sent to assist him. But Natalie would not get away so easily, he knew, and that was what kept him here. Rostov had said her safety depended upon his success today, and Hans believed him.

The plan was simple, really: von Hausen would make his appearance in this public place, and when he sat at this table to talk to Hans, he would be immediately spirited away by Petka, his icy female companion, and unidentified Soviet mercenaries milling incognito through the crowd.

Hans Brenner took another sip from his mug and again searched his surroundings. As he did so he caught sight of something that made his heart flail against his ribs. Slowly he set down his mug. Between one breath and the next, his simple plan had suddenly become extremely complicated.

He studied the large black Citroën parked a block down the street, trying not to look overly curious. Inside sat a driver who looked inescapably American, and even from this distance the young man looked terrified.

That young American driver was probably no coward, Hans thought. The boy probably sensed there would be a confrontation on this picturesque street within the next few minutes, and people would get hurt. Secret as Hans had thought his meeting with von Hausen would be, it seemed the Americans had discovered his plans and had arrived to thwart the seemingly simple abduction of the German scientist Edwin von Hausen.

Neither the Soviets nor the Americans were going to run the risk of letting von Hausen make the wrong choice. Hans's instructions were simple: deliver von Hausen. Whether that meant obstructing the Americans or killing von Hausen, it didn't matter to Lieutenant Rostov. Hans and Petka were under strict orders to either bring von Hausen in or dispose of him, and so even with this new wrinkle to the plan, von Hausen's choice was quite simple: his future was in Moscow. And Natalie's future was, at this moment, precariously in Hans Brenner's hands.

Suddenly Hans stilled, his hand motionless on the tablecloth and his eyes riveted on the tall man walking past him. For a moment he was transported back in time to his childhood, when he would go skiing in the Black Forest with his best friend beside him. At any other time he would have been pleased to remember, to have a passing figure remind him of his close friend and brother Rolf Schulmann—but not today.

Hans's breath came back in shallow bursts, but his insides tied themselves into knots and made him strangely ill. There were very few things that could disconcert him, and even fewer things that could make him so frightened that his body almost ceased to function. But sitting here and knowing that in the next few minutes he might very well be impelled to kill Rolf would definitely qualify as one of those things.

His hand shook on the tablecloth, and he couldn't pull his eyes away in time to keep from locking eyes with Rolf when the latter turned and saw him. In that fraction of a second Hans noted a similar whirlwind of emotion in Rolf's eyes: recognition, alarm, disbelief, and, finally, horror at the unspeakable implications. Hans saw his friend's step falter. Only once before had Hans seen Rolf waver, and that was during the war when a diabolical Gestapo officer had claimed that Marie Jacobson was dead. But Hans didn't have time to dwell on the memory. He knew he had only a few minutes to try to work out a solution that would not culminate in complete catastrophe. Von Hausen was due to arrive any minute.

When Rolf broke eye contact and continued down the street, Hans knew his friend was also trying to find a solution. It didn't matter, for the moment, how this awful circumstance had come about. The only thing that mattered was figuring out how both of them could survive—and keep their loved ones safe.

How could he be successful without consequently destroying Rolf, and therefore also Alma and Marie? What stroke of bad fortune, coincidence, or providence had so cruelly intervened to pit him against the people he cared about? Not only was it morally wrong that he should have to choose between Rolf and Natalie, it was physically impossible! If he chose to complete this mission he would save Natalie's life but Rolf would likely die. And yet if he allowed Rolf to go free, the Soviets would have no possible chance of securing the professor, and Natalie's life would be forfeit. It didn't even factor into the equation that Natalie would never be his; he realized he would still do anything for her.

Quickly Hans glanced at Petka and was relieved to see that the man hadn't noticed the exchange. Petka was not the brightest of fellows, and he most likely didn't suspect that the Americans were here.

Suddenly the man who was the focus of this morning's escalating insanity appeared in a doorway across the street. Edwin von Hausen hesitated and then stepped into the sunshine, crossed the street, and moved toward the café. But Rolf intercepted him, making Hans's worst nightmare a reality.

For just a moment Hans watched as Rolf put his arm around the man's shoulders and steered him toward the car, his manner both carefully courteous and urgent. Hans wished he could identify Petka's hidden companions so he could distract them long enough to let Rolf get away . . . and maybe even get away himself so he could go warn Natalie. Desperately he scanned the crowd.

Time was running out. Rolf was approaching the car, and if Hans didn't move to stop him in the next few seconds, Petka would do it for him. Hans closed his eyes and took a deep breath, and when he opened his eyes, he knew what to do.

Hans stood, but he didn't move toward Rolf and the professor. Ignoring Petka's rising concern, Hans took one step toward the silver-blond skier—the same woman who had shadowed him in Berlin. Pulling the Nagant revolver from beneath his coat, he threw an arm around her neck. She let out a surprised squeak and clawed at his arm and tried to jab at his eyes, her shrieks panic-stricken but her movements deliberate and professional. Hans dug the revolver into her fur-lined throat and spoke one command in Russian. *"Nilzya."* Don't.

The gun convinced her, and she went still against his chest. Petka dropped the paper and produced his own gun, and now Hans could see two other men dressed as skiers reaching underneath their jackets. He kept all three in sight as he moved to the middle of the street. His captive didn't impede his progress as he advanced, and as the surrounding tourists realized all was suddenly not right in Chamonix, they began to panic, fleeing from Hans as though he had waved the gun at them.

Hans's heart pounded against his chest as if it were trying to escape along with Chamonix's visitors. At the car Rolf turned and glanced at Hans for a fleeting second, and Hans mouthed, *"Schnell!"* Hurry!

Rolf lunged for the car, pulling the frightened professor with him. He flung the door open and practically threw the frail man inside, but then he hesitated just a moment. He looked again at Hans standing in the middle of the street with his hostage, and then he followed the professor into the car and closed the door.

The woman in Hans's grip began to whimper, babble, and plead, her almost indecipherable jumble of French, Russian, and dreadful English making it easier to ignore the terror in her voice. Hans jabbed the revolver into her throat and ordered her to be quiet.

Rolf was safe, but now Hans had a whole new set of enemies. He could release the woman and surrender, but he didn't imagine Petka and his men would even consider preserving his life, and if they gunned him down now, Natalie would disappear. His hand on the gun trembled dangerously, and he found himself silently wishing he still had the confidence he'd had as a Gebirgsjäger lieutenant during the war. He had faced death bravely then, he realized, with nothing more than a thought for his own safety. But this was different. Fear for his own life was not the principal reason for his anxiety, and he wondered if the determination he now felt was what Rolf had meant once when he said he'd be willing to do anything to protect the woman he loved.

Hans saw on Petka's face a contortion of fury and determination that convinced Hans that this woman was uncommonly significant to the Russian. The two nameless mercenaries separated, trying to move in around Hans, and he had the fleeting, ironic thought that this standoff reminded him of a scene from some old American western, where the bad guys and the good guys had their inevitable showdown in the middle of Dodge City, Tombstone, or whatever other sweltering American street with a saloon, a hitching post, and a distressed woman or two.

Against his chest the woman went completely still, as if she, too, realized that a showdown was inevitable. Hans dragged his hostage with him as he tried to keep the Soviets from flanking him. His leg hit a hastily vacated chair at the edge of the street, and he continued to negotiate his way backward, blindly struggling through the assortment of tables and overturned chairs, abandoned breakfasts and forgotten skis. He could either retreat inside the café and be trapped, or he could remove the gun from the woman's neck and begin firing, hoping that the woman wouldn't immediately produce her own weapon and finish him off at point-blank range. Either choice seemed a certain disaster. He wondered what Rolf would do in his position.

His prisoner whispered in French, "Let me go and I'll hold them off while you escape. I have a gun."

"Show it to me."

She produced it, and Hans wrestled it from her grip and tossed it into a snowbank.

"You don't trust me," she whimpered.

"Of course not," Hans growled. "Be quiet." He kept his eyes glued on Petka and the two Russians. "Speak again and I'll have no choice but to—"

He never finished. Before he could conclude his threat he heard several shots fired in quick succession, originating from various points of the compass, and he used the ensuing panic to drag his hostage into the café behind him, sending the terrified garçon scurrying for cover. Several more shots followed, and Hans felt a violent tug at the flesh of his upper arm as he dove for the floor, pulling the woman with him.

* * *

The Citroën pulled rapidly away with Rolf and the professor inside, and Rolf watched anxiously as they passed his friend on the street. Professor von Hausen began to moan, his eyes wide and scared like those of a hunted rabbit.

"Keep your head down, Professor." Again Rolf looked through the rear window at Hans. Rolf's head still reeled from the suddenness of the morning's events and the shock he'd felt at seeing his friend here.

From a side street another car joined theirs, carrying Sergeant Edward Finley and several mercenaries from the assault. He glanced one more time through the rear window as both vehicles turned the corner and the drama unfolding in the center of the village was hidden from his view. He ached for Hans and wondered what could have possessed his friend to assist the Soviets. There were many things Rolf didn't know about his friend, he realized. The war had separated them and now he was seeing the results of that separation. Why couldn't Hans have confided in him?

Suddenly Rolf had a terrible thought. What if Hans hadn't had a chance? Rolf's hands clenched into fists. "Stop the car."

"I beg your pardon?" The driver glanced at him in the rearview mirror.

"I said stop the car."

The driver applied the brakes, still dubious. "But, sir, the major said we were to bring the scientist back without any delay—"

"Matthews won't mind." Rolf clenched his teeth.

The Renault pulled to a stop near the side of the road, and Rolf leaped from the back seat, then strode purposefully toward the second car in line. It too pulled to a stop, and from the windows the men inside stared at him, genuinely surprised. Rolf wrenched open the back door. "Give me a weapon."

Sergeant Finley drawled, "Well, I don't know about that, Major Schulmann—"

"All right, then, bring your weapon and come with me."

"We've got our orders, and they don't include—"

Rolf reached into the back seat and hauled Finley to his feet. "Either give me a weapon or come with me now. Lieutenant Rostov's men are here, and if we capture any of them they can lead us to Rostov. I'm not sure Major Matthews would forgive us if we didn't try this while we had the chance."

"Over my dead body," Finley responded conversationally, and he straightened his jacket. "You've got your orders, and you will follow them."

Several other men had climbed from the car to watch the unexpected confrontation.

Finley stretched to look Rolf in the eye. "You're a Nazi criminal, Rolf Schulmann, and we don't take orders from a Nazi. Get back in your car."

Rolf didn't budge. "I don't have time to argue with you, Sergeant. We need to return to Chamonix right now, or we'll lose our chance—"

"So what's your plan, Schulmann?" Support came in the unexpected form of one of Finley's men. Sergeant Finley turned to glower at the man.

Rolf glanced back down the road. "I've got to go back. I'll take two of you with me—since your commanding officer won't trust me with a weapon." He gestured to the right, his hand taking in the mountains and the other side of the village. "The rest of you will cut off any attempt to escape into Italy."

The man nodded. "What about von Hausen? There's a chance the Reds will realize he's still in the vicinity."

"Then we'd better not fail—and we'd better hurry."

Rolf sprinted back down the road. The heels of his feet throbbed where the soles had been worn away by his long march from Sachsenhausen, but other than that, he felt closer to his normal self than he had in over a year. He was worried that it might already be too late, that Hans might already be lying wounded or dead on the city street, but he brushed the disturbing thought aside and focused on the task at hand.

* * *

"Let me go!"

In the dubious protection of the café, the silver-haired woman struggled like an angry tiger, pummeling Hans and shrieking hysterically. Hans pressed her face into the floor and tried to reason with her. "Everybody's shooting, mademoiselle—if I release you now, they'll shoot you as soon as you step through that doorway."

She stilled. Hans took aim at the doorway and waited, his heart beating wildly against his ribcage. The hostage huddled next to him, struggling to breathe around his viselike grip on her throat. She began to sob quietly. She murmured something about this being a simple assignment and laughed crazily to herself, the sound muffled against the floor. Hans was tired of telling her to be quiet, so he ignored her.

He glanced behind him at the proprietor, who cowered on the floor behind the counter. "Where's the back door?"

"It's blocked by the new snow, monsieur—"

"Any back window?"

"No, monsieur." The man looked like he would be sick.

Hans peered out of the café but was unable to see anything more than overturned chairs, empty road, and mountains behind. There was nobody in sight. He glanced down at the woman at his side, thoughtful.

"Mademoiselle, do you still want to help me?"

Suddenly mute, she nodded against the floor.

Hans turned to the man in the corner. "Do you have a gun?"

The man hesitated, and then nodded. "*Oui,* monsieur."

"Give it to me."

From behind the counter the man obeyed, sliding an ancient Beretta across the floor to Hans.

Hans checked to make sure it was loaded and then turned back to the woman. "Call to your comrades and tell them I'm coming out. Tell them I want to surrender."

The woman stared at him, and then at the doorway. Hans could feel thick warmth coursing down his arm, and he realized he was bleeding badly. He felt light-headed and tried not to think about the possibility of losing consciousness. He knew if that happened he would never wake up. "Go on."

"What if I refuse?"

Apparently the thought of freedom made her foolhardy. "I could keep you here indefinitely, mademoiselle. I have as much enthusiasm as your Russian friends, and I have a greater will to live—believe me." Hans hated to treat a woman like this, but he had the fleeting impression that this woman was one of the most dangerous players in this game. The room was beginning to spin around him, and he had to fight to make his eyes focus.

"All right."

The voice sounded distant, as if she were speaking to him from the other side of the street. Hans loosened his hold on her neck and she raised her head to watch him. She saw his arm, and the look in her eyes said she realized his predicament.

He removed the ammunition from his original gun and handed her the empty Nagant. "Tell them I gave you my gun and I'm ready to surrender." Hans spoke with difficulty around his tongue, which refused to get out of the way. "Tell them I'm unarmed and wounded." A little truth wouldn't hurt the deception.

He held the Frenchman's gun steady. "If you have to speak in Russian, speak slowly, so I can understand."

The woman nodded and turned to look outside. She called out her message loudly and slowly, and Hans Brenner listened carefully to her words. She turned back to Hans for further instructions.

"Tell them you're coming out. Tell them to come get me. Tell them . . . I can't walk out on my own." The room spun lazily around his words, and his throat felt thick. "Hurry."

She rose shakily to her feet, toting the useless gun.

A Western, starring John Wayne. Somehow Hans had gotten himself hurled right into the middle of the filming of an American cowboy movie, and it wasn't turning out to be the one where he survived. He thought crazily about Natalie. *What in the world was going to happen to Natalie?*

His former hostage said something unintelligible through the fog of his brain, laughed, and then disappeared. Hans readied his weapon as best he could, rising up on his elbows and focusing on the doorway's drifting rectangle of fuzzy light. He vowed he would get one good shot before the darkness overtook him, and he focused his waning attention on making sure it was the best one he'd ever taken.

He watched the sunlit doorway, blinked back tears, and thought again about Natalie, and he marveled that he was dying for a woman who never would have been his anyway. The gun slipped gently from his hand, and his last thought as the tall, contorted shadow blocked the rectangle of light and he drifted into complete blackness was that he wished he and Natalie had had a chance at eternity.

THIRTY-SIX

Once they had safely landed at Rhein-Main Military Air Base near Frankfurt, Rolf shook von Hausen's hand and left the German scientist safely ensconced in the Halifax with his military escort for the second leg of his journey to England.

Major Matthews met him on the tarmac. "Congratulations, Schulmann, on a job well done. You've solidified my good opinion of you and won yourself the gratitude of the United States."

"This is as far as I go, Major."

Mathews was surprised. "I need you to escort the professor to England."

"I can't go." Rolf shook his head. "A friend of mine is in trouble, and I need to return to France immediately." He walked with Matthews away from the plane. "Seems the Soviets got to my friend Hans Brenner, and I need to find out why."

Matthews glanced at him thoughtfully. "Will you tell me about it?"

"Hans has been my best friend since childhood. During the war he saved my life, and the lives of my son and my fiancée—Marie Jacobson." Rolf's eyes misted. "Hans is the one who found me half dead outside Berlin, and now he's entangled with the Russians in a way that pitted him against me at Chamonix." He paused. "When we saw each other there I knew we were both in trouble—Hans is one of the best men I know, but he is also one of the most ruthless, effective hunters you'll ever meet." He smiled faintly. "I'd never hold out any hope of success in a contest against him."

"What happened when you met him at Chamonix?" Major Matthews's expression betrayed his growing interest in the subject of Lieutenant Hans Brenner.

"He created a diversion, allowing me to take von Hausen and escape."

Matthews turned to examine Rolf thoughtfully. "Thus saving a close friend, but endangering his own life."

Rolf nodded. "He sacrificed his own success to defer to me." Rolf hesitated.

"So, since you've probably heard from Sergeant Finley by now about my little detour, yes, I disobeyed both you and Finley and returned to Chamonix. I was worried about my friend becoming bait for a pack of hungry wolves."

"You mean you know how to think on your feet." Matthews smiled dryly. "Forget about Finley. The prisoners you brought me might bring me one step closer to understanding the bizarre mindset of Lieutenant Rostov."

Behind him the Halifax coughed and sputtered. Rolf said thoughtfully, "Sir, I knew the Soviets must have found a way to manipulate Hans. Besides being a deadly operative, he happens to be a decent man—and one of the most loyal friends I've ever had. Believe me, he has no love for the Communists."

Matthews gave Rolf a faint smile. "I'm always interested in the methods the Soviets use to manipulate their victims." He deliberated for a moment and then continued. "I'm intrigued by this friend of yours, Mr. Schulmann, and someday I'd like to have an opportunity to meet him. Go help your friend, and let me know if there's anything I can do to assist either you or him. I'm assuming you'll be attending to that other matter you discussed with me?"

Rolf nodded. "That is, if the Americans have decided to allow me to go free . . ."

"You are an honorable man, Mr. Schulmann. You have the makings of a leader." Matthews extended his hand and Rolf took it. They shook hands firmly. "And if things get resolved in France, I'd like to discuss with you a plan that I've been formulating ever since I first had the privilege to meet you."

* * *

Lieutenant Viktor Rostov carefully hung up the phone and stared at the photographs on his desk. His son, Sasha, gazed soberly back at him from the first photo, dressed in his combat uniform, with a rifle in his hands and the ruins of Stalingrad behind him. Viktor felt the familiar surge of pride— his son was the Soviet hero Viktor always knew he would be, and even though his body lay buried in an unmarked grave near the city of his courage, Viktor knew his son's deeds would never be forgotten. Perhaps the heroism of a son would exonerate a father . . . and a sister, Viktor thought as his hand gently touched the picture of his Lucya.

She was all Rostov had left, and the German criminal Hans Brenner had betrayed him. And now, even though it would hurt him dreadfully, Viktor had to keep his promise.

Stalin would not harm his Lucya—Viktor had faith in the humanity of his glorious leader.

But when he reached again for the telephone, he couldn't keep his hand from shaking.

THIRTY-SEVEN

April 18, 1946

Hans Brenner felt the pressure on his arm and lashed out viciously, swiping the anonymous hand away and reaching for his weapon. It irked him terribly that somebody would try to wake him when he had been enjoying the most relaxing sleep he'd had in months.

But Hans couldn't find his gun. Thoroughly annoyed, he opened his eyes and saw Rolf grinning down at him.

"That's the third time you've tried to deck me, Hans Brenner."

Hans felt groggy and disoriented. By way of greeting he growled, "What'd you do with my Beretta?"

Rolf laughed. "Is that what all the violence is about?" Rolf sat down in a chair next to the bed. "I took it from you in Chamonix. What did you expect? Do you think I'm going to let you have a gun when you're acting like this?"

The fog began to clear from Hans's brain, and he stared at his friend as if he hadn't seen him in decades. Rolf gestured toward Hans's arm. "I took the liberty of getting a doctor for you. That arm took a bullet, but it tore straight through—even though you lost a lot of blood, it didn't cause too much damage. The doctor cleaned the wound, gave you antibiotics and a transfusion, and sewed you up. He said you should be feeling better in a day or two."

Hans reached out his hand and touched Rolf's shirt to make sure his friend's presence wasn't just another dream. "You're healed," he said in wonder.

Rolf nodded. "Thanks to Marie—and you, Hans, for getting her to me."

"It wasn't me."

"Natalie, then," Rolf corrected himself. "Thanks to her for sending a letter to Marie."

Suddenly Hans remembered. He sat up rapidly, fear washing over him like a tidal wave, but that wave was immediately followed by one of nausea, and he fell back onto the pillow. "Where are we?"

"My villa, St. Victor-sur-Loire."

Hans paled. "How long ago was Chamonix? And how did you—?"

"You didn't think I'd leave you to battle it out alone, did you?" Rolf's brow furrowed, as if he couldn't understand what Hans could possibly have been doing with the Soviets in the Rhône-Alpes. "We captured your Russian comrades, by the way."

Hans realized he was also curious about Rolf's involvement in the escapade, but Natalie's safety was foremost in his mind at the moment. "I need to leave—get back to Berlin . . ."

"Hans, you passed out up there. The tourist you terrified half to death said you threatened to kill her."

"I feel fine," Hans lied. "And that's not true—I never threatened to kill her. And she's definitely not a tourist."

Rolf frowned as he absorbed Hans's revelation. "You're not that strong, Hans. And if you're right and that woman is working for the Soviets, you're going to be in a lot of trouble with your employers when you get back to Berlin." Rolf took a deep breath. "If you leave now you're committing suicide, Hans. Please reconsider."

"Rolf—how long ago?"

"Yesterday."

Hans shot from underneath the covers, and the room immediately turned upside down. He steadied himself against the bedpost and then began searching frantically for his boots.

Rolf watched him for a few moments, concerned, but then he produced Hans's clothing from the armoire and laid it on the bed. "You're making a mistake working for the Communists." He said it carefully as he retrieved his friend's boots.

Hans ached inside but didn't explain. He grabbed for his shirt.

"Where have you been all these months, Hans? We've been worried sick about you."

Hans pushed his arm into his sleeve. "Last time I saw you, you were a major war criminal, Rolf. So working for the Americans absolved you of any wrongdoings, I guess."

"Not all."

As he buttoned his shirt Hans asked pensively, "You and Marie married?"

Rolf shook his head, and Hans saw the pain in his eyes. "There have been a few—complications," Rolf said slowly. "Setbacks. I've had to face up to a few wrong choices, and they're affecting my family's future rather dramatically."

Hans looked soberly at Rolf, and then he returned to pulling on his boots. "I'm sorry for you, my friend. But I guess God has something in mind to help you, doesn't He?"

"I hope so." Rolf retrieved Hans's coat from a hook and handed it to him. "He can help you, too—if you let Him."

Hans glanced up at Rolf and then back down to his boots. "I wish He would."

"Anything I can do to make you stay?"

"Not this time."

"What's going on, Hans?"

Hans hesitated, staring painfully at Rolf. Since they were children he and Rolf had shared everything: their games, their girlfriends, their school-work, their dreams . . . *Everything.* "Natalie is in danger."

"Nurse Natalie?" Rolf's eyes widened. "Why would she be in danger?"

Hans sighed. "The Soviets are using her to get to me, and my failure at Chamonix places her life in danger."

Rolf frowned. "You're going to try to reach her before they find out—"

"I think it's too late for that." Hans stood. "But I'm going to try to reach her before they do."

"You'll make it."

"How can you be so sure?"

Rolf shrugged. "You're a good man, Hans Brenner, and God is looking out for you—and for Natalie."

"I hope so." Hans hesitated. "Thanks for getting me out of there, Rolf. Seems you and I keep running into each other . . . saving each other's lives . . . ."

"That's the way it is supposed to be, Hans, and you know it. Don't start withdrawing your friendship now just because we might be working on opposite sides of a foolish arms struggle."

There. Rolf had voiced the fear that both of them had been holding inside—that their lives were heading down separate roads and their friend-ship was unraveling because of it.

"Rolf, I really have to go."

"I'm coming with you." Rolf reached for his jacket. "You need me right now."

"No, I don't," Hans disagreed. "You've been keeping Marie waiting too long, and I'm not about to let you get into any more trouble."

"Believe me, it's no trouble, Hans. I want to help you."

Hans's eyes smoldered and he folded his arms defiantly. "Do you realize how long I looked for you before I found your half-dead corpse on the road to Berlin? Do you realize how irritated I'm going to be if you go and get yourself killed after all you've put me through? No way are you coming with me, Rolf. I'm as stubborn as you are, and I say no."

Rolf smiled faintly. "How are you going to make it to Berlin?"

"I'll find a way." Suddenly Hans was not so confident. Yes, he could find a way back into Allied Berlin, but even with a good automobile and a miraculous absence of military checkpoints en route, Berlin was a grueling journey from Rolf's villa, and Rostov would have vented his frustration on Natalie long before Hans found his way back to the hospital.

"Have you considered flying?"

Hans guffawed. "Yes, Rolf, I have a private *Fieseler Storch* waiting for me in the courtyard—didn't you see it there? And if that doesn't get me there fast enough, maybe I'll just spread my arms and jump from your roof."

Rolf smiled good-naturedly. "The *Fieseler* was one of Hitler's most reliable aircraft, but I actually had in mind an American *Dauntless,* which happens to be on standby at the St. Étienne airfield—that is, if you're interested in flying in an *airplane.* But if you're determined to flap your arms . . ." Rolf retrieved his own jacket from a hook and walked toward the door.

Hans grinned. "Someday I'm going to have you explain to me how you go from being a Nazi war criminal to commanding a position of authority in the United States Army." Hans pulled on his jacket. "And I demand to know how your employers knew what the Russians had planned. How'd you discover—"

"Where von Hausen would be yesterday morning?" Rolf grinned.

Hans nodded.

"Someone claiming to be an American agent started asking too many questions in Charé."

Hans glared accusingly at Rolf. "You already knew I'd be there."

"You? No. The Soviets? Yes."

Shaking his head, Hans moved toward the door. His head felt disconnected and his arm throbbed, but inside, his heart was bursting with both his gratitude for Rolf's intervention and his anxiety for the safety of the beautiful woman who was the catalyst for his part in this drama.

"I'm indebted to you, Rolf. I hope that someday this new German republic the Allies are promising us means peace for people like you and me."

"Let's get you on that plane, Hans Brenner." Rolf laid a hand on his friend's shoulder. "The pilot has orders to take you wherever you need to go."

* * *

Colonel Mikhail Sergeyev spoke respectfully. "Please understand that we do not enjoy harming beautiful young women like your daughter, Professor."

Viktor faced the man steadily, but he felt his anger rise with each breath. At his sides his strong hands curled tightly, and he felt like flying at the man, attacking him with his fists and his fury and his fear all rolled into monstrous blows that would teach him what it was like to be forced against one's will and what it felt like to fear for the safety of a loved one. But this same rage and concern for his Lucya also stayed his fists as he thought of the swift reprisals possible from such an act. If he loved his daughter he would calm himself now, control his fury, and bow humbly before this representative of glorious Stalin. He would acknowledge the great blessing that his loved one was allowed to continue living and to begin life anew in the east. He would show gratitude for Stalin's forgiveness and for the opportunity to make reparation for his mistakes.

"Stalin is gracious, Comrade Sergeyev. I will not fail again. Before too long we will be in Moscow, drinking to victory and to the glory of Stalin and our country."

"And if that is so, with that drink you can also celebrate the reunification of your daughter and yourself." Colonel Sergeyev smiled approvingly. "You're right to put your country before your personal interests, comrade. Stalin would be pleased."

THIRTY-EIGHT

April 19, 1946

Marie Jacobson waited at the window of the office, mentally preparing herself for what she would learn from the man who had taken Rolf away from her.

She turned to face Major Matthews. He had a gentle face, she noted, the kind of face a woman could trust. He seemed genuinely pleased to see her.

"Miss Jacobson." He took her hand and shook it warmly. "I'm glad you came. I'm sorry it was necessary to keep you from knowing your fiancé's whereabouts for such a long time—I've heard so much about you from Mr. Schulmann." He gestured for her to follow him into his office, and he pulled out a chair for her. "I hope I haven't made you wait too long."

Marie assured him she'd just arrived. She didn't mention that her wait had begun over a month ago—when Rolf disappeared.

Matthews sat on the edge of his desk, facing her. "We had reason to keep his location a secret, Miss Jacobson, but, I'm happy to say, that reason has ceased to exist."

"I have to know he's all right."

"And so you terrorized Captain Henrie at Zehlendorf until he had no recourse but to help you. You asked questions from one end of Berlin to another, invading POW camps in American, British, and even French zones, demanding to know if Major James Matthews had Rolf Schulmann ensconced there. I'm supposed to be working for an intelligence organization, Miss Jacobson, and so it's a little unnerving to have a young woman so intent on finding me." The admiration in Matthews's eyes belied his accusations. "You're quite a determined lady."

"Where is Rolf? Is he here? I need to be allowed to see him."

"He's no longer here." Matthews looked at Marie sympathetically. "When he was released he left immediately for France. The United States no longer considers him a threat, but he knows that France doesn't appreciate his role in the Occupation. He went to Paris to voluntarily stand trial as a Nazi war criminal."

* * *

Night fell, and a Friday evening of revelry and relaxation began for all medical personnel not assigned graveyard duty at the hospital. In their barracks apartment Mabel folded her arms and scowled at her roommate. "You're going off and getting yourself in deeper trouble, Natalie Allred. If you want my advice . . ."

Natalie tossed her sketch pad and a pile of clothes into a suitcase. "I don't want your advice. I'm sure it's timely and all that—but Curly's going to be here in just a couple of minutes, and he'll be in a *roaring* hurry."

"Well, you're gonna get it, nonetheless." Mabel straightened stubbornly. "You shouldn't be leading that nice American on, making him think you have feelings for him and then discarding him like used tissue when you think you've found something better. From what I see you've got yourself torn in three different directions and it's not fair to any one of those blokes."

Natalie rolled her eyes, exasperated. "Curly knows my concerns, Mabel. As soon as we reach Nüremberg we're going to spend time talking about it—working it out. And whatever we decide, it's really none of your business." Natalie felt her stomach churn at the thought of what she was doing, but she tried not to dwell on the possible consequences of her departure from Berlin or the fear that clutched at her whenever she thought of Lieutenant Rostov discovering her escape.

He wouldn't hurt Hans. He said he *needed* Hans. She threw her coat across a chair and closed the suitcase, then knelt on its lid and attempted to pull the zipper closed. She adjusted her position and tried again. "Mind giving me a hand with this, Mabel?"

Mabel grunted and moved toward the suitcase. She grasped the zipper and pulled. "You remind me of myself—at a younger, more fashionable age, of course." Mabel glanced up at Natalie and then down again at the stubborn zipper.

Natalie was surprised at the sudden revelation from beneath the British receptionist's prickly façade. "What do you mean?"

Mabel shrugged. "I used to attract them like flies to sugar." She colored somewhat and tried to cover it with a frown. "I had my pick of decent fellows, but I picked the one that was most convenient—and look where it's got me."

For just a moment Natalie studied the older woman, her shoulders hunched as she struggled with the suitcase. She recalled Mabel had been through a nasty marriage and divorce and had transferred to the American hospital in order to escape an abusive, dependent ex. "What are you trying to tell me, Mabel?" Suddenly Natalie felt sorry for her.

"Don't make the same mistake I did. Don't rush into anything."

Natalie leaned back on the suitcase and looked soberly at her roommate. She wished she could explain the reasons for her escape. How was she supposed to explain how Rostov terrified her? Or that she was trying to protect Hans by pulling herself out of the equation? If Rostov saw that she wasn't waiting around, mooning over the German or anxious to do anything to keep him safe, then perhaps Rostov could no longer manipulate Hans by using Natalie's safety as leverage.

Natalie offered the only explanation she could: "Things have gotten complicated."

"Running away from your problems isn't gonna make things any less complicated." Mabel jerked at the zipper firmly. "And you're pulling Curly Miller into a mess he does not deserve."

"Mabel, leave it, okay?" Natalie felt her heartbeat accelerating, and her eyes misted. "I know what I'm doing . . ."

She heard the rumble of a car outside the barracks, followed by multiple footsteps and a heavy knock on the door. "There. See? Curly and Gregory are here and I'm still not dressed." Natalie slid off the suitcase, her insides systematically tying themselves into knots. Now that the moment was finally here, she wasn't so sure if running away with Curly had been the best of ideas . . .

Exasperated, Mabel abandoned the stubborn zipper and moved toward the door.

Natalie sprinted for the bedroom. She fought against the misgivings that had surfaced, compliments of Mabel's crusty concern, and focused on preparing herself to face Curly. She dropped to her bed and reached to untie her shoes, frustrated when her haste caused her fingers to fumble at the laces. As she worked at the tangle she heard voices at the front door, and Mabel's voice rose impatiently. "This is not the best time, gentlemen—Miss Allred is preparing for her flight."

Natalie heard an exclamation of surprise, and her fingers ceased to obey her commands. She could not hear the words, but the voice was unmistakable. Lieutenant Viktor Rostov had come for her.

"No, I will *not* call her to the door." The obstinate British woman had suddenly become a powerful ally, Natalie mused, and she wondered if even Viktor Rostov could force his way past her.

Rostov was not giving up easily. Natalie heard the rising threat in his voice and felt her heart skip a beat. He was obviously not going to be swayed from his purpose, and from the determination in his voice she realized she had very little time.

The thought horrified Natalie, and she quickly refastened her shoes and stood. And in that instant two things happened: first, she had the distinct impression that she was unquestionably in danger, and second, she was seized from behind by a being so powerful, so determined, that even if she had not been completely stunned by the attack she would have been unable to even consider trying any of the tricks she had used on the three Russians on that terrible night so long ago.

A steel vise around her body pinned her arms to her sides, and a strong hand across her mouth cut off any hope of alerting her roommate to her predicament. Staggered by the swiftness of the assault, Natalie could do nothing but kick as she was lifted from her feet and carried through the bathroom, out into the laundry area, and through the back door.

In the dimly-lit alley she writhed violently, kicking and struggling against a strength that overwhelmed her. She twisted her head back and forth, trying to free her mouth and nose, her motivation not as much to scream as to breathe. The powerful form restraining her lowered her onto her feet and pressed against the backs of her legs, forcing her to her knees. He did not let go, but enveloped her in a smothering bear hug that forced her into submission. And then he whispered in thick, anxious English against her ear: "Natalie, hold still. Listen to me."

She recognized the voice she'd thought she would never hear again, and she allowed herself to relax in Hans Brenner's arms.

He whispered, "Don't scream, okay?" Carefully he removed his hand from her mouth.

She whispered back, close to tears, "What are you trying to do, kidnap me?"

"I'm trying to save your life."

Natalie turned and looked at his face, inches from her own, and felt the overwhelming shock of his proximity after such a long absence. He'd changed, she realized. The face that hovered close to hers was clean-shaven and handsome, and he wore a surplus army shirt from the men's shower room. His black hair had been trimmed short, and the eyes that gazed into hers held a purpose that intrigued her, moving her almost to tears with its strength. He was a new man, inside and out, and it encouraged her.

"I need you to trust me, Natalie, or we're going to die."

"Would Rostov really—?"

"Yes, he would."

"He threatened to take me with him back to Russia . . . " Suddenly she sobbed, "Where have you *been*, Hans Brenner?" She wanted to reach up and touch that beautiful face, but his arms still held her imprisoned and she suddenly didn't want him to let go.

"Listen, Natalie, any moment Rostov's going to make it past that battle-ax and realize you're not in your room, and I'd hate to be crouched here discussing history when he flies through that door."

"I'm not going anywhere with you 'til you tell me why you ran off and left me . . ." She bit her tongue and fell silent.

Hans did not respond, and she felt her cheeks flush as he studied her carefully, his eyes penetrating hers with an intensity that overwhelmed her.

She stammered, "I mean . . . how could you run off and not tell Rolf and Marie where you were going? They've been worried sick about you—"

"Natalie—" Hans's voice wavered. "Be quiet. If you say anything more I'm going to kiss you, and if I start kissing you we're never going to get out of here in time."

Natalie fell obediently silent.

Hans helped her to her feet, took her hand, and led her at a run through the alley and away from the apartment.

"You're hurt." She glimpsed for the first time the bandages underneath his shirt.

"It's nothing."

"Hans," she whispered, "I missed you—"

"Where's your fiancé?"

"What?"

"Where's Curly?"

She glanced back once and saw Lieutenant Rostov rush through the door of the laundry room. He turned and looked in their direction just as Hans pulled her around a corner and out of sight.

There was no time to tell him what she had determined to tell Curly—that in spite of all Curly's goodness and affection for her, in spite of his willingness to take her to the temple, in spite of his certainty that God had meant for the two of them to be together, she could not marry him. Nor was there time to tell Hans how she felt about him . . .

"Natalie, where is Captain Miller?" Hans's voice was urgent.

"Why do you need him?"

"We're in trouble." They skirted the corner of a structure and entered the courtyard, making a beeline for the compound's entrance. Hans glanced back at Natalie's apartment, where Rostov's vehicle waited with the engine idling. "We're going to need protection and transportation if we want to get out of here alive."

"Curly's on his way." Natalie swallowed. "He was going to fly me to Frankfurt . . ."

"We've got to find him."

They moved quickly through the courtyard, empty because of the promise of Friday night entertainment elsewhere. Natalie glanced over her shoulder in time to see Rostov and two other men exit her apartment and run for their vehicle. Ever on the defensive, Mabel followed them out onto the porch, shouting obscenities and brandishing an umbrella.

Hans squeezed Natalie's hand protectively. "I missed you, too."

"Hans, what are we going to do? What if Rostov reaches us first?"

"We'll meet Curly at the gate—and hope he's timely."

Natalie looked expectantly past the lighted guard shack, praying to catch a glimpse of the lights on Curly's Jeep as he turned the corner of the hospital. "He's bringing Gregory Jameson with him."

"Even better."

Hans steered her toward the entrance to the medical compound, and as they approached the guard shack, Natalie finally heard the sound of an army Jeep. She waved frantically as Curly and his friend rounded a corner of the hospital and approached. Curly caught sight of her and swung the wheel in their direction. Natalie glanced triumphantly across her shoulder at Rostov's entourage, certain these unexpected reinforcements would curtail his determined approach. But to her horror the Renault carrying the Soviet lieutenant pulled from the curb and made a beeline for their position.

Curly pulled the Jeep to a stop, and he and Gregory stared open-mouthed at Hans and Natalie. Gregory opened his door to get out but then froze when he saw the Soviet car accelerating directly toward the Jeep. Hans gathered Natalie into his arms and threw her into the back seat and then flung himself after her. "Go, Captain Miller—*schnell!*"

Curly shifted gears and punched the gas, and the Jeep lurched forward, tires screaming as he maneuvered to avoid the vehicle that seemed intent on ramming them. His prompt reaction saved all but the corner of the Jeep's rear fender, but the impact still threw Natalie violently against the seat in front of her, striking her shoulder against the steel frame and knocking the breath from her body. Hans grabbed her and pushed her back onto the seat.

In the front seat Gregory hadn't had time to close his door, and the unexpected impact threw him from the vehicle. He rolled several times, and Natalie watched, horrified, while he struggled to his feet and tried to run after them.

"What in *thunder* . . ." Curly clung to the wheel, battling to control the Jeep. He glanced back as the Renault swerved around for another try, and he accelerated.

The Jeep turned the corner and startled a group of nurses walking away from the hospital. Natalie heard a few of them shriek and she looked back to see them scrambling out of the way of the swiftly advancing Renault.

Curly gunned the engine, swerving around potholes and bouncing over curbstones as he headed east. Still stunned by the unexpected attack, Curly mumbled something and gripped the steering wheel.

"Does that radio work?" Hans had regained his command of the English language.

Curly glanced at him in the rearview mirror. "What's going on, Brenner? And where have you been all these months?"

"Call for help, Captain."

"Who in tarnation's behind us?"

Hans lunged over the seat for the handset. "Either you call for help or I will. You have no idea the danger we're in."

Still in a state of shock, Curly passed the handset to Hans and then returned his attention to the wheel. Hans stared at the object for a few moments, trying to figure how to work an American model, and then he tossed it back at Curly. "*You* call for help, Captain. Call security and have them meet us at the nearest checkpoint."

"The nearest checkpoint is at Friedrichshain."

"Call now!"

Curly fished for the loose handset and held it to his mouth, fighting the wheel with one hand as he barked into the radio.

Hans tapped Natalie's shoulder and pointed. She turned and saw another vehicle pull into the road from a side street to follow the first, and she clutched at Hans's arm. From the driver's seat Curly shouted into the radio receiver, giving their approximate location and requesting assistance at the border, swerving the Jeep around a corner with one hand on the wheel. Both cars followed.

"You mind telling me what's going on, Brenner?"

"Captain! Watch where you're going."

The Jeep lurched around a colossal pothole, righted itself, and continued toward the American/Soviet checkpoint. Curly kept alternating his attention between the road in front and the two cars behind. Gregory had probably raised the alarm back at the medical compound, and between that and Curly's call for help Natalie prayed that soon there would be an army in pursuit.

"Who's that behind us, Brenner?"

"Lieutenant Rostov—Berlin NKGB." Hans reached for Natalie's hand, and she gratefully clung to it. "He's angry at me and he's ready to take it out on Natalie."

"And apparently on you too," Curly responded.

Natalie stole a look at Hans in the seat next to her. She had a multitude of unanswered questions for him, and even though his revelation that Rostov worked for Soviet intelligence was not new to her, his words made the reality of their predicament hit her like a blow from a sledgehammer.

Curly glanced back at Hans. "You came back to Berlin to protect Natalie?"

"Rostov means to abduct her."

Curly almost lost control of the Jeep. "Brenner, what in blazes did you do to get that man so angry?"

Natalie saw a third car pull out in front of the Jeep and come to a sudden, complete stop in the middle of the road. Curly slammed on the brakes and swerved, and amidst the screaming of tires and the smell of burning rubber, the Jeep with its three passengers slid sideways and pulled to an agonizing stop inches from the impromptu roadblock. Curly sat with his knuckles white on the wheel and his face a sickly green. Hans, however, leaped from the back of the vehicle and reached for Natalie. But before he set her on her feet, the other two vehicles corralled them in.

Rostov and two other men emerged from the first car. The man Natalie had often seen in the hospital waiting room emerged from the vehicle that had blocked the road, and then from the third vehicle came the silent, muscular man Natalie remembered from the night of her birthday party.

Hans backed Natalie protectively against the side of the Jeep and placed himself between her and the approaching giant. The ogre advanced, while Hans stood resolutely, his feet apart and his arms loose at his sides, and Natalie imagined that Hans would probably go down protecting her. He swung with all his strength, landing a devastating blow that staggered the giant. But the beast recovered promptly and attacked with an unbelievable rage, and for several moments Natalie could hardly see Hans for the brutal fury of arms and legs and muscle that enveloped him. She opened her mouth to cry out, but the sound had not left her lips before she heard a heavy whoosh above her head, followed by a solid metallic thud, and the muscle-bound ogre paused, looked at Natalie with a strange, pleading stare, and crumpled silently to the ground at her feet.

Natalie stared first at the motionless mound practically lying on her shoes, and then she peered above her head. Curly towered over her, leaning from the Jeep with a steel tire-iron brandished tightly in one fist.

Hans staggered to his feet and threw a grateful look in the American pilot's direction, and then he reached for Natalie's hand and turned to face Rostov.

Lieutenant Rostov addressed Curly first. "Come down from there, Captain Miller, before you drop that thing on the head of one of your friends." He laughed. "I'm impressed with your resourcefulness." He turned to Hans, and Hans wrapped his arms protectively around Natalie as Rostov spoke. "You are brave, Lieutenant Brenner, to hit my friend Vasik. He doesn't like that, which I'm sure is why he forgot my implicit orders to *restrain* you—not murder you. I'm sure when he wakes up it is going to be near impossible to convince him not to finish the job." Finally he turned to Natalie, and the look in his eyes made her stomach churn. "My dear Natalya, I'm so sorry." His studied her regretfully as he continued. "Your Hans Brenner has failed you—and he has failed me. So I must keep the promise I made . . ."

Curly jumped from the side of the Jeep. "Under whose authority are you here in the American Zone? And what is it you want with Nurse Allred and Mr. Brenner?"

Irritated, Lieutenant Rostov contemplated Curly as he might a pesky insect. He smiled tightly. "I have orders from the Soviet High Command to place Mr. Brenner under arrest for crimes against the Soviet Union." He glanced once at Natalie, and then back at Curly. "Your fiancée is also in a great deal of trouble, Mr. Miller. She is wanted as a possible suspect in these same crimes. I have orders to detain them both."

Confused, Curly stared first at Rostov, then at Hans, and then at Natalie. "What is he talking about, Nattie?"

She pleaded with him. "Don't believe him, Curly! He's lying. Hans and I have done nothing wrong"—she glared accusingly at Rostov—"and he knows it!"

Rostov ignored her. "I have my orders with me, Captain, if you wish to study them."

"Of course I do," Curly snapped, moving resolutely toward the officer. "You may have orders, but you're on American soil." His voice was firm. "You will not take either Natalie or Brenner until we've discussed this with the American authorities."

Natalie felt Hans stiffen, and suddenly he spoke sharply. "Curly, watch out!"

Rostov's hand disappeared inside his uniform jacket and reappeared holding a Czech vz. 27 semi-automatic pistol. He stood with the weapon at his side while two of his men overwhelmed Curly and forced him to the ground at Rostov's feet.

Curly's face went as gray as Rostov's shirt. "We're *allies*, Lieutenant—remember?"

Rostov snapped, "That is easily debated," and cocked his pistol.

"Viktor!" Natalie screamed, "No!" Horrified, she struggled free of Hans's embrace and ran toward Curly. She fell next to him on the ground and pleaded for Curly's life. "You can't kill him, Viktor."

"I have no choice, Miss Allred. Move aside."

"Please don't do this, Viktor." She wrapped her arms around Curly and turned beseeching eyes on Rostov. "You're a better man than this. Please . . ." She hesitated. "Remember Lucya's suffering. Someone took away the man she loved, and it broke your heart as well as hers." Natalie leaned forward, imploring him. "Please don't make yourself as evil as the men who took away your daughter's Anton! Please, Viktor—what would your daughter think of you?"

Viktor studied Natalie's face. Pleadingly she met his gaze and willed herself not to give in to the fear his scrutiny produced in her. He studied her for a long moment, and even though his eyes smoldered she could see the underlying turmoil in their depths.

"Natalya, if I let him go he will report to the Americans."

"But you don't have to be a murderer, Viktor. Please, think about your daughter and . . . and your Alyona . . ."

Viktor's gaze wavered, then the gun dropped to his side. He took a step backward and smiled sorrowfully at Natalie. "You know how to touch my heart, Nurse, in more ways than one." He motioned for his men to release Curly. "I'll let him go, Natalya Ivanovna, for *your* sake—although it may cost me my freedom."

Natalie's eyes shone her gratitude and relief, and she helped a stunned Curly Miller to his feet.

Viktor turned to Curly. "It is time to bid your beloved *adieu*, Captain—where she is going there is no chance you will ever meet again. I can give you one minute to say good-bye before I change my mind about allowing you to live." He nodded to Natalie. "I'll wait with Mr. Brenner at the car." He turned and strode away, and Hans followed after him under the insistent weapons of Rostov's men.

Natalie watched Curly, her eyes anguished. She reached and touched his arm, and for several seconds she tried to find the right words to portray her grief, her embarrassment, and her fear.

"Natalie." Curly spoke first. "For your sake, I'm glad Brenner came back."

She colored slightly and whispered, "Please, Curly—forgive me. I want what is best for both of us." She touched his cheek. "You don't know how

long I've struggled with this. You told me I need to be honest with you—
and up until now I haven't been honest." She willed him to understand. "I
love you, Curly. But even though I don't know if I can ever marry Hans, I—
I love him more . . . and if I married you I would be lying to you from the
moment I made that covenant."

"That's what you wanted to tell me when I called."

She nodded, uncomfortable.

"I'm sure Hans is a good man," Curly said softly. "He'll take care of
you. Besides . . ." Here Curly's face grew hard as he looked across the street
at the waiting Soviet officer leaning against the car and fingering his pistol.
"Maybe we'll meet again—and sooner than that Russian suspects." Curly
glanced down the empty street. "I radioed for help. Gregory has probably
sounded the alarm. Perhaps if we stall them, talk long enough for the army
to find us . . ."

Natalie shook her head. "Your life is in danger if we do. Please go,
Curly."

"I can't leave you here—with that man." Curly glowered again at Rostov.

"You don't have a choice. Besides, I couldn't bear for you to be killed . . ."

Curly took her face in his hands, and his eyes searched hers. "Do you
realize how awful I feel, leaving you here like this?"

"It'll be all right . . ."

"No, it won't. He's not going to get away with abducting an American
citizen. He's got no authority to take you across the border."

"Curly . . ." Natalie hesitated. "I think he does."

Curly was taken aback. "What do you mean, Nattie?"

She touched his hand. "Rostov knows things about me . . ."

Curly stared at her, uncomprehending. His look demanded an explanation from her, but she just shook her head.

Viktor checked his watch, pushed away from his car, and walked
purposefully toward them.

"Go, Curly! Please, please go!"

"I love you, Nattie. No matter how you feel about me, I love you."
With one last defiant glare at the approaching Soviet officer, Curly kissed
her gently, climbed into the Jeep, and drove quickly away.

THIRTY-NINE

After Lieutenant Rostov released him, Captain Charles Miller made a frantic beeline for the low-profile offices of the newly formed Central Intelligence Group in Berlin's American district.

"I'm here to report an abduction."

The clerk was unimpressed. "Inform the Military Police, and they'll file a missing persons report . . ." The man clearly considered night shift on a Friday night sufficient cause for incivility.

"No." Curly was resolute. "It happened right under my nose, Lieutenant, not thirty minutes ago. A Soviet officer abducted a German civilian and an American army nurse."

"Happens all the time—Russians kidnapping civilians, that is." The man reached calmly for a form. He handed it to Curly. "Fill this out and hand it in. You can sit over there . . ."

With hands still shaking, Curly filled out the form—names, ranks, descriptions, locations—and then he handed it back to the young man behind the desk.

The officer gave it a cursory glance and set it aside. "The staff duty officer will look at it when he arrives. Too late to do anything about it tonight anyway."

"What is your name, officer?"

"Second Lieutenant Paul Fisher, sir."

Curly captured the man by his shirtfront and brought him up close to his face. "You're gonna have a look at it *now,* Second Lieutenant Fisher, or I'm going to make sure you get night duty for the remainder of your career. Understand?"

Fisher brushed Curly off and straightened his uniform. "You can't do that."

"Read the report, Fisher. Immediately."

Fisher retrieved the report.

Curly jabbed a finger at Rostov's name. "Check that name against the Allied Commission's register. See if it's listed."

"That's not my job, Captain." Fisher's respect level had heightened barely a notch.

"Consider it a temporary promotion, Fisher." Curly hovered while the reluctant clerk unlocked a filing cabinet. Fisher glanced again at the report and then thumbed through a stack of papers. "Nothing here, Captain." He replaced the file and closed the drawer.

Curly felt his pulse quickening. "Any other lists you can check? Anything higher clearance?"

"Level Two, but there aren't many names on that list." Fisher sounded tired. "Rhein-Main usually handles those." He locked the cabinet door and returned to his desk.

"Check Level Two, Lieutenant. That's an order."

"Well, if you put it that way . . ." Fisher drawled, clearly irritated this time. He turned and left the room, reaching again for his keys.

Curly waited, pacing and wringing his hands. It didn't matter that this evening's drama had put his return flight to Nüremberg unforgivably behind schedule. Nor did he worry about Gregory's dramatic tumble from the moving Jeep. Gregory could take care of himself, he figured, but Natalie . . .

Heavenly Father . . . His prayer was silent, deep in the recesses of his agitated consciousness. *Please protect her, and please protect Brenner, who's been through a whole heck of a lot in this war, probably more than I'll ever know. Please help him want to learn about the gospel, so Natalie can someday have the temple marriage she so desperately wants . . .*

Five minutes later Fisher returned, and his expression had acquired a humility that surprised Curly. "I reported the name of your Soviet officer to the SDO in Frankfurt." He was apologetic. "It seems Rostov is a hot item after all."

Curly was marginally relieved. "Thank you, Lieutenant."

"I'll have the SDO analyze your report further as soon as he comes in, sir, and he'll coordinate a plan of action with Matthews." He cleared his throat. "I'm sorry I wasn't entirely cooperative."

"And I'm sorry I grabbed your shirt."

* * *

Lieutenant Paul Fisher's mention of Rostov's name sent the SDO in Berlin immediately to the phone, and by eleven o'clock Friday evening Major James Matthews had been informed that his Soviet nemesis had struck again—this time, surprisingly, without the advance knowledge of the CIG.

Fuming, Matthews rushed to his office at headquarters and contacted his agent in the Soviet Köpenick district, and while he waited impatiently for the man to pick up the phone he decided it was high time the United States did something to clip Viktor Rostov's wings.

"*Guten Morgen . . .*" The man sounded half asleep.

"Pull yourself together. I'm calling in a small favor."

The man recognized Matthews's voice, and his next words were spoken in English, tinged with a slightly British accent. "Must be an important one to call me at a time like this."

Matthews tapped the edge of his desk. "Find out what you can about the recent abductions of an American nurse and a former Nazi officer—Natalie Allred and Hans Brenner."

"Just happened, you say?"

"Tonight at about twenty-one hundred hours, on the American side of the Friedrichshain checkpoint."

"All right. Any other information you can give me?"

"Yes." Matthews's hand stilled on the desktop. "Seems this abduction might be retaliation for the failure of Rostov's agent to abduct a German scientist in Chamonix. That unlucky agent was Hans Brenner. In addition, Brenner is the close friend of the man who brought that scientist in for me." Matthews gripped the phone tightly. "I owe that man a whole lot more than I can ever repay. But I believe recovering his friend might be a good start."

"Give me an hour." The receiver clicked.

Matthews spent the next hour trying to formulate a plan. He sweated, fumed, and cursed. He thought about Rolf Schulmann, Hans Brenner, his son-in-law, and this whole convoluted, diabolical postwar conflict. He tried to imagine what Rostov was planning and what Rostov was thinking, and the exercise made his head ache. Lieutenant Viktor Rostov was the most complicated, illogical individual Matthews had ever known. And yet, Matthews thought ironically, if Rostov had been born an American citizen, with the same ruthless drive, the same sense of duty and honor, and the same dedication to country that he now possessed as a Soviet operative, he would've been irreplaceable to have around—especially in Matthews's line of work.

Matthews's agent was true to his word, calling the major in exactly one hour with confirmation of the dual kidnapping of former SS Lieutenant Hans Brenner and U.S. Army Nurse Natalie Allred. Rostov had them sequestered at a compound in Köpenick, and they were scheduled to board a plane for Moscow at noon the next day.

"That's not enough time," Matthews fumed. "Find a way to get me another twenty-four hours."

"Well now, Major, this 'little favor' is becoming a mite complicated."

Matthews resumed his pacing, but by the time his morning staff arrived he was nowhere near formulating a plan. Frustrated, he picked up the phone and called Berlin.

FORTY

April 20, 1946

In the Köpenick district of Berlin there is a large city park graced by inspiring stone architecture and cool, clear fountains. At one time it was not uncommon to see young mothers pushing perambulators along the park's paths or couples enjoying moments together on park benches, oblivious to the world passing them by. Crystalline fountains bubbled pleasantly near sculptures of pensive cherubs or soaring birds, shapes eternally captured in granite, marble, and Nazi-inspired red sandstone. The Köpenick district is sometimes called the "green lungs" of Berlin, with the largest land area and lowest population in the Soviet-controlled sector.

But on the morning of April twentieth, 1946, a visitor to that park would notice that the scene had changed. A mother and child out for a stroll was a rare sight. The fountains had not flowed for years, and the sculptures had been defaced and destroyed. A few patches of lush grass remained, littered with refuse, loose bricks, and one sleeping refugee.

Hans Brenner stood at the miniature window of his basement cell, surveying the park and its homeless resident. He empathized with the luckless man, having been homeless himself for a significant portion of his recent life. But even though he didn't miss the feel of rank, slimy grass on his back, or the occasional stray dog licking his ear, or the hunger pangs that clawed at his belly each morning, at this particular moment he would gladly have traded places with this man. Disheartened, Hans continued to survey his little patch of sunlight from the perspective of a rat.

The cell block crawled with those furry rodents, and to Hans they seemed to be the only happy residents of this basement prison.

He heard footsteps in the corridor outside his cell and a key scraping in the lock. He turned away from his window and stepped from his bed down to the concrete floor just in time to face Lieutenant Rostov entering his cell.

Rostov contemplated his prisoner, and he seemed ill at ease.

"I should've destroyed you long ago." Rostov frowned. "You've failed me and failed my country, and your failure is now *my* failure." His eyes were hard. "When I found out about Chamonix I was determined to kill you. I *would* have killed you last night."

"But you didn't, for Natalie's sake." Hans recalled Natalie's heartfelt petition for the safety of her fiancé, Captain Miller.

"I didn't kill you last night for Natalie's sake, Mr. Brenner, and this morning I do not kill you for my own." Rostov moved toward the cell's small table and deposited his visor cap on its surface. "It seems you may still be of use to me—perhaps more so than I had previously thought." He rested one hand on the back of the solitary wooden chair. "Last night, while you slept peacefully, I visited the *Universität zu Berlin* and researched the academic files of a student named Hans Brenner."

"You've been busy."

Rostov ignored the sarcasm. "I had no need of von Hausen's records—most of those are in the possession of the NKGB anyway—but except for your connection to von Hausen, your records have been largely ignored by my government."

Hans recalled several of the things he knew would be in his file from so many years ago, and his apprehension grew.

Rostov continued thoughtfully. "You kept detailed notes, it seems, of your work with von Hausen. There was one thing in particular that intrigued me . . ."

Hans felt the pulse in his neck pounding, and he waited anxiously for the officer's next words.

"You wrote that von Hausen had encountered a roadblock in his experiment. Frustrated, he told you he would abandon his hypothesis and report the experiment as a failure. But you dissuaded him, asking that he allow you to try one more time."

Hans suddenly felt tired, deflated. When he'd compiled those diaries he'd been swept up in the influence of Hitler's new world philosophy and had planned for the procedures, experiments, and results he recorded to be utilized in the interest of Germany's Third Reich. But his diligence had come back to haunt him, he realized now. His painstakingly detailed observations now served as a foundation for his future, a future that would be determined by the Russian now standing in front of him. He felt nauseated at the thought of residing against his will in Russia and working for the Soviet government.

"It was *you* who discovered the best way to isolate the necessary isotopes, Mr. Brenner. It was *you* who guided the project through to success—and then you convinced von Hausen's superiors that it was von Hausen who discovered the solution. I can only imagine you made such a career-destroying decision because of either a special fondness for your mentor or because of a misguided sense of compassion for a man you realized would be destroyed by failure. Hitler, I understand, was not the most forgiving of leaders."

"Von Hausen is the scientist," Hans said stiffly. "I was just his assistant."

"You're as knowledgeable of the process as von Hausen," Rostov responded emphatically, "and because of that you'll be as useful to the atomic commission as von Hausen would have been. That is reason enough to have you take von Hausen's place. In fact, as far as I'm concerned, Mr. Brenner, you're of *more* significance to my government then von Hausen would have been—and when you've demonstrated the uranium extraction process to the commission, I'm confident they will feel as I do."

With a heavy heart Hans said, "If I go with you to Russia, will you let Natalie go free?"

Hans's query agitated Rostov. He leaned wearily against the chair, contemplating Hans with a look that deepened Hans's trepidation. Hans tried to reason with him. "It would be an extension of your promise to me, Professor. Before I left for France you told me that if I brought you the man who could help you, you would not harm Natalie ever again." Hans grimaced. "It seems *I* am to be that man."

"I resent the implication, Mr. Brenner, that I have already harmed her."

"Physical torture is not the only way to break a person, Rostov. You, of all people, should know that."

"I assume you refer to my daughter's forced exile and how it influences my actions," Rostov snapped. "But Stalin will not harm my daughter. She will be returned to me unharmed when I return with *you* in custody."

"Perhaps you overestimate your government's generosity."

Rostov paced near the closed cell door, his movements revealing a mounting anger at Hans's words. "You will be transported to Novosibirsk, and you will see what a benevolent leader Stalin can be. And in regards to your Natalie . . ." Rostov paused, and Hans felt the ominous darkness that accompanies fear of the unknown. "Her given name is *Natalya Ivanovna Karagodina.* She is a Soviet citizen and she will return with me to Moscow."

Shocked, Hans moved closer to Rostov, his eyes threatening. "Now wait a moment, Professor—Natalie is an American citizen."

Rostov did not flinch in the face of Hans's fury. In fact, his eyes mirrored a barely controlled version of the same emotion. "Yes, Hans Brenner, she was raised as one. However, her mother, it seems, has kept the truth hidden from her all these years. Natalya Ivanovna was born in Petrograd."

"That can't be true. She told me herself that her father was an American—a cowboy in South Dakota."

"That is what she has been led all her life to believe, Hans Brenner. Her mother never told her that her *real* father—her Russian father—died a traitor's death before Natalya was even born."

Hans swallowed against his panic. "You still have no right to force her against her will—"

"I have every right," Rostov shot back. "At first I kept the revelation of her parentage to myself, in anticipation of your victory at Chamonix." Rostov's fury steadily increased until it seemed as if it would explode in the face of his prisoner. "But when I learned of your deliberate treachery I contacted my superiors and told them everything I'd discovered about the girl. My promise to you and Natalya is now impossible to keep, Mr. Brenner; I've been ordered by my superior officer to escort her to Moscow."

"You wouldn't dare." Hans took a menacing step in the direction of the Russian. "Your action would constitute a threat to the Allied forces that assisted you in your victory."

"She is a Soviet citizen and I can take her as I please," Rostov shot back. "It is Soviet law—all displaced Soviet nationals discovered in conquered territory are to be returned to their country of origin—and because of last year's agreement at Yalta between Comrade Stalin, President Roosevelt, and Winston Churchill, the Allied Commission would not dream of opposing me."

FORTY-ONE

Natalie didn't want a visitor that Saturday morning, and even if she had, Viktor Rostov didn't fit the bill.

"I brought you something to eat, Natalya." Rostov entered with a plate and mug. "I apologize I have little to offer—but I assumed you wouldn't be in the mood for a sumptuous feast."

Natalie stared dully at the crusty black bread and mug of tea. "I'm not hungry."

"Then I was right not to bring more." Rostov smiled. "I actually came this morning with the idea that we could keep each other company for a few minutes."

Natalie stood and moved away from the officer. "Why would I want to spend time with a monster?"

Rostov looked momentarily taken aback. Natalie turned and pleaded with him. "Viktor, your family is being stolen from you and you can't see that your government is to blame." Natalie took a deep breath, gauging her decision to continue by the surge of emotions in Rostov's eyes. "You try to be a good man one minute, and then you do cruel and unspeakable things the next. It's as if the part of your conscience that regulates behavior is defective—or has been blocked out by the idea that Stalin is right, socialism is good, and the end justifies the means."

"You don't have the right to judge me."

"Perhaps not," Natalie agreed. "But I have the right to express my opinions . . ."

"Only because I'm overly permissive"—Rostov's face darkened—"and will not punish you for expressing them. This is not America, Natalya Ivanovna."

Natalie felt the menace in his words. "Viktor, I can see your conflict; it's there in your eyes whenever you threaten me or Hans. You admitted yourself that some of the things you do are difficult—and yet you do them anyway."

Rostov scowled. "As a Soviet citizen you will find you must do what you're told *always*—even if your personal feelings cry out and beg for you to resist."

"But what motivation do you have for obedience, besides terror, suffering, and death?" Natalie realized her questions chafed at unhealed wounds Rostov carried.

"A better life, Natalya—and a strong country. An equal society is infinitely preferable to the selfish, capitalistic culture of the Americans, which rewards the rich and punishes the poor."

"Yes, but what about freedom?" Natalie knew she was still treading on dangerous ground, but she couldn't stop. "What about freedom to choose right instead of being compelled to do something terrible out of duty?"

"My government chooses what is right for me, and they are never wrong." Rostov's words were clipped.

"Are you saying it was right for them to murder Anton and exile your daughter?"

Rostov's silence thundered through Natalie's consciousness, but she didn't heed the warning. "Why do you stay, Viktor, and serve such a government? Why do you value duty over family, and tradition over freedom? Why don't you take your daughter and escape?"

Suddenly he moved menacingly toward her. Terrified, Natalie retreated until her back contacted the wall and she could retreat no more. Rostov moved to within inches of her face, and his eyes held in their blazing depths a hint of anguish that she realized he couldn't hide from her.

But even the sorrow in his eyes couldn't minimize the threat of his words: "I do not wish to hurt you—I have promised your Hans that I would not. It is a good thing I made that promise, Natalya Ivanovna, because your words make me long to teach you a lesson about duty and country that you will never forget."

He raised his hands, and she flinched. But he only rested them against the wall on either side of her head. "You're too outspoken in your opinions—you, a woman raised erroneously as an American, selfish in her judgments and actions, her every thought for the welfare of herself at the expense of everyone around her. Tell me, Natalya"—here he gave her a derisive sneer—"are you prepared to defend your opinions to the death? For that is where they are taking you—and within very little time of your repatriation, I fear."

"You'd kill me for my opinions?"

He studied her angrily, his mouth pressed into an uncompromising line and his hands balled into fists against the wall, and then he closed his eyes and lowered his head. For just a moment his anger receded, and he appeared to

Natalie to be a broken, humbled man. "*I could not carry through with such an order, my dearest Natalya, but be assured such an order would come.*"

Rostov pushed away from the wall, and when he looked at her again his eyes were contrite. "I do not mean to threaten you or scare you." He sighed heavily. "You are right: I *do* struggle with what I'm required to do, and I *do* wonder what kind of person I'm becoming. What would my daughter think of me if she were to discover some of the things I do for my country? Sometimes I cannot stand thinking of the evil man I have become—but perhaps I have always been an evil man . . ."

Natalie sank onto the edge of her cot and watched him carefully. She whispered, "I know your daughter loves you, Viktor, and does not condemn you for what you have to do."

Rostov studied her carefully. "I wish you wouldn't see me as a monster, Natalya Ivanovna. I wish there were something I could do to convince you that I'm human—a person with hopes and dreams, just like you, who is capable of loving someone and caring for someone . . ." He sighed glumly, and his expression hinted at a desire for reconciliation. "What can I do for you to improve your opinion of me?"

"Release Hans and let me go back."

Sorrowful, Rostov shook his head. "That I cannot do." He hesitated. "You have not found your relatives."

"No."

"Would you consider me less of a monster if I allowed you to visit your Aunt Clara's former home? It would mean a postponement of our flight to Moscow, and another day in Berlin means another day before I can request that my daughter be returned to me. But for you, Nurse Natalya, it is a sacrifice I'm willing to make—if it would soften your dislike."

Natalie felt a curious stirring in the pit of her stomach, and as she contemplated Rostov's offer she realized it was actually a significant concession on his part. And even though the excursion would only postpone the nightmare that Natalie knew awaited her and Hans, she still felt a twinge of gratitude toward the man who had suggested it.

She whispered, "Will you let Hans come with me?"

Rostov hesitated, and for just a moment his eyes flickered angrily. He stood and turned away from her, and his shoulders sagged with a strange heaviness that confused her. But he finally nodded, and without turning to look at her he said, "I want to be your friend, Natalya. Yes, Hans Brenner may come."

FORTY-TWO

In the basement of CIG headquarters, Curly Miller was startled awake on Saturday morning by a hand on his shoulder. Wide-eyed and disoriented, he swung his feet off the couch, rubbed at his eyes, and finally recognized his friend Gregory Jameson hovering over him.

"I figured you'd still be here," Gregory said.

Curly yawned and stretched. "Can't leave 'til this thing's resolved." He focused on his friend. "What are you doing here?"

"Fisher just received a call from Matthews. The major wants us to fly down there and meet with him at Rhein-Main."

"That's good news, isn't it?" Curly looked hopeful. "I mean, that suggests they have some idea how to get Natalie and Brenner back?"

Gregory shrugged. "He wants us there by nine."

Curly glanced at his watch and stood quickly.

"Wait," Gregory said softly. "There's something we need to do before we leave."

They looked at each other for just a moment, and then without speaking they both sank to their knees on the cold concrete floor.

* * *

Gregory flew with Curly to the military air base west of Frankfurt, where Major Matthews invited the two of them to a conference over late-morning breakfast.

Curly and Gregory declined the coffee Matthews offered, and Matthews smiled at the refusal, his eyes congenial. "Mormons?"

Gregory nodded. "We don't drink—"

Matthews waved his hand dismissively. "Never mind that. You two fellows realize how many Mormons there are here in Germany?"

Curly grinned. "We've met a few. In fact, Nurse Allred is a member of our church, and Hans Brenner has a friend who's also a Mormon."

"Wouldn't happen to be Rolf Schulmann, would it?" Matthews smiled at their surprise. "Like I said, you Mormons are everywhere."

Matthews sobered. "Lieutenant Rostov plans to transport your friends to Russia. My source told me that they were scheduled to depart the Soviet Köpenick district at noon today."

The two young pilots looked at each other in horror, but Matthews said, "However, it seems God is on your side this morning, gentlemen. Just two hours ago I received word that Rostov has postponed his flight for another twenty-four hours. My contact doesn't know the reason for the delay, but to me, the reason is irrelevant." Matthews leaned forward and watched Curly and Gregory closely. "What *is* relevant is that this delay gives us one more day to rescue your friends." He took a sip of his coffee and continued. "I have the suggestion of a plan, and it involves the participation of you two fine young men."

Curly said, "Major, if you have a plan for getting them back, we're ready to help in any way we can."

* * *

Lieutenant Viktor Rostov kept his word. Before the sun set he took Natalie and Hans to Bernaur Strasse. He allowed them to walk down the street where Natalie's aunt had lived while he and his soldiers stayed with the vehicles. Hans and Natalie stood in the middle of a shattered street and stared at the destruction that spanned from one end of their vision to the other.

If the mountain of rubble in front of them had once been a leather goods store, it didn't seem so now. It had been obliterated—consumed in a firestorm—and then pillaged during the ensuing war years. Natalie did not speak; she didn't cry. She just looked.

The building used to be a stately red brick in an endless row of shops and second-story apartments. According to Hans, during his university years this area had been a well-to-do borough for well-to-do customers.

Only one wall of the store remained: a sturdy connecting wall between that shop and its neighbor, jutting a ragged ten feet into the sky. On either side of the shop's remains Natalie could see similar walls—some with precarious portions of the second story structure still attached. Everywhere she looked lay piles of useless rubble, displaced bricks, and twisted metal.

While the rest of Berlin was beginning, ever so slowly, to pick itself up, brush itself off, and rebuild, this street had been left to decay. And Natalie knew why; these shops belonged to Jews, and most of the Jews would never return.

Natalie thought of Hitler's miserable extermination order, so carefully, so efficiently carried out until all that remained of her people was a whispered suggestion of the nation it had been before the war. But it did no good to mull over the injustice of it all. It had happened, even though it was so evil that one could not imagine it happening in a civilized world. And because of the incredible evil of it all, it was more likely to be forgotten. People tended to block out what was too horrific to think about, or to deny it ever occurred. Natalie herself felt so ill at the thought of what might have happened to her aunt and uncle and two cousins that she was also guilty of trying to suppress the thoughts.

She felt gentle hands on her shoulders. "Natalie?" The concern in Hans's voice showed he recognized her plight. "What are you going to do?"

Natalie shuddered as if trying to free herself from the awful burden of having to make a decision. She rested her head against Hans's shoulder and stared at the ruins. "I don't know."

She glanced up and down the street and saw only three people: a small child and a woman foraging in the gutter a block away, and an older gentleman sifting through rubble across the street and three doors down.

Hans released her and walked across the street toward the man. Natalie followed.

Hans said, "Let me give you a hand with that, father." He used the polite title for a distinguished man of advancing years as he bent to help grasp the edges of a twisted steel frame. He added his considerable strength to the meager efforts of the old man, and within a matter of moments the twisted object had been worked free of the rubble. Hans handed it to the man. "Is this your establishment?"

The man shrugged. "It used to be." He placed the sign on the edge of the garbage-strewn road. It read, FINE JEWELRY AND WATCHES.

"You're a jeweler?"

"A watchmaker. My partner was the jeweler." He peered up at the tall German next to him, taking in his black hair and dark eyes.

Hans asked, "Are you familiar with the other proprietors on this street?"

"Most of them." The man pointed to a chain dangling from one of the top corners of the sign. "I need to find the other one of these," he said, and he began searching through the rubble again. Natalie looked at the pile of twisted debris and wondered where the man thought he would hang the sign. "Did you know the family Bröder?" she asked hopefully.

The man nodded, straightened, and pointed across the street. "Abram had his leather goods shop right over there. They beat him and burned the place." The man shook his head sadly and continued. "We were the best of friends."

Hans looked at Natalie, and she saw the hope in his eyes that mirrored her own. He turned back to the man. "Where did they go?"

The man continued searching through the rubble while he answered, and Hans bent to assist him.

"They wanted us to go with them. The Sterns agreed to go, but we foolishly chose to stay." Natalie saw the man's hands trembling as he carefully stacked bricks.

Hans asked soberly, "What happened to your family?"

Natalie glanced at Hans, surprised. She'd been about to ask the man where her aunt and uncle had gone, but Hans had sensed the man's need to talk about his own experiences and had turned the discussion. Natalie realized that underneath his rough, unpolished exterior, Hans had a thoughtfulness to his nature that put her to shame.

"My wife didn't make it." The man's hands slowed. Hans supported the man's drooping shoulders with his large hands and helped him sit down on the curb. Hans sat down next to him. "What do you mean?"

Fascinated, Natalie joined the two men on the curb and listened as the watchmaker opened up to Hans, telling him tearfully of the Nazi marauders, the brutal beatings, the degradations, and, finally, his family's forced move into the ghetto and eventually to the camps.

"My wife didn't survive the camps, and my two sons disappeared while I was a prisoner." The man poured out his grief as the three of them rested together on the dirty curb.

Natalie glanced over at Rostov, leaning against his Renault with his arms folded and his eyes watchful. He seemed in no hurry, even though she knew he was granting this detour against his better judgment and against his ingrained sense of duty. His eyes met hers, and, feeling both flustered and grateful, she mouthed the English words *Thank you*. Solemnly he nodded his acknowledgement of her gratitude.

"You've been through a lot, father." Hans now indicated Natalie. "This woman has also suffered. Maybe you can help her. Do you have any news about her relatives—the Bröder family? You said they were your close friends . . ."

The man scratched his head. He seemed to be searching through his memories, trying to separate Natalie's family from the whirling storm of experiences that comprised the last seven years of his life. Finally he nodded and looked at Natalie. "I remember now. They wanted to go where the Germans wouldn't follow, and they decided the safest place would be France."

* * *

As it did every Saturday night, a Handley Page Halifax the British had loaned to their Soviet allies arrived at Rhein-Main Military Air Base near Frankfurt. It had originated that morning from the Soviet air base in Köpenick. This particular plane made routine deliveries every weekend between Soviet territory and the military air bases in Hamburg, Düsseldorf, and Frankfurt, and this particular Saturday was no exception. The plane finished its route at Rhein-Main, where the pilots would rest in the cargo hold for a few hours before returning to Köpenick.

What was *not* routine for the Russian pilot and copilot was the group of American GIs on the tarmac awaiting the plane's arrival, their mood uncommonly buoyant and welcoming. They greeted the two surprised Russians with bottles of vodka and jovial promises of a good-ol'-American night on the town, and the pilots' suspicions dimmed as liquor flowed and friendships grew. The GIs enticed them away from the airfield and into Frankfurt, where enough liquor to drown even a lonely Soviet pilot's sorrows materialized whenever they even hinted that they needed to return to their plane.

The Soviets and their American comrades spent most of the night in boisterous celebration, and when the two pilots recovered they found themselves locked in an underground bunker with nothing left to their names but their underwear, a few empty bottles, and a lousy hangover.

FORTY-THREE

April 20, 1946

Many do not like Paris the first time they visit. Springtime weather can be unpredictable, and the rain falls often and with discouraging force, driving both tourists and Parisians off the streets.

But Professor Jacobson had always loved Paris—perhaps because his own romance had blossomed there so many years ago, and perhaps because that was where his daughter Marie had been born . . .

He could hear the gentle rain falling now, whispering against the window of his office as if inviting him outside to enjoy its fragrance. Even in the middle of busy Paris, it would leave the air smelling of lilacs and fields of clover, and every time he inhaled the freshly washed air it reminded him of a day—a lifetime ago, when he was young and strong—when he had danced with his beautiful bride in the rain.

Jacobson stood and stretched. He reached for his overcoat. Soon he would be home in his cozy library, his fireplace blazing and a good book in his hands. He would read by the fire until late, and then he would write a letter to his daughter in Berlin.

He slipped his arms into his coat, picked up his umbrella and his briefcase, and turned to the door. He opened it and stepped into the hallway, reaching the top of the stairs at the same moment as a younger man who had been winding his way up the marble steps below. The man was well-dressed, Jacobson noted, with light brown hair neatly combed and a briefcase in one hand. He carried a hat and overcoat under his arm. Dark stains on the man's coat and hat confirmed the rainfall outside.

The visitor looked up at Jacobson. His eyes were an intense blue, pleasant, and definitely not the eyes of the young man Jacobson had imagined. His eyes revealed the intellect and responsibility of a person twice his age—the eyes of a man who has done much and seen more than life should offer a man of his years. Jacobson saw experience there, and sorrow. And as the newcomer's eyes locked with his own, Jacobson imagined he saw a flash of recognition.

The man hesitated on the steps, then smiled politely and spoke in flawless French. His voice was pleasant, but to Jacobson it seemed a bit sad. "Monsieur, please will you direct me to the office of President Félix Gouin's judicial secretary?"

Professor Jacobson pointed. "Straight down the hallway, take a left, and you'll see another flight of stairs. At the landing you'll come to . . . No, let me show you." He motioned for the man to follow. He offered a polite, "I see it's raining outside."

"A little."

"Are you from Paris?"

"I have a small villa near Lyon."

The professor was intrigued. This man didn't look like a Frenchman. In fact, if not for his perfect French, Jacobson would have suspected the man to be of German ancestry. He held the office door for the visitor and then followed him inside, letting the door close behind them. It was more than a curiosity now, he realized. He doubted they had met before, but there was something about him . . .

Abruptly the younger man paused, turned, and extended his hand toward the professor, an American gesture of friendship Jacobson had not been expecting. A bit taken aback, he accepted the proffered hand.

The man looked him directly in the eyes and said, "I can tell you're a good man, Professor Jacobson, and I want to thank you for everything—before it's too late and I never have another opportunity."

Jacobson started. He stared back at the man—with his deep blue eyes, his strong, handsome face, the military set of his shoulders—and suddenly he knew. He took a deep breath, and with all the courage he could muster he brought his other hand firmly over their clasped hands. His voice didn't sound like his own as he said, "And I want to thank you for my daughter's life, Rolf Schulmann, before"—his voice caught in his throat—"before it is, as you say, too late."

They stood that way for just a brief moment, eyes locked as they gave each other the respect they each deserved, and then with a mutual understanding they ended their handshake and Rolf Schulmann turned away. Jacobson watched as the man his daughter loved so deeply set down his briefcase, removed a sheaf of typewritten papers, and walked to the desk holding the stack in his hand.

He placed his offering on the desk in front of the secretary and stepped back. His voice was steady. "Please inform President Gouin that the names he and de Gaulle requested are all listed here. I have provided him with all known collabos in the Rhône-Alpes region directly linked to the Belley département from the time the Germans crossed the Demarcation Line in '42 to the invasion of Normandy. And please let him know that Major Schulmann brought them personally. I'll be staying at the Hotel Vienne, room three forty-seven, if he has any further . . . questions."

The meaning was obvious to Professor Jacobson. The German major was turning himself in.

Astonished, Professor Jacobson watched as Schulmann donned his hat and coat, retrieved his briefcase, and turned toward the door. Rolf Schulmann looked again at Jacobson as he passed, and he nodded deferentially, touching the brim of his hat with the utmost respect. Then he was gone.

* * *

When they arrested him the gendarmes didn't abuse him as they might have—Professor Jacobson insisted on that. Former Nazi Major Rolf Schulmann came quietly, humbly, as if he were accustomed to being dragged from his room in chains. Jacobson noticed he had arrived at head-quarters fully dressed; Schulmann had known they would come, and had not even removed his shoes.

Jacobson set a wooden chair just inside the cell door and sank heavily onto its surface. For several moments neither he nor the German spoke. The air was thick with unspoken questions and the knowledge of what—and who—lay between them.

Rolf Schulmann spoke first, and Jacobson could hear the emotion in his voice. "She looks just like you."

Jacobson studied him soberly. "And I can see that you love her."

"But that's not enough, is it?"

"No, it's not." Jacobson laid his hands carefully in his lap. "My daughter has told me a lot about you, Mr. Schulmann," Jacobson continued uncomfortably. "Because of her love for you I would like to get to know you better."

Schulmann acknowledged his comment with a nod but didn't answer. The professor continued carefully. "Now that the war is finally over, it seems that we have time to talk about you—and about Marie."

"What do you wish to know?"

Jacobson shrugged. "Your military career. Your family. Why you were sent to a concentration camp . . ." He folded his arms. "And everything that happened to my daughter while she was in your custody."

Schulmann studied him carefully. Jacobson knew that this man had understood Jacobson's implied question. Had Major Schulmann treated Marie with respect while she was his prisoner, or had things happened that had compromised her dignity?

"I'll make no excuses, Professor." The words were carefully spoken. "I'll tell you what happened and let you decide. That's the only way I can be fair to Marie."

Mr. Schulmann recounted his life, starting with his childhood in Schönenberg, his family's move to Chicago and his subsequent education there, and the way he was caught up in the frenzy of the Nazi Party and the madness that followed. He described his conversion to The Church of Jesus Christ of Latter-day Saints, detailing his encounter with the missionaries and Hélène's and his subsequent desire to be baptized. He described his loneliness after Hélène passed away trying to give birth to their second child and his worry for his surviving son's safety while he was stationed in France. He spoke of Félix Larouche, Marie's Résistance fiancé, and of the disaster in the mountains above Izieu. And then he described in careful detail exactly how he had interrogated Marie and how he had tried to mitigate her torture at the hands of the Gestapo. He explained his decision to hide her away from the Gestapo until he could decide what to do with her. He spoke of their time together in Schönenberg and of his growing love for her. He told the professor of Marie's courage when she'd protected his son from danger and of her decision to return to France with him to visit Félix's mother.

He talked about Marie's disappearance and his efforts to find her, and he described the final brief moments they had together as he was sentenced to die. He explained how the death sentence was unofficially postponed during the frenzied panic of the Allied invasion of June sixth, and he briefly described the months that followed in Sachsenhausen.

Jacobson observed that Schulmann didn't try to augment his suffering or dramatize his own heroics. Nor was he asking for pity or forgiveness. He was merely telling his story—factually, straightforwardly, with no embellishments. Against his will, Jacobson felt his respect for the man rise a notch or two. He asked, "Do you realize what your marriage to my daughter would do to her?"

Soberly, Schulmann replied, "Yes, I do."

"But can you understand the danger from a father's point of view?" Jacobson persisted. "As a father the idea that my daughter might spend her whole married life ostracized, shunned, and seen as an object of ridicule, the wife of a Nazi . . ." Jacobson took a deep breath. "Everywhere you go you will always be seen as a Nazi. There is no place in this world you can settle that she will not be treated as a traitor for marrying you. And you, Mr. Schulmann, will be hunted for the rest of your life, whether by governments terrorized by Hitler's evil regime or by vigilante types looking to collect a bounty. Do you honestly think I can, in good conscience, allow my daughter to be put through that kind of hell?"

"Of course not." Schulmann's voice remained humble.

"Your children would be intimidated at school, made to feel the brunt of the anger of their classmates' parents. Your innocent children will become the next generation of victims, Mr. Schulmann, and they will be taught to hate you for the evil things that other Germans did during the war. Are you prepared to deal with *their* suffering? Are you prepared to put your family through the horror of narrow-minded intolerance, prejudice, and hatred?"

Schulmann watched him silently as he finished, and Jacobson could see the sorrow in his eyes.

Schulmann took a deep breath and leaned toward the professor. "Everything you've said is true." He paused. "You're definitely in a position to know, and to be honest, I dread having to go through all of that myself, let alone drag your daughter, our children, and Hélène's son through that kind of a future. Not only will there be hurtful, angry remarks and prejudice, but there will also be death threats, expulsions, and lawlessness. There will be constant danger to my family, both day and night. I won't be able to leave for work in the morning without wondering if I'm kissing my wife and children for the last time. And, even though you were too refined to mention it, there will be extreme danger to you yourself, Professor. You will also bear the effects of your daughter's and my decision . . .

"I've agonized over this very subject ever since I was again reunited with Marie. I've lain awake at night wondering what to do about it all. I've wished I could live my life over, with the knowledge I have now, and make decisions that would not haunt me and devastate the ones I love. I've tried to imagine how I would feel if *my* daughter fell in love with a Nazi . . . And the thought terrifies me. I have no excuses for the decisions I've made. None at all."

Schulmann shook his head sorrowfully. "I don't know why God didn't allow me to learn about Him at an earlier age. I've wondered what my life would've been like if I'd had that opportunity. And, to be honest, maybe He did try to give me that opportunity earlier and I was not in a frame of mind to recognize His whisperings. I'm grateful to Him for not giving up on me, even though He eventually had to broadside me with the message in order for me to hear it.

"But aren't we forgetting something, Professor?" Schulmann's eyes remained steady on Jacobson. "We have the light and knowledge that only the gospel can bring, and we have the ability to see God's hand in all things. We can ask Him for protection, and if we're keeping His commandments to the best of our ability, we have assurance that He won't abandon us. Doesn't the Bible say God has 'not given us the spirit of fear; but of power, and of love, and of a sound mind'?

"Professor, I cannot promise you, the father of the woman I love, that your daughter will be protected from life's harsh realities. And you're right to worry that she'll have more than her fair share of them if she marries me. I can't promise you that nothing will ever harm her or our children. I can't promise you that I'll be allowed to grow old with her. Neither can I promise you that our children will grow up unscathed by the hate and prejudice of which you speak. There are only two things I *can* promise you, Professor Jacobson: that your daughter and your grandchildren will never receive anything but love from me, and that our family will stay close to the Savior Jesus Christ. Marie and I will try our hardest to pattern our lives after Him, and we will teach our children to do the same. Your daughter will be as safe as I can possibly make her, Professor. Of that I give you my word."

Professor Jacobson met Schulmann's gaze and contemplated his words. They rang true, and he realized he was struggling with the fact that this man, who had done so much to undermine the French people's struggle for freedom during the war, could show such faith and conviction, and such love. He didn't doubt this man cared for his daughter. In fact, Rolf Schulmann had the love for Marie that he'd always hoped Marie would find in a husband. What was Heavenly Father thinking, throwing a Nazi officer and his daughter together?

Schulmann's voice interrupted his reverie. "Your daughter has been a blessing to me, Professor Jacobson. She said something to me, once, while I still had her in my custody in Belley. She said, 'You have kindness in you, Major Schulmann.'" Rolf's voice wavered, and he cleared his throat. "I've wanted to tell you what her simple words have meant to me over the years. I believe that was the moment I began to fall in love with her."

FORTY-FOUR

April 21, 1946

She heard footsteps outside her cell door, and an anonymous voice ordered her to dress and prepare for immediate departure.

Fearfully, Natalie swung her legs to the cold concrete, reached for her slacks, and pulled them on. She picked up her shoes and then she hesitated, her heart pounding and her breath tight in her chest. She dropped her shoes onto the jumbled blanket on her cot and slid to her knees, folded her arms, and leaned her face into the mattress.

"Protect us, Heavenly Father, please . . . soften Viktor's heart . . ." And then in a surge of goodwill that took her completely by surprise, "And please . . . be merciful to his innocent daughter, Lucya."

Lieutenant Rostov arrived two minutes later and escorted her out of the building.

"Where is Hans?"

"Be patient, Natalya."

"What's going to happen to him, Viktor?"

"He will leave for Novosibirsk within the hour."

"What is he going to do for the Soviet Union?"

"My dear Natalya." Viktor smiled tightly. "That's really none of your business. You shouldn't even be asking."

"Where are you taking me?"

"You're full of questions this morning," Rostov snapped. "I'm allowing you a chance to bid your friend farewell, but I am not required to explain anything to you."

Natalie saw Hans standing under the watchful care of Vasik, and her heart leaped into her throat. She ran toward him.

Rostov said, "You have fifteen seconds, Natalya."

"Natalie, I—I'm so sorry." Hans buried his face in her hair. "I can't help you anymore. I don't know how to save you from him." With his voice betraying his agony, he whispered, "No matter what happens, please remember that I love you."

Behind them Lieutenant Rostov's voice sounded impatient. "Don't waste my time."

Hans continued, his whisper urgent now. "Natalie, there's something I've been meaning to tell you and I've never had the chance . . ." He shifted his balance slightly, and she felt the agony in his next words. "I'm a different man now, Natalie—different from the gutter rat who called you a dragon so many months ago . . ." He hesitated, and his arm tightened around her. "When I left Berlin, after you told me about you and Curly—"

Rostov interrupted. "Brenner, that's enough. Release her and step away."

Hans did not let her go. Natalie could hear Rostov and his trusted Vasik approaching, and her body went completely cold. She began to shake uncontrollably. Suddenly, desperately, she wanted Hans to understand her feelings for him, and she blurted, "Hans, I'm so sorry . . . Curly and I aren't—"

Vasik's leering face suddenly filled her vision and she was brutally wrenched from Hans's embrace. She stumbled, righting herself in time to see Vasik wrestle a struggling Hans to the ground. But even while being brutally shackled, Hans continued to fight, launching himself bodily into the monster and pummeling him with knees, head, elbows, torso, and handcuffs until his giant captor felled him with one violent, heavy fist to the side of his face. The last thing Natalie saw before Rostov captured her and dragged her to his car was Hans on his face in front of the towering form that could not possibly be considered human.

* * *

In the back seat Natalie shrank as far from Rostov as she could, her mind still numb with shock. "Are you going to kill him?"

"No, Natalya, I need Mr. Brenner to fulfill his obligation to my government."

"Why are you taking out your frustrations at your government's tyranny on Hans?"

Rostov smiled faintly. "It is *your* government also, Natalya, and I would again recommend that you stifle your tendency to speak treason—if you do, there is a greater chance you'll live a long and productive life."

"Please, Viktor—where are you taking me?"

He stretched his arm along the space between them and contemplated her soberly. "I've received permission to take you with me back to Moscow."

"Like a war trophy?" She began to cry, choking on her words. "Viktor, I beg of you . . ." She had never been so frightened in her life. "I'm not that kind of woman. Please don't make me do things I've promised God I will not do . . ."

Rostov watched her sorrowfully. He turned his body to face her squarely. "There is something I've never told you about me." He sighed. "I'm a sick man, Nurse Natalya, and the doctors have told me I won't live much longer. You will stay with me and help me . . ." Suddenly his words seemed awkward. "I—want you to help me live . . . for my daughter's sake." He hesitated again and then continued almost pleadingly. "I would never force you to—to love me that way."

Natalie watched him and felt, for just a moment, a whisper of compassion for the Soviet lieutenant.

"You said my father was a naval officer, and that he was killed?"

"According to my sources in Moscow, that is correct."

"What about my mother, Viktor? If what you say is true, then she needs me even more." Natalie shuddered. "Think of your daughter, Lucya. How did you feel when she was taken away from you? Are you prepared to cause my mother the same agony *you* are experiencing? What if I never see her again and she always wonders what happened to me?"

The lieutenant was clearly uncomfortable with her reference to the similarities between her predicament and that of his daughter.

"Viktor, please reconsider . . ." She could hardly breathe. "Please at least let me go with Hans and—"

"Never." He straightened in his seat and his eyes went hard. "It is because of Hans Brenner that you're in this predicament, Miss Allred. If he had succeeded . . ." Natalie felt a wall rising between them as effectively as if Rostov had deliberately placed and mortared each stone himself. "Natalya Ivanovna, do not speak that name again."

Silently Natalie watched him, desperate for anything to say that would convince him to listen to her. She remembered how her mention of his dead wife, Alyona, had influenced him to let Curly live, but as clearly as if the warning had been written on the stone wall between them she sensed that if she attempted the same ploy now she might never see another sunrise.

She kept silent. She watched as they passed through the gate of a Soviet military compound and pulled to a stop near an imposing structure guarded by Red Army soldiers.

A young officer appeared at the entrance and hurried toward the car, his eyes worried. He leaned near the lieutenant's window and spoke urgently in Russian. Rostov responded shortly, opened his door, and stood.

The officer continued his frantic dialogue, and Rostov turned on the boy, impatiently silencing him with one word. Then Rostov asked a question, and the officer hesitated, anxious. He licked his lips and almost whispered a response.

Rostov's rage exploded. Ignoring Natalie still inside the vehicle, he slammed his door and strode up the steps and into the building, the nervous young officer close on his heels.

After a few silent minutes the driver glanced through the rearview mirror at Natalie and cleared his throat awkwardly. He spoke apologetically, obviously trying to explain something to her, and then he also left the car, indicating with his hands for her to stay where she was. Terrified, Natalie huddled in the farthest corner of her seat and wrapped her arms around her torso, watching the door of the building.

She could not make her brain function past her terror. The thought of what might be her fate overwhelmed her, and she tried unsuccessfully to divert her thoughts to more pleasant things—her mother, her relatives, Hans Brenner . . .

It didn't help that every pleasant thing that meant anything to her was tied up in this nightmarish quagmire. She knew an attempt to escape would be futile. The guards standing nearby watched her steadily, and she knew that even if she did leave the car they would hardly stand idly by and allow her to walk—or run—away.

She worried about Hans. She pictured him folded at Vasik's feet, and it made her physically ill.

She heard footsteps and saw a figure descending the building's steps and approaching the car. Diminutive and unimpressive, with sagging jowls and dull grey eyes, he wore a business suit and held a set of keys in his hand.

He spoke quickly to a guard, selected a key and unlocked the driver's door, slipped into the seat, and started the engine. He glanced back at Natalie, his expression betraying nothing, and then he pulled away from the curb.

She took a chance. She whispered in English, "Where are we going?"

"Orders." The man responded in her tongue. "I am to deliver you to the airport for transport to Moscow."

Defeated, Natalie leaned her head to the side and silently watched the city pass by.

At the nearby Köpenick air base, Natalie's driver pulled the car close to the steps of a waiting Halifax, its engines idling and propellers running. She moved past Russian sentries guarding the plane and ascended the steps.

At the plane's door hovered an impressive young soldier dressed in the uniform of a Soviet political officer. He smiled kindly at her as she approached. "Miss Allred!" Although he had to shout to be heard above the roar of the engines, he addressed her formally and in the politest Russian-accented English she had ever heard. The breeze ruffled his light brown hair, and he gestured for her to hurry. Once she was beside him, he shouted into her ear, "My name is Alex Petrov. Lieutenant Rostov asked me to relay his regrets that urgent business prevents him from joining you on your flight—he wishes for me to accompany you and your friend to Moscow."

"My friend?"

Petrov nodded and reached for her arm, hurrying her along. "Lieutenant Rostov will join you tomorrow . . ."

Natalie didn't hear the remainder of the man's words. She walked through the door, ignoring the pilot and copilot busy in the open cockpit on her left, several Russian guards standing and lounging on her right, and bags and crates of supplies stacked in a cage at the rear of the plane. Instead her gaze locked on the still form near that cage, and she lunged toward the chained figure of Hans Brenner, his face bruised and bloody and his head drooping unconscious against the frame of the airplane.

With her heart crying out and her eyes riveted to her objective, she was not expecting the sudden interference of the gigantic creature responsible for Hans's predicament. When Vasik rose up in front of her she cried out, almost colliding with his broad chest before she was able to arrest her forward motion.

Grimly he leered down at her, his teeth hideously decayed and his nose a swollen, pulpy mess in the center of a bruised face. From the pummeled looks of the giant Natalie assumed Hans had been able to effectively resist his attacker for some time before succumbing, and the thought made her yearn to be with Hans where he lay so still in his restraints.

But Vasik forced her to a seat and she obediently sat next to him. He ogled her steadily while the young Alex Petrov secured the door and instructed the guards to take their seats. Petrov nodded politely at Natalie as he passed to secure the door of the cargo cage at the rear of the plane. Natalie glanced through the window and watched miserably as the airstrip passed away under the taxiing wings of the Halifax.

In the distance she could see the outlines of ruined Berlin, and she knew it would be a long time before she was missed at the hospital. Dr. Hayes had approved her travel to Nüremberg and would not be expecting her return for at least a week. She turned and strained to look past the leering Vasik toward Hans. His head rolled with the movement of the plane, and he opened his eyelids once before fading again into painful oblivion.

Grief-stricken, she turned her attention back to the window and caught a glimpse of a car pulling onto the tarmac and paralleling the plane, increasing speed to stay even as the Halifax taxied for the runway. The car moved closer to the plane and she saw a figure in the back seat of the car, straining forward as if to urge the driver to greater speed, and as she squinted to get a better look, she realized that the figure was Lieutenant Viktor Rostov.

The car careened to a halt, and Natalie watched as Rostov threw open his door and launched himself from the car, sprinting toward the plane with a speed and determination that surprised Natalie. His face was ugly with anger, and as he ran he waved his arms violently and shouted unintelligible threats at the now-retreating plane. And then Natalie saw him stumble, hesitate, clutch at his chest, and fall to his knees on the runway.

Without warning the dirty curtain over her window dropped closed, blocking her view of the frantic Rostov. She looked up at Petrov, surprised, but his expression remained unreadable. "Pardon my intrusion, Miss Allred, but you must take this opportunity to rest—this will be a long flight." Abruptly the political officer turned from her and busied himself closing the curtains of five more windows in the passenger bay before sitting across from Natalie and leaning his head against the side of the plane.

Curious, she followed him with her eyes as the plane separated from the ground, and as she watched him the young man expelled a gentle breath and settled back into his seat. For just a moment he stayed there with his eyes closed, and then suddenly Natalie found him gazing at her solemnly. She was too surprised to drop her gaze, realizing he'd discovered her observations. His clear blue eyes narrowed, and for just a moment she imagined a hint of warning in their depths before he looked away.

While around her the Russian soldiers produced previously stowed bottles of spirits and celebrated their return to Mother Russia, Natalie sat silently and worried about Hans, wondered about Rostov's final, frantic pursuit, and pondered the unexpected, silent warning in the young political officer's eyes.

* * *

Hans felt his body bounce violently and strike the floor. He groaned, his tortured skull pounding and the shackles cutting into the bruised flesh of his wrists. Ignoring the excruciating agony, he raised his hands to his face and wiped blood from his crusted eyelids and then tried to focus around a milky fog.

It seemed Professor Rostov's vested interest in the usefulness of his brain did not extend to the health of his limbs. Gently, carefully, he moved his extremities, testing his range of motion as much as physically possible in the limited space. It took several minutes for him to realize that he was lying near the cargo hold of an airplane—and the engine's roar against his throbbing ear, the shimmies, and the constant vibrations were not some diabolical new torture. Disorientation was followed by several minutes of panic—if he was on a plane, that meant he was on his way to Russia and would never see her again.

Then, from his position against the rough metal floor, Hans caught a glimpse, through a forest of military footwear, of a trim ankle, and he swallowed painfully. His eyes followed the ankle until it disappeared inside the pant leg, and then followed the pant leg until it disappeared behind Vasik. The gorilla had his face turned away from Hans, seemingly enthralled by the rest of Natalie—the part Hans could not see from his position on the floor.

Natalie was here. Hans closed his eyes.

The plane again hit a violent pocket of turbulence, and his head slammed against the floor. At moments like this Vasik seemed to find Hans more interesting than Natalie, and now the monster grinned down at Hans's discomfort. Hans gazed back steadily and didn't let his expression betray the agony in his skull.

The plane began to descend, and Hans's tortured ears screamed for relief from the mounting pressure. Still he stared back steadily at his tormentor, and even though Hans's face remained calm, his heart pounded and he pleaded with God, begging Him to somehow intervene in his and Natalie's behalf.

His head felt the turbulence of their descent through the metal flooring, and he braced for an impact that would most certainly break his neck. He closed his eyes and held his breath, and when the impact finally came he was surprised—his captors had chosen to put charitable human beings in the cockpit.

The plane taxied to a stop and Hans watched as a very young Soviet officer stood, politely offered his hand to Natalie, and escorted her immediately from the plane. The two pilots stood next and turned to follow the officer to the door, and suddenly one of them turned and caught Hans's eye. Underneath the Soviet cap, flight jacket, and Russian pilot's insignia, Hans recognized U.S. Army Pilot Captain Charles Miller. And right behind him was Gregory Jameson.

In the same moment Hans recognized the pilots and they disappeared through the open doorway, the world around him exploded into complete mayhem. GIs in full combat gear raided the small plane, and the cacophony of their shouting and the Russian guards' foul, astonished curses added to the confusion. Most of the unfortunate Soviets were too drunk to resist, and after they absorbed the shocking revelation that they had not landed in Moscow, they relinquished their weapons and surrendered.

But Vasik obviously didn't agree with the concept of either defeat or surrender. The Americans foolishly left only six men in the plane to apprehend the volcano, which erupted in the most deadly explosion Hans had ever witnessed from a human form.

Disabled GIs flew in all directions, and one landed near Hans with a brutally broken arm and an expression on his face that could only be described as outright shock and awe.

Hans tapped him politely on the shoulder with his manacled hands. He remembered to speak English. "Give me your gun, please."

The young man shook his head, his eyes bright with pain. Hans wondered if the boy had been trained never to relinquish his weapon. Another American soldier received Vasik's loving regard in his midsection and disappeared through the door of the plane.

Only one frightened soldier remained to subdue the Ukrainian, and Hans returned his attention to the disabled man near him. "Got something against living, Private?"

"We're under orders not to shoot any Russkies . . ."

"You mean you're under orders not to *kill* any Russians, right?"

The boy nodded, grimacing in pain.

"I promise I won't kill him." Hans reached imploringly for the man's gun. "But if you give me your weapon, I promise to disable him for you."

At the door Hans saw the Soviet officer who had escorted Natalie from the plane. *Young and inexperienced,* Hans thought, and a bit uncomfortable in the uniform he's wearing . . .

Hans watched as the officer raised both hands and tried to reason with Vasik, and Hans again prodded the disabled soldier. "That man's an American agent, isn't he?"

The young boy struggled to rise. "I don't know. I just do what I'm told . . ."

Hans saw Vasik lock his hands around the young officer's throat. Hans tried one more time. "I really need your gun, Private—*right now,* if you don't mind."

The soldier agreed. He awkwardly stretched his intact left arm across his body and managed to work his sidearm free. Hans took the Colt revolver and hefted it reverently against the palm of his hand. It was a real cowboy weapon!

Ignoring the agonizing pain, Hans raised the weapon with his right hand, of necessity dragging his fettered left along with it. Grateful his trigger finger still functioned, he took careful aim at the momentarily motionless paws wrapped around the neck of the young undercover agent who was now dangling precariously in midair. Hans moved his aim a fraction of a centimeter to the right and carefully squeezed the trigger, expertly shooting the gorilla through both thick wrists.

For a man who made his living with his hands, it was a death sentence. Hans turned his attention away from Vasik's agony and subsequent detainment back to the miraculous gadget he held in his hand. Finally he reversed it and reluctantly handed it back to the private. "If you ever want to trade," Hans said hopefully, "I have a Luger hidden back in Berlin . . ."

"An honest-to-goodness Luger?" The boy's pain-filled eyes brightened. "Wait 'til I tell my kid brother back home!"

FORTY-FIVE

Natalie stood with Curly outside the officer's lounge. She felt awkward, self-conscious, and eternally grateful. "You continue to surprise me, Curly Miller." She smiled softly. "You and Gregory kept us from a rather nasty fate."

He smiled back at her. "I can only imagine."

The conversation was uncomfortable. Natalie's gaze wavered as she tried to think what she could say to lessen the awkwardness of the situation. She brightened. "I'm impressed, Curly. You and Gregory disguised yourselves so completely—and that agent was such a good actor—I never imagined this could be a rescue."

Curly sobered. "You didn't think we'd just leave you there, did you?"

"Of course not." Natalie shook her head. "I knew you'd try to get us out. That's the way you are." Suddenly she touched his arm, and her eyes pleaded with him. "How am I ever going to thank you?"

He shrugged, and even though the meeting was obviously painful for him also, she could see that he was pleased with her gratitude. Gently he took her hand in his. "Listen, Natalie, I didn't do this so you'd run back to me." He searched for a way to express his feelings. "You mean the world to me, and I still haven't figured how I'm going to get over you—but I did what I had to, that's all. No way was I going to let you and Brenner disappear . . ."

"I know, Curly. And I appreciate it. You didn't abandon us."

Curly touched her cheek softly. "I have a feeling Hans Brenner never will, either."

* * *

Natalie met briefly with Major Matthews, and at his insistence she told him all about her connection with both Hans Brenner and Lieutenant Viktor Rostov.

She started with the uncomfortable and embarrassing drama involving the three Russian soldiers and Hans's timely intervention. She told Matthews about Lieutenant Rostov—the visits, the roses, and the threats in an attempt to use her as a bargaining chip against Hans. Natalie admitted she had no idea why Rostov was so determined to capture him. She did not mention Rostov's assertion of her Russian parentage.

Matthews asked Natalie if she'd be willing, for her own safety, to wait to return to Berlin, and she admitted she'd been hoping to use her accumulated leave of absence to look for her relatives in France. Major Matthews promised her that he would call and explain everything to Dr. Hayes at the hospital.

Matthews took her hand in his as the meeting drew to a close. "Nurse Allred, I'm so pleased that you're safe. I hope you'll find what you're looking for in France."

"I hope so, too, Major." She hesitated. "Can you give me any idea how Mr. Brenner is doing? I mean, he seemed to be in a lot of pain when they removed him from the plane . . ."

He smiled reassuringly. "I'll take you to him."

Natalie hugged him gratefully.

That afternoon Natalie stood in the doorway of Hans's hospital room and watched him sleep. Major Matthews touched her shoulder. "I have to make a phone call." He walked away.

Natalie moved into the room and sank into a chair next to Hans's bed. She resisted the impulse to reach out and trace the curve of his jaw, scruffy with several days' stubble and multiple bruises. Vasik had really damaged Hans this time, Natalie realized, and she wondered if caressing the high cheekbone or the broad forehead would hurt him too much. His ear was ripped and partially bandaged, he had a bandage on the side of his head, and his nose looked like it might have been broken. His arms carried multiple lacerations, and his strong, beautiful hands were discolored and the knuckles twice their normal size. Several fingers had been broken and the doctors had set them and strapped them to splints. Hans's bruised chest was wrapped in multiple layers of clean white gauze. Natalie wondered how many ribs had been broken and tried not to imagine the scope of internal damage possible by the blunt force of a gorilla bent on maximum destruction.

Gently, carefully, she rested the side of her head against his torso, and she felt him stir. His hand came up and lay softly against her head and neck. She lifted her chin and they studied each other silently. Natalie had no desire to break the silence, and neither, it seemed, did Hans. For the first time in more days then she could recall she felt completely safe. They rested that way until Natalie could hear Major Matthews's footsteps returning to the room.

"You're awake, Lieutenant." Matthews swept into the room with a cheering smile for Natalie and an encouraging hand on Hans's bruised shoulder. "You speak English, Lieutenant?"

"When I feel like it."

Matthews chuckled. "How are you feeling?"

"Like I've been forced through a sausage grinder."

Matthews laughed. "You look like it, too. In fact—" Matthews reached for an empty chair. "Even though I'm tremendously interested in your association with Lieutenant Viktor Rostov, I'm going to let you heal for a few days before I discuss the subject with you." He turned to Natalie with another smile. "I believe Nurse Allred will take very good care of you until you're feeling better."

"I don't want Natalie to take care of me."

"Hans!" Natalie sat up, hurt. "I'm not the best nurse in the army, but I think I know a few things about cracked ribs and broken noses."

"Natalie, that's not what I meant." Hans smiled faintly. "You need to stay away from me until Rostov's captured—"

"No, I need to stay right here by your side."

"Listen, Natalie . . ." Hans hesitated. "I know you're a good nurse—and I would trust you with my life. But you want to go to France. You'll be safe in France. Curly can take you there and help you find your relatives."

"Hans, I—"

Matthews interrupted. "Captain Miller is returning to Nüremberg, Mr. Brenner, and then he'll be headed to Berlin. He won't be back for another week at least."

"How is Natalie supposed to get to France?"

"I'd be honored to get Natalie on a flight that's leaving soon, if that's her wish. She won't be alone, either—I'm sending Rolf Schulmann's fiancée to Paris along with a military lawyer, and Natalie can billet at the army base there—"

Hans grimaced painfully as he struggled to prop himself up on one elbow. "Why is Marie going to France?"

"Lie down, Mr. Brenner, or you'll never get well." Matthews pushed Hans back onto his pillow. "She's going there to be with her fiancé."

"He turned himself in, didn't he?" Hans swallowed a curse. "Misplaced sense of honor . . ." he grumbled, shaking his head. "What was he thinking? Doesn't he realize a guilty verdict could mean the death penalty?" Hans rubbed at his bruised neck, swallowing painfully. "France has an exceptionally nasty form of capital punishment, too."

"Rolf Schulmann is a good man."

Hans looked at Matthews. "When is the trial going to be?"

"Miss Jacobson has agreed to inform me as soon as she knows." Matthews stood. "Miss Allred, you look exhausted, and I suppose Mr. Brenner is also in need of rest. I need to take you back to the office and make you comfortable for a few hours while I plan for a meeting with Lieutenant Rostov."

"Major Matthews . . ." Natalie began, worried. "What if Rostov—"

"He won't threaten me." Matthews smiled reassuringly. "Rostov and I reached an understanding long ago: we may be adversaries, but before that we were friends. Besides, he's been pestering my secretary for this rendezvous ever since your friend Curly stole you away from him. I'm sure he's anxious that we discuss the situation like—how does he say it?—like 'two civilized human beings.'"

FORTY-SIX

April 22, 1946

From his position on the upper bank of the Havel, Lieutenant Rostov watched as Major Matthews selected a stone from the bank of the river and weighed it expertly in his hand. Matthews brought back his arm and shoulder and then launched the stone in a smooth, graceful arch toward the lazy current of the narrow eddy. Viktor watched, amazed, as the stone barely touched the surface of the water, skipped gracefully into the air, and then again contacted the surface and bounced. The stone's dance continued, each spring tighter than the last, until finally the magical pebble encountered the river's main flow and disappeared beneath its frantic run.

Viktor walked to Matthews's side. He said in English, "How did you do that?"

Matthews turned and glanced at him. "It's all in the wrist. See? Let me show you." He stooped down, selected another pebble, and held it up for Viktor to see. Viktor selected a smooth stone similar to Matthews's.

"Now hold it between your fingers like this." Matthews demonstrated for him, and Viktor forced his long fingers to mimic the shorter, fleshier ones of the American officer.

"Know how to throw a baseball?" Matthews asked.

"Yes—a little."

"Well, it's somewhat like throwing a baseball—except there needs to be a fluid connection from your shoulder all the way down to your fingers." Matthews twisted his torso, demonstrating in slow motion. He brought back his arm. "Don't throw over your head, or the rock's going to sink like a—well, like a stone."

Viktor smiled faintly. He watched Matthews's movements and copied him carefully.

"Throw to the side, and use your whole arm but not necessarily all your strength. And flick it off the tips of your fingers to give it a spin."

Matthews launched the stone, and Viktor counted seven perfect bounces.

"Impressive."

Matthews laughed. "You need to lighten up, Viktor—you sound like you're at the *Politburo* meeting describing the situation in Poland."

Viktor hurled his rock. It slammed into the surface of the river, rebounded in a tremendous jump followed by a half-hearted stumble, and then disappeared into the murky darkness. Viktor scowled at the location of his stone's betrayal and then looked accusingly at Matthews. "I threw it exactly as you instructed."

"It takes significant practice." Matthews slapped him encouragingly on the back. "My father showed me how to skip stones when I was four."

Viktor looked out silently over the river.

"I was sorry to hear about your wife, Viktor. How long has it been?"

"Over two years," Rostov answered softly.

"A retreating German Luftwaffe unit, you said? Strafing the neighborhood in a last-ditch attempt to—"

"Your gift of white roses was fitting. She loved white roses."

"It was the least I could do. I know how much Alyona meant to you."

Viktor turned his back on the river to face Matthews. "Major, you're a father, aren't you?"

"I am." Matthews sobered, watching Viktor steadily. "I have a daughter— a few years older than yours, I believe. Your Lucya is seventeen?"

Viktor folded his arms, carefully hiding the slight tremble in his hands. "Because you have a daughter you can understand a father's concern for his daughter's safety."

"That's true."

"I brought a recent photo of my daughter."

"I'd like to see it."

Viktor reached into a pocket and handed a mutilated photograph to Matthews.

The major took it and frowned. "Looks like it's been sent through the wringer." He indicated the torn, folded, and dirty object. Several holes had been gouged through the girl's image. "How did it get like this?"

"I received that photograph in the mail yesterday, Major. It was like this when I received it."

Matthews swore softly. "What fiend would treat your daughter's image with such disrespect?"

"Look at the picture."

Matthews looked down at the photograph in his hands, and Viktor watched the American's face and felt the familiar tightening in his chest that he had felt when he first saw the picture. He did not need to look at the photograph to know what his old friend was seeing. He knew of the dismal, overcast sky, made even more depressing by the photograph's lack of color. He knew of the steam billowing over his daughter's bowed head, originating from the engine somewhere in the distance behind her. He knew of her thin frame clothed in a shapeless, loose-fitting outfit and her feet struggling to climb into the train. He knew of the large hand on her elbow and the soldier's face close to her own, taunting her. And he knew of the terror in Lucya's gentle eyes—eyes that looked exactly like those of her mother and of Natalya Ivanovna.

Major Matthews silently returned the photograph. He turned and began to walk along the bank of the river, and Viktor walked beside him.

"Your heroic rescue of Lieutenant Brenner and Miss Allred is not going to help my daughter, Major."

"I'm aware of that."

"She has suffered more than your daughter will ever suffer—and I cannot—" Rostov's voice broke. "I cannot allow your western cowboy tactics to endanger her life any further." He turned to face Matthews squarely. "I am ready to negotiate a trade."

Matthews shook his head. "I'm not here to negotiate with you, Lieutenant."

"My top mole hidden in your intelligence organization for Hans Brenner and Natalie Allred."

"No." Matthews grimaced. "I'm confident we'll uncover your agent without your help. And even if we never do, I am not trading Brenner and the nurse."

Viktor took a deep, wavering breath. "Mr. Brenner, then." He realized that Natalie might be forever out of his reach unless he presented the American major with the evidence he had accumulated against her. But for some reason he hesitated. For some inexplicable reason he could not bring himself to betray Natalya's heritage to this man, even though doing so would guarantee her return to him. Something hidden deep in the recesses of his blackened soul cried out against the betrayal and blocked the words from leaving his lips.

"No, Viktor. Again, no."

Suddenly Viktor felt nauseated. "My superiors see you as a dangerous, heartless man, Major Matthews, but I have always thought you reasonable." He forced himself to breathe steadily around his fear. "I'm prepared to offer you even *more*, Major, if it will help you to reconsider an exchange. Along with the identity of our agent, I'm prepared to give you back the German nuclear scientist Klaus Lichtermann—if only you will help me save my daughter's life by returning the young Nazi lieutenant." Viktor hesitated. "I'll protect Mr. Brenner with my life, if it's his well-being that makes you worry."

He saw the suspicion in the American officer's eyes, and he thought of his mother's long-ago words to an impressionable little boy, admonishing him to be a man of his word and to take care of the ones he loved. Viktor knew his past conduct would make it difficult to convince the major of his reliability now, and suddenly he wished that, like his mother, he believed in a supreme deity he could turn to for comfort and advice.

"I believe you know how to keep your word, Viktor . . ."

Rostov knew that was a major concession on Matthews's part.

The major continued. "But the issue here is not whether I should give up the lieutenant or whether or not you'd keep him safe—"

"The issue is my daughter," Rostov snapped, and he felt the panic in his chest accelerating his heart's dangerous rhythm.

"Again, I am sorry for your suffering, Lieutenant. But the answer is no." Major Matthews's voice took on a threatening edge. "And if I ever hear of you approaching either Mr. Brenner or Miss Allred again, I'll have you arrested for treaty violations, abductions, and murders that go far beyond the scope of a former Nazi and an American nurse."

Viktor stared down the major and realized he was tired of this game. He had been prepared to sacrifice a top agent in order to secure Hans Brenner and, ultimately, his daughter's freedom. To him it seemed more than a fair exchange—especially with Lichtermann included—and yet this obstinate American continued to thwart his efforts. This meeting was not going as Viktor had intended. What possessed his former comrade to turn down such a generous offer? An acclaimed German nuclear scientist and a vital operative's name and location, offered in exchange for a mere laboratory assistant?

The fear for his daughter's safety was compelling Viktor to make dangerous concessions he would not normally consider.

You understand, of course, that there is no room for failure.

Colonel Sergeyev's words, threateningly intoned so long ago, still haunted him—especially with the recent exile of his daughter and the senseless loss of her Anton. In fact, Viktor had failed so many times in this assignment that he was surprised it was not *he* in that mutilated photograph, headed for the frozen east and a life of hard labor.

"What has happened to you, Viktor?" Major Matthews's disappointed voice interrupted Viktor's thoughts. Matthews shook his head sadly. "What has happened to the principled Soviet officer who lobbied with me for Allied postwar cooperation? What happened to the intelligent and affable Viktor Rostov who was my equal at the Yalta Conference, who negotiated peace among feuding leaders with me? What happened to the moral fortitude of the man whose character I never had to question? What has happened to you, Viktor, that you would embark on such a ruthless, bloodthirsty career?"

"My path was chosen for me." Viktor's jaw felt tight. "Besides, my daughter's safety is worthy of my continued obedience to Comrade Stalin."

"I'm sorry for your daughter. I truly am." Matthews's voice hardened. "But I will *never* agree to an exchange—either for Lieutenant Brenner or for anybody else I manage to save from your clutches. You have chosen a lonely road, Lieutenant—one that I cannot advocate and do not envy you taking."

"There is no chance for compromise?"

Matthews's voice was clipped. "None whatsoever."

"Then I believe this meeting is at an end." Viktor held out his hand, and Matthews took it firmly in his own. Viktor said, "Even though the problem is left unresolved, you're truly a worthy adversary, Major James Matthews."

"And I'm honored to oppose such a noble enemy as you."

Viktor turned to go, moving up the embankment toward the tree line. Suddenly he hesitated, and following a singular, silent prompting that caught him entirely off guard, he turned and said, "His name is Sergeant Edward Finley, posing as adjutant to your superior, General Grayson."

Matthews made a valiant attempt to mask his surprise at the unexpected gift. If they hadn't been friends during the war, Viktor might have missed the faint spasm in the older man's left cheek at the shock of the mole's exposure. "I'm sure he's not the only one," Matthews responded evenly.

Rostov smiled tightly, turned, and walked away.

FORTY-SEVEN

April 22, 1946

When Professor Jacobson opened his door and saw Marie standing there, he gathered his daughter into his arms and held her close. His relief at having her safely home was only a small part of his emotion. He didn't want her to see the anguish in his eyes, because as much as he hated to admit it to himself, his concern for his daughter had been expanded to include apprehension for the complicated, honorable man she loved.

Marie clung to him. "Where is he, Daddy?" He ached at the agony in her voice. "In Frankfurt they told me he came here. I know you must've seen him."

Jacobson gently wiped a tear from her cheek. "Unfortunately, he was transferred today to the St.-Joseph Prison in Lyon. His trial is soon . . ."

She pulled away and looked up at him. "I need to find a way to help him, and in order to do that I . . ." Her voice wavered. "I have to know what they're accusing him of."

Professor Jacobson nodded. "I can let you read the indictment, along with evidence we have discovered in Nazi files."

"Do you think he's guilty?"

The look in his daughter's eyes cut him deeply. "He has many good things about him, as you said."

Marie shook her head. "Please don't ignore my question, Daddy. Do you think he's guilty?"

Jacobson dropped his eyes. "I'm confused, Marie—I don't know what to think." He tried to soften the blow of his words. "Mr. Schulmann has the finest representation available. But the accusations are phenomenal . . ." He hesitated. "And there is a good chance he will be found guilty."

Marie clung to her father's arm. "I need to see those documents right away, and then I have to find someone who can help him . . ."

"It's not going to be easy, Marie."

"I know." Her eyes were haunted. "But I have to try!"

Professor Jacobson took Marie to his office and sat her at his desk. He produced everything he had in his possession that concerned the Nazi criminal Rolf Schulmann. He turned on the lamp and then went to the hearth, stoked the fire, and left the office, closing the door and leaving Marie to her terrible task.

* * *

Marie couldn't take her eyes off the pages, and her stomach tied itself in knots as she read. Her head pounded and her heart screamed that these horrible accusations could not be true. Her Rolf would never be capable of such atrocities!

Besides, he had promised her long ago that he would never do these things. He had convinced her that he would not jeopardize the trust he had developed with God. And even with the horrific facts glaringly recorded in front of her, Marie believed in Rolf's promises.

She stayed hunched over her reading until late, with her father's clock ticking in the background and the warmth of the fireplace behind her fading as the flames turned into glowing yellow embers. When she finally stood and turned away, she knew what she had to do.

FORTY-EIGHT

April 30, 1946

In Paris she had been directed to Lyon, where her determined research had finally uncovered an address in Belley. The prefect in Belley, Monsieur de Lorme, had pointed her in the right direction. And now it seemed strange to be standing alone on this humble stoop, her hands trembling with anticipation. Her mind refused to accept that her long months of worry and searching might finally be at an end—that she might be about to face the relatives her mother was praying Natalie would find.

Natalie knocked, and after a few moments she heard footsteps approaching. She stepped back expectantly as the door opened. "Madame Bröder?"

But the woman bore no familial traits. This wasn't her aunt. Natalie's face fell.

The woman eyed her expectantly, and Natalie realized that communicating with this woman might be extremely difficult. Hadn't Rolf mentioned that Hans spoke French? Now she really wished Hans was here with her. She wished she had waited for him. But Matthews had assured her that most Europeans spoke at least one language besides their native tongue. Natalie prayed that for this woman, English would be the one.

"Good day, Madame. I'm sorry to intrude, but I was hoping to talk to Monsieur Abram Bröder—or a member of his family."

The woman's brow furrowed. She clearly had not understood a single word.

Natalie asked simply, "English?"

The woman shook her head and turned away from the door. She called into the interior of the home, and a young teenage boy soon appeared to stand beside her.

"May I help you?" he asked.

Natalie breathed a sigh of relief. "I'm so glad you can understand me!"

He looked pleased. "I speak the English from the school." He beamed at her.

She pressed forward. "Do you know the family of Monsieur Abram Bröder? They used to live here in this house."

From the look on the boy's face it was obvious she had challenged his elementary vocabulary. Natalie repeated her question and then watched anxiously while he translated each of her words in his head. He smiled and nodded happily each time a word was deciphered to his satisfaction. Finally he turned to the woman and spoke in a barrage that seemed to encompass much more than the scope of Natalie's simple question. The woman replied at length, glancing at Natalie every few moments.

Finally the boy turned back to her, licked his lips nervously, and began to formulate the strange English words. "Monsieur Bröder is not live here. He is given the *boches* . . ." The boy scratched his head. "The Germans they take his family."

Natalie felt her legs go weak. She steadied herself against the doorframe and tried to form her next question. "Wh-when . . . ?"

The boy didn't have to consult with the woman this time. He looked at his hand and then held up two fingers. "Two year."

Two years. Natalie remembered that once, in the hospital, Rolf Schulmann had mentioned casually that Hitler had focused a great part of his Jewish Solution on the deportation of Jews hiding in southern France. She felt sick.

She thanked the boy and turned to go.

* * *

Natalie returned to the Belley prefect and found Monsieur de Lorme. She informed the prefect head that his instructions had taken her to the home of her relatives but that her aunt and uncle no longer lived there. "The boy told me the Germans took them away," she reported.

Bulky and self-important, de Lorme peered at her. His dark eyes looked completely bored beneath his dense eyebrows, and his beard seemed to be constantly in motion, as if he had adopted the American habit of chewing gum.

"What do you want me to do about it, mademoiselle?" The dull lifelessness of his gaze meant he either already knew of their disappearance or he didn't care. What could possibly be so important about the disappearance of four little Jews? At least he knew how to speak her language.

"I was hoping there would be some record—any information about the deportation of the Bröders . . ."

"My dear girl"—de Lorme rolled his eyes heavenward—"this whole prefect was under Nazi control in '44, and the German major in charge of the Belley département was exceptionally ruthless. Many Jews were displaced or deported. Fortunately, the Nazis were remarkably efficient at keeping records. Everything that happened here would have been included in the German major's records, and those records have all been moved to other localities—especially any information relating to the *rafles* . . ."

"*Rafles?*"

De Lorme sighed, irritated at her ignorance. "Deportations of foreign nationals—relocation of the Jews."

At the risk of inviting more of his displeasure, Natalie pressed the head of Belley's prefect until he told her that Jews deported from Belley in the spring of 1944 would have been processed at the waystation at Drancy, north of Paris.

Heart heavy, Natalie thanked the man and left for the train station.

She was surprised to find Marie Jacobson on the platform. Natalie's first thought when she saw Marie sitting alone with her hands clasped tightly in her lap and her eyes staring straight ahead was that a Belley train platform was a curious place for Marie to be sitting if her fiancé was in a prison in Paris. Her second thought was that she longed to open her heart to Rolf Schulmann's intended, tell her everything, and beg her for her assistance.

Marie turned, and Natalie saw tears glistening in her eyes. Natalie hesitated, not wanting to burden Marie with her own worries when it was obvious Marie had more than her own share. But Marie leaped to her feet and ran to her.

"Natalie Allred!" She took Natalie into her arms. "Who would've thought when we said good-bye in Paris that we'd run into each other again in Belley!" The woman's pleasure at seeing her was obvious, and with the greeting Natalie's pent-up store of emotions burst.

Softly, silently, she sobbed on Marie's shoulder, and Marie continued to hold her close until Natalie had cried all she could possibly cry. Her anxiety for her relatives, and for Hans, lying in agony in a hospital bed because he had cared enough for her to try to save her, all added up to one gigantic sorrow that suddenly became the storm of the century.

Finally Natalie pulled away to face Marie. She wiped her face on a sleeve. "Isn't it curious how life continues forward when loved ones disappear—as if they never existed, as if they never even lived, or breathed, or *loved?*" She wiped at her eyes and tried to smile at Marie. "Everyone I talk to shrugs off my worry, as if to say, 'Life goes on.'"

Marie tried to reassure her. "Everyone has their own sorrows, Natalie—everyone lost loved ones during the war, and the anguish can be so unbearable they can't stand the thought of any more heartache." Marie touched her shoulder gently. "You and I are luckier than most—my Rolf is still alive, and his son is my greatest treasure. Because of your letter I have been happier over the past months than most people have been since before the war began. And your Hans returned from the dead and was there to protect you when you needed him most." Marie sighed. "Do you realize how blessed we are? We're treasured by two of the most valiant sons of our Heavenly Father—two men who constantly put our welfare and the welfare of each other ahead of their own safety. Two men who epitomize the Savior's words—'*Greater love hath no man than this, that a man lay down his life for his friends.*'"

Natalie remembered the few peaceful moments she'd shared with Hans in the hospital in Frankfurt, with Hans holding her close to him while they shared a poignant moment of silent, intimate camaraderie, and she nodded her agreement to Marie's words. "If only it were possible . . ." She hesitated. "Marie, Hans is such a good man. I—I care for him deeply, and I wish . . ."

"What, Natalie?"

Natalie sat down slowly on the nearest bench, her hand resting on its rough surface and her eyes on the other woman. "I broke up with Curly, and I haven't been able to tell Hans yet. So much has happened, and every time I try to tell him, something interrupts us . . . and I start to think that maybe I'm not *supposed* to tell him . . . that it's easier with him not knowing . . ."

"Why would it be better if Hans doesn't know?"

"He told me he loves me."

Marie smiled gently. "If Hans Brenner loves you, then you're officially the second luckiest woman alive."

Natalie flinched. "And yet, because I love him back, I endanger the eternal marriage I've dreamed of since I learned about the Church." She brushed at a loose strand of hair. "I used to think I was in love with Curly because he could take me to the temple—now I know I'm in love with someone else, and my dream of an eternal marriage is as unattainable as it was before I was baptized."

Marie sat down beside her. "You're worried Hans will pressure you if he knows you're not marrying Curly."

Natalie nodded. "And what makes it even worse"—here Natalie had to take a moment to compose her feelings—"I love him so much that I cannot imagine *not* marrying him!"

Marie looked at Natalie thoughtfully. "When you told me on the plane what had happened to Hans—why he had been missing for so many months, and what he's been through with that Soviet officer—I was shocked.

For the past few years Hans has endured a lot, Natalie, and it's usually been for the people he cares about most—people like you and me, and Rolf, and little Alma . . ." Marie swallowed. "Rolf told me once that he thinks Hans is closer to believing in God than Hans is ready to admit—even to his closest and best friend. And if that is so, then you shouldn't discount the possibility that his regard for you might be the incentive he needs to finally take those important steps that will make eternal marriage possible."

"Because of me?" Natalie agonized. "You think he would join the Church because he loved me? What about because he knows it's right?"

"What would be so terrible about having a *reason* to find out if something is right?" Marie reasoned calmly. "Didn't Nephi have a reason for following his father, Lehi, into the wilderness? Wasn't it because he loved and respected his father and wanted to please him?" Marie touched her hand. "You're a wonderful woman, Natalie, and I can see how Hans fell in love with you. I believe he is already changing, and from what I know of him, when he decides to make those promises to God and to you, you can be positive he will keep them for the rest of his life."

Natalie silently digested Marie's words, and even though she still had her concerns, she realized that her growing love for Hans seemed to make the idea of his eventual conversion more plausible. She heard the train whistle and looked up.

Marie said, "So you didn't find them here?"

Natalie shook her head. "Why are *you* here, Marie?"

"I'm trying to . . . help Rolf." Marie looked down at her hands. "He's been accused of unspeakable crimes—things he could not possibly have done, and I'm trying to find someone who might be able to speak in his behalf."

"Why are you looking here? Isn't Rolf in Paris?"

"He's been transferred to Lyon. His trial begins soon."

"Then why are you here? Shouldn't you be there with him?"

Marie struggled with her emotions. "He has *nobody,* Natalie—nobody to help him. But I believe there's somebody who can testify that he's not the monster they say he is. I've been in Belley looking for the Résistance leader Jacques Bellamont. Rolf said once that Jacques was a friend—and Rolf sent Jacques to protect me the morning the Gestapo captured me in Beaune-la-Rolande. But apparently Jacques left Belley some time ago. So now I'm going to Lyon to look for a woman who might know his whereabouts."

"Will you stay and attend the trial?"

"I don't know, Natalie." The train whistle sounded, and Marie brushed a wisp of hair from her eyes. "I must find Jacques—I cannot stand the thought of sitting in the courtroom without Jacques there to help Rolf."

Natalie frowned. "Why were you looking for Jacques here in Belley?"

"Because this is where he fought during the war."

A horrific suggestion lurked in the recesses of Natalie's consciousness, and her voice began to tremble. "And you said he was Rolf's friend during the war?"

Marie nodded. "It took a while, though. It's rather exceptional for a Maquisard and a Nazi major to be on speaking terms."

"Marie . . ." Natalie slowly stood and looked down at the woman on the bench. "What unspeakable crimes has Rolf been accused of?" She already knew, and she felt the cold, bitter taste of the knowledge creeping toward her mouth. "What was Rolf doing in Belley during the war?"

Marie saw the look on Natalie's face and her brow knit with concern. "He was the Nazi officer in command of the Belley département."

Natalie took a step backward. She felt the blood drain from her face, and her chest go cold. Even a premonition of the truth had not saved her from the brute force of its revelation. Her body turned of its own accord and she walked numbly toward the train, away from Marie, nothing penetrating her consciousness but the words of the young boy at the front door of her aunt's home—*Monsieur Bröder is not live here . . . The Germans they take his family.*

Marie stood and ran after her. "Natalie, I am so sorry. I wasn't thinking properly." She touched Natalie's shoulder, but Natalie didn't respond. "I assumed when you said your aunt wasn't here, that it meant she and her family hadn't lived in Belley after all."

Natalie turned numbly to Marie, her eyes dry. "According to the prefect, they were deported in the spring of '44—along with many other Jews. The prefect said that the Nazi major who ordered the *rafle* was 'exceptionally ruthless' . . ."

Marie stared at her, horrorstruck. "That cannot be true, Natalie. That man was either mistaken or he didn't know Rolf. I cannot accept that Rolf would do that to the Jews. I *will not* accept it."

Natalie hugged her arms around her body and closed her eyes, as if with the act she could block out the absurd idea that Rolf Schulmann, the kind, gentle, and desperately ill German officer whose life had been prolonged only through God's gentle grace, should be responsible for the murder of her Aunt Clara, Uncle Abram, and cousins Aimée and Leah.

FORTY-NINE

May 2, 1946

There are many reasons one might visit Lyon, deep in the southern half of France: it is considered one of the Renaissance capitals of the world, with its Roman architecture and amphitheaters and its penchant for good food and good times. Sixteenth-century red-tiled structures, flowing rivers bisected with ancient stone bridges, and art museums give the burgeoning community international appeal.

On the second day of May 1946, there was another compelling reason besides architecture and art for a handful of internationals to visit Lyon. The former headquarters of the Section Four Gestapo, situated on the historic Avenue Berthelot, the *École de Santé* was the gathering place for the highly publicized trial of former Allgemeine SS officer and accused war criminal Major Rolf Ahren Schulmann.

Rolf stood in the designated spot for the accused, a four-by-six wooden box with a padlocked gate and heavy glass panels rising eight feet toward the ceiling, separating him from the rest of the court like a fish in a bowl. If he looked upward he would see the hefty oak beams crisscrossing high above him on the ceiling's massive surface, as much for aesthetics as structure. And in each space between, improved lighting transformed the Nazi headquarters he had known in 1944 into a hall of justice for the conquered, run first by the victors and now by the victimized.

If he looked through the glass that surrounded his little box, he could see the heavy oak-trimmed balconies, filled to overflowing with curious onlookers who had heard, by word-of-mouth, that an important Nazi *boche* had been captured and was going to be tried this morning for his role in France's suffering. They would sit in on the spectacle for at least the first day or two, just to determine if this particular German had done enough during his forcible stay in France to merit their attention. What they really wanted to know was if Rolf's crimes were dreadful enough to earn him the guillotine.

Rolf searched the faces in the balcony, a part of his bruised heart yearning for a glimpse of the beautiful face that had been a part of his dreams since the middle of the war. But when he didn't see her he convinced himself he was glad—Marie should not be here, should not be forced to hear the diabolical things they would say about him. If she didn't come he wouldn't have to wonder if the things they accused him of would change her opinion of him forever.

But as Head Judge Aubert Pomeroy entered the courtroom with his two associate judges, Rolf looked neither up at the impressive ceiling nor at the balconies with their curious crowds. Rather, he kept his attention on the tribunal as Judge Pomeroy reached into a jar and selected the names of seven Frenchmen and two American diplomats who would act as Rolf's jurors. Pomeroy called the jurors forward to take their places in the designated location next to the judges' bench.

Judge Pomeroy called the room to order, and the proceedings of the nation of France against Rolf Ahren Schulmann officially began.

The prosecuting attorney for the French provisional government rose at the invitation of the tribunal and delineated Rolf Schulmann's crimes, painting the Nazi major's wrongdoings and the need for swift retribution in grandiloquent terms worthy of a French High Court instead of simply a war crimes tribunal.

Rolf's attorney moved to the podium. Professor Jacobson had chosen Monsieur Pierre Lamoreau himself, and Rolf had been impressed with the man's meticulous attention to the case. In the days preceding the trial Lamoreau had visited Rolf's cell multiple times, sometimes with Monsieur Jacobson and sometimes alone. A Frenchman and a former judicial committee member under de Gaulle, Monsieur Lamoreau had recently fallen on hard times under Félix Gouin's interim presidency, which had decided that Lamoreau possessed neither the experience nor the loyalties necessary to continue in his post. So in his unemployed state and inspired by the continuing war crimes trials in Nüremberg, Lamoreau had volunteered to head a judicial committee for the defense of former collabos and Nazis rounded up by de Gaulle and his predecessors and, along with his accumulated team of starving, multinational lawyers, had made a name for himself as lead counsel on the finest defense team available to the accused.

Monsieur Lamoreau humbly addressed the judges. "Messieurs, I'll address the accusations leveled against the prisoner by the Provisional Government of France.

"During this last devastating war, Allgemeine SS Major Rolf Schulmann was a Nazi. That is an undisputed fact. But the foremost subject being disputed here today is not only whether my client Monsieur Schulmann did, of his own will and choice, carry out the crimes as delineated in the indictment, but also whether he carried them out at all.

"The main accusations against my client as outlined by the prosecutor are as follows:

"Accusation number one: On the morning of March 24 of the year 1944, Schulmann organized and implemented a *rafle* in his département of Belley, with the intent of arresting and deporting forty-seven Jews to the Nazi concentration camps in the east. As a result of his actions, forty-seven foreign-born and naturalized French residents of Jewish origin lost their homes, their financial savings, their possessions, and most likely their lives. Few if any of those French citizens have returned to claim their homes in Belley, and so it has been hypothesized by the prosecution that even though denied by the defendant, these displaced elements were arrested as planned, transported by train to Nazi concentration camps, and ultimately eliminated along with more than six million other Jews under Hitler's diabolical regime.

"Accusation number two: On the morning of April 6, 1944, Schulmann ordered and implemented a roundup of forty-four orphan children and seven adults from a Jewish children's home in the hills above Izieu, east of Lyon. These children were deported in the same manner as purportedly the before-mentioned Jewish nationals from Belley. According to the accusation, it is documented fact that every one of these souls, minus one adult, lost their lives in the camps.

"Accusation number three: Schulmann apprehended, interrogated, imprisoned, and allegedly executed multiple Communist factions and Allied agents as part of his illegal and oppressive occupation of southern France, from the time the Germans crossed the Demarcation Line in '42 until the time he surrendered control of the area to his Gestapo counterparts under the direction of Klaus Barbie and Section Four Headquarters."

Monsieur Lamoreau glanced once at Rolf in his cage, then returned his attention to the solemn panel of judges. "I'm here to prove to you, until there is not a whisper of remaining doubt, that the accused, Mr. Rolf Schulmann, is not guilty of any one of these crimes; that Monsieur Schulmann did *not* uphold his government's oppressive agenda either for the elimination of the Jews or for the oppression of the French people; that he is neither a war criminal nor a murderer; that in fact he worked actively *against* the implementation of the diabolical *rafle* system introduced by the Nazis against the helpless Jews, and that he did, in fact, earn himself the worthy, magnanimous, and deadly title of 'traitor' to Hitler's Third Reich."

FIFTY

Madame Donatienne Guilbert used to live in a comfortable home on the rue de St. Andre near the outskirts of Belley, but her neighbor explained to Marie that after Madame Guilbert's home was raided and Résistance leaders arrested in '44, Nazi Major Rolf Schulmann ordered her to leave the city or face arrest. Madame Guilbert chose to move to Lyon.

Marie remembered this woman's white hair, wizened features, and fearless grey eyes, and now Marie stood with Natalie on the threshold of Madame Guilbert's modest apartment, noticing how the brave woman's eyes had sunken into age-ravaged folds.

"But, mademoiselle, you were arrested," the old woman said, awestruck.

Marie nodded. "I was sent to one of the camps." She kept it deceptively simple, anxious to ask the question that had brought her to this woman's home. "I'm looking for the man you knew as 'Bruno.' He is Monsieur Jacques Bellamont, and he was the leader of the mountain Maquis at the time I was in Belley." She hesitated, and then added, "He was the friend of my fiancé, Félix Larouche."

The woman nodded, her eyes suddenly reminiscing. "I remember Félix. And I remember Bruno—Jacques." She smiled sadly. "And even though I didn't remember your name, I remember *you*. For just a moment you were with us, and then, like a candle flame snuffed out, you were gone."

Marie shuddered at the woman's description of her capture, and she glanced once at Natalie before again addressing the Frenchwoman. "I must ask you, Madame Guilbert, if you know where Jacques has been living." She swallowed. "A good man needs his help right now, and I'm afraid that if I don't find him soon this good man is going to die."

Madame Guilbert didn't ask any questions, and Marie was glad, because her heart was already racing in her chest, anxious to resolve this thing. Madame Guilbert said simply, "I do know where he is. At least, I know the city . . ." A fit of coughing wracked the woman's slender frame and cut off her words.

Anxious, Marie waited for the woman's coughing to subside.

Finally Madame Guilbert managed, "He is married, and he resides with his new wife in Paris."

"Paris?" Marie was at the same time elated and dismayed. "Paris is such a large city, madame. Is there any other direction you might give me? Any address? Any street name? Perhaps a borough?"

The woman shook her head. "I am sorry, Marie Jacobson. But that is all I know."

* * *

In spite of the promises made by Lamoreau to the tribunal during his remarks on that opening day, as the days passed it became obvious to the prosecution that Lamoreau had almost no witnesses to back up his claim of Rolf Schulmann's innocence. Where was one to find a witness that Schulmann had not caused the removal of forty-four innocent children and their caregivers, if all who had been there had either been Jews who had been executed or Nazis currently running for their lives?

Lamoreau read a sworn statement from Madame Zlatin, head of the children's home in Izieu. She had been providentially absent from the home on the morning of April 6, 1944, but she stated that she had once met the German major in Izieu near the end of '43. He had approached her with the unhappy news that a woman who had recently been hired to work with the children had been arrested by his soldiers and would not be returning to the home. He had apologized to her and her husband for leaving them shorthanded and had asked politely to be shown the children's home. After a tour of the place he had praised her for her kindness to the orphans in her care and had offered to send her a truckload of much-needed supplies in the near future.

The prosecution countered that the major's seemingly polite visit with the woman and her now-deceased husband had been with the sole object of gathering information about the children's home for use in the *rafle* the following year. Obviously Schulmann had been interested in finding out the numbers of available children and caregivers and their ethnic origins.

Amid occasional unruly threats from the balcony audience, Rolf described what had transpired in each of the cases mentioned. He accepted responsibility for the seizure of Jewish possessions and for the disappearance of the many Jewish residents, but he denied having arrested them. He claimed that through a trusted friend they had been forewarned of his plans and had fled the city. He understood why they would not have wanted to return to their homes and possibly face a repeat of the March 24 *rafle*.

Rolf next told the devastating story of the Izieu children, confirming Madame Zlatin's words that he had gone there soon after arresting an American agent, Marie Jacobson, in December 1943. He told of his anguish when he arrived at the home on the morning of April 6 the following year, only to discover that the Gestapo had been there first and that the children were gone.

Rolf explained that he felt responsible for the tragedy. Captain Bernard Dresdner, assigned to Section Four Headquarters, had weaseled his way into the good graces of Rolf's superiors and of Klaus Barbie, and Barbie had allowed the vile captain to interfere in Rolf's département. But Rolf should have found a way to stop him.

As the trial progressed, Rolf could see the strain of his defense wearing his attorney down. During a break Lamoreau confided to his client that he was running out of ideas, and that soon the outcome of this trial would have to be placed squarely in the hands of Rolf's God.

That afternoon, while the Frenchman battled valiantly in his defense, Rolf prayed for help. He knew his inaction and naïveté at the time of Dresdner's arrival had led ultimately and catastrophically to the children's deaths. He had been officially in charge of the Belley département and should have kept a tighter leash on the vile Gestapo captain. He had come to terms with the probable outcome of this trial weeks ago—with the possibility that not only would he be found guilty by this tribunal, but he would face execution because of it.

He thought back to his recent visit with Elder Ezra Benson of the Quorum of the Twelve Apostles, and the memory brought back the peace he had felt in that great man's presence. He remembered how kind the Apostle had been, treating him like a beloved brother instead of a Nazi war criminal, listening to what Rolf had to say with the deference due to an equal and not a monster. And Rolf remembered Elder Benson's reference to Joseph Smith and to heavenly tribunals. Now Rolf dropped his head, closed his eyes, and silently told his Father in Heaven that it really didn't matter what this French tribunal decided—his greatest desire was to be found innocent in Heavenly Father's eyes.

* * *

With Natalie beside her, Marie stood across the Avenue Berthelot from the former Section Four headquarters, thinking about the day, so many lifetimes ago, when her life had been prolonged by Rolf's and Hans's courage.

She touched Natalie's elbow and pointed at the building across the street. "Natalie, if it hadn't been for Rolf's and Hans's intervention, I would have died in that building." Her hand tightened on Natalie's elbow as her emotions overwhelmed her. "And now, because of unthinkable accusations against Rolf, and because I can't find Jacques Bellamont, it might be *Rolf* who dies here instead of me." Her voice wavered as she clung to Natalie for support. "I don't think I can stand this . . ."

They walked together across the street and into the lobby, and then Natalie's step faltered. "I can't do it, Marie—I can't go in there and look at him. Please don't make me go in there."

"Natalie, we don't know what happened in Belley."

Natalie took a deep breath. "I'll wait for you right here."

Marie climbed the back steps to the balcony. She stood in the shadows and watched the proceedings with a heavy soul, her heart aching for the man who sat with his head bowed and his face solemn, his strong body humbled by the weight of a responsibility he refused to deny or relegate to another.

She did not stay long. Every minute she stood in the balcony was a minute of searching wasted. Much as her heart cried out to stay here with Rolf, she needed to find Jacques Bellamont.

"Dear Father in Heaven," she whispered, "please help me find Jacques!"

* * *

That evening Monsieur Jacobson came to visit Rolf in his cell. He brought his usual chair and placed it by the open door, and then he sat down wearily and leaned forward into his hands.

"Things aren't going well, Mr. Schulmann." Jacobson dropped his head and stared at the floor. "I've been meaning to tell you, Rolf, the opinion I have of you."

"No need, sir. I already know how you feel."

Professor Jacobson looked up at Rolf and shook his head. "I've told you my concerns and my fears for my daughter. But I've never told you my opinion of you. You're the reason I have my daughter alive today, Rolf

Schulmann, and that fact alone would drive me to admire you. But since I've come to know you better, that admiration has grown until I can no longer deny that you may be one of the best men I've known."

Jacobson took a deep breath. "You've been charged with hideous crimes, Mr. Schulmann. But when I look in your eyes I don't see the cold, evil emptiness I have seen in the eyes of so many Nazis sitting in that same box in that same courtroom, espousing their innocence. I don't see the fear that knowledge of one's crimes can etch into one's very being for all to see. I don't see the hate for the victims of an unrepentant soul, nor do I see the cold apathy of a spirit past feeling remorse for the suffering he has caused.

"In short, Mr. Schulmann, either you're the most cold-blooded, cold-hearted, and calculated killer I've ever known, or you're as innocent as my daughter says."

There was a long moment of silence. Rolf watched Marie's father as he sat with his shoulders hunched, obviously deep in thought. And when the professor spoke again his words elicited a love so profound that Rolf had to catch his breath and fight to hold back his tears.

"A verdict of guilt in this trial might eventually take the decision out of my hands, but I wanted you to know that, whatever this tribunal decides, in *my* book, you're an honorable man." Jacobson fought against his own emotions. "And if you're set free, I will give you and my daughter my blessing."

Wearily he stood and picked up his chair. "I'll pray that if you truly are innocent, you'll be released so that my daughter may have the chance to marry such an honorable man."

FIFTY-ONE

May 4, 1946

North of Paris sits a high-rise, low-rent housing project surrounding three sides of an open court. While during the Occupation Parisian landlords cinched up their belts and blamed their vacancies on the Nazi occupation, practically every unit at this particular community remained full to overflowing throughout the war. Even though most people would consider a place to sleep a blessing in a time of exceptional hardship, tenants of Drancy didn't see it as such, and even though the units remained filled beyond capacity, there was a paradoxical turnover rate as new residents arrived and old residents left on a daily basis.

Drancy, five kilometers outside the metropolitan center of Paris, was the official departure point for all Jews the Nazis deported from France.

Natalie and Marie had to wait for several minutes before Natalie's repeated knocks produced a response. The office door was finally opened by a diminutive gentleman, bald and emaciated, his gaunt features emphasized by the bright eyes that stared out at them from his skull.

Marie asked in French, "Are you the proprietor of Drancy?"

"I am."

"We're searching for the names of relatives we believe passed through this camp in the spring of '44. Are you the individual we need to see?"

The man nodded. "If they came through here, I'd know about it." He invited them in, and Natalie preceded Marie through the door.

The proprietor's office was small, cramped, humid, and incredibly cluttered, and Marie stood awestruck, staring at the most paper she'd ever seen in one room, stacked in piles that reached from the floor nearly to the ceiling. Pile after pile lined the walls, climbed over the desk and hearth, filled every crack and cranny between books on the bookshelves, covered the windowsills, and filled the chairs that at one time had been meant for humans.

"I apologize," the man said. "The office is small." He shuffled around his desk, removed a stack of papers from his own chair, and sat laboriously down. He looked across at the two visitors and asked, "What is the name, please?"

"Bröder Abram," Marie responded, and she glanced at Natalie.

The man turned and searched the stacks with his eyes, and Marie felt Natalie's despair. It was going to take a ridiculous amount of time to find anything in this office.

The man leaned slowly from his chair and sifted through a stack. He mumbled, "It will depend on the origin of your relatives. They came mostly from Paris, with but a few from the surrounding départements."

His manner of speech was as slow as his movements, and it took all the patience Marie could muster to stand still and listen to him.

"Where did your relatives originate?"

Marie translated for Natalie.

"Belley."

"Vicinity of Lyon . . ." The man was almost speaking to himself. "Belley . . . Aix-les-Bains . . . Izieu . . ." He pulled a stack of papers off the mountain of paper and laid it carefully in front of him. "Bröder Abram . . ." he repeated again, and he sifted through the stack in front of him.

Marie watched, amazed, as the man pulled several papers from the stack. Obviously this man saw order in all this clutter. He held the pages in his hands and glanced through them carefully. "I have several Bröder Abrams. Does he have a wife?"

"Clara." Natalie didn't wait for Marie to finish the translation. "And children: Aimée and Leah."

The man nodded and read each paper laboriously. Finally he set the papers on the table. He shook his head and said to Marie, "None of these Bröder Abrams is the man you seek."

"What do you mean?"

He shrugged. "These men do not have wives named Clara, or children with the names you mentioned." The man carefully placed the papers back in the center of the stack while Marie explained the situation to Natalie.

Natalie spoke to Marie. "Perhaps there is another Bröder Abram." She sounded both distressed and hopeful. "But if there is no other man by that name, then my relatives might still be alive. On the other hand, if he"—she nodded at the proprietor—"didn't look closely enough, he may have missed them and I will never know. Please ask him to look again."

When Marie translated Natalie's request for him, the man looked annoyed. "I am certain there were no more prisoners by that name, mademoiselle."

No translation was needed. Natalie stepped back. She mumbled, *"Merci,"* and fled from the office. Marie followed her, leaving the proprietor to his clutter.

Natalie stood with her hands clasped tightly, her breathing ragged and her face pale. Marie looked around and could feel a deep despair permeating the air of the compound. It filled her lungs like a gaseous poison and made her heart sad. Here was where Jews in France, victims of *rafles* like the one in Belley, were sorted, demoralized and processed, and then ultimately loaded on buses and trains and removed from Drancy and eventually from this world.

"Where did they go, Marie?" Natalie's voice was little more than a whisper. "If they're not listed in the records for this camp, where would they have been taken?"

Marie placed a comforting hand on her shoulder. "No record of your relatives ever coming to Drancy is a *good* thing, Natalie. I wonder if they're still alive." She tried to sound hopeful. "What if Rolf never did arrest them? What if Rolf found a way to *save* them?"

"Marie . . ."

"He believes in God, Natalie, and wouldn't do anything that would offend God. He told me once during the war that he suspected that the Jews were being exterminated, and he would never knowingly send an innocent man to be murdered. He would not do it. *He would not do it!*"

Natalie studied Marie silently, her eyes red but her face appearing determined. "Soon Hans and Major Matthews will be at the trial." She straightened resolutely. "I'll wait there for Hans and Matthews to arrive from Frankfurt, and then I'll attend Rolf's trial."

Marie squeezed her shoulder reassuringly. "Rolf will be grateful to have you there to support him—and I'm sure you'll find answers. I'll be there as soon as I find Jacques Bellamont, and we'll attend his trial together and see for ourselves what *really* happened in Belley."

FIFTY-TWO

May 5, 1946

At first Professor Jacobson thought the graceful figure running toward him through the crowd and across the *Place de la République* was part of the Paris May Day parade. Then she looked up at his window and he noticed the anxiety in his daughter's face. He turned from the window and descended the stairs to let her in.

She fell into his arms. "I was there!" she sobbed, and then she had to calm herself before she could continue. "For just a moment I was there, and I saw you, and the judges, and *him* . . ." She wiped her eyes and stared at her father. "Why are you here?" Suddenly she went white.

"The judge called a recess for the weekend. The trial will resume tomorrow morning in Lyon. Both of us should be there."

"I can't—I need to find someone who can help him."

"Here, in Paris?"

She nodded, anguished. "Somewhere, among all these people . . ." Her arm took in the masses of people lining the streets for the parade. "Somehow I have to find a Maquis leader"—her voice caught—"who is perhaps the only man alive who can tell the tribunal what really happened in Belley."

Jacobson touched her face gently. "Marie, honey, God knows what really happened in Belley. We can only do the best we can with what we have, and Monsieur Lamoreau is doing that now. You've done your best, and now we need to leave it in the hands of Lamoreau and God." He smoothed away the moisture from her cheek. "You and I need to be there to support him, whatever the tribunal decides."

Marie examined his face, her eyes wet with tears. "You believe him?"

"I believe him." The professor smiled. He bent and kissed her forehead. "What else can I believe, when my beloved daughter loves him so wholeheartedly?"

* * *

As the evening approached, Marie stood on the steps of her father's flat, watching a massive throng of French Communist Party protesters pass her on their way to a rally.

Her heart was empty and her body exhausted. She'd tried everything, every potential lead, and still she hadn't found the man she sought.

She wanted to pray—but she felt her heart yearning to lash out, to cry against God for abandoning a man who believed in Him. Rolf Schulmann had never abandoned God. So why hadn't God allowed Marie to find the one person whose testimony could save the man she loved?

But it wasn't God's fault. *She* was the one who had failed, and her failure had betrayed the man who had sacrificed himself for her. In her hour of need Rolf had found a way to save *her,* and now that the tables were turned she couldn't find a way to save him. The thought that she would have to return to Lyon empty-handed and continue to watch as a good man was accused of unspeakable crimes, humiliated in front of an indifferent audience while her heart died along with him, was more than she could endure.

She lowered her head and humbled herself before a Heavenly Father she had wrongfully accused of abandoning His suffering son.

She didn't look up as the multitudes of Parisians moved along the *Place de la République* with their banners, proclaiming France a nation with a glorious future of Communism, nor did she care when they continued to pass her, holding torches and banners high as they marched. It was a parade that occurred in the strangest of circumstances, the second one of the day and considerably less ostentatious than the May Day parade had been. But the passionate voices and the sounds of a thousand marching feet indicated that something extraordinary was happening on the streets of Paris. They showed that it was time for a change, that Communists had a right to be included in the new republic of France. Many had given their lives for freedom, and it was time that they be recognized as heroes.

But as they passed, Marie suddenly felt a curious desire to look up, to see with her own eyes the kind of people who would espouse a Communist society above freedom of choice. And as she did so, she saw one individual march by who filled her empty heart and made her strength again flow, and she began to run, her own voice calling frantically through the din.

"Jacques! Jacques Bellamont! Jacques!"

FIFTY-THREE

May 6, 1946

Monsieur Lamoreau arrived at the courtroom the next morning in high spirits, an uncommon lilt to his step and a smile on his face. He crossed immediately to Professor Jacobson's seat and leaned close to the man's ear, whispering with great intensity until Judge Pomeroy and his two associates were seated, the jury had assembled, and court was brought to order.

Rolf didn't usually look into the balcony. He'd abandoned that depressing habit after the second day of his trial, when it had dawned on him that he wasn't going to find a friendly face in the crowd. But for some reason he did look up this morning, and what he saw there made his wounded heart begin to soar.

Dressed in the stylish suit she'd worn the day she returned to him in Berlin, Marie watched him from the first row. She leaned toward the railing as she met his gaze, and the love and encouragement he saw in her dark eyes momentarily washed away the anguish, embarrassment, and fear of his predicament. For one blessed moment her presence made him feel completely at peace. As much as he feared how the trial's revelations would hurt her tender spirit, he was grateful to her for having the courage to come.

Next to Marie lounged the last man Rolf ever thought he'd see again— Maquis leader Jacques Bellamont, his scarred face as serious and ever-watchful as it had been during the Occupation, as if he were still staging guerilla warfare instead of sitting calmly in a courtroom. Rolf stared at him, astonished that Jacques would be at his trial. With his face characteristically serious, the Frenchman brought two fingers slowly to his brow and silently saluted his German comrade-at-arms.

Still reeling from the shock of seeing Marie and Jacques, Rolf caught a movement at the edge of his vision and turned to see Major James Matthews of the American Central Intelligence Group climbing the stairs to the visitor's balcony, followed by Hans Brenner.

Hans walked with a limp, and he had new scars across his cheek, his forehead, and the side of his head. Rolf thought about the drama in Chamonix and surmised that Hans had not been as successful as he'd hoped in his evasion of Soviet reprisal.

But when he saw the person climbing the stairs at Hans's side, Rolf concluded that Hans's flight to Berlin had not been a complete failure: Hans had his arm around the shoulders of Rolf's nurse from the hospital. Natalie, Hans, and Major Matthews took seats at the opposite end of the balcony from Jacques and Marie, near the back of the already crowded area. Hans held Natalie close and grinned down at Rolf.

Between the two groups of familiar and cherished faces, suddenly it seemed to Rolf as though the whole balcony was crowded with his supporters. The illusion cheered him, lifting the gloomy cloud that had become his constant companion throughout the proceedings.

At the direction of Judge Pomeroy, Monsieur Lamoreau was called to the podium.

"My witness list has grown, monsieurs," Lamoreau cheerfully announced to the judges. "And for my first witness this morning I wish to call to the stand one of these recent arrivals, a Monsieur Leon Reifman."

Rolf turned and watched as a young man walked toward the witness box. Rolf decided he looked younger than he actually was, and he wondered if people often thought him just a boy. But his sallow face, prominent cheekbones, and deep-set eyes held the intelligence and experience of an older man and attested to the war's toll on his body. He walked with a slight limp, although his slender torso remained erect. He climbed into the witness chair and glanced about the room, his dark eyes taking in Rolf, the attorneys, the prosecutor's table, the judges' bench, the jury, and the balcony with its spectators.

"Monsieur Reifman, will you please introduce yourself to the court?"

The young man nodded. "I am Leon Reifman, and I live in Marseilles."

"How long have you lived in Marseilles?"

"Two years."

"And how did you hear about this trial?"

Reifman said, "My friend Madame Zlatin received a letter from Monsieur William Jacobson, asking her if she knew anyone who would be willing to testify at the trial of the Nazi major in charge of the Belley district. Madame Zlatin told him about me, and Monsieur Jacobson came to Marseilles late last night to ask me to come."

Lamoreau asked, "How do you know Madame Zlatin, who with her husband ran *La Maison d'Izieu* near Belley?"

"I lived at the children's home with my sister, my parents, and my little nephew. We helped with the children in the home."

"And where are your sister, your parents, and your nephew now?"

The young man flinched slightly. "They were deported by the Germans."

"I'm sorry about your family. Will you tell me what happened at *La Maison d'Izieu* on the morning of April sixth, 1944?"

Leon Reifman nodded and swallowed again, his Adam's apple rising and falling as he did so. "That morning we were starting breakfast, and I came to the top of the stairs and saw my sister talking with two men near the front door. One of them called up to me 'Come down, we want to talk to you,' but my sister signaled for me not to. She looked frightened."

Rolf could picture the Gestapo strong-arming the terrified children away from their breakfast, away from their beautiful home, and into the backs of filthy army trucks. He felt sick inside.

Leon continued. "I went through the infirmary and out onto the terrace, but there was a German soldier standing outside, so I ran into another bedroom and jumped into the garden. That's where I hurt my ankle.

"I hid in the bushes at the edge of the garden, and the soldiers came and looked for me. Once I thought one of the soldiers looked straight at me, but he didn't say anything, only walked away.

"I could see the children in the trucks. Monsieur Zlatin was trying to talk to one of the soldiers, but the soldier hit him with his gun and told him to be still. Then he threw Monsieur Zlatin into the trucks with the children, and the other teachers were thrown in as well."

Lamoreau asked, "What happened to the trucks and the children? What happened to your sister, and your parents and nephew?"

Leon's voice wavered. "The soldiers drove away with them, down the mountain toward the village. I never saw them again."

"Did they all leave?"

"The Gestapo? No, monsieur." Leon shook his head. "Several stayed, and they started looking for me again, and then Monsieur Schulmann arrived." He indicated Rolf.

"Monsieur Schulmann was not present when the children were taken?"

"No, monsieur."

"What did Monsieur Schulmann do when he arrived?"

Leon glanced at Rolf. "He went inside the house, and the soldiers left the garden and went into the house also."

"Did you see anything else after that?"

The boy nodded and looked at Rolf again. "I watched as they came back out. Monsieur Schulmann was wearing handcuffs, and the Gestapo officer struck him in the face."

"Did they say anything as they were leaving the house?"

"Yes, monsieur. I heard everything."

"What did they say, Monsieur Reifman?"

Leon shrugged. "Monsieur Schulmann said the other man would pay for taking the children away, and the other man hit Monsieur Schulmann in the face and told him that he was a traitor."

* * *

Although Lamoreau had insisted that Rolf's attempt at deportation of the forty-seven Jews on March twenty-fourth failed purposefully, and that he had actually forewarned the intended victims, the prosecution disputed the claim. They offered Rolf's own statement as evidence, extracted from his report to Klaus Barbie in Lyon, insisting that Rolf would have carried out his orders exactly as planned if there had not been extenuating circumstances, mainly an earlier-than-normal school holiday and lack of properly updated registrations for the Jews in his district. Besides, very few of those affected by his actions had ever returned, which meant that somehow the major had been able to track them down and eventually deport them as ordered.

Lamoreau called a young woman to the stand. Rolf's brow furrowed as he tried to determine why she seemed familiar. He didn't think he'd ever seen her before, except perhaps in a photograph. She was graceful and slender, her green dress fashionable and her light brown hair stylish. She wore net gloves and clutched a black leather purse in both hands as she slid onto the witness chair.

Her blue eyes met his, and Rolf sat back, stunned at a dual revelation that brought the long ago and recent past together in a collision so tremendous that it took his breath away.

Lamoreau approached the woman and asked her to introduce herself to the court.

"My name is Aimée Bellamont. I reside with my husband, Monsieur Jacques Bellamont, in Paris."

"Where were you living on March twenty-fourth, 1944?"

"East of Lyon—in Belley."

"Do you know this man, Madame Bellamont?" Lamoreau pointed in the direction of the prisoner's cage.

"I know him from reputation alone, monsieur. He was the German officer in charge in Belley. I have never met him personally."

"What *is* his reputation, madame?"

Aimée's eyes misted, and she smiled softly. "He is the man who saved my life, and the lives of my sister, my mother, and my father."

"How did he do that?"

Aimée brushed at her cheeks and glanced into the balcony, her eyes focusing on her husband in the front row. "My husband was a Résistance fighter during the war. When a new Nazi major came to be in charge in Belley, my husband did his best to undermine his efforts." Aimée paused. "But then they came to an agreement."

"What sort of agreement, madame?"

"Major Schulmann found my fiancé and informed him that there would be a *rafle*. He showed Jacques the list he had received from Gestapo head-quarters. He begged Jacques to warn the people on the list."

"Did your fiancé do what Major Schulmann requested?"

Aimée nodded. "He warned everyone he could find."

Lamoreau moved closer to the woman. "Not many of the people on that list have returned to their homes, Madame Bellamont. The prosecution argues that because these individuals have disappeared, Major Schulmann's actions that morning make him a criminal and a murderer." The lawyer paused. "In your opinion, is Major Schulmann guilty of these crimes?"

One more time Aimée Bellamont met Rolf's gaze, and she smiled at him. "In my opinion, sir, the major's actions on that cold morning make him a hero."

* * *

Lamoreau called Jacques Bellamont to the stand. Jacques uncurled his lanky frame from his seat in the balcony, slipped past a dozen pairs of knees, and negotiated his way through the crowd on the stairs. He didn't glance at Rolf as he passed, nor did his eyes sweep the room as he lowered himself into the witness chair. Instead, his eyes remained steady on the opposing counsel, as if challenging the prosecutor to a private, personal war.

Rolf's attorney walked to the witness box. "Monsieur Bellamont, your wife has testified that you helped Monsieur Schulmann notify these forty-seven Jewish citizens of the deportations."

Jacques finally turned his attention to Lamoreau. "That is correct."

"Who told you about the *rafle* planned by the Germans?"

"Monsieur Schulmann himself."

At Lamoreau's request, Jacques described the night Rolf had raided the meeting at Madame Guilbert's residence, arresting every Maquis leader present along with a wounded British pilot. He told how Rolf had singled him out and talked to him privately, showing him a list of forty-seven names and advising him that in the morning his soldiers would detain and deport every person whose name was on that list. He told of Rolf's request for his assistance in warning the people on the list, and of Rolf's promise to release Jacques's men in return.

Jacques also testified of Rolf's aid to the Résistance, beginning with the staged execution of the captured Maquis leaders and their release into the Rhône-Alpes and the gift of a loaded supply truck. Jacques then described how Rolf had contacted him in April of '44, requesting his assistance in smuggling an Allied agent woman and the mother of a deceased Résistance leader out of the country. He also described Rolf's request that he send a wireless transmission to a Maquis operator's location known to be in the hands of the Germans, with a message meant to confuse the Germans and make them believe that an American woman they had captured might secretly be working for the Nazis.

The prosecution reminded Judge Pomeroy and his associates that Rolf and Jacques were friends. They could very easily have known each other before the war—didn't Rolf's family own a villa in nearby St. Victor-sur-Loire? In the chaotic final years of the war the two men could have concocted this story to protect Rolf in the event of Allied capture and trial, portraying him as a principled, religious, and innocent victim of the wiles of an evil dictator.

The prosecutor faced Jacques. "You say that you personally warned every family and every individual on that list, thus saving your fiancée and all forty-six other Jews from deportation."

Jacques scowled. "I said that I warned *almost* every person on the list. There was one family that I could not reach in time."

"Can you remember the name of that family?"

"Yes. It was the family of Monsieur Gustav Stern."

The prosecutor looked triumphant. "And that is one of many families on that list that never returned to Belley."

Jacques smirked. "That is because he and his wife live near Aimée's family in Paris. In '44 Monsieur Schulmann warned them himself and allowed Monsieur Stern and his family twenty minutes to escape." He glanced contemptuously at the prosecutor.

For a moment the prosecutor hesitated. "Perhaps, Monsieur Bellamont . . ." His voice had taken on a defensive edge. ". . . perhaps it is just coincidence that your neighbors have the same name?"

"Or perhaps they didn't die at Auschwitz as the prosecution claims."

The prosecutor pressed Jacques further. "Perhaps you're lying to me in order to defend a guilty man—a friend's execution at the guillotine would weigh heavy on your mind, wouldn't it?"

"In *this* case, with *this* friend, it would." Jacques glanced at Rolf and then back at the prosecutor. "And my memory is better than you think, but I have to admit that remembering *all* the names on that list would be a daunting task."

"So if you were pressed you wouldn't be able to correctly identify the names on the list of individuals you supposedly warned to escape."

"I did not say that, monsieur. I only said I'm incapable of reciting the names of forty-seven people off the top of my head."

The prosecutor gave him a derisive smile. "If I gave you a random list of three hundred names, including the names on that list, would you be able to identify the names of the forty-seven victims?"

"You mean, the forty-seven souls fortunate enough to reside in Major Schulmann's district? Yes, I could identify all of them."

The prosecutor indicated the judges and jury with a grand sweep of his arm. "But Monsieur Bellamont, you just informed this tribunal—"

"I have the official order in my pocket, monsieur—signed by Klaus Barbie himself."

The prosecutor froze in his tracks. He turned to face Jacques.

Jacques clarified. "That night Rolf gave me the letter he had received from Gestapo headquarters—he said he had made a copy for himself just in case . . ." Here Jacques grinned at Rolf. "Just in case I destroyed the list in a fit of rage. Why would he entrust a Maquisard with the official list, you wonder? Because he wanted to convince me that it was not his doing, this round-up of the Jews. I decided to keep the list. I brought it with me—if you'd like to see it."

"I would, monsieur."

Jacques produced a discolored, wrinkled document from his breast pocket, unfolded and smoothed it carefully on his lap, and then handed it to the lawyer. "I apologize that it has been slightly mutilated—it has been on my person since the day it was first placed in my hands."

Speechless, the prosecutor accepted the document and studied it. He glanced once at Jacques Bellamont and then across the room at Rolf. He hesitated and then offered it to Monsieur Lamoreau.

Lamoreau shook his head. "Thank you," he said with a smile. "I have already seen it."

The prosecutor handed the list to the lead judge, turned, and walked back toward Bellamont. "I'm curious, monsieur. Why would you keep such a thing? Why would you carry it around with you wherever you go?"

Jacques folded his arms and leaned back in his chair, his expression thoughtful. "To remind me."

"Of what?"

"That good people exist even in evil circumstances. That I am the friend of a good man who risked his own life for the sake of forty-seven Jews and one American woman. That this good man risked death on all sides by consorting with his enemy. That my wife—my Aimée—is alive because of Rolf Schulmann's courage."

FIFTY-FOUR

After days of damaging testimony, Monsieur Lamoreau had finally enjoyed a session of almost complete triumph. At the close of the day the lead judge instructed the attorneys to prepare closing arguments for the following morning, and Rolf was escorted from the courtroom.

Natalie flew to her feet, her hand rigid on Hans's shoulder as she strained to see past the people around her.

"Who are you looking for?" Hans stood up beside her, stretching his stiff back and limbs.

"Jacques Bellamont." Natalie continued to search the dense crowd. "Actually, his wife. She has the same name as one of my missing cousins, and she lived in Belley during the war . . ." She searched the crowd. "But she left the room after she testified, and Monsieur Bellamont has disappeared . . ."

Hans nodded, then grabbed Natalie's hand and strong-armed a path through the multitude to the head of the stairs.

"Do you see him, Hans?" Natalie's voice was almost lost in the din. Hans shook his head, intent on finding Jacques and Aimée. He steered her through the crushing throng choking the stairs, navigating between bodies and around blockades until they reached the foyer. Hans breathed deeply of the clear air as he ushered Natalie from the building, and as he scanned the crowded street he saw the Frenchman they sought behind the wheel of a car, maneuvering away from the swarming masses. Hans dropped Natalie's hand and ran.

He called out to Jacques, waving his arms, and he could have sworn Jacques had seen him. But Jacques accelerated and soon he had left Hans far behind.

Disappointed, Hans turned and walked back toward the courthouse. He saw Natalie standing with Marie on the steps and he watched them as he approached, intrigued by the differences between the two women. Both were Americans, but from entirely different backgrounds—while Marie was more French than American, in Natalie's American veins coursed dangerous Soviet blood. Marie's doe-brown eyes carried a soft, gentle expression, deceptively masking the courageous adventurer who had survived the war, while Natalie's blue eyes were capable of a dragon's fire, a cover for the vulnerable woman inside.

He had to tell her. Even if he could never have her, he had to let her know how he had changed. He just prayed she would not conclude he'd done it to manipulate her feelings for him.

He approached the two and heard the woman who meant the world to him say gently, "You were my strength in Belley, Marie. Why shouldn't I have a chance to be yours now?"

"He is my reason for living. If he were to be found guilty now . . ." Marie shuddered, and Natalie pulled her into her arms.

She said soothingly, "Your friend Jacques gave a compelling testimony. As did Leon Reifman and Jacques' wife . . ."

"But what do *you* think of Rolf now, Natalie?" Marie's voice came muffled from Natalie's shoulder.

Natalie gave a half smile. "I know what I *want* to think, and after seeing the woman Jacques married . . ." She hesitated, glancing across at Hans before continuing. "Marie, Hans and I need to speak with Monsieur Bellamont and his wife. Do you know where they went?"

Hans scowled and waved an arm down the street. "He saw me coming and hit the accelerator as if I were a demon bent on his destruction."

Marie looked up at him. "My dear Hans"—she smiled at him through her tears—"have you looked in a mirror lately? If you were running after me I would probably do the same thing." She stepped away from Natalie. "Besides, Jacques has placed his wife and himself in a dangerous situation. He's a French Communist who has just testified in behalf of a German officer. How was he to know that the large, half-crazed madman covered in war wounds lumbering down the street after him was not a fellow Communist bent on his demise?"

"I'm not half-crazed," Hans growled.

Marie laughed. "Don't worry, Hans. He promised to return for the verdict."

FIFTY-FIVE

May 7, 1946

When Hans Brenner was just a boy, he heard the old Sussex legend of Saint George, who fought and defeated a terrible dragon. Even though the knight was victorious, he was overcome by his many wounds and died. Where his blood was spilt, beautiful white lilies of the valley grew, and the delicate clusters of little bells spread their intoxicating perfume across the countryside.

Hans watched a Frenchwoman walk across the street with a basket of white flowers, followed by another vendor, and another. Perhaps the legend of the knight and the dragon was the catalyst for the tradition of giving out *muguet*—these delicate white flowers—in the beautiful month of May.

Natalie approached, walking down the steps of her apartment building toward him, and he ached inside, realizing that there was at least one dragon too precious to be slain. How he wished he could spend the rest of his life protecting this dragon from harm!

She seemed both surprised and pleased to see him standing there, clean and bathed, shaved and combed, and in a new suit and tie. He stood with one foot on the steps and a bouquet of *muguet* in the hand resting hopefully across his raised knee.

"Oh Hans, how thoughtful!" She looked at the flowers, and then she threw her arms around his neck, catching him completely off guard. He forgot to move the bouquet. Natalie laughed and pulled back. "*Now* look what we did, Mr. Brenner—the poor little flowers!"

"We need to talk, Natalie. Right now. Are you coming peacefully or do I have to kidnap you again?"

Natalie giggled. "Closing arguments start at nine."

Hans nodded. He looked down at the flowers, and they both watched soberly as several petals fell, bruised, to the steps.

Natalie took the bouquet and said softly, "You're worried about Rolf."

"I'm worried." His hands found her shoulders and rested there. "Rolf should never have had to go through this. He's got the honesty of a saint and the courage of a martyr—not to mention a religious streak as wide as the Rhône."

"Do you think he's guilty?"

"Not any more than I am, Natalie." Hans shifted uncomfortably. "He was required to fight against your people. So was I. He did what he was told, and so did I." Hans hesitated, and then he dropped his arms. "But he never fought against *children,* Natalie—and he never knowingly sent innocent civilians to their deaths. You can be certain of that. He did not send your relatives to the trains."

She was watching him closely, and her eyes seemed to plead with him. "Hans, you have such a power over me. You make me want to believe in Rolf's goodness and his innocence." She touched his arm. "And I almost believed for myself when I saw Jacques' wife and realized there might be more to her than just a familiar name. She lived in Belley and was one of Rolf's supposed victims, and when I was in Belley I was told that my relatives were arrested by the Germans . . ."

"But we don't know for sure that that's true."

"Why would they tell me that if it weren't true?"

"It's easy to hate the Germans these days."

The anguish in Natalie's voice broke his heart. "Hans, after the trial, I would so much like to see you again—but I understand, with Lieutenant Rostov still around, how dangerous that will be in Germany."

"Lieutenant Rostov is a ruthless man." Hans looked way from her, his answer noncommittal.

"A ruthless man with a heartbreaking purpose." Natalie smiled sadly and fingered a bruised flower. "He buys his daughter's every breath through his obedience to his government."

"There is nothing more dangerous than a good man dedicated to an evil cause." Suddenly Hans couldn't look at her. "Natalie, I will not interfere with your marriage to Curly."

"Hans . . ."

He shook his head. "Ever since I came back, I've been trying to explain something important to you. I must tell you *now*—before something else happens to interfere."

Hans took her hand and they crossed the street and entered a grassy park near the riverbank. Through oak and maple boughs they could see a stone footbridge spanning the tranquil Saône River, the stone arches of its foundation a deterrent to all but the smallest of watercraft.

Hans led her to the bridge. "When I left Berlin last year, I needed to find out more about the Mormon Church—not only because of what you and Curly and Gregory did for Rolf, but also because of something that had happened several months before I met you."

He walked with her toward the center of the bridge. "Near the end of the war Rolf was sentenced to death for treason, but Marie always had faith that he was still alive. I decided to look for him after the war, and I discovered that a group of prisoners from Sachsenhausen had been forced to march toward the Baltic Sea. I followed them.

"I had a lot of things to think about. In Switzerland, Marie had told me she wanted to marry Rolf for eternity; I realized I wanted to know more about love that can last forever."

Hans leaned against the waist-high stone wall. "I wanted to find out what made Rolf such a good man. I had a lot of bad habits, Natalie—I did things that Rolf and Marie would never consider. And I began to wonder if God was so angry at me for my sins that He was refusing to help me find my friend.

"I became discouraged—not just about my own mistakes but about not finding Rolf. I reached the Belower Woods and discovered hundreds of shallow trenches between the trees where prisoners had spent the night. I thought about Rolf, cold and sick, probably dying, and I crawled inside one of the trenches. And then I . . . I . . ." Hans stopped.

"What is it, Hans?"

"I *prayed,* Natalie." Suddenly embarrassed, Hans turned his eyes away from her to gaze out over the river. "I didn't know how to pray, except for what I had observed Rolf do when he didn't know I was watching. He would kneel and hold his hands together, like this . . ." Hans knelt on the stone footbridge at Natalie's feet and clasped his hands in front of him. "And he always bowed his head and seemed to be talking to a friend." Hans's expression became thoughtful. "And so that night in the Belower Woods in that awful trench I decided it was time for me to pray.

"I didn't know if God would listen to someone like me, but I talked to Him anyway. I talked to Him like I used to talk to Rolf, and I pretended God was sitting there with me on that chilly night.

"I told God that Marie needed Rolf—and that I needed God's help to find Rolf before it was too late. And then I told God that I wanted to be a better person and that I would stop drinking and smoking . . .

"I didn't *want* to stop, Natalie—but Rolf had mentioned God didn't like it, so I promised God that if He would help me find Rolf I would give up those things and try to do only the things Rolf would do.

"Then I started feeling really bad, like I really needed a drink, or a cigarette, and the memory of all the enticing things I used to do over- whelmed me. I fought those feelings for hours." Anguished, Hans looked up into Natalie's face. "That was one of the longest nights of my life. I felt lonely, and dirty, and very sick—but I kept telling God how badly I needed Rolf to be all right, and how I was willing to change if He would help me find Rolf."

"Hans," she whispered, "in Berlin we were friends, remember? Why didn't we talk about this then?"

"We should have," he agreed. "But I was so worried about Rolf, and at that time it just didn't seem like something I should discuss with . . ."

"An American nurse?"

He smiled faintly. "I was beginning to think about you a lot, Natalie— and after what we discussed about temple marriage, and honesty . . ." Hans sighed. "I didn't want you to think I was trying to manipulate you into loving me in return."

He rose to his feet and returned to leaning against the wall. "And when Marie arrived to care for Rolf and you told me you had agreed to marry Curly, I decided that I was no longer needed in Berlin—and I left.

"I went to Baiersbronn in the Schwarzwald region—I decided to talk with another Mormon I had met once—Rolf's branch president, Horst Wagner."

Natalie joined Hans against the wall. "You left Berlin to talk with a Mormon branch president?"

Hans nodded. "I trusted him—he was courageous and kind, and he had once done me a favor. I figured if anyone could teach me about God, and repentance, and eternity"—Hans hesitated—"Horst Wagner would be that man."

There was a long moment of silence between them. Natalie studied him carefully while the river slid silently, lazily away beneath them. Along the avenue an occasional automobile passed the small park along the riverbank, and somewhere in the distance, perhaps near the convergence of the Saône and the Rhône, a boat's whistle gave a long, moaning sigh. The early morning sun had risen higher in the sky, the light reflecting off the faces of Lyon's famous Romanesque architecture and the glassy surface of the river. It turned Natalie's hair to burnished copper.

"Herr Wagner allowed me to stay with him and his wife for several weeks. I helped him with his congregation's needs—I chopped wood, repaired roofs, cleaned chimneys, harvested apples, loaded hay into barns, and felt more useful than I had ever felt in my life.

"One morning I was chopping wood for a sister, and she ran from the house with a baby in her arms—he must have been no more than a year old—and she asked me, 'Are you one of the elders of the Church? Please, will you give my son a blessing?'

"I was stunned. I told her I was not a member, but I would find President Wagner and bring him to this sister's house. She began to cry and showed me her son. He was struggling to breathe, and his body was limp."

Hans hesitated, and his face gradually flushed with emotion. "I took the baby from her arms and we hurried to the Wagner house, but President Wagner had already left to help another sister in a nearby community.

"We knelt down—the mother, Frau Wagner, and I—and the mother begged me to ask Heavenly Father to save that baby. I was uncomfortable, but I did what I could. I told Heavenly Father that I was not a member of His Church but that I needed Him to tell President Wagner that this baby needed a blessing. I was naïve, Natalie—I guess I thought Heavenly Father worked that way.

"I ran to find a doctor. But by the time I returned, the baby . . . the baby . . ." Hans could not continue. Natalie slowly touched his hand, and he captured it tightly in his own.

"Hans, I'm so sorry."

He looked at her quizzically. "About what?"

She was confused. "Didn't the baby die? I thought you said—"

"The baby was *fine,* Natalie." Hans grinned at her. "When I returned with the doctor, the baby was toddling around happily eating Frau Wagner's bread. I stood there in the doorway and watched him play, and I started to get this nice feeling inside—that a miracle had just happened . . ."

"So President Wagner came home and gave him a blessing?"

Hans shook his head. "He didn't come home until late that night—but when he arrived, the first thing he did was ask me if Frau Schroeder's baby was all right." Suddenly Hans could not see Natalie past his tears. "That morning he'd been giving another sister a blessing, and in the middle of his prayer he felt impressed that he needed to also ask for Frau Schroeder's baby to be healed. Horst didn't understand, but the feeling kept coming until he added that petition to his prayer."

Hans struggled to compose himself. He was not in the habit of showing such emotion in front of anyone—but for some reason it didn't seem to be bothering Natalie. She seemed engrossed in his story and waited eagerly for him to continue.

She crept closer and asked, "Hans, what happened?"

"I asked President Wagner to baptize me."

Natalie took it well. The pallor in her face affected her high cheekbones for only a few moments, and her gaze wavered only slightly. Her voice, though, trembled when she asked, "Have you told Rolf? Or Marie?"

Hans shook his head. "I had to do this alone. I had to know for myself that I was ready . . ."

Suddenly he could no longer continue, and impulsively he gathered Natalie into his arms and held her close to him. In the silence he could hear the wind rustling through the trees at the river's edge, the soft lapping of the water against the granite pillars supporting the footbridge underneath their feet, and a bird chattering incessantly overhead.

Natalie said, "Hans, why didn't you tell me sooner?"

Hans sighed. "I have *tried,* dear princess, I have tried. Ever since last November, when I saw you crossing the hospital courtyard one night in a rainstorm."

"Last *November?*" She stilled. "You came back?"

He nodded. "The last time we talked you looked so scared, and I was worried about you. I came back because I had to know—that you were all right." He looked intently at her. "I *do* love you, Natalie. More than I thought it was possible to love a woman. And when I returned to Berlin and saw you walking across the courtyard in the rain, and you were so beautiful, and so precious to me . . ."

"Hans . . ." Natalie's voice wavered. "I wish you'd talked to me that night. I wish you had let me know you were there." Her hand moved to his face, carefully avoiding the more pummeled areas as she smoothed his weathered skin with her fingers. "I was so worried about you."

"I *wanted* to talk to you, Natalie—to tell you everything that had happened in Baiersbronn. But you were engaged to Curly, and I didn't want you to think I'd been baptized just for you."

Her eyes bright, Natalie leaned close until her cheek touched his and her breath warmed his ear. Her proximity sent his senses reeling, and he could not stop his arms from pulling her closer. She whispered simply, "Curly and I are not getting married."

It was Hans's turn to lose his ability to function. The echo of her words reverberated through his head and into his racing heart, and he felt her cheek against the side of his face and her warmth in his arms, and he couldn't figure how to make either his body or his mind respond to the revelation. It perplexed him, frightened him, stunned him, and encouraged him all at the same time, and he marveled that his system could experience such a dramatic response to her simple words. Finally he mumbled awkwardly, "Poor Curly . . ."

His response made Natalie giggle. "Curly is going to make some lucky girl a wonderful husband someday," she whispered. "It just can't ever be me." She rested her hands on his shoulders and smiled up at him. "We've both been struggling with what we had to say to each other, and I'm glad we've finally shared our secrets. I love you, too, Hans Brenner," she whispered. "And I'm glad you've taken such an important step in your life. You have the makings of greatness in you—and I see a strength in your eyes that takes my breath away."

Across the riverbank park Hans heard an automobile stop near the door of the apartment building, and he watched as the door opened and the driver emerged, adjusted the *chapeau mou* on his head, and leaned against the car to watch the entrance to the building.

Natalie saw the man and whispered sadly, "He is an associate of Professor Jacobson—he's here to take us to the trial. Hans . . ." She suddenly had tears in her eyes and clutched at his lapel. "After the trial we have so much to discuss . . . What are we going to do?"

He gathered her closer. "Natalie, I'm holding in my arms the answer to my prayers." He gave a long, wavering sigh.

Hopefully she whispered, "Then you'll be there when I get back to Berlin."

He hesitated a second too long.

"You are going back to Berlin after the trial, aren't you?"

Hans nodded, and Natalie clutched at him. "Hans, I need to know you will be there for me when I return."

"Natalie . . ." He struggled to form his words. "Major Matthews doesn't think you should go back to Berlin. He thinks Rostov will be watching for you." His hands rubbed her back gently. "Matthews has interceded with your superiors, and after you visit your relatives in Paris—if Aimée is indeed your missing cousin—the Army is transferring you to a hospital in America."

"No." She began to cry. "How am I supposed to live away from you? How am I supposed to go through that again? How am I supposed to survive each day not knowing if you're safe, or if you're hurting, or dying . . ."

"You'll be all right." He tried to reassure her. "I want you to think about me—about *us*—while you're away, and I will find a way to come to you in America."

"When, Hans? When will you come?"

Again Hans hesitated, and this time he knew he had no answer for her. He struggled to put into words the infinitesimal hope that gleamed through the inevitable horror of the next few months.

"Surely Major Matthews can find a way to get exit papers for you?"

Hans shook his head once. "I have something I need to accomplish in order to receive those exit papers." He leaned close to her, his face inches from her own. He felt her trembling against him, and suddenly he wanted the terrible task that awaited him ended so that he could finally hold her peacefully in his arms—without people looking on, or drivers waiting, or friends calling, or danger threatening, or death looming—and he crossed the remaining inches between them and kissed her with every ounce of anxiety and fear and frustration and longing and hope he'd harbored ever since she'd first worked her way into his heart. She clung to him and returned the same emotions, and he knew that even though they had a treacherous road still ahead of them, somehow, *someday,* everything was going to be all right.

FIFTY-SIX

Two days after the closing remarks of both the prosecutor and Rolf's attorney, Rolf was summoned by Judge Pomeroy to stand before the tribunal to hear its verdict.

Every seat of the visitors' balcony was filled. Onlookers stood two-deep against the back wall and crowded the steps. Every eye watched the German Nazi—who might or might not have been a criminal—as he was delivered to the front of the courtroom to face his tribunal. Every face showed anticipation of the verdict, and except for the clanking and rattling of the prisoner's shackles as he moved toward the judges' bench, the room was deathly still.

Rolf saw Hans and Natalie on one end of the balcony, and Jacques and Aimée on the other, and Major Matthews and another American officer he didn't recognize somewhere in the center. But his eyes searched frantically for the face of the one person whose support he needed desperately at that moment, and he found Marie again on the front row. His gaze locked with hers, and Marie smiled bravely down at him, but even from this distance Rolf could see that her face was pale and her eyes wet.

Her lips moved silently, and he recognized the English words, *I love you.*

Her words gave him the courage he needed to stand straight and tall in front of Judge Pomeroy and his associates. Even though his legs felt weak and breathing was excruciating, he felt the strength of her presence and her love for him, and he knew that he was not going through this ordeal alone.

His attorney stood supportively next to his left shoulder, and suddenly Marie's father was standing resolutely at his right. Surprised, Rolf looked at him and saw the tears in his eyes.

Jacobson smiled at Rolf. "If you will permit me, sir."

Rolf could hardly speak in the face of such kindness. "Thank you, Professor." Together the three men stood and waited for the verdict.

Solemnly Judge Pomeroy faced Rolf. "Rolf Ahren Schulmann, I must be frank: there are certain accusations against you that warrant death at the guillotine. The subject of your guilt has been debated extensively by this tribunal, and even though your innocence has been argued heatedly by Monsieur Lamoreau for many days, and he has been fortunate enough to produce several excellent witnesses in your behalf, under no circumstances can we pronounce you innocent of all wrongdoing."

Rolf could not look at Marie. Judge Pomeroy's words fell as heavily on Rolf's shoulders as if he had already pronounced him guilty of murder. Rolf again felt the shock that had overwhelmed him two years before when he'd learned that the children at the Izieu children's home had been deported to their deaths. He remembered again the bitterly cold morning in Belley when he'd organized a round-up of forty-seven Jews, and he remembered his desperate, silent prayers as he reasoned with Gustav Stern, a Jewish father frantic beyond reason at the possibility that his family would be taken from him. And Rolf thought about his little boy, who had been returned to him for just a small moment and who now would be left without a father.

Courageously Rolf straightened, and his apprehension gave way to a sliver of peace. No matter what happened to him, his son would not be without a mother. Marie would hold Alma close to her heart and care for him, and Rolf wouldn't have to worry about whether he would grow up to be an honorable man. Mostly it was *Marie* he worried about, and the thought that he would never be her husband was more unbearable than the probability of imminent death.

"Mr. Schulmann, in regards to the accusations against you: as head representative of this tribunal, acting under authority of the interim presidency of the nation of France, and in conjunction with my two associates and your jury, I pronounce the following judgment upon you."

Judge Pomeroy produced spectacles and balanced them on his nose. He pulled a document in front of him and continued. "In regards to accusation number one—implementation of a *rafle* among the citizens of Belley on the morning of March twenty-fourth, nineteen hundred and forty-four—the tribunal finds it necessary to divide the accusation into three separate categories with three separate verdicts. Therefore the first accusation against you is divided as follows:

"Accusation one-A: Implementation of a Nazi *rafle* among the citizens of Belley, with the intent of deporting forty-seven Jews to camps in German-occupied territory.

"Accusation one-B: Willful disregard for the dignity of citizens of France, and the confiscation of personal effects and properties of private French citizens for the gain of the oppressors.

"Accusation one-C: Deportation of forty-seven Jews to concentration camps, resulting in the death of these individuals at the hands of the Nazi oppressors.

"Mr. Schulmann, in regards to these accusations, this tribunal finds you *guilty* of the following: implementation of the Nazi *rafle* system in Belley, and willful disregard for the dignity of a French citizen's rights to privacy and property—on these two points I will deliver your sentence in a few moments.

"Because of the lack of irrefutable evidence that these forty-seven persons were actually deported, and because of the appearance of *one* of these persons, and the testimony of various witnesses that other persons from the list are alive and accounted for, the tribunal finds you *not guilty* of the deportation of the forty-seven individuals whose names appear on the list."

Here Judge Pomeroy paused as a murmur rippled through the throng packed into the balcony.

"In regards to accusation number two," he finally continued, "the deportation of forty-four children and their caregivers from the Izieu children's home on April sixth, 1944—this tribunal finds you *not guilty.*"

Indignant howls rose from scattered locations throughout the courtroom, followed by a veritable beehive of buzzing commentary among neighbors. Judge Pomeroy raised baleful eyes toward the culprits, and the room soon returned to silence.

Pomeroy cleared his throat and continued. "Accusation number three." He adjusted his spectacles. "The apprehension, interrogation, and supposed execution of Allied agents and Communist factions." He glanced once at Rolf. "It is the opinion of this tribunal that the prosecution of Monsieur Schulmann for crimes committed against Allied agents belongs in the courts of Great Britain and the United States. We have received official notice that the United States government suspends any and all legal action against Monsieur Schulmann at this time. Great Britain has not responded to the subject, and this court is not willing to wait for it to do so. Finally, a Communist party member has testified in this court that Monsieur Schulmann orchestrated an escape of Maquis guerillas during the war and aided that organization in its operations against the Germans. The court has received no evidence to the contrary. Therefore, in the case of accusation number three, this tribunal finds Rolf Schulmann *not guilty.*"

Pandemonium erupted in the visitors' gallery and Judge Pomeroy's intimidating glare did little to quell the consternation. Finally he threatened to clear the courtroom. That, coupled with a surge of gendarmes fighting their way through the quagmire on the stairs, brought everybody back to their seats. Judge Pomeroy glared one last time at the assembly and then said, "Rolf Schulmann, God must be looking out for you. I, at least, do not see what good it would do for you to lose your head. However, you have been found guilty of odious crimes against a large number of French citizens, and I must sentence you to either five years in prison or complete monetary restitution to the forty-seven victims of your *rafle*."

He hesitated. "I understand that you own considerable business assets in France, including significant real estate in the area of St. Victor-sur-Loire, all left untouched by the Nazis because of your position."

Rolf found his voice. "Yes, sir."

"The tribunal hereby seizes all assets listed in the name of Monsieur Rolf Schulmann held by French banks or located on French soil, to be distributed among either the victims themselves or any relatives who bring this tribunal proof of their relationship to the people on the list. Mr. Schulmann, you're free to go." The sound of the judge's gavel struck Rolf's consciousness with the force of a wrecking ball, and he stood, stunned, while his guards unlocked his hands and feet.

Marie Jacobson leaped to her feet and fought her way down from the balcony. She struggled through the crowd, forcing a path through and wrestling her way down the stairs until finally she wrapped her arms around her beloved. Rolf wept, holding her close against him and whispering her name over and over. She held his face in her hands, and her eyes looked deep into his, sparkling with a joy she could not confine to her eyes. "I'm so proud of you, Rolf Schulmann!" She kissed him, and Rolf felt the confusion, frustration, and despair of the past weeks lift from his chest and disappear as effectively as if it had been a raging flame snuffed with a single, life-saving breath.

Professor Jacobson approached the pair, smiling. His eyes were also wet as he watched his daughter's and his future son-in-law's joy. He placed a hand on Rolf's shoulder. "My daughter will never divulge this, so I'll tell you: she has been in France almost since the day you were arrested in Paris, combing Nazi records and visiting cities, towns, and countrysides for friends who might speak on your behalf. She finally found the witnesses she sought—in a manner so timely it can only be attributed to God's watchful care of a good man."

Rolf touched Marie's cheek gently, gratitude and wonder written in his eyes. "Now it is *you* saving *my* life, Marie Jacobson." His voice broke.

Rolf felt a strong hand on his shoulder and turned to face the familiar rough-cut features of his Maquis friend Jacques Bellamont. With a welcoming grin Rolf extended his hand toward the Frenchman, but Jacques ignored it, instead pulling Rolf and Marie into a colossal bear hug. "Marie found my hiding place and convinced me that I needed to save you from yourself one more time," he said. Then Jacques reached to pull his wife into the circle. "And since my Aimée is alive because of you, she could not be talked out of coming along."

Rolf smiled at Aimée. "Even though I've never had a chance to meet you before today, I knew you from a photograph I'd seen back in the days when your husband was my enemy."

Jacques laughed. "Who says I'm not still your mortal enemy, Major Schulmann? What makes you think something as insignificant as your friendship would change all of that?" He clobbered Rolf's shoulder with one great fist. "I rather prefer the old days, with me always one step ahead of your idiot troops and you always at the receiving end of my contributions to Germany's downfall."

Rolf smiled, although memories of his time in Belley still hovered painfully just below the surface. He again addressed Aimée. "I told you I'd seen you in a photograph, but there is something else about you that is familiar to me."

Before Rolf could continue, Hans and Natalie made their way out of the throng exiting the balcony and hurried forward to join the happy circle. Natalie made a beeline toward Rolf, but as she approached, her eyes met Aimée's, and her footsteps faltered. Rolf saw her eyebrows furrow as she contemplated Jacques's wife, and then for a long moment is seemed as if she stopped breathing.

"She has your same eyes, Nurse Natalie." Rolf said it gently, and Natalie burst into tears and threw herself into Aimée's arms.

At first Aimée seemed perplexed, although her hand came up to comfort the obviously emotional woman who clung to her. Aimée glanced questioningly at Rolf, as if requesting an explanation for Natalie's tears.

"You're alive!" Natalie sobbed, burying her face in the younger woman's shoulder. "You're *alive!*" Natalie took Aimée's face in both her hands and stared into her eyes. "Your mother . . . your father, your sister—are they here?" Her voice caught.

Aimée looked to Rolf to translate, and Rolf did so.

Aimée nodded. "Paris."

Natalie hesitated, and then she switched to her elementary German and explained, "You are my cousin—I'm from America. I—search for you . . . I was worried you were dead."

Aimée studied the woman carefully, her brow slightly furrowed, and then she too reverted to the language of her childhood and whispered softly,

"You're the daughter of my Aunt Anna!" And she smiled through her sudden tears.

"My mother is worried about her beloved sister, Clara," Natalie murmured. "I came to France to find your family." The women embraced again, and Hans turned accusingly to Rolf.

"You knew about Natalie's relatives?"

Rolf shrugged. "Natalie told me about them one night in the hospital—after you disappeared."

Hans slugged him in the same shoulder Jacques had, and Rolf howled. Hans accused, "You could've saved us a lot of trouble if you'd just informed Natalie her relatives were alive and well in France!"

"Hans, I had no idea they were here!" Rolf rubbed his shoulder. "How was I to know that Jacques's fiancée in Belley two years ago—whom I'd never met—and my American nurse's missing cousin were one and the same?"

Marie squeezed Rolf's hand and said softly, "Seems your actions in Belley have come back to repay you. Whoever would have thought that your decision to save the lives of a young woman and her family would have had such far-reaching consequences? That courageous choice affected not only your future safety, but the life of your friends and brother as well."

Rolf turned to Marie and brought her face close to his. His eyes shone with tears. "You speak of my choice. *My* choice! But what of your decision to parachute into France? What of your decision to accept an assignment so dangerous that you knew you might not make it out of France alive? What of *your* courage, Marie, when you protected my son?" He traced the line of her jaw with a trembling finger. "What if you had decided you could not love me? Where would I be now, Marie Jacobson, if it had not been for *your* courageous decisions?"

Marie reached and captured his hand and held it against her cheek, and as Hans and Natalie and Aimée and Jacques celebrated their reunion amidst the commotion of an emptying courtroom, Rolf and Marie held each other close while Marie's father looked contentedly on.

FIFTY-SEVEN

May 10, 1946

Rolf was grateful for the unexpected interruption at three in the morning. Sleep was not coming easily, and he dreaded having to endure six more hours of solitude before Monsieur Jacobson arrived with Marie and they were prepared to leave. So when three young men dressed in dark suits, American shirts, and new ties knocked on his door and presented him with a summons, he was eager for the diversion of a swift ride east across the Rhône.

They took him to a small château somewhere between Aix-les-Bains and his old Nazi command in Belley and introduced him to Lieutenant Major William J. Carlisle, associate to Major Matthews and unofficial recruiting officer for the American Central Intelligence Group.

"I attended the last day of your trial, Mr. Schulmann," Carlisle said as he offered mugs of hot coffee all around. He offered Rolf a glass of water. "Matthews informed me of your religions beliefs. Seems someone's looking out for you."

Without wasting any time, the lieutenant major outlined the reason for the night-shrouded rendezvous. "Mr. Schulmann, President Truman has finally agreed to the creation of a national intelligence organization—one that we anticipate will become powerful enough to counteract the threat posed by the Soviet NKGB. He has agreed to allow us to recruit, train, and supervise agents who will be assigned to areas in the United States and the international field.

"We're prepared to recruit hundreds of young agents—men and women who are zealous in their patriotism and their mistrust of Stalin and his Communist regime. However, we're woefully behind the Soviets in the area of intelligence, and we're in desperate need of experienced agents who are ready at this moment to join the team."

He studied Rolf closely. "Pending a favorable outcome to your trial, Major Matthews recommended that you be offered American citizenship and a career with the United States Central Intelligence Group, under Major Matthews's command. Now that you're a free man, I'm authorized by Matthews to extend that offer to you. Of course, you would not divulge your affiliation to anyone but your wife—once you're married, of course."

Carlisle continued. "Because we are reasonable people, we want to give you a fair offer, Mr. Schulmann. In the eyes of the United States government you're a valuable individual, and we're prepared to offer you compensation for your service."

"What am I supposed to do for the CIG?"

"That depends on whether or not we can trust you implicitly. We've been shocked recently by the news that someone you knew—a sergeant named Edward Finley, who happened to accompany you on your successful foray into Chamonix—has been exposed as a Soviet agent."

"Does Major Matthews trust me?"

"Unconditionally. But SS Major Schellenberg was not convinced we could trust you."

"Schellenberg arrested me for treason."

"That's my point exactly. You were a *traitor.*"

"Would you prefer I'd been completely loyal to the Führer?"

Carlisle smiled. "Are you interested in hearing what we're willing to offer you?"

"As long as it involves time off to go fishing and play catch with my son, I'm interested."

"Family man, huh?" Carlisle said good-naturedly. "All right. You work for us and we'll give you a fair salary, we'll make sure you have time with your son and your gal, and we'll give you back your family's business assets in Chicago and Germany. All we ask is that you continue with us for as long as we need you."

"Where? Here in Europe? Or in America?"

Carlisle tapped his fingers against each other. "Matthews hasn't decided yet. We have a pressing need for you in London, although if you ask me, you'd be safest in some obscure Arizona cowboy town—with a new name and a new background, of course."

"Of course." Rolf Schulmann leaned back in his chair, his eyes trained on the man in front of him. "Now tell me what you want me to do."

FIFTY-EIGHT

May 10, 1946

It doesn't take a cool May breeze or a stunning Parisian sunset or a victory celebration to turn a simple dinner with friends into a memorable evening.
Sometimes all it takes is an assembly of people who have dedicated the last
several years to fighting for each other's lives. Add to that a forthcoming
wedding, a reunion of long-lost relatives, and a judicial pardon for a courageous
man, and one has the makings of a celebration that will never be forgotten—at
least by the six individuals fortunate enough to have such compelling reasons to
celebrate.

The informal *rencontre* took place on the evening of the tenth at a
well-known Paris café on the banks of the River Seine. Present were
Jacques and Aimée Bellamont, Hans Brenner, Natalie Allred, Marie
Jacobson, and Rolf Schulmann.

After a pleasurable dinner and conversation in the café, Hans walked
away from the rest of the group, across the street in the direction of the
Seine, and he remembered the pleasure of his arms around the young
American nurse again and her eyes looking up into his. The thought of her
made his heart do strange and wonderful things in his chest.

He heard a step behind him, and Rolf's cheerful voice brought him
back to the present. "Look, Hans, the fine citizens of Paris have replaced the
glass in the rose windows of the Notre Dame."

Hans looked up and saw the west façade of the gothic masterpiece
looming above him in the fading light. Above the Gallery of Kings the
setting sun had become imprisoned in the multifaceted panes of exquisite
color, bursting into his senses with an explosion of light so magnificent that
he took a physical step backward. He found his voice. "Seems they've
decided the Germans are no longer a threat to their precious cathedral."

"I'm glad it wasn't destroyed," Rolf said. "I heard that when the Allies entered Paris, Hitler ordered his generals to destroy the city, but his command was not obeyed." Rolf leaned against a railing and contemplated his friend standing next to him. "It takes a courageous man to listen to his heart and make right choices when ordered to do otherwise."

Hans leaned over the rail in front of him and looked down at the moving current of the river below. A newfangled *bateaux-mouche* vessel slow-danced with the current, offering its curious tourists an engrossing vista of the *Île de la Cité* and its celebrated *Notre Dame de Paris*. The tourists watched the rose window's mesmerizing display, and Hans watched the tourists.

"Hans," Rolf said softly, "I was referring to *you*."

Hans sniffed. He indicated the boat. "Somebody's making a fortune off those foreigners."

"Natalie said you have something to tell me."

Hans smiled. "She didn't tell you herself?"

"Tell me what, Hans?"

Hans clasped his hands in front of him over the rail and concentrated on breathing slowly, evenly. He knew the time was right, and he was grateful to Natalie for giving him a nudge in the right direction. He turned to face his friend.

It didn't take long to tell Rolf everything. There wasn't much to tell, after all. Hans considered his own conversion much less magnificent than the miracle that had broadsided Rolf so many years ago, and so he didn't waste time on details. Hans told Rolf that he had visited President Wagner in Baiersbronn, that he had joined the Church, that he had been ordained an elder, and that his hope was that Natalie would accept him for who he was and that someday they could be married in the temple in America.

Rolf listened silently, and when he didn't immediately respond, Hans felt himself continuing against his better judgment. "Rolf, there's something you need to know. I'm only here today because of you." His folded his arms and gave Rolf a faint smile. "You taught me that God hears and answers prayers, and that He helps us when we petition Him in behalf of our loved ones. I don't know if you realized you were teaching me, but you were. Every time you fell to your knees, every time you picked up that book of yours or refused a cigarette or treated a woman with respect—you were teaching me. And when I saw that you were willing to sacrifice *everything* to save Marie, I realized that, more than anything, I wanted to be like you."

Hans glanced across the river at the cathedral and then turned and smiled at Rolf. "I had to break through a whole lot of stubbornness, my brother, before I was ready to accept what you taught, but with your help, and Marie's, and Natalie's . . . I finally did."

Hans stopped, embarrassed, and Rolf continued to watch him silently. Hans realized that his friend's silence didn't bother him as it might have otherwise, and he was suddenly overwhelmed with the same comfortable warmth that had surprised him that morning over ten months ago when he'd knelt in a plywood shelter to pray for Rolf's return to health. And with that warm comfort, he also had a curious sensation, one that both worried him and comforted him: he received the impression that, no matter what the next few months held for him and for Natalie, everything was eventually going to be all right.

Finally Rolf spoke, his voice thick with emotion. "Marie and my son are only alive because of you, Hans. I have a chance to marry my sweetheart because of *your* sacrifices—because you were willing to trust in a God that you didn't even understand." His eyes misted. "Don't think I didn't notice, Hans Brenner—the way you never complained when I feigned eye fatigue to keep you reading my Book of Mormon. Don't think I didn't notice that you'd been praying for me—you were rather devious about it, though; I only caught you at it once." He smiled at his friend. "You're the man I have always wished *I* could be—you're one of the most unselfish and giving people I know. I'm proud to call you my friend."

It was not the profound response Hans had been dreading, nor was it a thoughtless dismissal of his experience. In Hans's estimation his friend's simple reply was perfect, and he was eternally grateful to Rolf for it.

Rolf grasped his shoulder. "Hans Brenner, you're now truly my brother."

They clasped hands, and suddenly, impulsively, Rolf strong-armed Hans into a mighty embrace.

"Brothers," Hans said, and his voice became choked with unaccustomed emotion.

"True brothers in the gospel," Rolf agreed. "And for eternity."

"I'm going to miss you, Rolf, while you're in America. You're leaving tonight for the Schwarzwald, right?"

"I've been away from my boy too long."

"And then what?"

Rolf smiled. "And then the three of us—four, including Professor Jacobson—will be on the fastest airplane to America—Marie and I have waited long enough." He punched Hans's shoulder. "And soon, if I'm not mistaken, you and Natalie will be there too."

Hans grinned. "And if that happens, you will attend our wedding?"

Rolf hesitated, and in the brief silence Hans sensed that something was not as it should be. He felt the feeling intensify and corkscrew into a tight pain in his stomach. "That is my fondest wish, Hans Brenner." His friend's voice sounded unnaturally tight. Rolf looked away, and the feeling of unease wrenched abominably in Hans's gut, and suddenly he knew that the answer his friend offered him only encompassed a segment of the whole truth. *What had the Americans done to Rolf?*

Probably no more than they'd done to Hans. Hans dropped his eyes and stared at the river below. He recalled vividly his dark-shrouded rendezvous with the Americans in a remote villa, and suddenly he understood that Rolf had also been secretly to that villa, and therefore had secrets of his own to hide, secrets that even in the presence of his brother could never be revealed. Hans recalled Major Matthew's unpleasant words during that conference: *You're going to have to get used to not knowing everything—even about your closest friends. I know that's a lot to ask of you, but it's going to have to be something we agree to up front.*

Marie appeared at her fiancé's side, and Rolf placed his arm around her shoulders. "We need to get going," she said softly.

Hans swallowed his fear and bantered, "You're sure Marie will still have you, Rolf? After all you've put her through?" He managed a grin in Marie's direction.

Marie gave him a faint smile and bit her lip.

Jacques and Aimée joined them at the rail, and Rolf and Marie turned with them to watch the sunset across the Seine.

Natalie approached Hans and squeezed his arm. "Thank you, Hans, for the flowers. They're beautiful."

"Too bad we crushed them," Hans mumbled, thinking about the morning at the bridge.

"Oh no, Hans, I'm talking about these."

Surprised, Hans glanced down at a bouquet held loosely in her hands. It was a gorgeous display of lilies of the valley, fragrant lilacs, and multicolored roses, and he felt his pulse quicken as he looked at it. Much as he would have liked to accept responsibility for this expensive offering, these flowers were not from him. He was about to divulge this information to Natalie when something about the arrangement caught his eye. And as he looked closer, he saw, nestled in the exact center of the bouquet, a single white rose, stunningly perfect, and with all of its thorns removed.

His throat went dry. "When did these arrive, Natalie?"

"A few minutes ago." Natalie sensed his sudden anxiety and her brow furrowed slightly. "The vendor delivered them to our table while you were out here with Rolf. A pretty young woman with the most curious silver-blond hair. She spoke only French, but she pointed toward you."

Hans could hardly see past the wave of nausea that enveloped him, and he grasped for the rail. Carefully he bent and kissed her, and as he pulled her protectively closer to him he tried desperately to recreate the feeling of peace he had had just moments before. *Someday everything will be all right . . .*

"Hans, when will you come to America?" The anguish in her voice wrenched at his heartstrings. "In a few weeks I'll be home, and I don't know how I'm going to survive being separated from you again."

"I don't know." He felt his voice quiver. "Natalie, my dear Natalie, I need to know if . . . if . . . ." The arms that held her began to tremble.

"If I love you enough to wait for you?" she prompted bravely, and he nodded, agonized and relieved all at once. He touched her face, his fingers gently tracing the curve of her jaw as he waited for her answer.

Wistfully she said, "If only there needn't be any more separations. If only you and I could find a way to escape reality's nightmare."

"But it won't always be a nightmare, my Natalie—if you will promise to wait for me, I promise you that, as soon as I can, I'll find you and we will be married in the temple in America. And then we will have children and we will grow very, very old together."

Natalie turned her face into his hand, and against the rough warmth she closed her eyes and whispered, "Maybe we'd better discuss this marriage thing further, Hans Brenner."

* * *

Rolf and Marie left to collect her father for the drive to Germany. Jacques and Aimée spirited Natalie away, and all Hans had remaining to remind him of his fiancée for the duration of his foreseeable future was her promise to be his bride, her warmth in his arms, and her kisses on his lips.

He didn't look up as a black *Fiat Topolino* separated itself from traffic and slowed next to the bridge, but he pushed numbly away from the railing and moved toward the vehicle. As he did so Hans glanced one last time at the ancient cathedral across the Seine, its façade half shrouded in approaching darkness and its unique flying buttresses cast in deepening shadow. The south rose window had already deepened to dull grey, and the famous west rose's glittering jewels had begun to fade. Only the carved Virgin and Child, standing between two protective stone angels in the center of that window, still glowed with an ethereal light. *Everything will be all right.*

His eyes lingered on the west window, wrapped like a halo around the form of mother and son, and then Hans turned to the waiting automobile. Its engine still purred, but the driver had emerged and was opening the rear door. He was dressed as a French chauffeur, but the uniform didn't hide the man's identity from Hans.

Quietly Hans said, "I remember you."

"I'm not surprised." The young man closed the door behind Hans and returned to the driver's seat. He paused with his hands gripping the steering wheel and glanced through the rearview mirror at Hans. "You ready for this, comrade?"

"Do you realize what he's going to do to me?" Hans swallowed. "How could anybody be ready for this?"

The driver nodded silently. "It's not going to be easy for you at first, sir. I've had to convince him I'm one of them, which means I'm not going to be your favorite person in a few minutes."

"I wasn't expecting it so soon . . ." Hans knew his voice was trembling.

The man was apologetic. "Matthews leaked the news of your whereabouts to him through an agent in the Soviet Köpenick district, and Lieutenant Rostov made his move. We had to act now." He cleared his throat and continued awkwardly. "Listen, Hans, I've wanted to thank you for your intervention in my behalf. You saved me from that monster on the plane. And I want to apologize in advance for—"

"Is Natalie safe?" Hans interrupted gruffly.

"Matthews guarantees it."

"But why the white rose?"

"White rose?" The driver glanced at Hans, puzzled.

Hans let out a soft moan. "In the bouquet Rostov's agent handed Natalie." Hans's palms were sweating. "The white rose has special significance to the professor, since the death of his wife."

"How did he know your location this evening?" The driver gripped the steering wheel and swore softly. "If Rostov's on to us . . ."

"Please, let's just get this over with, all right?" Hans could hardly breathe.

His driver nodded soberly and turned back to the steering wheel. He pressed on the gas, pulled the vehicle away from the riverbank, and carefully merged into traffic.

FIFTY-NINE

Sunday, May 12, 1946

It seemed entirely fitting that, after the horror and anguish of more than two years of fear, persecution, uncertainty, imprisonment, separation, sickness, and finally Rolf's trial, they should be standing here again on a peaceful Sunday morning on this mountainside above the awakening community of Baiersbronn. Marie was wrapped in her beloved's arms, and the twinkling lights of the greeting-card vision below them faded obediently into the soft glow of a morning sunrise.

There were a few distinct differences, Marie surmised, as she felt Rolf's chest rise and fall against her back and listened to his regular breathing next to her ear. *This* particular sun rose on a warm spring day, while the last Sunday morning she had stood here with Rolf the world had awakened cold and gray. The breeze that moved her hair against her face did not sting with the ice particles of winter, and both she and Rolf were slightly older and infinitely wiser than they'd been on that early war-torn December morning in 1943.

But the greatest difference between that Sunday morning and this was at that precise moment pulling urgently at Marie's skirt, clamoring to go to the bathroom.

Marie laughed, disengaging Rolf's arms from her waist to bend down to Alma's height. "All right, *liebling,* I hear you." She glanced up at Rolf and saw the amusement in his eyes. She grinned at him. "Nature calls louder from your son than from the valley below."

Rolf laughed. "I agree. In a minute we'll go."

He cleared his throat and pulled Marie up to face him. "I have something I have wanted to formally ask you for a very, very long time." He smiled at her, leaned close, and said softly, "Marie Jacobson, will you marry me?"

It didn't matter that the answer was already understood. She began to cry. For just a moment she remembered another proposal, a lifetime ago, with Rolf close to her like this, his tortured expression imploring her to understand the man inside the Nazi uniform, but she could not. She also recalled his gentle words as he was being arrested for treason: *I love you.*

Rolf captured her face in his hands, and the look in his eyes showed that he knew her thoughts. "Please don't make me beg ever again, Marie."

She threw her arms around his neck and leaned her face against his. "Yes, Rolf—a million times yes!"

She felt him shudder, as if with her acceptance his body had suddenly been made whole again, and he kissed her.

She thought of a naïve American girl dropping into France to test a new system of wartime codes, unaware that the secret code she tested would be her *least* important test over the next two and a half years. She thought of a seasoned German officer, his heart torn between his convictions and his obligation to his country, seeking the guidance of the Spirit and fighting against impossible odds to save this naïve girl from his government's evil and from her own prejudice, and loving her enough to sacrifice his life to save hers.

Rolf whispered, "I love you, Marie," and his sigh released all the pent-up agony from Marie's heart as well as from his. Then Rolf bent down and took his son's hand, and the three of them returned to join Marie's father, who had sensed the significance of this little detour and had opted to wait in the car below.

HISTORICAL NOTES

PROLOGUE

Allied planes bombed rail centers in Germany on April 12, 1944. Literary license has Allied planes bombing production centers as part of the D-day operations of June 6, thus possibly prolonging Rolf's life.

Anton Kaindl: Last commandant of the Sachsenhausen Death Camp. When asked at his war-crimes trial where he planned to march the prisoners, he told judges what he told Rolf Schulmann in this novel: they were to be marched to the Baltic Sea and drowned. There is a possibility this was not true; the International Red Cross had been advised of the march by camp administration two days before the march and had been asked to provide food for the prisoners. It's possible the SS was simply trying to stay ahead of the Russians and move evidence as far away from the camp as they could. It's also possible motives were exactly as Kaindl said.

The Sachsenhausen Death March began on the night of April 20–21, 1945. Approximately 33,000 prisoners took part in the march, including women and children. Sick prisoners were either executed or abandoned at the camp.

German criminals were required to form a camp people's unit to help guard their fellow prisoners on the march. They were given weapons, but the SS guards didn't trust them with ammunition. For more about Sachsenhausen, please see the following:

> www.scrapbookpages.com/Sachsenhausen/ConcentrationCamp/Death%20March.html
> www.zchor.org/sachsenhausen/sachsenhausen.htm
> www.tankbooks.com/ehlich/ehlichchapter8.htm
> www.scrapbookpages.com/Sachsenhausen/Trials.html
> www.jewishvirtuallibrary.org/jsource/Holocaust/Sach.html

At least once during the march Allied planes dropped leaflets warning SS guards not to shoot any more prisoners. The shooting diminished somewhat.

In the Belower Woods, about 250 German prisoners were officially freed. The next day SS guards abandoned the remainder of prisoners and fled advancing Red Army troops.

ONE

Kreuzberg district: In the American sector of Berlin, and bordering both the British sector on the north and the Russian sector on the east. There was some intermingling of the personnel—both civilian and military—among these sectors, although because of rising political tensions the Americans and British tended to interact more than the Americans and the Russians.

Military Labor Service Units: German POWs were conscripted into service by the United States to repair damage caused by the war.

Hitler Youth program: The *Hitlerjugend* was a military group for German boys and girls until the end of the war.

Volkssturm: Units composed of senior citizens conscripted into the German army—mostly a last-ditch effort by Hitler to oppose the approaching Allies.

Kübelwagen: A Volkswagen model produced during the war, on a VW chassis originally inspired by Hitler for "affordable" family cars (one of the forerunners to the VW Bug). This model would have been used as a military vehicle, being to the Germans what the Jeep was to the Americans.

TWO

Operations officer for the Soviet NKGB in Berlin: In early 1945 Stalin approved the attachment of operational officers to Soviet occupied districts in Berlin and other foreign locations. These operations officers would have been subordinate to the Directorate of the NKGB in Moscow. By the end of 1945 there were only six operations officers under the First Directorate who would be stationed in Germany. Two more arrived in January of 1946 (see Murphy, *Battleground Berlin,* 33–34).

NKGB (People's Commissariat for State Security): Closely related to the NKVD (People's Commissariat for Internal Affairs). To make it deceptively simple, the NKVD would have focused on state security and police control in the USSR, and the NKGB would have focused on counterintelligence operations on foreign soil. Both the NKVD and the NKGB later became the MGB (Ministry of State Security) in March of 1946 when the Soviet Union disbanded all "People's Commissariats." The MGB later became the KGB (see Murphy, *Battleground*

Berlin, chapter 2). In Beevor, *The Fall of Berlin, 1946,* the NKVD is credited for abduction of German scientists. The author surmises that the NKVD is better known in western history and often considered an umbrella organization to the NKGB. Historians often used the terms *NKVD* and *NKGB* interchangeably.

Aleksandr Mikhailovich Korotkov: Soviet intelligence officer; head resident of the NKGB in Karlshorst.

On January 23, 1946, Stalin and other top Russian officials met with the head of the Soviet atomic project to discuss ways "to build the bomb quickly and not to count the cost" (David Holloway, *Stalin and the Bomb: The Soviet Union and Atomic Energy 1939–1956,* New Haven: Yale University Press, 1994; as quoted in Murphy, *Battleground Berlin,* 36). They decided that more intense efforts would be necessary to acquire German scientists and personnel talented in the area of nuclear physics (see Murphy, 13–14; 472, note 47).

Hero of the Soviet Union: The highest honor awarded a Soviet citizen. Comparable in some ways to Hitler's Iron Cross.

OSS: Office of Strategic Services; forerunner to the CIA.

American recruiting efforts: The U.S. and Great Britain also recruited former enemies after the war, including former SS and Gestapo officers—such as Klaus Barbie, known as the "Butcher of Lyon." U.S. records defend this decision, stating that, regardless of past crimes, certain individuals were necessary as informants and operatives in the fledgling U.S. intelligence organizations. The Soviet Union's spy capabilities were seen as light-years ahead of those of the Americans, and the Americans recruited many Germans in an effort to undermine these capabilities. During the last days of the OSS, U.S. intelligence was not allowed to recruit former members of the SS or Gestapo. This changed in the ensuing years of the CIG and CIC (see Murphy, *Battleground Berlin,* and http://www.paperlessarchives.com/barbie.html).

SOE: Britain's spy organization throughout World War II.

The Strange Case of Dr. Jekyll and Mr. Hyde: Published in 1886 by Robert Louis Stevenson. The phrase "Jekyll and Hyde" means a person with a dangerously split personality.

THREE

Dacha (pronounced "Da-cha"): Small Russian farm, usually inhabited during the summer. Some dachas are incredibly small, with the garden plot, the cottage, and any outbuildings taking up no more space than an average American home.

Commander Zhukov: Red Army military governor of the Soviet Occupation Zone in Germany. His term began June 10, 1945 (see Beevor, *The Fall of Berlin 1945*; and Murphy, *Battleground Berlin*).

Lucya: Traditionally derived from *Ludmila*. A person with this name would only be called *Lucya* by her husband or father, and even then probably only when he is considering how much he loves and misses her. The author chooses to call Rostov's daughter *Lucya* consistently throughout the book for simplicity, and because the author has a very beautiful Russian sister with the same name.

A postwar ruling by the U.S. military forbade Americans from marrying Germans. This ruling actually remained in effect, with few exceptions, until near the end of 1946. For information on General Eisenhower's "non-fraternization" policy, please see:

http://en.wikipedia.org/wiki/History_of_Germany_since_1945
http://en.wikipedia.org/wiki/Eisenhower_and_German_POWs

Soviet atomic project: The Soviets ordered the roundup of German scientists in early 1945 for the benefit of the Soviet Union's atomic bomb research. The Soviets tested their first atomic bomb in 1949 (see http://en.wikipedia.org/wiki/Soviet_atomic_bomb_project).

FOUR

Izieu: A tiny community near the Rhône River in the Rhône-Alpes region of southern France, the location of *La Maison d'Izieu,* an orphanage for Jewish children whose parents were missing because of the war. See http://www.annefrank.dk/children/new_page_5d.htm.

Friedrichshain and Treptow districts: Districts of divided Berlin located in the Russian sector.

SIX

Bernaur Strasse, Berlin: Fictitious address. The real Bernaur Strasse in Berlin is actually part of the demarcation line between former East and West Berlin, and part of the Berlin Wall ran along Bernaur Street. It remains as a memorial.

TDY: Temporary duty assignment for military personnel.

Nuremberg trials: Trials were held in Nüremberg between 1945 and 1949, with the most publicized trial of Nazi war criminals held between November 1945 and October 1, 1946 (see Rice, *Nazi War Criminals;* and Rosenbaum, *Prosecuting Nazi War Criminals*).

Neukölln district: In the American sector, south of the fictitious hospital.

Treptow: A district in the Soviet sector bordering the American sector.

Red Army Zone/American Zone: A detailed map of the separations of Berlin from 1945 onward can be found in Murphy, *Battleground Berlin*, 7.

Finger-biting incident: In post-WWII Hungary, a similar incident happened to a 19-year-old girl. Two Russian soldiers entered the home of the girl while she was there with her younger sister and their mother. While one soldier detained the sister and mother, the other attacked the 19-year-old in her bedroom, only to have his finger bitten completely off by the determined girl. The younger sister escaped and ran for help, and the two soldiers fled the house without causing any additional harm to the women. The mother happened to be friends with a Russian officer billeting at a next-door neighbor's house, and the sister had run to bring him. The officer promised the woman he would find her daughter's attackers, and he did so by searching among his men for the one missing a finger. The soldier was found and arrested. The 19-year-old girl is now a grandmother, and her daughter lives in America and is the author's aunt.

EIGHT

Eisenhower has been accused of withholding postwar humanitarian aid from the starving Germans in a spirit of revenge; he has been credited with saying, "I say let Germany find out what it means to start a war" ("Trouble in Germany," *Time Magazine*, October 22, 1945) and has been accused of gross disregard for the Geneva Convention's mandate that a conquering power has a moral obligation to care for the needs of the conquered nation. However, the author is of the opinion, based on the writings of Eisenhower biographer and historian Stephen Ambrose, that General Eisenhower actually attempted to care for the German population but found himself completely overwhelmed by the numbers of German civilians in need of assistance. Without records that were destroyed by the U.S. Army in the late 1940s, it is impossible to be certain which view is correct (see http://en.wikipedia.org/wiki/Eisenhower_and_German_POWs).

ELEVEN

Liliane Gerenstein: The eleven-year-old girl at *La Maison d'Izieu* who wrote the "Letter to God," found in a drawer at the home. Liliane died, along with the other children, at Auschwitz. Her mother was deported earlier, and her father eventually immigrated to the United States and died in 1979 (see Morgan, *An Uncertain Hour*, 274; http://www.izieu.com/new_page_5.htm).

Klaus Barbie: Head of the Gestapo stationed in Lyon. Referred to as the "Butcher of Lyon" for his intense interrogation methods and murders. His responsibilities included not only implementation of the Final Solution in southern France but also the discovery and disbandment of French Résistance cells in the area (see Morgan, *An Uncertain Hour*).

Charles de Gaulle: Leader of the Free French (French Résistance)—the government he led from Britain and Algiers for a good portion of the war. He attempted to unify the many different resistance movements in France with moderate success—enough that Britain, which recognized de Gaulle's government over that of Vichy, was willing to assist in the Résistance's efforts by sending supplies and agents.

De Gaulle returned to France in June 1944 and was acknowledged president of the French Provisional Government until he resigned in January 1946 (see Morgan, *An Uncertain Hour;* Beevor, *Paris After the Liberation*).

THIRTEEN

Kristallnacht: November 9–10, 1938. The Nazi response to the murder of an embassy representative in Paris by a Polish-German Jew was thereafter referred to as *Kristallnacht,* or "The Night of Breaking Glass" (see http://en.wikipedia.org /wiki/Kristallnacht; http://www.historyplace.com/worldwar2/timeline/knacht.htm; http://www.roizen.com/ron/grynszpan.htm).

Reinhard Heydrich: Chief of Reich security (see http://en.wikipedia.org /wiki/Reinhard_Heydrich).

Universität zu Berlin: The University of Berlin, founded in 1810. During Hitler's reign it became a university for Nazi studies.

FOURTEEN

MP: Military policeman.

During the war the Nazis kept extraordinary records—very helpful to the Allies.

Gendarmes: French military police.

FIFTEEN

French *collabo* trials: de Gaulle didn't wait for the outcome of the trials in Nüremberg to begin his own war crimes tribunal.

SIXTEEN

Maquis: A guerilla branch of the French Résistance that often resided in the mountains, the Rhône-Alpes being especially thick with members of the organization. See Morgan, *An Uncertain Hour,* for more on the Maquis movement, the Rhône-Alpes, and Communism in France.

Candy bomber: The "Candy Man" of the Berlin airlift had not yet fastened his white handkerchiefs to bundles of candy and dropped them to the children of West Berlin at the time of Alma's 1945 flight down the corridors of the hospital. But it seemed like a nice idea—and a fitting tribute to Retired World War II Air Force Pilot Col. Gail Halvorsen, nicknamed "The Candy Bomber," who dropped candy and gum to Berlin's children in 1948 and 1949, and who also served as dean of student affairs at Brigham Young University in the '80s (see http://www.talkingproud.us/HistoryBerlinCandyBomber.html).

NINETEEN

American POW camp west of Berlin: This is a fictitious camp, although the Allies had multitudes of POW camps throughout the Berlin area as well as in the United States, France, Great Britain, and most other occupied territories.

TWENTY

When Viktor Rostov asks Natalie to address him as "Viktor Nikolayevich" instead of "Lieutenant Rostov," he is coming dangerously close to breaking Russian protocol. He is her superior, and she his victim. But underneath his devotion to duty he feels a connection to her that he cannot deny, and his request that she call him by the less-formal (but still respectable) Viktor Nikolayevich is his attempt to have her see him as more than just a military authority. He wants her to be strictly compliant—but perhaps not as afraid of him as she might have been if he always insisted she call him "Lieutenant Rostov."

TWENTY-ONE

Hammond Lieberman: Fictional character.

Tchaikovsky: In 1878 Pyotr (Peter) Ilyich Tchaikovsky wrote a violin concerto considered unplayable by many professional violinists at the time, and it didn't gain popularity until much later.

Stravinsky: Russian composer Igor Stravinsky's Symphony in C was completed in 1940, while Stravinsky was in exile in the United States. The premier performance of this symphony was by the Chicago Symphony Orchestra in 1940.

Justice Jackson: Robert H. Jackson was the chief prosecutor for the United States at the Nüremberg trials presided over by the International Military Tribunal.

TWENTY-TWO

Krauts: Derogatory nickname for the Germans used by the Allies.

Troika: Richly decorated lacquer box made by Russian artisans.

TWENTY-THREE

POW camps in Britain: Approximately 1,500 POW camps were built in Great Britain—several in East Sussex, where Brighton is located. German prisoners held in those camps would have been those prisoners not considered high security risks by the British government. The camp near Brighton mentioned in this novel is entirely the author's creation. Even though a camp #114 actually existed, several camps in different areas had the same numbers (see http://news.bbc.co.uk /2/hi/uk_news/england/2136096.stm; http://www.islandfarm.fsnet.co.uk /LIST%20OF%20UK%20POW%20CAMPS1.htm).

Russians and German watches: Soviet soldiers saw German watches as war trophies and would wear the ones they found (see Anonymous, *A Woman in Berlin: Eight Weeks in the Conquered City*).

Gerainya: Hero (masculine version: *Geroi*). In Russia the idea of a person being heroic would have conveyed the same feeling that "royalty" does to a westerner. By using this title for Natalie, Rostov was not just protecting her from his guards at the border. He was also giving her a veiled threat by alluding to her Soviet citizen status (from an interview with Shirley Freeman, Russian language, culture, and research assistant).

TWENTY-FOUR

Elder Benson's visit to Frankfurt: On March 17, 1946, Frederick W. Babbel wrote that Elder Benson visited with Saints in Frankfurt who were so emaciated that it was "almost like shaking hands with a skeleton" (Babbel, *On Wings of Faith,* 166). Elder Benson wrote in his personal journal of the horrific conditions of the Saints, and Rolf's report to Elder Benson is based on that account (see Benson, *A Labor of Love,* 50–51).

TWENTY-SIX

Iron Cross: Highest honor awarded by Hitler.

When Rostov comments to Hans that Hitler didn't keep his promise to the Soviets, he is referring to two possible treaty violations on the part of Germany:

1. The Neutrality Agreement between Germany and the USSR signed on April 24, 1926, pledged neutrality on the part of each nation in the event of an attack on the other by a third party nation. Renewed in 1931 and ratified two years later, this treaty became a foundation for the following:

2. On August 23, 1939, Hitler's representative Foreign Minister von Ribbentrop and Soviet Foreign Minister Molotov signed a non-aggression treaty that specifically stated that the countries would not use aggressive tactics against each other either as individual entities or together with any other aggressors. This was referred to as the Molotov-Ribbentrop Pact.

On August 13, 1942, Soviet President Stalin wrote to United States President Roosevelt petitioning Roosevelt for assistance in the West because Hitler had broken his 1939 non-aggression promise to the Soviets (see http://www.americaslibrary.gov /cgi-bin/page.cgi/jb/wwii/stalin_1 and http://www.historyplace.com/worldwar2 /timeline/pact.htm).

Dismantling munitions factories: Hans is referring to his work as a POW for the Soviets—the USSR dismantled many German factories and transported them by rail to the Soviet Union for reassembly. They considered it partial recompense for Soviet suffering caused by Hitler (see Murphy, *Battleground Berlin*, 10–14).

Twenty-Eight

Occupied France: France surrendered to the Germans on June 22, 1940. At that time the Germans divided France into two zones: occupied France to the north and unoccupied France to the south.

Major-General Walther Schellenberg: SS officer in charge of intelligence, with the specific responsibility given him by Reinhard Heydrich to ferret out and eliminate resistance factions in foreign occupied territories. Schellenberg actually was detained and interrogated by the American OSS in 1945. For purposes of this novel, the author assumes that time period continues into the spring of 1946 (see Jewish Virtual Library, http://www.jewishvirtuallibrary.org/jsource/biography/Hmueller.html; http://www.jewishvirtuallibrary.org/jsource/biography/Schellenberg.html).

Denazification: The Allied Control Council in Berlin officially began using this process in January 1946. Denazification was a plan to completely rid Germany and Austria of Nazi influence and punish Nazi Party members (see http://en.wikipedia.org/wiki/denazification; http://www.germanculture.com.ua /library/history/bl_Nüremberg_trials_denazi.htm).

Rhein-Main Air Base: Construction of this air base began in 1909 as a site for dirigibles. It was later utilized by Hitler's Luftwaffe and was heavily bombed by the Allies in 1944 and early 1945. After Germany surrendered, the United States worked to repair the base, adding and lengthening runways and rebuilding hangars and the base's infrastructure (see http://www.globalsecurity.org/military/facility/rhein-main.htm).

Adjutant: An officer whose duty was to act as an aide to a higher ranking officer.

THIRTY

Rolf's visit with Elder Benson in Frankfurt on March 17, 1947—see chapter 24 notes.

Destruction of Frankfurt and preservation of the mission home: The story of an intact bomb in the courtyard of the Frankfurt Mission Home can be found in Frank Babbel's account of Elder Ezra Taft Benson's European mission (*On Wings of Faith*, 44–45). For purposes of the story, the author has the bomb still in the courtyard on March 17, 1946. She doesn't know if the bomb had actually been removed by this time.

Allgemeine SS: The branch of the SS that dealt with, among other things, intelligence operations (as opposed to the Waffen SS that did most of the fighting).

Doctrine & Covenants 121:1–3: Only portions used, and spaces removed for convenience of storytelling.

THIRTY-ONE

Charé: Fictitious village situated near Chamonix in the Rhône-Alpes.

American-inspired jazz: After the Great War, France was influenced by American jazz (see http://www.bbc.co.uk/dna/h2g2/alabaster/A507719).

THIRTY-THREE

Bergmütze: A cap worn by the German Alpine Elite. It had flaps that could be pulled down over the ears and neck in the cold, and a visor for sunny days.

Café *La Rochette:* Fictitious café located in Chamonix in the Rhône-Alpes.

THIRTY-FOUR

Shirley Freeman was invaluable for her research into the Kronstadt Rebellion of 1921 (see also W. H. Chamberlin, *The Russian Revolution* [New York, 1965], 2:495; http://dwardmac.pitzer.edu/Anarchist_Archives/bright/berkman/kronstadt/berkkron .html).

Petrograd: At the beginning of WWI the name of the city of Saint Petersburg was changed to Petrograd. In 1924 Petrograd was changed to Leningrad, and then again to Saint Petersburg on September 6, 1991 (see http://www.saint-petersburg.com /history/1914-1924.asp#Name-change and http://en.wikipedia.org/wiki/Petrograd).

Natalie: "Natalie" is a stretch of the Americanized form of the Russian name *Natalya,* also westernized as "Natasha." In this case, the author wanted to convey the idea that Natalie's mother didn't want Natalie to know she'd been born in Russia and so called her "Natalie" from the time the two arrived in the United States. When Lieutenant Rostov finds out about Natalie's heritage, he immediately begins calling her by her formal Russian name—*Natalya Ivanovna.* According to the author's sources, he probably should always adhere to that complete patronymic, unless she is his wife or daughter. However, the author has chosen to drop the patronymic (on pain of death from any who are intimately familiar with Russian culture!) in many instances for better readability. The same holds true for "Viktor Nikolayevich"—usually the author has Natalie just say "Viktor," although this crime against Russian language protocol might get the author banished to Siberia herself.

The first day of the Chicago World's Fair was May 27, 1933.

Perry Como: A popular 1946 entertainer known throughout the world.

Rachmaninoff: A Russian/American pianist and composer, 1873–1943.

Anton Rubinstein: A Russian pianist, teacher, conductor, and composer, 1829–1894.

THIRTY-FIVE

John Wayne: Although he appeared in many films before this one, John Wayne's role in the 1939 Western *Stagecoach* is considered to be the one that made him a world-wide star (see http://en.wikipedia.org/wiki/John_Wayne_filmography_%281926-1940%29).

THIRTY-SEVEN

St. Victor-sur-Loire: A small community on the banks of the Loire River near Lyon.

Fieseler Storch: A German aircraft—Model 156 (see Chant, *Aircraft of World War II,* 131).

Douglas SBD *Dauntless:* An Allied warplane (see Chant, *Aircraft of World War II,* 116–17).

THIRTY-EIGHT

Curly commented that Rostov was "on American soil." When the U.S. has control of an area, the military and the government consider that area American soil, just as an American embassy in another country would be considered by the U.S. to be an extension of the United States of America.

THIRTY-NINE

Central Intelligence Group (CIG): Established by President Truman in January 1946—a descendant of the wartime OSS and a forerunner to the CIA (the CIA was officially established in 1947; see Murphy, *Battleground Berlin*).

FORTY

Red sandstone: When Hitler came to power, he imported a significant amount of red sandstone with the intention of creating statues and monuments dedicated to the strength, power, and might of the Third Reich. Ironically, when the Red Army invaded Germany in the closing months of the war, they used Hitler's unused sandstone to create monuments to the might, power, and strength of the Soviet Union and to Hitler's downfall. Many of these monuments have been preserved or are being renovated in the former East German Democratic Republic.

Novosibirsk: Considered the "Capital of Siberia." Many German scientists were relocated to Novosibirsk in 1945 and 1946 to assist the Soviets with the development of nuclear weaponry.

Yalta Conference: The second of three conferences held between the three major Allied powers: the Soviet Union, the United States, and Great Britain. Also referred to as the Crimea Conference, it took place at Stalin's invitation at the Black Sea resort of Yalta beginning on February 4, 1945. President Roosevelt attended, along with Premier Stalin and Prime Minister Churchill. The purpose of the conference was to decide how the three Allies would govern postwar Germany. A key decision was that all Soviet Union and Yugoslavian citizens were to be returned to their respective countries, whether or not they were willing to go (see http://en.wikipedia.org/wiki/Yalta_Conference).

FORTY-THREE

President Félix Gouin: Interim president of the provisional French government after General de Gaulle resigned unexpectedly in January 1946. Gouin remained president only until the elections later that year, at which time the presidency of the provisional government went to Georges Bidault (see Beevor, *Paris After the Liberation*).

Hotel Vienne: Fictitious Parisian hotel.

FORTY-FOUR

War trophy: During Europeans' traumatic postwar experiences with the conquering Soviets, it was not uncommon for "valuable" civilians of the conquered nations to be commandeered for some useful purpose in the Soviet Union. The author surmises that it was a "spoils if war" attitude akin to the Soviet practice of abducting scientists. Even if Natalie had not been subject to the rulings of the Yalta Conference as a Soviet-born citizen, the situation with Rostov in this novel would have been realistic. After the war ended, a relative of the author—a nurse in Hungary—was similarly carted away by a Soviet officer and his wife, who took a fancy to her and decided that a young nurse from a conquered nation would be a useful asset. Luckily, the nurse escaped her captors at the train station and returned to her family.

The young private's interest in Hans's Luger: Many American GIs considered a German Luger a war trophy.

FORTY-SIX

Politburo: The highest governing organization of the USSR—this committee was organized by the Bolshevik Party (Lenin's party) in the early 1900s.

Soviet mole in the American CIG: The NKVD/NKGB was expert at planting its spies in American intelligence's inexperienced ranks. David E. Murphy states in his book *Battleground Berlin* that "it appears that the Soviets were well-informed of [American Intelligence in Berlin's] operations" (17–19).

FORTY-SEVEN

St.-Joseph Prison in Lyon: The site of Klaus Barbie's incarceration before his trial in the 1980s (see Morgan, *An Uncertain Hour,* 21).

FORTY-EIGHT

Rafle: The systematic roundup of Jews and other "undesirables" from Germany and other Nazi-occupied territories.

"Greater love hath no man than this, that a man lay down his life for his friends" (John 15:13).

Boche (pronounced like "beau"): French slang for German soldiers in WWII.

FORTY-NINE

Trial scenes: Details for Rolf Schulmann's trial were compiled using the proceedings of the Nüremberg trials beginning in 1945 and descriptions of the war crimes trial held for Section Four chief Klaus Barbie in 1987 (see Rice, *Nazi War Criminals;* Rosenbaum, *Prosecuting Nazi War Criminals;* and Morgan, *An Uncertain Hour,* 15–17). Barbie's trial was held in Paris in the *Salle des Pas Perdus* (Hall of Lost Steps) to accommodate the vast throngs expected to attend. Artistic license—and perhaps a bit of poetic justice—places Rolf's trial in the former Gestapo headquarters in Lyon.

Guillotine: Used for capital punishment in France until it was officially abolished in 1981.

FIFTY

Sabina Zlatin was a licensed nurse who began taking displaced Jewish children into her home after the 1940 armistice. The local prefect warned her that the Germans would be a danger and suggested that she take her children into the Italian Zone. With the kind help of Marcel Wiltzer, the *sous-prefet* of Belley, Madame Zlatin and her husband, Miron, found a home used for Catholic retreats above the small community in Izieu. Wiltzer told them that Germans had never bothered the village. Madame Zlatin moved her operation to the Izieu site and began to take in more children. (See Morgan, *An Uncertain Hour,* 262–75, for the story of the children's home in Izieu.)

Beaune-la-Rolande: A small community outside Paris.

FIFTY-TWO

May Day Parade in Paris, 1946—Held on the *Place de la République* on the morning of May 5 (see Beevor, *Paris After the Liberation,* 232). Lilies of the valley were sold by the bushel throughout France.

French Communist Rally: This demonstration/parade was actually held on the evening of May 5, 1946, at 6:00 P.M. on the *Place de la Concorde* in Paris. For purposes of this story the author has moved that rally nearer to the apartment of Professor Jacobson (see Beevor, *Paris After the Liberation,* 232–33).

FIFTY-THREE

Leon Reifman: A young medical student thought by the Germans to be one of the children at Izieu (see Morgan, *An Uncertain Hour,* 262–75).

FIFTY-FIVE

Lily of the Valley (*Convallaria majalis;* French: *Muguet*): Native to Europe, this plant blooms with delicate, bell-like flowers in the spring and has red berries in the fall. During the month of May it is a tradition in some parts of Europe to give this flower as a gift—often in conjunction with the May Day holiday. (See Beevor, *Paris After the Liberation*, 232.)

FIFTY-SIX

Confiscation of Rolf's personal possessions: A similar situation occurred in France in August 1946 with Colonel Passy (code name for André Dewavrin, American intelligence expert accused by the French of embezzlement) (see Beevor, *Paris After the Liberation*, 234–37).

BIBLIOGRAPHY

Anonymous. *A Woman in Berlin: Eight Weeks in the Conquered City.* Trans. Philip Boehm, New York: Metropolitan Books, 2005.

Babbel, Frederick W. *On Wings of Faith: My Daily Walk with a Prophet.* Salt Lake City: Bookcraft, 1972.

Beevor, Antony, and Artemis Cooper. *Paris After the Liberation, 1944–1949.* New York: Penguin, 1994.

————. *The Fall of Berlin, 1945.* New York: Penguin Putnam, 2002.

Benson, Ezra Taft. *A Labor of Love: The 1946 European Mission of Ezra Taft Benson.* Salt Lake City: Deseret Book, 1989.

Boll, Heinrich. *The Silent Angel (Der Engel Schwieg).* Cologne, Germany: Verlag Kiepenheuer & Witsch, 1992.

Brown, James Good. *The Mighty Men of the 381st Heroes All: A Chaplain's Inside Story of the Men of the 381st Bomber Group.* Salt Lake City: Publishers Press, 1989.

Chant, Chris. *Aircraft of World War II.* London: Amber Books Ltd., 1999.

Dew, Sheri L. *Ezra Taft Benson: A Biography.* Salt Lake City: Deseret Book, 1987.

Eisenberg, Carolyn. *Drawing the Line: The American Decision to Divide Germany, 1944–1949.* Cambridge: Cambridge University Press, 1996.

Freeman, Robert C., and Dennis A. Wright, *Saints at War.* American Fork, Utah: Covenant Communications, 2001.

McIntosh, Elizabeth P. *Sisterhood of Spies: The Women of the OSS.* New York: Random House, 1998.

Morgan, Ted. *An Uncertain Hour: The French, the Germans, the Jews, the Klaus Barbie Trial, and the City of Lyon, 1940–1945.* New York: William Morrow and Company, 1990.

Murphy, David E., Sergei A. Kondrashev, and George Bailey. *Battleground Berlin: CIA vs. KGB in the Cold War.* London: Yale University Press, 1997.

Nibley, Hugh, and Alex Nibley. *Sergeant Nibley, PhD: Memories of an Unlikely Screaming Eagle.* Salt Lake City: Shadow Mountain, 2006.

O'Donnell, Patrick K. *Operatives, Spies, and Saboteurs: The Unknown Story of the Men and Women of WWII's OSS.* New York: Free Press, 2004.

Rice, Earle Jr. *Nazi War Criminals.* San Diego, CA: Lucent Books, 1998.

Rosenbaum, Alan S. *Prosecuting Nazi War Criminals.* Boulder, CO: Westview Press, 1993.

Rottman, Gordon L. *FUBAR: Soldier Slang of World War II.* Westminster, MD: Osprey Publishing, 2007.

Rushton, Patricia, Lynn Clark Callister, and Maile K. Wilson. *Latter-day Saint Nurses at War: A Story of Caring and Sacrifice.* Provo, UT: BYU Religious Studies Center, 2005.

Stafford, David. *End Game, 1945: The Missing Final Chapter of World War II.* New York: Little, Brown, and Company, 2007.

SELECTED INTERNET RESEARCH:

Concentration Camps:
www.scrapbookpages.com/Sachsenhausen/ConcentrationCamp/Death%20March.html
www.zchor.org/sachsenhausen/sachsenhausen.htm
www.tankbooks.com/ehlich/ehlichchapter8.htm
www.scrapbookpages.com/Sachsenhausen/Trials.html
www.jewishvirtuallibrary.org/jsource/Holocaust/Sach.html

U.S. Recruiting Efforts / Klaus Barbie:
http://www.paperlessarchives.com/barbie.html

Izieu Children's Home:
http://www.annefrank.dk/children/new_page_5d.htm
http://www.izieu.com/new_page_5.htm

Eisenhower:
http://en.wikipedia.org/wiki/History_of_Germany_since_1945
http://en.wikipedia.org/wiki/Eisenhower_and_German_POWs

Soviet Atomic Project:
http://en.wikipedia.org/wiki/Soviet_atomic_bomb_project

Kristallnacht:
http://en.wikipedia.org/wiki/Kristallnacht
http://www.historyplace.com/worldwar2/timeline/knacht.htm

Candy Bomber:
http://www.talkingproud.us/HistoryBerlinCandyBomber.html

Allied POW Camps:
http://news.bbc.co.uk/2/hi/uk_news/england/2136096.stm
http://www.islandfarm.fsnet.co.uk/LIST%20OF%20UK%20POW%20CAMPS1.htm

Rhein-Main Air Base:
http://www.globalsecurity.org/military/facility/rhein-main.htm

German–Soviet Non-aggression Pact:
http://www.americaslibrary.gov/cgi-bin/page.cgi/jb/wwii/stalin_1
http://www.historyplace.com/worldwar2/timeline/pact.htm

Major-General Walther Schellenberg:
http://www.jewishvirtuallibrary.org/jsource/biography/Hmueller.html
http://www.jewishvirtuallibrary.org/jsource/biography/Schellenberg.html

Denazification & the Allied Control Council in Berlin:
http://en.wikipedia.org/wiki/Denazification
http://www.germanculture.com.ua/library/history/bl_Nüremberg_trials_denazi.htm

Yalta Conference:
http://en.wikipedia.org/wiki/Yalta_Conference

Petrograd:
http://www.saint-petersburg.com/history/1914-1924.asp#Name-change
http://en.wikipedia.org/wiki/Petrograd

Kronstadt Rebellion:
http://dwardmac.pitzer.edu/Anarchist_Archives/bright/berkman/kronstadt/berkkron
.html

Uranium Ore and Acquisition of German Nuclear Scientists:
http://en.wikipedia.org/wiki/Russian_Alsos

ABOUT THE AUTHOR

Sandra Grey was born in Inglewood, California, to a very large two-generation military family. Her paternal grandfather served in World War II, and her father is a retired air force major who trained to be a spy during the Cold War.

Sandra remembers as a child finding her mother at the kitchen sink one Halloween, conversing intimately with a stranger—a tall man with red hair and a red mustache. After Sandra's initial shock wore off, she realized that this stranger sounded just like her father and had his eyes. Her father's never-used, government-supplied spy disguise kit had been recommissioned to be his Halloween costume. The most clandestine action that spy kit ever saw was when Sandra's mother arrived at the airport to pick up her husband after spy school, and she found herself being ruthlessly stalked by a tall, handsome, red-haired stranger.

Sandra graduated from Brigham Young University with a degree in humanities and has followed her insatiable curiosity and love of history on adventures from Asia to Alaska, Mexico to Europe, and Russia to Brazil. Sandra currently lives with her husband and their own large family in St. Johns, Arizona, and is satisfied to leave all covert action to the characters in her novels.